He hesitated a little too long and now he was out of time...

Mark only had a few seconds to spare, as he raced down the stairs. His heart exploded outward, and his breath came in short, wheezing snorts. His feet moved as if he floated on air, he leapt toward the bottom when he had a couple of stairs to go, and grabbed the banister for support. The paneling and bloody doors were all the same, gray and cold and filled with windows, as he raced down the infinitely symmetrical packed hallways, to the second level and then to the first, echoing a life filled with sameness and regularity. The large tile squares that permeated across the floor helped him skip from one moment to the next. A march played over and over in his head, and his feet kept time with the downbeat.

He should have traveled more and toured the world. He wasn't sure why he thought of that now, but there it was, dangling in the open atmosphere, as he hung in the air for milliseconds before his feet struck the next level, and he continued on with his journey. He hadn't even traveled out of the US. He had never even been to Ireland, England, or Scotland. What a mess. He had no hope of ever fulfilling his destiny, if he couldn't even be bothered to take a plane across the Atlantic. One catastrophe after another filled his world, but he would redeem himself, and it would start right now. His right ankle throbbed, and his hips surged, as he circumnavigated around children and random pedestrians.

Mark bounded down the stairs, his footfalls resembling a herd of buffalo in the middle of a large pasture, his feet shuffling as the bloody staircase carried on beneath him and disappeared under metal ridges before it appeared once more on the opposite end. It was beautiful in its simplicity, as the movement proved both steady and promising.

His feet struck bottom, and he pushed through the door and tripped on the threshold. He stumbled and swerved, but he didn't go down. His watch beeped, informing him he had only a minute left. A warning Mark had put in place, knowing the situation would come to this, and that he'd need the additional incentive to race to safety.

His head cleared as the deep breaths neared, and time marched on. The end surrounded him, filling his lungs up with smoldering fire and smoke.

Mark pumped his arms at his sides, and lengthened his stride. A stitch developed, and he felt pins and needles around his ankles. Even his knees screamed, as he jerked onward, like a soldier on the battlefield racing away from the enemy. He shoved his way around the revolving door, and his feet touched the sidewalk the instant his whole world changed.

The Pru became a shell of its former self.

Lynette Sommer ends her carefully calculated Power-Point presentation in the Hancock Tower with a pink slip shoved across her desk and a standing order to vacate the premises immediately. Richard Lancaster, III races through The Pru with a tie stuffed down the front of his khakis and an overzealous security guard hot on his trail. At the Boston Public Library, Carl Razer finds himself in the midst of a manic encounter from a teenage book enthusiast who has let the glitter and glamor of *Twilight* destroy what is left of his brain cells. And then it gets progressively worse, as three homegrown terrorists—Matthew, Mark, and John—destroy three vital Boston landmarks—The Hancock Tower, the Pru, and the Boston Public Library—with the drop of a backpack and the flick of a switch...

KUDOS for *Simultaneous Meltdown*

In *Simultaneous Meltdown* by Robert Downs, Lynette Sommers, Richard Lancaster, III, and Carl Razer are all having a very bad day. Lynette gets fired, Richard gets caught stealing, and Carl gets accosted by a *Twilight* obsessed teenager demanding to check out the book from the library after someone else has already checked out the last copy. What the three don't know is that their day is going to get a lot worse when three home-grown terrorists decide to blow up the buildings they're in. Written in Downs's unique voice, the story is told from the point of view of the victims, the police, and the terrorists, and will keep you on your toes from beginning to end. ~ *Taylor Jones, The Review Team of Taylor Jones & Regan Murphy*

Simultaneous Meltdown by Robert Downs is the story of three victims, three terrorists, and a couple of policemen whose investigation goes awry. When Lynette Sommers gives an honest presentation of her employer's shady dealings, she is promptly fired. Richard Lancaster, III, is a loser who can't even steal a necktie (one he doesn't even need) without getting caught. And Carl Razer barely makes enough to survive with his job at the public library, certainly not enough to put up with all the weirdos. But all their lives are about to take a disastrous twist when Matthew, Mark, and John decide to blow up the three buildings where Lynette, Richard, and Carl happen to be at the time. The three victims survive, but barely, and their lives go downhill from there. Then the police assigned to investigate the terrorist bombings are sure they have their man, but they don't, and unless they change their tune, it is unlikely they are ever going to solve the case. Riveting, compelling, and intense, *Simul-*

taneous Meltdown will keep you shaking your head and guessing from the very first page to the last. ~ *Regan Murphy, The Review Team of Taylor Jones & Regan Murphy*

ACKNOWLEDGMENTS

NaNoWriMo 2012 quite possibly saved my writing career and breathed life into this novel. I rediscovered the joy of writing by setting everything else aside and making the cursor glide across the page. Thank you to Black Opal Books for, once again, taking a chance on me. This is our fifth book together, and I hope there are many more to come. Lauri and Faith and the rest of the team have been fantastic, and I can't sing their praises loudly enough.

I owe my dad a huge debt of gratitude. He has single-handedly built me a steady stream of readers in Fairmont who look forward to my next book, and he's called in so many favors to help me out I know he's lost count. My brother and his lovely wife as well as my mom and dad provided great feedback on my cover. My entire family who has endlessly promoted my writing and my Facebook page. My readers who ensure I don't spend all of my time talking to myself, and my fellow writers for providing tips, trade secrets, and countless rounds of encouragement. And I'd like to thank God, who always makes the impossible possible. Any errors in judgment have, and always will be, my own.

Simultaneous Meltdown

Robert Downs

A Black Opal Books Publication

GENRE: MYSTERY/THRILLER/SUSPENSE

This is a work of fiction. Names, places, characters and incidents are either the product of the author's imagination or are used fictitiously, and any resemblance to any actual persons, living or dead, businesses, organizations, events or locales is entirely coincidental. All trademarks, service marks, registered trademarks, and registered service marks are the property of their respective owners and are used herein for identification purposes only. The publisher does not have any control over or assume any responsibility for author or third-party websites or their contents.

SIMULTANEOUS MELTDOWN
Copyright © 2018 by Robert Downs
Cover Design by Jackson Cover Designs
All cover art copyright © 2018
All Rights Reserved
Print ISBN: 978-1-644370-35-3

First Publication: NOVEMBER 2018

Published by Black Opal Books **http://www.blackopalbooks.com**

DEDICATION

For my brother,
who helped me put the pieces back together

Chapter 1

Lynette Sommer stood before a sea of familiar faces. Male faces. Each one had turned his attention directly toward her. She clicked through the PowerPoint slides, each one culminating, building on the one before it. Most of the eyes were glazed over, or at least turned in the opposite direction. Hunched over bodies covered leather seats. A few yawns filled the crowd. No hands shot up to stop her, but not a soul seemed intrigued by what she had to say. Even her boss, sitting at the head of the table who had seemed to support her and told her she was a star pupil within the firm, seemed to have backed off. Of course, he hadn't seen her presentation ahead of time. No pre-brief. She had given him some of the finer points and run a few ideas by him before she delved in and sprinted toward the finish.

She still had a dozen slides to go, and more than twenty minutes left in her presentation. The seconds ticked by on a clock at the opposite end of the room.

Cold air pumped through the floor, and she shivered. Lynette gripped the remote in her hand tighter, emphasized a few pertinent points, and then walked to the other side of the screen, careful to avoid the projector light. Her wool skirt rubbed her thighs as she walked. The conference table was long and black, nearly the full size of the room, and the leather chairs swiveled. The men's eyes focused on empty notepads, or on the reception area behind the glass wall. The glass reflected multiple smartphones.

She didn't like losing.

She'd lost before: softball games and soccer matches. Lynette left it all on the field, sprinting toward the net or around the bases, her arms like pistons at her sides. She'd always been quick, a natural runner. The track coach had tried to recruit her, after watching her sprint around the soccer field like a tornado searching for land. But her heart lived in fields of green and seas of dirt, square white bags and wide nets, in polyester shorts and shirts.

The faces in front of her now, though, felt dirty, used up. The men cold and dead, lines and creases fully formed on their faces with mouths closed in silent trepidation. The one at the head of the table scrolled through his phone with the flick of his index finger.

She'd practiced the presentation over and over, used a mirror, and whatever else she could think of, as she hit the high points and skirted past the low ones. She'd gone over the finer details of the slides, point by point, with her head held high and her mouth opened wide. Yet, she didn't feel at ease. Instead, Lynette felt tightly wound, on edge, the carpet nearly catching a heel, her lips nearly numb, and her face almost there as well. The air shot up through the vents and smacked her face with each turn of her heel. She'd given presentations in this conference room for literally four years, and each had gone better than this calamity. She'd seen faces turned up toward her, eager faces, happy, with a smile of encouragement here, or a polite nod there. But not now. Now she felt as though there were seventeen guns pointed in her direction, and all she needed was one itchy trigger finger.

Sweat cascaded down her fingers and smacked the blue carpet. Lynette clicked to the next slide.

"This company is hiding money, plain and simple, gentlemen. It's cooking the books to deliver consistently successful quarters. Each quarter one to three cents ahead of projections. And it's fraud. Hidden beneath these numbers is another Enron or Worldcom. A disaster awaiting the right financial auditor. When this one tanks, you don't want to be floundering for one of the life rafts."

She'd shown them charts, numbers, and graphs to back up her data. A specific line on Xanthic's balance sheet and income statement—the same line, in fact—was off each time. She wasn't sure how anyone could have missed it. It had taken her less than a day to discover the error of Xanthic's ways. The executives were slick and polished and aided by slippery politicians with fat bank accounts and college mistresses, salesmen who talked one game and delivered another. Instead of running a company, they should have been running for office. Congress. A place where golden parachutes were passed around like umbrellas before a spring rain.

Not being able to account for every dollar bothered her. Having the trail of gold shoved right under her nose made her fists clench and her heart race.

"Thank you, Lynette."

"But I'm not finished. I have—"

Her boss bowed his head. "You most certainly are."

❧❧❧

He'd seen the tie in a Bergdorf's catalog. Not this exact same tie but similar. It had a slightly different hue, but the pattern and colors were the same. He'd walked through the Pru looking for the perfect tie, waiting for his wife who was with her friends, and most likely garnering her own slice of turtle cheesecake rather than sharing, her small fork poised over the smattering of whipped cream and caramel. But he couldn't blame her. Richard Lancaster III had a mouth full of sweet teeth.

His hand stroked the fabric, rubbing it up and down, lovingly like a dog named Bud. Not that he'd ever had a dog named Bud, or even owned a dog, for that matter. He was allergic. Damn near blew away his nostrils every time one of those furry beasts pranced next to him, or stuffed its soft face in his crotch. Still, it hadn't prevented him from petting every dog he saw and sneezing all over both hands and several T-shirts.

He did have trouble staying on point. That's what his last evaluation had said. He hated his boss, the evil little man with the twitchy eye, a short man with a big personality and a large mole at the end of his nose that always said hello before he did. He might as well have been Rudolph, his boss, although the man probably wasn't as smart or as surefooted as the furry reindeer. Not as smart as the tie was.

It stared at him, longingly, like some girlfriend he could no longer name. Like some college party he had attended years ago, where the festivities and women and booze ran together to the point that he could no longer separate one from another when he worshipped bikini tops and round bottoms. But he could still dream about drunk girls, keg stands, secondhand smoke, and eyes the size of paper plates from the marijuana intake.

He'd always had trouble with his eyes. He'd needed glasses for what was most of his natural life. That's what he'd always told people. Bad eyes, bad teeth, and chubby hands. Of course, his candy habit attributed to the bad teeth, or what he liked to refer to as his lack of self-control. When bits of chocolate stained his lips, he thought he'd pass out from the sheer ecstasy of it. That's what this tie was. Pure ecstasy. Sure, it wasn't the original version, but it was a damn good second-place finisher, and he had just the spot for it in his closet.

Richard looked over his shoulder and then peered up into the corners. This was supposed to be some midrange store, and there wasn't a clerk in sight, except for one behind the counter, but he engaged in some conversation with a chatty gal with a too-wide smile and exaggerated movements that bordered on eccentric. Her clothes further enhanced her eccentricity with loud colors, mismatched between her top and bottom. Her hands shot out in one direction, and then another, almost as if her arms were no longer a part of her body. She ran her hand through her hair too many times, and she liked to wiggle her ass whenever the mood suited her, which was about every six seconds. She had a nice ass, sure, but she didn't need to flaunt it like some half-crazed Loony Tune. Her laugh resembled a hyena's.

He hadn't been helped. Not at all. And what he could really use right now was assistance and a second opinion. His wife told him he had a problem pulling the trigger. That he just needed to make a decision, instead of dancing around the subject, and analyzing every shopping outcome for fifteen minutes. She wasn't going to be around for another forty minutes, if memory served him correctly.

Richard didn't just want the tie: He needed it.

The other clerk remained in the back. He'd wandered in that direction ten minutes ago, doing God knows what. Or maybe the more accurate analogy was to God knows whom. Since a female of undetermined beauty—he couldn't see her face, although she was another one with a nice rear end—followed him back there about a minute later and neither managed to reappear. She tried to be discreet about it, but she might as well have had a sign floating on top of her head, or some halo painted in black—certainly not a golden one—and held together with Scotch tape. She walked with nothing short of determination, her steps quick and forceful, and she hadn't bothered to look back. Not once. To get to the back room, she had to walk across the entire store, circumnavigating racks, with other men around herded in small groups of one or two staring at this shirt or that pair of pants. But the herds weren't there now, probably because neither clerk bothered to do a thing called work, and so they had left while Richard remained. It might as well have been a bar, or some game show called, *Spot the Pretty Girl with the Nice Caboose.*

ↄ∾ↄ

Carl Razer had walked up and down these same aisles for five years. Narrow aisles. Some might even say cramped. Books of all sizes lined the shelves. Enough books to last a lifetime, even if you were an avid reader, which he was. He devoured books the way an alcoholic might devour cocktails in one of his weaker moments, with a girl on his arm and a glass in his hand. His hands shook with anticipation, from the sheer number of books and brightly-colored spines, and he pushed his cart in front of him. It, too, was stacked with books, and damn close to overflowing.

The pay wasn't great (although the hours were), and if it wasn't for sharing an apartment (or in this case a room the size of a closet in downtown Boston), there was no way he could afford the rent. As it was, Carl was nearly behind, every month. But the joy of books, and the sea of customers—all ages, shapes, sizes, and races—that traipsed through the Boston Public Library made it worthwhile, and made his days run together. Not having a car certainly made things easier. It was a beautiful thing, the freedom. Walking whenever and wherever he wanted, taking the T to Harvard Square or Porter, or out on the Green Line to Brookline. Boston and its immediate suburbs were at his disposal, as long as he had a plan and his Charlie Card.

Boston was one of the few cities left where a person didn't need to own a car. He'd die in this walkable city, in his hole-in-the-wall apartment, where traffic noise often kept him up at night, or put him to sleep, with honking horns and sirens and screeching tires throughout the night and into the dawn. But at least Boston slept. He'd visited the city that never sleeps, where the bums ran free, and he'd decided it was not meant to be, after some errant field trip for some undetermined amount of time. Boston proved comfortable for him. He'd grown up here, still had a number of high school friends in the area, and he'd even bumped into Ben Affleck and Jennifer Garner—not at the same time.

He'd talked about the weather, the Sox, and whatever else crossed his mind for the couple minutes that he was in line. Not until later, after the clerk had a look of surprise painted on his face, did he realize that he had just spoken with a genuine celebrity and one-half of a powerful couple.

That's who he dealt with now. Another powerful couple. The two had come out of nowhere, all legs and arms and sour expressions, with their heads tilted and their lips moving in unison and their hands jerking in an indeterminate pattern. Their eyes flittered around before settling on Carl, and his books: the cart wheels squeaking, the stack of books wobbling, his grip tightening. The two barreled toward him like two moving trucks in the middle of the downtown tunnel. He barely even had enough time to blink.

"Can I help you?"

"Yes, you most certainly can," the male said. "Where is the *Twilight* series?"

Carl removed his hands from the cart. "It's currently checked out. Would you like to add your name to the waiting list?"

"What do you mean it's checked out? You haven't even looked it up on the computer."

"I don't need to look it up on the computer, sir." The last word left his lips before he could stop it, even though the kid wasn't a day over seventeen.

"Don't call me sir," the kid said. "Maybe you should check again."

The girl snickered and then smacked her lips.

"I checked about half an hour ago for another customer," Carl said.

"Well, I'd like for you to check now." The kid turned and pointed his hand in every direction but the information desk. "What are you waiting for?"

A million thoughts flowed through Carl's head. The most prominent of which being that these two should have been in school. That some teacher in some Boston public school missed the two of them, although the tall blond one was probably missed a bit less than the pixie-haired brunette with the full lips.

⚜

Richard Lancaster III breathed in and out, deeply, using his diaphragm. He'd learned the breathing technique through a yoga instructor, or ex-girlfriend, or an ex-girlfriend who just happened to be a yoga instructor. He'd stood around, maybe a bit too openly, and certainly a bit less naturally with his shoulders slumped slightly. Despite staring from afar at the tedious mating ritual and hovering ten feet away for approximately five minutes, he didn't seem to be getting anywhere. One clerk was still in the back, probably snogging with the dark-haired girl with the round bottom, and the other one still chatted away with a nonpaying customer like it was open mike night at Mickey's.

The breathing thing didn't help. He didn't want to close his eyes, just in case he fell asleep standing up, which had happened to him once before. He took one last look over his shoulder, noticed that no one seemed to be paying attention to him—not the least bit surprising—not even the girl on the other side of the counter—standing next to her conquest even as her right hand dipped below the counter's depths—who flirted rather openly with the less-than-friendly clerk with the long hair and squinty eyes. One more glance confirmed what he needed to know: He could bring in a jackhammer and no one would notice.

With a quick jerk of his hand, he swiped the tie from the open drawer.

Darting in the general direction of the main entrance, Richard Lancaster III took a slight detour around an elderly gentleman who strode through the threshold. Before he'd even hit the other side of the entrance, the alarm sounded in a monotone voice, mentioning that he should return to the counter, and something about a clerical error. The only error was the clerk who now looked up, eyes wide, forgetting the girl next to him, and the passionate exchange that had grown more and more animated.

"What the hell—" the kid yelled.

He skipped right over the whole motto about the customer always comes first, and he extracted himself from behind the counter and raised his voice when his first set of instructions didn't take hold. But Richard was already in motion, running away from the crazy clerk who didn't bother to pay attention earlier, but who now had an intense interest in the goings-on around him, and who moved about as well as an eel on dry land.

While the little shit slipped, Richard sprinted. He ran all out with his arms pumping at his sides, the tie carefully stuffed down the front of his trousers, and bouncing around like a Miracle-Gro plant, juking and jiving with each twist of his hip.

"Hey, you—"

The kid continued yelling, his voice and intonation nasally, and a bunch of other people joined in. Richard couldn't hear over the general uproar, the folks squawking on cell phones, the teenagers without inside voices talking and chattering over one another, and the voice inside of his head that helped him maneuver around the ever-curious crowd with open mouths.

A smaller kid—not the one who didn't bother to pay attention, but a smaller version of the space-cadet employee—dove at his feet like he was sliding into second base just ahead of the throw of the catcher, and Richard went down hard against the tile. His hip struck home, and then his thigh and his side ached and screamed, or maybe it was the mom next to him who yelled loud enough to break glass.

Richard shoved both palms on the ground and bounced back up, both knees aching and his heart racing, slipped in between a crowd of soccer moms eight deep and three wide—not that he counted—who chattered and waved and pushed strollers. He elbowed one, three elbowed him, and then he passed through the melee and rushed around a corner.

He didn't even bother to look behind him.

Chapter 2

Rug rats filled the streets. Little tots and tykes, and bigger ones carried wooden sticks that resembled baseball bats. A slight breeze filled the air, blasted around, whistled through trees, and culminated in a giant roar. Or that was the rats. One kid stood directly in the middle of the other kids with a hand in his glove and bent slightly forward, and one toddler held a bat as he stood positioned near a white, rubber pentagon with his knees bent and the wood pointed toward the sky. Youngsters from the opposite end of the street taunted the smallest of the group, as he wielded a wooden stick larger and heavier than he was. He swung at a white ball with red laces and whiffed. Nothing but air and a rush of wind. He swung again, and again he missed, swinging harder than the time before, twirling around and nearly falling down.

John laughed. The kid bit his bottom lip, concentrating, and swung harder than the two times before, but this time ball connected with bat, and it arced well beyond the one who tossed the ball. John shook his head, fascinated. And then he strode toward the darkened abode in front of him with the cracked shutters, brown patches of lawn, and filmy windows with the hairline fractures. The house offered no hint of a reply.

It wasn't his house, but then he'd never worried about formalities.

Two other cars parked on the street out of reach of the kids' errant balls. Chanting and taunting echoed in the middle of the road.

The location was predetermined, picked by one of the other two men. All that John cared about was the task in front of him, the job, and success. Hope. Political messages and hidden agendas filled with underlying letters and conflicting opinions. The truth would come out, or he would help it. Either way, he planned for a large parade.

Most of his life John was an outcast, a misfit standing on the outside, looking in between the bars, or cheering from the stands. He wasn't awkward, but most folks saw him that way. He no longer fit the obstinate mold, and he moved his toys and sandbox to the other side of the fence. And that was hardest for him to comprehend: Times had changed, and he hadn't always changed with them. He felt out of control, and the task at hand was a way to gain it back. He could rise above the pansies and the fruitcakes and send a message to the masses to spark enthusiasm. It had gotten out of control. Politics. No one seemed to know, or care, or even realize that the economy sank faster than the Titanic. With his hand poised over the handle, he was ready to flush and watch hopes and dreams flow down the drain. All he needed was the right amount of force.

⁊⊃℮⊃

"You're late," Matthew said.

"Traffic," John replied, as if this explained every bit of lateness that had ever existed.

Matthew's hand gripped the rail, as he shuffled up the stairs. A single porch light flickered, the swing swung, and claw marks covered the bottom of the wooden door.

"Cold feet?"

John shook his head. "I'm ready. Been ready."

Matthew slapped his comrade's back. "Born ready?"

John grinned, finally. His teeth were stained yellow. "Maybe."

Matthew stepped inside. The house was as cold inside as it was outside. Even colder. He couldn't see his breath, but he could feel the heat slowly leaving his body and drifting toward the pockmarked ceiling. He didn't shiver. Shivering was for the weak and served no real purpose. For what he had in mind, he would need every last bit of his strength.

The idiot was late. John wasn't the smartest of the three. His SAT score was in the 1300 range, instead of 1450. A mere amateur. He probably didn't even know what he was doing, or understand the message they wanted to send. And he was focused on the kids, when his attention should have been focused on the task laid out before them. John's left hand had a slight twitch. Maybe it was excitement, or something else entirely. He'd barely lifted his eyes, as he walked through the door. This was Matthew's mission, and John was a by-stander, a pawn in the overall political agenda. He and his 1300 SAT score were too stupid to realize the obvious. Matthew wouldn't bother spelling it out for him.

This was Matthew's plan. He'd come up with it, he'd recruited the other two men, and he was the one in the best position to execute said plan. Maybe his strength would lift the other two, or maybe it wouldn't. It didn't really matter.

What mattered was how it all worked out. If he could get the herd to follow orders, the masses would believe.

Belief was such a fleeting thing. One minute they were all gung-ho GI Joe, and the next minute they cocooned back within themselves sucking thumbs and punching stairwells. He couldn't stand Americans and their short-term memories. Americans focused around what was absolutely best for them, even if it was to the detriment of everyone else. The simpletons were lazy and cocky and overweight.

Imposing democracy where it was neither wanted nor even encouraged proved futile and terribly childish. Fighting a war against a country that never asked for the invasion set America up for failure time and time again. The path to ignorance was often paved with good intentions, and those in power exhibited more obliviousness than a cheerleader with an inferiority complex. To right the wrongs of America, he needed to destroy the country from the inside out, and what better way to reign supreme than to destroy its bloody symbols of wealth and power. Boston performed a tea party, and now it needed to fall in fiery waves of ash.

Once the flames licked the sky, the real healing could begin. In the meantime, the only sound Matthew heard was the whine of consumption and carburetors. Each new thought made him even more frightful of the one that came before it, but once chaos arose, the rest of the world would take notice.

All he wanted was to point the universe in a new direction, and he'd stand tall with the detonator in his right hand. When America fell, he'd welcome the transition with open arms and appropriate motivation.

He blinked, and the vision of destruction vanished. But a sense of serenity took its place, and he nodded his head as he savored the moment.

He'd found the house on Craigslist, located in Framingham, a shit town off The Pike, on a direct line west of

Boston, where the houses were cheaper and bigger. A few fucks a bit more trusting than the others. The entire neighborhood sighed in perfect harmony.

The For Sale sign in the yard beckoned him with open arms. He picked the lock and thrust the door open with his right hand.

ഗ്രൈ

The triumvirate stood on three sides of the table. The room stood at the bottom of a flight of stairs in an open space filled with cinderblocks and junk and a single bulb emitting a soft glow. The light winked off the concrete. The chain from the bulb broke off in Matthew's hand, and dropped to the hard floor.

"Do you have it?" Matthew asked.

John shook his head. "I thought you were bringing it."

"Why me?"

"Why not you?" John asked.

The man had to be joking. That's all there was to it. One idiot often begets another, and John was the biggest idiot of all. If Matthew could have ended the man's miserable existence right there, he would have. But he needed him for the plan, even if the card table didn't.

John finally nodded. His loopy grin was covered in cheeks and teeth. The bulb didn't seem to notice.

"Well, can I see it?" Matthew asked.

The man shook his head.

"Could you act like you're more than five years old?" Mark said. "It might save the rest of us a bloody bit of trouble. I ain't got time for your games."

The basement was cold, dark, and dank. It stank of a combination of excrement and mold. Spider-webs congregated overhead and in three of the four corners.

"Did someone die here?" John asked.

Matthew nodded. "Yes, years ago."

"A child?"

"Yes. How did you know?"

"I can still feel a presence," John said.

Matthew glared. "You can't feel shit."

"Don't test my patience."

The room was silent again.

The table was long and massive, and covered with materials that resembled plastic putty. Orange putty stood on the table, garnering for attention, and wires of different lengths skirted out in different directions like Christmas lights. And backpacks. Three dark ones—the exact same size and color—spread out on the table before him. Three watches. Silver. And matching outfits to blend in with the surrounding population, a population filled with commuters and financial experts and individuals much too focused on themselves to worry about the agenda of anyone else. Idiots with Starbucks mugs and white Dunkin' Donuts cups filled to the brim with black liquid, cream, and sugar.

The outfits, while not identical, were similar. The pants and tops were blue, and the hats black. A single logo covered the caps.

The compound was previously stolen. John wasn't exactly trustworthy, and he wasn't exactly a genius. But he was highly motivated and could articulate when the situation warranted it. Other times, his mouth moved faster than his brain, darting off in different directions, and never quite returning home. One tangent begot another until his original thought had gotten lost along the way, or shoved under the radiator.

John's body was covered in moles and pockmarks. He wouldn't tell Matthew the pockmarks' origin. The moles, however, were more easily attributable to genetics. John's eyes drifted this way and that, like a misfiring musket. Sweat filled his palm before he rubbed it on his pants. His lips were chapped, and his right eye was about to water. He closed his eyes and massaged his forehead.

"Where's the dead body?" John asked.

"We're back to that now, are we?"

John massaged his forehead with more force. "It was never found, was it?"

"No, it wasn't. Are you going to start a search?"

"I can still feel her presence."

Matthew shook his head. "No, you can't."

"How would you know what I can and can't do?"

Matthew exhaled. "Because you're an idiot."

ᘓᘚᘓ

As if that explained everything. It was, in fact, a copout. It didn't explain anything at all. But then Matthew never made any sense. It was all about him. The lion and the lemmings. The ones headed straight for a cliff before even realizing their toes were already over the edge. John hated shepherds, but he hated sheep even more. When he lifted his eyes, he jerked his head.

Sure, he was the pseudo-leader of this particular operation, but that didn't mean he was the true leader, the one Mark turned to. Matthew was the most articulate and a forward thinker, and even had the highest SAT score, but he was still a consummate moron with a complete lack of interpersonal skills. What he had in his brain he lacked in vision and actual follow through. He was a walking computer without a mouse.

"Let's get this stuff distributed," John said, "so I can drive into the city."

"Bloody hell, I thought we had already established that I'm driving."

"You've already been in two accidents this year."

Mark bumped a backpack. "What does that bloody well have to do with anything?"

John placed his hands on the table. "You can't be trusted behind the wheel of an automobile. Your fuse is almost up."

"I'm a perfectly good driver," Mark said. "It's the others I'm worried about."

Typical American response: It was always someone else's fault. The response was even automatic without the slightest hint of remorse, spoken like a man who would die before he reached forty-five. In a fiery crash against a concrete barrier. John swallowed the response before it left his lips. His eyes drifted down to his hands, and he bent his fingers at the knuckle, as his nails scraped across wood.

The Semtex, wires, watches, clothes, and backpacks were passed around like beads at Mardi Gras. Having been to Bourbon Street on three occasions, John needed another visit, a bag filled with beads, and a second-floor balcony overlooking the street before he missed out on yet another opportunity to view an inebriated college student's hooters.

John removed his suit first, and the others followed. The new clothes resembled jogging suits, bright blue in hue, with Sox ball caps. The red B was both striking and tasteful. No smiles were offered or exchanged, and fewer words as well.

The three placed clothes in a fourth backpack, an orange one, along with the leftover supplies and extra wires.

ოჳҽჳ

The drive into Boston was meaningless, redundant, and filled with multiple entry and exit points. Massholes weaved in and out of open lanes in gaps barely wide enough for a tractor lacking both blinkers and common sense. Toll collectors collected $1.00, or $1.25, the booths green and sturdy. Mark spoke followed by Matthew, over the sounds of silence and the occasional horn.

Mark peered out the window. "It's another gray day."

"Do you need me to go over the bloody plan again?"

Mark expelled a hurried breath. "I'm not bloody retarded."

John gripped the wheel tighter, as a jerk—minus the turn signal—swerved into his lane. He flipped the radio off and the blinker on. The sea of SUVs moved in a stop and go fashion on six lanes of interstate filled with overhead passes and masses of frustrated drivers. Weaving in and out only added to the aggravation.

Billboards plastered on the side of the highway advertised endeavors like concerts and restaurants and lawyers and shopping centers and fast food joints with heart attack burgers.

John gripped the wheel tighter. "Traffic is a bloody catastrophe."

"That's The Pike—"

"Where horns and aggressive driving are highly encouraged."

Time passed rather quickly. The cars appeared rather endlessly, merging in with the rest of the spectators every few miles or so, as the sea of tadpoles went about their daily lives.

Chapter 3

"What do you mean I'm fired?" Lynette asked.

Her boss shrugged. He actually shrugged. His broad shoulders moved up and down, the air between them filled with electricity. A human resources rep with severely pulled back hair sat beside him, and they had both barged in her office moments ago. Literally. The two couldn't have moved faster with an electric scooter. Their mouths formed thin red lines. Lynette's door shut in a rather abrupt manner, and the rep carried a stack of paperwork with her that was half the size of her torso. The rep was a medium-sized woman with a serious expression and little else. Her eyes were beady behind big, round glasses. Shifty. Her movements were jagged and serrated and limited in nature, as she shoved a stack of papers in front of Lynette before she even dropped in the chair on the other side of her desk. The rep's voice was devoid of all emotion. Lynette's office felt like it was ninety degrees, and her left leg shook.

Lynette hadn't even managed to get her bearings. Her computer had entered sleep mode, with random icons moving about the screen, the stack of paperwork on her desk long and onerous, the new pile butting up against the old. The papers shifted slightly beneath the warm air, and in the ongoing silence her computer pinged. She heard voices down the hall. Loud voices. A printer whirred to life somewhere in a cubicle, and a copier rose from the dead. But her office was completely silent. A paperclip hitting her desk would have provided more noise. With her comfortable chair now considerably less so, Lynette shifted in her seat, and crossed her legs the other way—left over right.

A finger tapped her desk.

The rep sneered. Literally. She actually sneered, her lips pulling back from her teeth, with her face cinched up tighter than a Ziploc freezer bag. "I thought you understood the term."

"But it's Friday afternoon." Lynette had plans for Saturday, or at least she thought she did, and Sunday seemed rather promising as well.

"All the better for you to enjoy the weekend."

Lynette shook her head, adjusting the cobwebs. "How long?"

"Permanently."

This is ridiculous. She'd never been fired in her life, not even when she dropped an entire tray of plates in the middle of Red Lobster on a Saturday evening. "When will I be escorted from the building?"

"You have until the end of the day to pack your things," the rep said.

"Benefits package?"

"Do you think you actually deserve benefits?" the rep paused. The air continued its jagged edge. "It's all explained in the stack of papers."

Lynette's mind whirred faster than the computer, and her left leg picked up speed. "How come your stack is still larger?"

The rep said nothing. Of course, she wouldn't. Her index finger poked the bridge of her round glasses. As for Lynette's boss, he hadn't even looked at her once. He'd kept his head bowed, and his arms folded across his chest—the shrug of his shoulders the only indication he still breathed. He studied his cuticles for more than three minutes, and appeared in a state of perpetual shock. She was sure it was just an act. She'd seen the same song and dance before with other employees, but she had no idea it would affect her. That she'd flush her life down the toilet over a single PowerPoint presentation. She was Xanthic's top performer, or at least that was what her last performance review had said. Maybe the same statement was used on every evaluation of every appraisal. Top performer today, fired tomorrow. She'd never asked about the others.

"I'm not the only one being fired, am I?"

The rep stood up and opened the door. "I think we're done here."

୧୬୧୬

Richard had a close call with some random kid's arbitrary arms attacking his legs like an octopus. He'd turned the corner at full speed, and he'd rammed into this punk adolescent with ear buds jammed in his ears, and a dire expression plastered on his face. A mom had intervened and pulled her child back, before the kid ended up on the bottom end of his shoe. The mom had severe hair and a stern expression—similar to a drill sergeant—and Richard received the evil eye as he flew on by.

Footsteps slammed behind him. One set. Two. He didn't look back. The thought of the enemy close at hand made his stomach churn. He heard one shout and then another. Different voices. And then a third shout, the same voice as the first. He maneuvered around a couple who were too busy holding hands to notice the commotion around them. He saw an opening up ahead and he went for it, nudging a stroller in one direction, a toddler in another, and a cane with the stroller. The squeaking either came from his shoes, or the toddler, and he attempted to block it out, as his legs churned and his stomach burned.

The green exit sign marked his ultimate destination.

He shot up the stairs taking them two at a time. A hand reached out behind him and grabbed onto his shirt, before the fingers slipped through the fabric. A firm hand, but it didn't have the strength to carry on. Richard shifted to his right, a couple of folks screamed next to him, older folks and then a younger couple held hands with puckered lips and doe eyes. A few folks pointed, and a baby cried—not the same one as before. This one had a high-pitched squeal and flailing arms. The world around him blurred, just as another hand reached out for him.

The arm tugged his collar, his head jerked back, he thrust an elbow, a grunt ensued, fingers slipped, his feet churned, and then he raced forward with his arms pumping and his breath wheezing.

The presence behind slapped at his heels, the voice focused on him. The tie shifted in his pants, moving this way and that, freedom and justice and the American way. His right foot itched followed by his left. A young woman with a cell phone jammed into her palm waltzed in front of him, dancing along to some ridiculous song. He jived when he should have shucked, and he slammed into her, her breasts smashed against his chest. Both of them dropped to the ground in a sea of arms and legs. Flailing. She fell on her back like a turtle. He, on the other hand, proved a bit more nimble. He shot up, while she shot off her mouth. But Richard ran and maneuvered before the panting behind him could ultimately close the void. His breathing came in fits and starts, and he felt the stitch at his side grow stronger. The stitch had exacerbated after the collision, as the young woman cussed at him.

Darting through a dense crowd—most of whom spoke in a foreign tongue—he stuck his elbows out at his sides, parting the waves in front of him, as colorful language offered a firm reply and middle fingers saluted. A sea of blue and green glass windows blurred by, offering up sights on the street below. His hands whistled through the air, as a series of whispers surrounded him. An escalator rocketed upward, and he hurtled after it.

When the moving machine stopped, he took off and leapt a bench, minus any couples holding hands, and he hugged a plant, as he smacked his forehead on a branch, before he bent backward in slow motion and headed for the home stretch. He turned a corner on the third floor at full speed, slid down one escalator, and pumped his legs toward another. He rounded one kiosk and then weaved his way through another. A wind chime assaulted his face, and he tripped over a shoe. He curved one corner, took a sharp turn at another, and bounded down another moving stairwell to ground level.

The glass doors stood in front of him, offering him a vision of the outside, as traffic and pedestrians whispered by, the cement sidewalk his ultimate destination. He glimpsed freedom, and he offered it his right hand.

Richard pumped his arms harder, moving them faster and faster through the air, concentrating on the doors in front of him, and the group of pedestrians that had congregated toward one side. The doors were close, so close, and his first smile in days appeared across his face. More people around him pointed, as the screaming reached a crescendo—or that was the whistling through his ears—and the stitch at his side blared. Or it could have been the insistent voice behind him. Incessant. Just a few feet behind him. The heavy panting and deep breathing and monotone speech and pounding feet propelled him forward ten feet from the outside doors.

It had its own heartbeat.

The stitch.

A blur rushed beside him, a man in a red hat, tan pants, and white jacket. The first indication that something was seriously wrong. The second indication was that the ocean of folks in front of him had congregated together, banded, men and women and children standing together as one with elbows locked and feet spread. He tripped. His arms flapped out in front of him, catching the tile before his body smacked the floor, and then an arm reached out for him. Grasping. Folks around him began to cheer.

That was when he, Richard Lancaster III, knew that his life was officially over.

c✐c✐

"What are you doing back here?" Carl asked.

"Maybe I wasn't clear the first time—"

"Oh, I think you were perfectly clear."

"Then maybe you should hand over *Twilight*, make things a little easier on yourself."

He'd never known anyone to be this passionate about *Twilight*. Sure, he'd heard of Twihards, the long lines for opening night at the movies, the online fanatics who were as passionate as loyal *Star Wars* fans, the readers who followed and watched the various *Twilight* reviews as they played out on the internet, but this was a firsthand experience, and as far as Carl knew, the hooded teenager hadn't even read the novels yet. He was several years behind the pop fiction curve: It was already the middle of the *Fifty Shades of Grey* phenomenon, and its ensuing trilogy. He hadn't seen any *Fifty Shades* fanatics, and he wasn't quite sure he was ready to deal with bondage and leather and lace on full display.

Carl clenched his fists 'til his knuckles turned white, and he started seeing spots on the far back wall.

"Is that a water pistol?" Carl asked.

The teenager shook his head. "Man, this is real."

This was the first time he'd ever been held up in the library. In fact, he'd never even heard of the library holdup thing before. If anyone had told him this was how his day would have played out, he would have driven them to the insane asylum himself, and he'd have handed said detainee three pink pills and possibly two yellow ones.

Carl tried to shove the cart in front of the teenager with the cocky attitude and overly large pupils, but he had no cart. For that matter, he didn't even have a book. He was clearly in a state of shock, because the whole world slowed down to an absolute crawl, and he saw a little leprechaun dancing on the top shelf. Real time didn't seem so real, and the books that surrounded him appeared to laugh. A table stood between the teenager and him. He placed his hands on it to hold himself up.

The teenager had walked in wearing a BC sweatshirt, his massive ears jammed up against the hood, and he suddenly shifted his eyes, his voice even rising an octave. The kid had only spoken a few sentences, and now the pistol smiled with each movement. His jeans were about four sizes too big, and it couldn't have been much more than friction that allowed them to hold their current position. The jeans appeared worn and frayed, and the sweatshirt had probably seen better days in Dorchester.

The kid rubbed his nose with the butt of his pistol.

"All the novels are checked out," Carl said. He needed to say something, anything, to end this nightmare. There was even the possibility of downloading books off the internet. If it hadn't been for the stupid Big Six, and their stupid quotas, it would have made his job even easier. Then, he wouldn't have to deal with stupid kids with stupid guns in the middle of the stupid day. "You know, you can download it directly from the library's website with your e-reader."

The kid squinted. "What the hell's an e-reader?"

Great, so he'd managed to be held up, in a library, with an undersized kid in an oversized outfit, over a stupid *Twilight* series that frankly he didn't even think was all that great, or really even all that well-written—although it certainly was written well for its intended audience, and it certainly wasn't anyone that had attended BC, at least not that he was aware of anyway—and he'd managed to discover the one reader who had never heard of an e-reader before.

"It's a Kindle."

"What the hell's a Kindle?"

Carl started to cry. He just broke down right in the middle of the library, next to the children's section, his arm too far away to pick up a book from the shelf, with some beady-eyed six-year-old less than twenty paces away, his face stuffed in a Dr. Seuss book, reading it on a small plush chair with his legs dangling and his arms hanging.

The kid hadn't even bothered to look up once. So Carl closed his eyes and hoped this kid with the gun would disappear.

Maybe he did deserve to die.

Chapter 4

John gathered with the other two on the steps of the Boston Public Library, Copley Square, downtown Boston. He'd parked several blocks away. A Ford Mustang rental to be exact. Don't ask. He'd walked in wanting a compact vehicle, since the streets of downtown Boston were tricky enough as it was, and finding parking—not the least of which relied on luck—was an entirely other matter that took a direct act from the parking gods themselves before he could find a space. He managed to find one immediately, setting a record, at least for himself, and he managed his first whistle in years. Just a little one, since he'd received looks of complete horror from strangers on the sidewalk, one of whom carried a Dunkin' Donuts cup. Mark, shortest of the three, had actually slapped him on the back.

But back to the Mustang. It had to be the most ironic thing imaginable. He'd never managed a car upgrade in his life. Sure, he'd heard about them, but it had never happened to him personally. It even caused the whistle before the slap on the back. Of course, the backpack had alleviated the sting of the slap, but in the end it made it worse, because the damn Semtex and all the wires jammed into his spine and forced him to bend over. A sharp intake of breath gathered in the back of his throat.

After exhaling, John stood up taller and walked a little straighter.

He'd shot Mark a look of pure horror. Mark responded with a belly laugh, doubling over at the waist and hugging his chest. And it wasn't a small one either. It was a rather large one that took several seconds to subside, the bending, bobbing, and chuckling working in unison.

John shook his head. He'd need better friends in the future. Not that he was a social creature by nature, even though most humans were. He was more of an elitist, or maybe he was just aloof. The argument had ensued in grade school, and more than once, about him being human. It was discussed in third grade, so it wasn't exactly an informed debate, but all the same it had stuck with him through the better part of his formative years. That had been a tough year for him, third grade, and none of the following years seemed to get any easier, especially the high school ones.

John stood with his back against the pillar and his eyes on the little church across the way. He shoved his left thumb in the pocket of his jogging pants, and removed the smile from his face. In lieu of sunglasses, he shielded his eyes with the back of his hand. He dropped the backpack next to his feet and even kicked it once or twice. Dissension clouded his mind, and perspiration filled his heart. He smacked his lips, and flicked his thumb against his thigh. A passerby stopped and stared at him for more than twenty seconds before moving on.

ↄﾟↄﾟↄ

Matthew dealt with two idiots. That was the plain and simple fact of it. And one of the two decided it was a good idea to whistle. Not just a brief one, low and through his teeth, but a louder one that actually sustained itself for a couple of notes and turned two or three heads.

Even the drive was an exercise in terror, as far as he was concerned. Matthew was used to Boston drivers: their overaggressive nature, the manner in which they whipped in and out of lanes, the horn honking that felt like it rivaled Chicago, and where in small towns like Concord the term "sense of entitlement" developed a whole new meaning. He'd run into an individual from Concord, a man who was probably the devil incarnate behind the wheel, when he had actually stopped to let an old lady cross the street—the man nearly had a heart attack screaming and cursing and gesturing through the windshield with his lips floating and his face contorted in rage—and his wife wasn't any better and offered up one-fingered salutes just for the hell of it. She screamed and gestured as much as he had, and quite possibly burst a blood vessel, and at one point he'd actually gotten two fingers, one from a man who was probably in his fifties, and the other from the wife who appeared a few years his junior. The whole situation stuck with him now, even though it was years later, and he was still stuck riding and driving around in this cramp-induced city with more than its fair share of aggressive drivers—one of whom was named John. The man honked his horn loud enough to raise the ghost of Babe Ruth, and he'd even offered up a few curse words when merely a middle finger wouldn't do. The man in Concord would be proud.

And now he had to deal with a different kind of idiot. A simple one. The nightmare triumvirate. He just hoped Mark could do his job, because he wasn't about to deal with the consequences if he couldn't.

Matthew stood one step above the other two with his knapsack facing the doors behind him, his cheeks brisk from the cold, and every word out of his mouth even and measured.

☙❧❦

The jacket and explosives made him appear bulkier than he really was. John didn't mind looking fat, but he preferred to do it on his own terms, thank you very much. And this hadn't even been his bright idea to begin with. It was Matthew, the tallest one—always the fault of the tall guys who figured height represented power and privilege and standing on the next step up somehow made him superior—and he was stuck behind the wheel of the car. Now he stood on the steps with the other two, passing time on the second step up from the bottom, out of the way of direct traffic. If it were up to him, he would have leaned against one of the pillars, with his back perfectly propped, and where he had a view of all of Copley Square. A rather nice view, if he did say so himself. A church stood across the way, a small one, and he considered that ironic as well, surrounded by taller buildings on one side and a throughway on the other, if he'd considered the notion more thoroughly instead of dismissing it. But he didn't.

Sure, it was a great plan, but that's because he was involved in it. He was the idea man, more than just a wingman, and it was his damn idea, even if Matthew decided to take all the credit along with most of the bills.

John had on a Timex. He hated Timex. What he really wanted was a Rolex, ever since he was old enough to know what a Rolex was, but he could never afford one, and at the rate his life progressed, he wasn't sure he ever would. Sure, it was a pipe dream, but it was his dream. And that was really all that mattered. Despite the cold outside, wind, and even the occasional snow flurry, sweat dripped down his face, plummeting off his cheeks and onto his jacket. The sweat would mix rather well with the explosives, wires, and whatever else managed to find its way into his life, like dust and lint and coffee stains. He needed a pink and white Dunkin' Donuts cup, instead of an empty palm shoved against the outside of his pocket, and a vicious expression painted across his face. Standing and waiting was worse than having his teeth cleaned with a razor blade.

The Sox cap made him feel a bit better about himself, despite the awful season that plagued them this year, and if management didn't straighten things out, the dreadful spell would continue like herpes on a twenty-dollar whore. It was a fungus, a cancer, a mold induced coma that had taken over the Sox, similar to the curse of the Bambino, even though that particular calamity lifted with their 2004 World Series win and come-from-behind triumph over the damn Yankees.

A series of church bells rang, and it was by some miracle that he managed to hear this, but the cars and the loud pedestrians and the visions that continued to plague his life had subsided for just a moment, and filled his world with a clanging that bordered on the ferocious, and managed to twist his world around. Consistency was what John's world needed, and a little hope went a long way.

Matthew's voice below jarred his thoughts, and shoved the syncopated rhythm in another direction. His pack clicked with his rocking motion, and the air blew a stream of current through his hair.

He looked down at his watch, and Matthew and Mark looked at him. One of the men nodded, and then the three split up. Getting lost rather quickly in the crowd, with his Sox hat plastered against his head, proved easy—being vertically challenged didn't hurt matters either, and his nondescript face helped further. The hard part was breaking through the added security of Hancock Tower. It was worse since 9/11, and it showed no signs of letting up. But then he had already factored this into his journey, and he had developed a rather unique plan.

The Semtex hugged his back like a long-lost lover, his movements calculated and sure, and his mind drifted ahead to better times and better memories long past.

ℯ⌔ℯ⌔

Matthew bounded up the stairs, the concrete steps that extended in either direction and that could hold an entire battalion of military soldiers marching off to war. He'd thought about war, and what it meant, and how it had gotten out of hand by a series of politicians that gave no regard to the average American. What was executed either with, or without Congressional support, by Presidents, or their cabinets, and which often resulted in the deaths of innocents, women and children holding baskets and bottles, and soldiers with friends and families and little ones waiting back home.

The system was broken.

It was fucking annihilated by some Arab in some desert that was hotter than a waffle maker, where sand dunes inherited the Earth, and where water wasn't just enjoyed, it was a sacred commodity worshipped by the entire nation. He thought about the men, the soldiers who were trained to fight, and who, in some cases, ended up dying not on the fields of battle, but on the streets of Tikrit by handmade IEDs stuffed with nails and screws and whatever else those fucking towelheads could find, and then placed in the way of military vehicles, or strapped to some six-year-old before he was shoved in the face of some pimple-faced lieutenant, who hadn't even gotten to experience two virgins let alone the sixty or so that were promised to the six-year-old Arab for blowing himself to hell and back. Once the body was blown to bits, the pieces were picked up from the streets and shoved in a casket with the American flag draped on top and heaved on a cargo plane and flown back to our nation and buried in Arlington with a simple white tombstone as the rest of the row filled with more dead figures than our Congressional legislation could ever hope to account for.

Incredible. But he was bound and determined to level the playing field, even if it meant he had to make a few sacrifices to ensure his message was received with wicked precision. His message was simple: War wasn't the answer. It didn't matter if it occurred on the streets of Tikrit or Baghdad or Beirut or Cairo. He wasn't a pacifist, but America couldn't solve its problems by bombing its way to an increased oil supply in countries where children were brought up to hate democracy and our overindulgent ways. If he could break the idiots in power, the hope for a better tomorrow existed, otherwise the bloody shitstorm would continue.

Matthew walked through the Boston Public Library's plastic devices that were on either side of the door, standing like two sentries ready to take on the world, or at least a handful of Boston's finest book thieves. He marched in the direction of the stairs, the Semtex bobbing, his heart racing, the sweat dripping in buckets down his face, as a blast of warm air smacked him between his eyelashes. He nearly took a step backward before he pressed onward, working his way up to the third floor, the library warm and welcoming despite its vast expanse of cold marble outside, the pink floors peering up at him with sharp, fierce gazes. He thrust his thumbs between the laces of the knapsack to steady himself and center his mind along with the rest of his body.

His right cheek twitched, moving back and forth of its own accord, the knapsack heavier on his shoulders, his lips pressed in a firm, thin line, the sweat pooling on his jacket, mocking him, the beads glistening and dripping as he walked across the cold, hard floor, weaving his way between wooden tables and chairs and still bodies. A blast of warm air struck him on the chin, and the sensation of heat remained even when the air didn't. But he pressed through the vast expanse, the large room with the high ceilings and the welcoming feeling and the books lined up like soldiers on the shelf. He placed the knapsack there on the third floor, removed a few pounds of the plastic explosive, and then placed the rest in a central location, the sack sitting ominously for any and all to view.

A simple detonator throbbed in his pocket.

❧❧❧

John had waltzed past the Hancock Tower security guard, sitting like a statue behind a marble countertop, flipping through a magazine, no doubt filled with a series of ads, or comments about the state of the world, or the state of women, and their lack of suitable attire. He had seen a few on the beaches of Nantucket wearing barely-there bikinis with straw hats and drinking from glasses with their backsides turned away from the water. But this was winter in Boston, not Miami, or Malibu, so the bikinis were shoved in bureaus or boxes waiting on next year, and a lone guard sat behind a u-shaped desk. The guard wore glasses, and he was skinny, all limbs, which managed to stick out a bit when he leaned back in his chair. The guard stared at a series of monitors, his hand hovering over a control panel. A suspicious expression plastered his face, one eye stared more intently than the other, the glasses added yet another dimension to the picture, the freckles rather prominent on his pockmarked skin, his uniform crisp and pressed firmly against his thin frame with a red logo in front of a gray background.

One eyebrow lifted. "Who are you?"

John hesitated for a split second, his movements more calculated. He even managed to bow his head slightly as he reviewed a pseudo clipboard. He skimmed the fake list with his thick finger. "I have a delivery for the thirty-second floor."

The guard's head lifted and his eyes narrowed.

John shifted his eyes down to the list before he lifted them once more. "Roger Smith."

The guard's nametag said Gary or Jerry. "You're telling me Roger is getting flowers?"

"If you'd like to call him up and ask him himself, you may do so." John tapped his Timex and glanced at the digital readout. "I'll wait."

"Roger has never gotten flowers before."

"There's always a first time for everything," John said.

Gary took a sip from his Dunkin' Donuts cup. "I know every individual who walks into or out of this building, and I haven't seen you before."

John expelled a single breath of air. "The other delivery person was fired. Embezzlement."

Gary grimaced, like he'd been stuck with a cattle prod turned to a reasonably high frequency. "You're trying to tell me Carol embezzled money?"

John nodded, head bowed. "It's always the ones you never stop to consider…" His voice trailed off.

Gary harrumphed. "She was a good woman."

"The best," John replied.

"You know, I should really deliver them myself. Company policy."

"You're certainly welcome to do so. But that would mean you'd have to put down your *Maxim* magazine, and leave your station unattended." John twirled the flowers in his hand. "You wouldn't want that, would you?"

Gary completed a full circle in his swivel chair, his face filled with concentration. "My partner should be coming back shortly."

John glared. "I'm sure he will be—"

"You can wait."

John tapped his Timex once more. "I really can't."

"It's not a suggestion."

"Do you really want Roger angry?" John asked. "He resembles the Tasmanian Devil when he's angry, and I'm not sure you're ready to deal with those particular consequences."

Gary's eyes narrowed. "How do you know Roger?"

"I do my homework."

"As a flower delivery person?"

John flashed his best smile. "I'm much more than a flower delivery person."

Gary executed another harrumph and flicked his fingers in a dismissive gesture.

John was stuck on an elevator with an old woman who had just farted. His eyes burned and watered, and if he was close enough to it, he would have punched the emergency stop button. Maybe he'd suffocate. He'd die in some stinking elevator with an old woman who passed gas with the same amount of enthusiasm that cheerleaders showed at a pep rally. Worse than the smell, though, was her smile. Like she shared some great secret with the rest of the elevator.

His jacket clung to him. The small space and three teenagers jammed around him, as did the little kid that jerked on his pants, and resembled a gremlin with his toothless gaze and wide eyes. Three tugs and then a brief intermission before the next round of tugging began. If John had believed in suicide bombing, he would have blown himself to the heavens along with the surrounding pedestrians. Getting his tonsils pulled for the next six years would have been better than this. Instead, he suffered his fate at the hands of an old bag with a crooked smile, and the kid humping his thigh with his toothless grin and lifeless stare.

One drink at an Irish pub never sounded so good. No, he'd better make that two.

The ride would never end. John was sure of it. The road to the top was paved with good intentions and a crowded atmosphere. But that was before the elevator, the kid with an affinity for tugging, and an old bag with an affinity for passing gas in crowded spaces. Even the operator—with one hand hovering near the buttons and the other underneath his nose—was not amused by the situation. His hat was pulled low, and he had yet to make eye contact.

When the elevator finally did stop, John stumbled outside, sucking in a series of deep breaths, each one more blissful than the last. He wasn't on it for more than a few minutes, but it felt like forever, and his lungs ached. Time kicked him in the balls. The foul, lingering odor constituted his every thought and most of his senses. The stench was all he could think about. It had probably burned off half his nose hairs.

On the other side, the air was clear, clean, and filled with emotion. A spectacular view, nearly perfect in its simplicity and filled with a sense of openness and wonder, completed the picture. The skyline extended for miles, and churches appeared on the horizon. The city had very distinct lines, and points of interest popped out like pictures on a map. He'd always wanted to visit Bunker Hill Monument. It stood off in the distance, laughing at him, punching toward the sky, and yet he couldn't turn away. Each thought brought him closer to his final destination, and each sensation made his heart flip.

The backpack weighed heavily on his shoulders, yet the burden didn't even faze him. The sheer majestic simplicity of what he was about to do couldn't escape him either.

Nothing would.

His steps proved lighter and breezier, as the crowd parted before him.

သာသာ

The deal was twenty minutes. That was all the time he had. No more, no less. The devices were rigged to explode simultaneously, and failing that, he was the one with the kill switch, still throbbing in his pocket, beating as fast as a frog's throat. His heart palpitated with each thud.

Matthew pictured the end. Winning. He foresaw everything and accounted for every little hiccup or bump in the plan, and he circumvented every wrong turn. A sense of madness wasn't complete without a little forethought. He was the one in the group with vision. No other alternative and certainly no backup plan. It was this...or nothing. And nothing seemed terrible, a round for losers, and what the second-place finisher in the prom king contest faced: a sea of blank expressions. Endless possibilities ensued. Before the twenty minutes ended, Matthew wondered about the outcome, and how it would all go down on the Copley Square playground. He stood off to the side, wide, sturdy steps beneath his feet, his back to a sea of buildings across the square with a full view of the proceedings about to unfold. The seconds ticked by on his Timex, and the countdown continued in his head. There was a plan to meet at the Starbucks across the street, but he wanted to witness the destruction firsthand, and bask in all of its infinite glory. No viewing booth ensued for second place.

He had hoped it would come to this. In fact, he had planned it this way, and there was no way to lead him astray. He was happy once, but he failed miserably in his endeavor with death and destruction his only motivator. But maybe, just maybe, he ended up exactly where he was supposed to for the first time in his life. But he hoped it wouldn't be the last.

If he couldn't bend an entire nation to his will, he didn't have a chance at happiness. If he couldn't bomb the idiots in power into submission, he deserved to end up locked away for the rest of his days. If he couldn't create a sea of chaos and a pile of ashes, only to rebuild on top of what he already destroyed, he deserved to die in front of a group of men with swords and shotguns. If he couldn't build hope where none had existed before, he didn't deserve to lead naptime in kindergarten class, let alone an entire nation of misfits and miscreants.

The seconds ticked by at an impossibly slow pace. A counteraction to the adrenaline coursing through his system and rushing in one direction followed by another. He hadn't been this excited in a long time. Maybe ever. His heart rocked against his ribs, and blind power consumed him.

Matthew held the detonator in his right hand, and looked down at his left wrist. Only a few seconds left. He lingered longer on the top step than he should have. The chaos around him stunted his thoughts and emotions. He was too close, and filled with anticipation and adrenaline. He backpedaled down the stone stairs, his momentum carrying him. He counted down the seconds in his head, and when he reached one, he pushed the button. He stood two steps from the bottom, and still the explosion rocketed him backward.

The impact thrust against his chest, and launched him into the air. He called out, but his voice was lost in a swirl of chaos, fire, and smoke. His back and butt slammed against the concrete, his legs straight and splayed out on either side of him with his face pointed toward the sky and his mouth opened wide. His left knee ached more than his right. Too shocked to stand, he lay splayed on his back with the cold concrete beneath him as snowflakes floated down and painted his face. The white mixed with the red, black, gray, and the smoky haze.

The Boston Public Library was a giant fireball. The stone structure, which some might even refer to as magnificent, was a shell of its former self, and the pillars out front, which at one time were glorious, lost much of their luster, snapping and cracking like twigs in a bonfire. Stone and cement rained down from the heavens, struck the sidewalk, and splattered like grapefruit.

Too frozen to move, Matthew picked up his head and stared with his mouth open and his eyes wide at the chaos surrounding him. The fiery inferno lifted toward the sky, the passerby dodged him far and wide, he crushed the detonator against his palm, as splintered plastic cut into his hand. It went better than he had planned.

Flames shot out of the middle of the library, a fiery blaze that gained strength and momentum. He couldn't find his voice, even though his mouth moved, and words flowed from between his lips. Sitting made sense, nothing else did. People passed him with mouths opened, possibly in shock, darting in every direction, as more debris rained down, paraded around him, and the sky filled with gray and flames. He sensed traffic in front of him. He felt the fear and panic that hung in the air like fog, creeping from the smoldering building to the sidewalk below. The outstretched tentacles of the smoky gray destroyed the purpose of his otherwise meaningful existence, as the ringing in his ears plugged and fermented in his brain. The charred remains of the once magnificent structure filled his nostrils with heartache and pain.

A stranger lifted Matthew up off the ground. And he shook from head to foot, as his mind kept time with a syncopated rhythm. He hadn't even realized his whole body had resorted to convulsions and that he had left a piece of himself within the confines of the library, possibly even on the pink floor or the stairwell, as he raced to the bottom and out the glass front door. He felt exposed, vulnerable, and nearly immobile. Catatonic. That was the word for it. Maybe it wasn't the right word, but it was a word, and so it stayed in his brain, floating and reaching out before yanking on his shoulder. The little voice in his head screamed in protest.

In front of him, all he saw was madness.

തൗൽ

The elevator dragged along in slow motion. The numbers counted down, as the countdown continued in his head. John ticked off the precious seconds, and he realized he would make it outside with less than a minute to go. It was close, too close, but the wait to go down was longer than he anticipated, and the aftereffects of his previous ride in the elevator still lingered heavy on his conscience. The view was spectacular, and he spent a minute indulging in it, like a little kid watching *Sesame Street* for the first time and clapping along to every song. He counted down the numbers in his head, and he estimated the pattern of his otherwise bane existence.

If he had any sense, he would have been an architect. John loved the shape, and the energy that buildings created. The way simple pillars added an entire personality to a structure, or even the simple placement of windows—the type used changed a building from a humble structure into a masterpiece—and the way each structure caught the light a certain way. He'd always had a creative eye, but he never indulged in creative endeavors thanks to his father. The stilted conversations and one-way rages lingered heavy on his mind, as though they had happened yesterday. His dad was strict, a man who liked to use his belt first and ask questions later. The man believed morale in the household would improve as long as the right number of beatings ensued. No one could ever please him. John hadn't even bothered to try. In fact, he'd focused on whatever made him the angriest and whatever he could do to set him off in an alcohol-induced rage for his own entertainment. It was a game, similar to Parcheesi or Backgammon, only with higher stakes and uneven results that left him hollow and empty inside.

John tapped his foot and stared out at the display. This simple measure helped him take control over his emotions. He'd been known to lose it on more than one occasion, another gift from his father. His heart rate increased, as he stood still, waiting on this ridiculous contraption, and still tasted the lingering effects of his ride up: The stench clung to the roof of his mouth like barbed wire. He started to sweat, his face hotter than the rest of his body, even though he no longer had his backpack, or the Semtex, and he felt a warm breeze directly against his face. He had no idea where the breeze came from, or where it would go next. He could only hope he wasn't too late.

The elevator clicked and jerked slightly as it reached bottom. A metallic ping ensued as the doors opened. John pushed toward the sanctity and freedom of the glass doors, shoving anyone and everyone out of his way, no longer caring about protocol, or propriety, or women and children first. His arms pumped at his sides as he rushed through the throng.

Saving himself was his highest priority.

Hancock Tower would end up a shell of its former self, and he smiled at the possibility of corrupt workers and innocent bystanders blown to oblivion in a master-piece of his own creation, as sixty stories worth of blue glass smacked the asphalt on a Tuesday afternoon.

The tops of his feet slammed the insides of his running shoes. His breathing lost its steady quality, growing more erratic with each step, as he shoved air in and out of his nose. But he saw the doors ahead, the guard sitting duti-fully at his station, his face buried in *Maxim*, not even bothering to look up as John stormed by. He struck the doors with great force, enough to dislocate his shoulder, but his shoulder held, and his breathing softened…or that was the adrenaline talking?…and then he gasped, breathed the fresh air, and bent over at the waist. He had his arms pointed in an angular fashion as he panted and sucked in breaths through his open mouth. The cold air swirled and mixed with the hot breath he expelled from between his lips.

Behind him, Hancock Tower exploded. Windows and doors burst, flames sought more oxygen, glass rained down around him, and people screamed and hurdled in every direction. He hadn't noticed the people before, but there they were with ear-piercing cries, as he coughed and gagged and sucked in every bit of air his lungs could take.

John turned his head away from the cartoonish nature of the latest catastrophe. He covered his face with both hands and peeked through the gaps between his fingers. A thunderous clap echoed throughout the confined space, and, with his hands on his hips, he grinned at the latest sins of mankind.

ᘓᘓᘓ

Mark only had a few seconds to spare, as he raced down the stairs. His heart exploded outward, and his breath came in short, wheezing snorts. His feet moved as if he floated on air, he leapt toward the bottom when he had a couple of stairs to go, and grabbed the banister for support. The paneling and bloody doors were all the same, gray and cold and filled with windows, as he raced down the infinitely symmetrical packed hallways, to the second level and then to the first, echoing a life filled with sameness and regularity. The large tile squares that permeated across the floor helped him skip from one moment to the next. A march played over and over in his head, and his feet kept time with the downbeat.

He should have traveled more and toured the world. He wasn't sure why he thought of that now, but there it was, dangling in the open atmosphere, as he hung in the air for milliseconds before his feet struck the next level, and he continued on with his journey. He hadn't even traveled out of the US. He had never even been to Ireland, England, or Scotland. What a mess. He had no hope of ever fulfilling his destiny, if he couldn't even be bothered to take a plane across the Atlantic. One catastrophe after another filled his world, but he would redeem himself, and it would start right now. His right ankle throbbed, and his hips surged, as he circumnavigated around children and random pedestrians.

Mark bounded down the stairs, his footfalls resembling a herd of buffalo in the middle of a large pasture, his feet shuffling as the bloody staircase carried on beneath him and disappeared under metal ridges before it appeared once more on the opposite end. It was beautiful in its simplicity, as the movement proved both steady and promising.

His feet struck bottom, and he pushed through the door and tripped on the threshold. He stumbled and swerved, but he didn't go down. His watch beeped, informing him he had only a minute left. A warning Mark had put in place, knowing the situation would come to this, and that he'd need the additional incentive to race to safety.

His head cleared as the deep breaths neared, and time marched on. The end surrounded him, filling his lungs up with smoldering fire and smoke.

Mark pumped his arms at his sides, and lengthened his stride. A stitch developed, and he felt pins and needles around his ankles. Even his knees screamed, as he jerked onward, like a soldier on the battlefield racing away from the enemy. He shoved his way around the revolving door, and his feet touched the sidewalk the instant his whole world changed.

The Pru became a shell of its former self.

Chapter 5

Carl needed a smoke break. His world revolved around the inhalation of tar and nicotine and other carcinogens. He smoked Marlboro Reds, and sometimes when the mood struck him, Camels. He had a system: He never smoked more than one cigarette, and he allowed himself one smoke break every two hours. He didn't need more than that, and he certainly couldn't settle for less.

It wasn't an addiction. Carl could quit anytime he wanted to. It just helped him alleviate stress, and it helped him keep the weight off. It also helped him run faster in his youth, so cigarettes weren't as bad as the news reports and Surgeon General's warnings had him believe. Plus, he controlled the cigarettes, the cigarettes didn't control him. He even switched brands for a period of time, just to prove he could.

He had adjusted his smoke break rule after the teenager and the plastic pistol. He'd never seen someone so bent out of shape over *Twilight*. Short of psychiatric help, he couldn't offer the kid, or his handgun, any hope or alternative medication. And he certainly wasn't going to offer him one of his cigarettes. The little shit could find his own. His favorite bench was fifty feet away. A stupid rule to discourage smoking. Like he couldn't walk the extra forty-eight feet without government assistance.

Carl inhaled and exhaled, the smoke forming an "O" as it left his lips. He'd practiced this for nearly two months before he perfected it. He even had a few smokers raise their eyebrows, or toss a few compliments in his direction. He closed his eyes, savoring the taste on his lips, the calm sensation, and the out-of-body experience.

The last drag was always better than all the ones before it. If he wasn't such a stickler for the rules, he'd have ended up smoking two or three cigarettes a long time ago, just for the sheer pleasure of that last drag.

As he stubbed out his cigarette, the door behind him exploded, and he smacked into the wooden bench, his hip smacking one of the hard edges, before he rocketed sideways and propelled forward, and his other hip slammed into the concrete, ultimately ending with his head against the rough edges of the stone wall, a dizzy sensation, a blackout, and one large bruise. When he came to, the building behind him was a giant comet, and stone and debris littered all around him. It might as well have been Armageddon or the Apocalypse or some shit. And that was when he realized those infernal cancer sticks—as the Prius-driving, environmentally-conscious, tree-hugging shits liked to refer to them—had just saved his life.

It was a sign that he was on the right path, and so he tossed his hands up in the air and uttered a hallelujah and an amen. He twerked, and he shimmied, and he even thrust his elbows out in either direction.

∽∾∽

She had 'til the end of the day to have her stuff removed from her office. But Lynette immediately started packing her belongings into boxes, not even bothering to wait for the final bell, knowing that the sooner she removed herself from her situation, the sooner she could start her new life. A number of visitors stopped by her office. But not her boss. He had looked in the other direction, shirking away from her and averting his eyes, as she grabbed a couple of boxes from storage, paraded back to her office with cartons in tow, and started clearing out her desk. She dumped the contents of her desk drawers one at a time: pens, pencils, notepads, staplers, pictures, trophies, highlighters, and a thumb drive found the bottom of the box. And then she moved on to the next drawer, dumping magazines—*Cosmo* was a personal favorite—along with Tylenol, Ibuprofen, and Benadryl—the changing of the seasons was the worst time of year for her—Sharpies, more pictures and awards, including one for longevity—fifteen years with the company, like that mattered—a couple of dry-erase markers, an iPod, and part of her CD collection bounced into the box.

When she reduced her life down to material possessions, the box and her world seemed emptier than she ever could have imagined. The thought hollowed out her insides, and caused her world to turn to ash.

Lynette cursed her boss under her breath. She had given so much of her time, energy, and heart to Xanthic. She'd delayed starting a family. She'd worked weekends and weeknights. She'd given up vacations, tropical island tours, a cruise, postponed her wedding by six months when a project needed her undivided attention, as if she were the only one who had discovered the tricks of the trade. She'd nearly lost her husband to the demands of her job. He'd literally given her an ultimatum—cut back or cut him out—and she'd managed to talk him down, the same way she might negotiate a merger. She actually negotiated with her husband. He'd demanded sex two more nights a week for a year, and she had caved to keep him happy. She would have given him blowjobs for a month just to keep the peace. And here she was being let go, literally tossed out on her ass, her pencil skirt not long enough to billow up around her, her hose clinging to her legs and trapping heat, her mind wandering to and fro, her entire universe being shoved into cardboard. The curse words started flying, one four-letter word after another, as she slammed another drawer into the pit of despair and lost dreams. And then she kicked the beast—box—aside, almost poking a hole in it with her black high heel. She punctured both the box and her dream in less than a few hours, and her cardboard reality shattered.

Lynette grabbed the other box, jerked it across the carpet, snagged it on the separated piece, a section that she had wanted replaced for months, and her boss had continued to appease her with words instead of actions—a common theme. He talked out of one side of his mouth and acted out of the other. He had literally nodded his head, told her it would be fixed, and then it wasn't. And when she spoke to her boss again, he had waved her off, dismissing her with a flick of his wrist and a turn of his head, right before he picked up his phone and placed a call before she had even closed the door behind her.

He was a bastard. Her boss. He treated her like an outsider ever since he had stepped foot in the corner office, the one overlooking downtown Boston with a panoramic view, the one with the dark furniture, dark desk, and glass coffee table. A man's office. An office from which he excluded her, except when he summoned her to his chambers and talked incessantly. The good ole boy network was alive and well in Hancock Tower, and Lynette was left with little to show for it. The golfing took place on Friday afternoons, often twice a month. She hated golf, but she gave it a go and took lessons. She could hold her own on the golf course: hitting the fairway with precision and striking the ball solid. Sure, she couldn't chip worth a damn, but she could putt, and her iron play proved solid. Some of the other executives, men, couldn't match her. Fucking men. She had done everything she could to fit in, and still it hadn't been enough. And now she cleared out her desk, cussed up a storm, the heat nearly suffocated her to the point that she thought she had a hot flash, even with the fan blast, sweat dripped off her face and between her arms, her nose warm to the touch, her cheeks more than likely a solid pink. In fact, if she had been asked even just a couple of days ago, she would have said things were looking on the up and up, and now she was the former help, and being kicked to the curb for actually telling the truth. The bastards. This company deserved a toilet bowl and a squeegee.

She hadn't glanced through the benefits package yet. She wouldn't glance through it until she had at least three drinks and one long cry. If she were a vindictive individual—which she certainly wasn't—she would have made them pay, and pay dearly, suing the company, along with the golden parachute bastard for everything he had.

Lynette grinned, as she swiped the contents off the top of her desk into the awaiting box. Pictures and pens and papers and a mouse pad and a glass paperweight disappeared beneath the flaps. Some of it—the pictures and paperweight—cracked, but she didn't care. She'd sort all of it out later after she had a few drinks and maybe a pint of ice cream. She unplugged her coffeepot—which she used to make hot water for her tea—and then slammed into the door with her backside, jerked it open, and walked out with the coffeepot in her arms, cradling it in both hands. Her entire universe dwindled to a series of inanimate objects.

She marched down the stairs—thirty-two flights but she wasn't counting—becoming angrier and cursing more and more under her breath with each step, her heels clicked and her teeth clacked and her stomach rumbled, and out the door. After literally fifteen flights or so, she thought she heard a series of pops and screams, but she focused on the stairs, the clicking and the clacking, and her march toward oblivion.

Before she even trudged outside, though, chaos had literally intervened. There were men dressed in suits and khakis, and businesswomen in suits and skirts and high heels and pink and white and cream colored blouses with mouths opened wide, skirting in all directions. Broken glass covered the sidewalk like pigeon shit. And all she thought about was how insane it was. And then she could actually see. Her eyes opened wide as she noticed the glass with the bright blue tint from Hancock Tower, and maybe that's where the popping came from, the glass breaking even before it struck the pavement, raining down in softball-sized pieces of hail and other chunks bigger and heavier than she was. And then her eyes moved from the glass, and noticed the red. It literally covered the entire sidewalk, as it splattered across the concrete canvas and seeped into the cracks.

It was insane: the screaming and colliding and broken bodies and crumpled catastrophes. And then Lynette screamed, too, and ran with the rest of the businessmen and women in their colored suits, some tailored, and some of which weren't. And then she laughed. She ran and laughed and clung to her coffeepot like it was her long-lost friend, and smiled like it was her birthday, even though it wasn't for another six months, and then a thought entered her mind, rocketed through her brain like a spaceship headed straight for the sun: Maybe the bastards had gotten exactly what they deserved. Her boss had finally taken the easy way out, and he had evaporated into thin air. Maybe the rep from human resources took the journey along with him toward the blue-gray sky.

She stopped on the sidewalk, on the other side of the street after she'd darted across, nearly slamming into a Prius, and then a minivan, and then a Ford pickup, as folks rubbernecked with wide eyes, parted lips, and glazed expressions. Lynette waited until she reached the other side with her feet on stable ground, and once she was there, she looked up, counting the floors as she went, and then she had to recount, because she thought maybe she had gotten it wrong in the crazy aftermath of glass and red and people. But she counted twice more, each time coming up with the same number, and then she realized, as she clutched the still warm coffeepot to her chest, her thoughts scattered around her like broken glass, pigeon shit, and dazed mannequins. It took over a minute for it to literally sink in, but then it did, and she realized that was her floor. She was there only moments ago, tossing her belongings, some of her favorite possessions, pictures that she enjoyed looking at every day, and magazines that she hadn't gotten around to reading. And then she realized the laughing had ceased. Instead, she cried, as the tears rained down her cheeks, like the glass and the shit that struck the pavement, as a sea of tears and shattered dreams surrounded her.

She hiccupped, and the waterworks continued once more.

ഇൽ

He struggled in the backseat, twisting his wrists and jerking his shoulders. He, Richard Lancaster III—son of the founder of Lancaster Financial, before his dad sold the business, and then he'd up and died less than three months later, no longer able to face the monotony and burden of doing nothing—was in the back of a police cruiser with his hands cuffed behind his back and his knee jammed against the door. He was actually being led away from the Pru like a common thief. His dad had died on the golf course, a private club less than four miles from home, on the fifteenth green in the middle of the best round of his life. He was on fire, they'd said. He'd nailed every green, sank nearly every putt, and he'd even chipped in from number thirteen. It was absurd. Sure, his old man loved golf, even more so than a few drinks around the bar with the Sox or the Patriots on the tube. His dad wasn't a Harvard man, MIT grad, or even a BU fan. He went to a blue-collar school for a blue-collar degree, and he drank his beer and liquor with a gleam in his eye. The old man died, but his legend lived on.

When his dad sold the business, and when he'd made out his will, he'd left all of his money to his current wife and the string of exes. The old bastard had screwed him from the grave. But Richard Lancaster III had a signed letter in a gray envelope. And in it his dad had given him an ultimatum: He'd told him if he could hold down a job for ten consecutive years, he'd have a small sum waiting for him. That was how his old man had put it. And yet his ex-wives had to do nothing for the pot of gold at the end of the bikini waxes. The trophy wives with the trophy haircuts with the trophy tans and the trophy eyes had it made in the sun, rolling around in hundred-dollar-bills and tanning oil and soaking up the rays in their string bikinis, or topless, and for all he knew bottomless, while he was handcuffed and hogtied in the backseat of a police cruiser, squirming. His right leg twitched even more than his left.

Sure, it wasn't that bad, but it was bad enough. He'd end up in some interview room in some precinct, and he'd have a cup of water, or a cup of burnt coffee shoved across the table, sitting in a metal chair in front of a metal table with the chair scraping across the cement floor with a one-way mirror off to the side—like in the movies—with a cop with a bad haircut—probably some ten-dollar job at the county barbershop—staring at him like he was a common criminal from the streets of Roxbury. The cop would whip out the tie he'd stuffed down the front of his pants—evidence was how he'd present it—with a smile on his face and a glimmer in his eye, and he'd be fucked three ways from Wednesday. And then he'd spend a few months in jail and pay a four, or maybe even a five figure sum—money that he didn't have—and then he'd be right back where he started, except he'd be in debt, jobless, gutless, and digging himself out of some bottomless, never-ending pit in the middle of a graveyard on a Saturday afternoon with a shovel in his hand and a towel shoved down the back of his pants and a tie wrapped around his neck with a guard at the other end watching his every move. That was his life, and the sea of cars in front of him further proved his point. He bowed his head, as the cop in front of him slammed on his brakes, the screech heard round the world, the rubber burning and horn honking and choice words added for good measure. When he looked up, taillights winked at him. And he wondered just how much worse his life could get. His eyes fixated on a particular point on the horizon, and he mumbled a string of forgotten phrases under his breath.

He gripped his right knee to minimize the twitching.

Just when he thought it couldn't get any worse, it did. The radio on the dashboard squawked, an all-points bulletin from what he could gather, and then the cop flipped the siren, and his world filled with squealing and squawking, the radio blasting through the speakers, tires wailing, all four wheels turning, as the cop maneuvered the cruiser around, before barreling back in the direction from which he had come.

Chapter 6

It's never good to be the first one on the scene. That was his mantra from day one. He'd always wanted to be the second one, the one after the initial responder. That way the scene was never his, but it also proved he wasn't ignoring the calls, and that he had arrived as quickly as possible. He'd snap his fingers, say gosh darn it to let the sucker who had arrived first know he had tried his best, and he'd say a little prayer under his breath. It had worked for countless crime scenes. Too many to mention.

Addison Thomas was lucky, but he liked to attribute it to more than just luck. He had inherent skill, a sixth sense for where the next crime would take place, and he'd always managed to strategically place himself just out of reach. He'd peel into the lot, or the street, or wherever he needed to go with his siren blaring and his hands tight on the wheel. He oozed southern charm, even if he'd never crossed the Mason-Dixon line. It was a good system. In fact, it was one of the best systems he had ever come up with, and now here he was—through some fluke, or bad luck, since the gods no longer looked upon him favorably, although he rather liked where he was, thank you Bing Crosby—with his back against the wall and a blazing inferno staring down at him. This situation had gone horribly wrong. Catastrophic even. And he somehow managed—through some stroke of horrendous luck, he guessed—to be the first one on the scene. He couldn't snap his fingers and pass the scene off on someone else. This was his rodeo, thank you, Bing Crosby.

And it wasn't just some small neighborhood crime. Flames whizzed through the Pru, and debris splattered the air. Screaming women, men, and offspring everywhere, cut and bleeding, and an unconscious older man with a gray-haired woman standing near him and rubbing the side of his head. And he stood in his shirt and tie, with his hand in the air surveying the situation and weaving his way through the madness, as a hand reached out to grab him. Everyone at the scene looked to him, Addison Thomas, for guidance and answers to a series of questions he still tried to work out for himself. The puzzle proved even more terrible than he had initially imagined.

What the fuck had just happened?

He wanted to cry, to bend over, to break down in the middle of the street, with cars lined up in either direction, people gawking and screaming, with babies and children crying and voices rising. He wanted to shed a few tears of his own, to isolate and harness his true feelings along with the gravity of the catastrophe as it played out before him like a plunge from the forty-fourth floor. This was the biggest clusterfuck he had ever seen, and somehow he managed to end up in the middle of it with no end in sight. His master plan tanked faster than the Sox in September.

This was his scene, and it was his worst nightmare. He wanted to cry and puke, in that order. He felt certain he would faint. He rocked back and forth as a snowflake smacked his lips and his eyes watered. Saltiness dribbled down his cheek, and froze against his face. But he stood his ground with the concrete hard and harsh beneath him, and silently cursed whoever on the other end listened. If this was the end, he wanted a refund and a pat on the back.

He needed a megaphone or a battering ram, and Addison had neither.

∽∾∽

He'd been on the job for six months. In that time, he'd seen rather dire situations. Women, children, babies, homes and commercial buildings up in flames, neighbors staring in horror at abodes with flames reaching toward the heavens, windows that exploded, Scooby-Doo bathrobes, red flannel robes, and silk camisoles lining the streets of desperation. But nothing could have prepared Daniel Pinder for the scene in front of him. The Hancock exploded outward, the streets were in chaos, glass and a river of blood covered the pedestrian pathway, traffic was jammed, several cars were jackknifed with rubberneckers turned toward the horror, and pedestrians were everywhere, mostly businessmen and women in sharp suits and gray skirts and hundred-dollar haircuts. He made the sign of the cross on his chest, pulled the golden cross that his mom gave him on his thirteenth birthday from around his neck, brought it to his lips, and kissed it. Not once but twice for good luck. And still the feeling of emptiness would not subside.

His heart slammed in his chest as he breathed deep, recalled his training, recalled better days and happier times—short skirts and summer tans—and kids and swing sets, and picnics and sandwiches and glasses of lemonade, and the Boston Common and Public Gardens, with oceans of green and rivers of trees. Walking with his girlfriend along the trails and pathways, holding hands, his heart slamming in his chest, his hand clammy but the woman beside him either not knowing or not caring, as she moved with such grace and ease that she practically glided across the concrete, and the heat not moving a hair or an inch of her long, brown locks that cascaded down her back. Her hair was what he first noticed about her, from across the room at a college party that he wouldn't have even attended if his roommate hadn't been such an ass.

Daniel stopped between classes—at the wall where every poster of every party that had ever existed was labeled and punctured the plasterboard—to tie his shoes, because at that particular time at that particular location he had noticed that his shoes were untied, and so he stopped and when he looked back up that flier pierced him right between the eyes. He didn't think he would go, and had even talked himself out of going on multiple occasions, and analyzed the situation from a hundred different angles, and even warmed to the idea of not going, until his roommate had walked in the room, turned on his stereo, and called him a bastard.

Most likely, he'd had another fight with his on-again, but mostly off-again girlfriend, and they were definitely off, he had said, before he called Daniel an ass, and his roommate brought up the night Daniel had snored louder than a freight train, and that was it. He couldn't take it anymore, and so he had stormed out into the night, to the party no less, with no idea what he would do once he got there.

Forgetting the bastard roommate, though, was at the top of his list of activities. He had known a few people at the party, and he had a drink or two to blow off a bit of steam and blend in with the rest of the crowd, and then he had seen her, with her back turned away from him, her long hair cascaded around her, and he had worked up the courage to go and talk to her, because he'd never seen anyone like her before. And it had nearly been the end of him. Her smile was all lips and teeth and carried enough wattage to light up a Christmas tree, and when she tugged on a strand of her long brown hair, he thought the world was about to expire.

This was a new kind of madness, and he was fairly certain it would be the end of him as well. But in a different way and certainly filled with more harrowing fanatics and forged fantasies.

The truck stopped, and he was already out with his feet smacking the ground, running toward the flames, the only one, other than the men in fireproof suits behind him in yellow and gray with helmets astray. The rules pounded through his head like he had just heard them yesterday: remove any civilians and then contain and extinguish the flames. The thirtieth floor of The Hancock was no more.

Daniel tilted his head up in the direction of the latest horrific noise of grinding metal and twisted steel, as a couple floors above were blown to bits. The Hancock appeared ready to collapse, and his body prepared to follow suit.

జ్ఞ

Leo Nivea couldn't believe someone had blown up the Boston Public Library. The columns out front were blown to smithereens, along with all three floors. Traffic reached a freakish standstill, with bodies twisted this way and that, focused on the horror, and then there were the runners.

People stormed in every direction: some had arms in the air, some didn't, shirking in all directions, men and women, children and babies pushed in strollers, and dogs walked on leashes were all coaxed toward safety. Concrete slammed against the walkway, and cars splintered on the street below. He'd lived in Boston nineteen years, and he'd never seen a scene in Copley Square like this one.

Leo extracted himself from his vehicle, once he was able to navigate his cruiser through the masses of misfits, although definitely not all, since chaos exploded to the nth degree, and even with his blasted siren and horn honking and finger waving he couldn't break through the herd. At least there were no dead bodies crushed under pillars or splayed out on the walkway. No one was hit by concrete or passing motor vehicles.

Fucktards and shitstorms of epic proportions filled his world. He chewed on his cuticle, and plowed his way through the madness and sadness. He bumped his shoulders, and an outstretched hand struck his chest, and his lips expelled what was left of his hope.

It just didn't make any sense.

But then nothing did.

And maybe nothing ever would again.

Chapter 7

Mark grabbed a table at Starbucks across Copley Square, where the chaos had already erupted. It was easy to predict Americans and how they reacted. They wouldn't, at least not from sanity's point of view. Instead, women and children and dogs on leashes ran in whatever direction led to the most complications, and nobody stopped to give a damn about anyone else. Anarchy. And then the ERTs arrived, who would at least inject a bit of sanity into the situation, and then after the scene was processed—bodies moved and stretchers pulled apart and pointed questions asked in hushed tones—the real fun began.

And after everyone was accounted for—those that had survived, and those that had not—the cops chased their tails in pointed circles and then a genius would try to piece together exactly what had happened by reconstructing the scene and determining point of origin. And in the process of discovery...well, before they had gotten all that far...news crews would get word of what had happened, and they would show up in droves, with blondes, redheads, and camera crews, and interview whomever they could find.

Insanity.

He had changed in the Starbucks bathroom, ready to watch whatever transpired out the window, as he grabbed a backless seat, while everyone and anyone ran from Starbucks like it was about to blow. Even a barista behind the counter exited through the back door, the cashier had told him. It was his job to report back to the two remaining workers with spreadsheets and dead body counts, as he abandoned his post to rubberneck or chicken-leg it on the sidewalk.

Mark shifted in his seat. The coffee in front of him was bitter, with a hint of a metallic-aftertaste, and his face became hot, despite the lack of heat in the room every time the door opened and another customer stepped through the threshold. If he wasn't careful, he'd start sweating, mixing one odor with another. What he wanted was to observe the festivities with his two compatriots, the idiot driver and the mastermind, who were just as crazy as he was, and possibly even crazier, and bask in the glory that they had actually pulled it off. All the planning and preparation, none of which was his doing, and it went exactly as Matthew had expected. No problems or hiccups, other than John now walked with a slight limp, his left leg dragging. He'd explained—not that either Mark or Matthew cared—that before he entered the men's restroom, he bounded down stairs two at a time, and he'd steamrolled for the glass doors, full speed ahead, with the adrenaline carrying him toward the sanctity of life, past the security guard, and right onto the sidewalk, just as the glass doors blew outward, and a lake of glass rained down around him. He had brushed himself off and had walked away like nothing bad had happened.

"Fucking brilliant," John had said. "The adrenaline has finally worn off."

His ankle was being held together by pins and needles, and John was fairly certain he needed a surgeon to operate. That he needed the gas—and possibly a shrink—and that he needed to go under, and the surgeon needed to operate in the next twenty-four hours, or there was a good chance he would die. Always dramatic, that one. Most of the time, John had no idea what erupted from his lips, even as he spouted off like a drunken Midwesterner describing the tornado that had just blown through the middle of his trailer park and had taken little Timmy with it.

ഗംഗ

Mark—the idiot—had a stupid grin plastered on his face, and he sipped from a steaming paper cup, as if it were a glass of chardonnay, with his gaze focused on the ensuing insanity. He had a hand stuffed in his pocket, as if that were the answer to all his problems—maybe he'd find a quarter or a dime—and Mark alternated between the lopsided grin and the coldhearted stare, as if he couldn't decide which one was more appropriate. He'd picked a seat that was directly under a fan, thereby establishing his idiot candidacy, and a far-off gaze took hold for the better part of his natural existence. It was meant to be, or it wasn't, but he had managed to withhold a few rights of his own. He'd even managed to get them similar hats. At least he'd talked Mark out of that harebrained scheme that lacked in both tact and persona, possibly of the non-grata variety.

The parading in Copley Square had taken on a new level of folly, and John was glad he'd brought his digital camera with the zoom lens—the one that could take a reasonably accurate photo from a quarter-mile away. The detail, while not quite clear, still made for a wonderful scrapbook, flipping through the pages when he was as old as his grandfather, with a little squirt on each knee, providing him comfort and possibly even a sense of purity. He could look back on the trials of his youth with both awe and wonderment.

John slapped Mark on the back, and procured the stool to his left in the opposite direction of the door with a plop of his pack and a shake of his head. His shirt was tighter around the middle than he wanted to admit, his hairline receded, and he experienced the first signs of crow's feet.

The bottom of his right eye twitched and throbbed at a level that was clearly out of touch with reality. He'd heard it was related to caffeine, stress, or not enough sleep. Since he had his eye on a Venti-sized cappuccino, he could have located the source of all his problems, although many of his hitches still sat on the bench on the edge of the square. A rather-loud moron less than ten feet away dropped all pretense of humility and exacerbated his Boston accent, dropping more Rs than a teenage texter. John held his breath for five seconds and clenched his jaw for ten, before he throttled a middle-aged man with a battering ram for a hand and a mouth as wide as the Charles.

The streets weren't forgiving. Stealing was more than just an unpunished sin: It was a way of life. He'd stolen his first candy bar when he was seven years old. He liked to tell people it was a dare, but it wasn't. He had merely seen it sitting on a shelf in the back of a convenience store, and he had claimed it as his own. He had gotten in his first fight when he was nine, the kind of fight with bleeding lips, busted teeth, and scarred and bruised cheeks. A kid nearly two years older, several inches taller, and several pounds heavier walloped him on the side of his head, and he had decided to hit back. Probably not the smartest move, but then John wasn't known for his intelligence. He had spit blood after about four or five punches, the blows to his head made him woozy, and the one that knocked him on his ass had been a doozy. But he kept fighting, learning, and evolving, until three years later the odds turned in his favor. Slow to learn and quick of temper didn't exactly make for the best combination, but he had adapted with every growth spurt. He lost his virginity at fourteen. It was over and done with quickly, and he had sought the same high—both sex and fighting—again and again. But he did try, probably too much in some cases, only to end up flat on his face with a broken nose. Pleasure was a gift he hadn't always given, yet he appreciated the effort the most, and that kept him looking to score with the entire dance team. He had stolen from his mother's purse, the local convenience store, ripped off sons and daughters and husbands and wives, married women with aging faces and unfulfilled dreams, and talked multiple women out of their underwear—once in the backseat of a Mercedes while the engine ran. All of it had changed him, probably more than it should have.

John experienced the good with the bad, and in either case his life turned out for the better, even if he did have a permanent scar on the back of his left thigh. This occurred when he dove through an open window, stumbled over loose shingles, and snagged the back of his leg on the rain gutter before he dangled over the edge of the roof, bled, and promptly fell into a rhododendron bush. The woman might have been worth it—he had promptly forgotten if she was—but the scar remained a permanent fixture in his lothario existence. But hope faded along with most of his dreams.

The look on his face was as real as the cup of coffee in his hand—the line was shorter than he expected—as he took the seat to the left of the short one with the stupid grin and vacant look on his face, the counter a little too close to the window for his taste, even if it did have the occasional woman bending over at the waist.

John sipped from the steaming cup that was a tad too

sweet, and nudged Mark with his right elbow. The sound of arrogant chatter filled the small space, as he peered over his right shoulder.

⌖

Two freaking idiots. Both with caffeine jammed in front of their faces, both with scars that had cut deeper than the continental divide and caused earthquakes on a vast expanse of shaky ground. Both had waited for the heavens to open up and the rivers to turn blood red, as the camera sat perched with an unobstructed view of the outside. The matching suits were all right, except the bright blue color was ridiculous. The aftermath, though, was brilliant, and his plan came together perfectly. That's right: It was his fucking plan. The two imbeciles tried to take credit for it, especially John, but he'd shove tar down their throats and rip off their dicks before that ever happened. If the stupid fucks wanted credit, they'd have to earn it.

His collar hugged his neck, and muted ambiance smacked him in the chest. Matthew brushed a lock of blond hair out of his eyes, and focused on the ultimate prize with more than a hint of satisfaction. He waited in line with the rest of the dimes and suits, and pinched his nose with his left hand. The horde moved, and he considered pushing through to the other side, even if it meant he received a slew of angry stares. After he placed his Venti-sized order, he slipped over to the other side of the counter.

Caffeine reminded him of varnish remover, but he discovered it was a necessary evil whenever he needed an adrenaline boost. It was all so inconsequential, and it had ended way too quickly. But now he basked in the glory of the idiots running around like a bunch of hens looking for a rooster. He had a secret thought: The world was filled with roosters. The damn fowls popped up everywhere, crowing at whatever ungodly hour of the morning, yapping like their bloody lives depended on it, head back, eyes pointed high, belting toward the sky. Hypocrites. The world was filled with them. The bastards were everywhere and nowhere, and searching for whatever greener pastures were currently located on the other side of the field, or in this case the Common. And it was a big fucking field. The vastness of it pissed him off. An insurgency, a bloody revolution, that's what this was, and he would lead the charge, with whatever musket or vision happened to accompany him on his journey, with his grand plan, bright ideas, and determined nature.

He closed his eyes, and grinned the mother of all grins.

A loud voice near his right ear jerked his head to the side. He grabbed his cup and shoved his way through the muck. He didn't even notice the hardened expressions, or the ones with lighter tones around the edges.

Steamed milk and hot liquid filled his nostrils. A damned shame that the world had come to steamed milk. Matthew had a hard enough time facing idiots, without facing whatever sissy drinks might cross their chapped lips.

If he hadn't put a stop to it, the idiot John, or Mark, would have dressed the three of them like triplets. He slapped Mark, or John, across the face, even as he'd suggested it, and before the words lingered in the air for more than a few seconds, the slap reverberated even louder in the compact room. The retard had actually bared his teeth at him, so he'd slapped him again, and the second time the meaning registered—and silence lingered. The table did not wobble. It's not like all of this was difficult. He had a simple job to do, and the retard had nearly failed at it. He shouldn't have let the bastard drive, but it wasn't like he had a whole lot of choice in the matter, since it was John's rental, and the retard had bloody insisted. If crying arose, a bloody nose would have followed.

Matthew counted on the anger to soothe his tormented soul. "What the bloody hell are you two doing?"

Two beats of silence ensued.

"Watching the festivities," John said.

Matthew slid the stool to the right and hovered near the edge of the small space. His view was slightly blocked, and so was his mind. "The camera?"

John sipped from his cup and stared straight ahead. "It's for the memories."

Matthew punched Mark on the shoulder. "What about the bloody internet?"

Social media was askew with what had happened, and the two retards already managed a few too many posts with only a small firewall separating the good from the bad. Pictures plastered Facebook and Twitter with unintelligible stories and misguided captions tossed across the universe. Selfies popped up like gray clouds in a darkened sky.

"It's expensive."

Matthew jabbed John on the cheek and steamed liquid splattered the table. "Or maybe you're just bloody retarded." The stupid bastard had repeated the sixth grade.

"Maybe you two should draw a little more attention to us," Mark said. "I could even draw you a map."

John bowed his head and shrugged his shoulders. "It's hot."

"Not outside."

John pushed his cup back. "My drink."

"Maybe you should fucking blow on it," Matthew said.

Mark tapped the table. "Why do you have to use so many curse words?"

"Because it's the only way to toss out the retard." Matthew needed a quadratic equation to keep his two compatriots in line.

John's head bent lower. "I did my job."

"And a damn fine one at that. But you're not exactly playing with the big boys yet."

John needed extra assistance with two syllable words.

"It went off without a hitch," John replied.

Matthew nodded and took a large gulp from his cup. "And so it did."

"That was in no small part because of me."

Matthew bumped Mark into John. "You wanted to get us the same bloody outfits. Look what you two retards are wearing. I mean, really."

He had chosen his own clothes for the occasion, and he was glad he had. If he resembled the other two any more so than he already did, he needed to wipe his brain with a magnet and stick a fork against his forehead.

"It's important to look good for the pictures."

"What pictures?"

"The news crews." John pointed and his voice rose. "Don't you see the vans?"

Matthew slapped John's cheek. "Put your fucking hand down."

Of course, Matthew wanted to know how the vultures had learned about it so quickly. The internet held few se-crets, and the Twitter feeds and Facebook posts and selfie sticks alerted the news before the first body or window fell. Maybe it was exactly what he needed to get his mes-sage across: the news crews. He wanted the whole world to hear it, and he wasn't about to take no for answer. In fact, he was bound and determined to work all the way toward yes. Even if it meant he had to go through a few nays first.

Chapter 8

Emergency personnel crammed the stairwell, moving up and down the stone steps rapidly in both directions. A constant thrum of voices and footsteps filled the toxic air. Air filled with smoke, charred remains, and the remnants of whatever started the fire, before it exploded outward and upward. The origin of the fire was one of several floors, or multiple floors all at once. It just didn't seem possible, but then the possibilities made Addison's world turn on its head, as he screamed and ran in the opposite direction. But that was in his youth, when he lacked basic common sense and interior motivation, and an endless cycle of failure filled his world.

A continuous line of stretchers, more than a hundred dead bodies. The emergency crew was topnotch, each one focused on removing the innocent and injured, before the crew dragged dead bodies down steps and stairwells. Not the elevators. Being trapped in an elevator was his worst nightmare, and when smoke filled his lungs, it was time to move on with hand guns and grenades. Playing nice never worked when it involved bastards with machine guns, C-4, and .44 Magnums.

A never-ending cycle of disorganization and despair broadcasted across multiple news channels. One continuous vision of darkness intercepted Addison's cosmos, and he couldn't blink fast enough to end the maze, like rats moving in perfect tandem through a series of openings and walls, or down elevator shafts, flowing and moving at whatever speed made the most sense. A continuous line of mammals focused on the nearest exit point. Maybe Addison's head would explode, and save him a bit of trouble.

Each crime scene was hard, and this one felt harder than the others, because of the scale of it, and the level of political games. Masquerading at the top, political pushing and shoving, and it being an election year, actually somewhat close to the big day—even though he hated politics and did whatever he could to avoid the shenanigans—added a new layer of pressure to this horrific occasion. All he needed was a way out. Retirement never sounded so good, or so imminent. Less than a year away from the big day, he'd already started planning his exit strategy. When it was time to go, he'd just walk right out the front door, and he wouldn't look back. He wouldn't turn his head. He didn't want a party. He didn't want some of the women—especially the secretary he worked with side-by-side, and for all these years—to give it a second thought, but he knew she would. She was a crier. That one. She had more than enough tears for five funerals, so he'd save everyone the trouble: There would be no going away. Not even an event at the Irish pub down the street, drinking beers after the little exit, with no brouhaha, or aftermath. Leaving was the easiest thing to do, if Addison played his cards right, and ducked out at the end of the day on a Friday before a long weekend.

The blast reverberated in the charred remains left behind. Ashes, particles, and soot filled the air, entire sections of floors and walls just vanished. His conclusion: the fires were centrally located. He nearly gagged on the thought and the number of dead bodies.

The complete lack of compassion nearly destroyed Addison.

He'd probably lose whatever hair he had left at a faster clip now from the stress. Addison struggled to keep the few hairs he had left, and he decided to go down without a fight. He didn't want chemicals, or extra vitamins—other than the ones he already swallowed—and he didn't want to use a special shampoo, since even that possibility made him feel like he was giving in. It hadn't always been all about his hair, but it was now, thank you, Bing Crosby.

A powerful gust smacked him in the face, as he stood on the road with his back to Boylston Street. A line of cars marched forward along with the occasional biker and a stream of pedestrians searching for the nearest T station. He stepped out of the way as a large dog passed and its owner trailed behind. The owner was small, in complete contradiction to the dog, and the leash was long.

Addison was determined to discover what had happened, even though right now, at this particular point in his miserable fucking existence, he didn't have a clue.

౭৲ঌ৲ঌ

"How did you manage to survive?" Leo asked.

"Smoke break."

"Cigarettes?"

Carl nodded. "They saved my life."

Leo stood sixty feet beyond the back door with a rail thin man who twitched from the waist up. Carl's lips held a blunt object. It was lit and smelled like shit, as did the rest of the contaminated air. A series of familiar faces gathered round just out of earshot. The building behind him moaned once or twice.

Leo spit empty sunflower shells on the grass, and turned up his collar when the breeze turned bitter. The gray sky shielded his eyes from the harshest rays, and the Android in his hands had a line of notes and more than one question left unanswered. He planned to understand a few more before the day was over, and the trail of bodies ended. "Are you crazy?" Leo asked.

Carl shook his head, the blunt object dangling from his lips. The object moved, as did Carl. "I don't think so. Why? Are you?"

"You're telling me that you just happened to be smoking outside when your place of employment blew up behind you?" Leo wasn't sure how the muckety-mucks would feel about luck. "And you were the only one on break—"

"I like to smoke in peace." The stick moved along with his lips. "Besides, no one else in the library smokes, and I'd just gotten through dealing with some rather threatening teenagers."

"Threatening in what way?"

"One of them pointed a loaded pistol at me."

Leo's Android stood at attention and waited on the next word. "Why?"

Carl's voice lacked mirth. "He wanted *Twilight*."

Leo stopped tapping on the contraption. "As in darkness?"

Carl sighed and flicked ash on the concrete. "As in the vampire novel by Stephenie Meyer—"

Leo scrolled through a previous section. "But you were in the children's section."

Carl nodded, as did the blunt object. "True. But the kid didn't want to hear that. He was rather insistent in his pursuit of reading material."

Leo narrowed his eyes. "You've gotta be fucking kidding me."

"That's not going in my statement, is it?"

Leo stared at Carl for several beats, his collar digging into his neck, and zipped his jacket higher, as flurries splattered the front. He didn't bother to brush his hand across the front.

Carl took a long drag. "You don't think he did it, do you?"

"Did what?" In Leo's experience teenagers didn't resort to blowing up public libraries, but then this scenario gave normal the middle finger.

Carl heaved out a breath. "Started the fire."

Leo looked over his left shoulder. "This doesn't resemble any fire I've ever seen before."

Carl stubbed out the nub and dropped it in the nearest receptacle. A woman scrunched up her nose as she walked by. "Then what was it?"

Leo took another look over his left shoulder. "It blew out the door in your direction, didn't it?" Carl nodded. "Did you ever consider that it could have been a bomb?"

⌀⌀⌀

Lynette literally couldn't stop crying. The tears flowed down her cheeks like a river of forgotten dreams. She laughed one minute—after having stuffed the pot in her backseat, her two boxes probably blown up, burnt, or just gone—and she glared off into the distance, contemplating her next move, now that the door was firmly shut and suffocated. Her world constricted, and the coffeepot was her only friend. She had laughed at what had happened to Hancock Tower, but it wasn't like any laughing she had ever done before. This sniggering was based on hysteria, shock, or some combination of the two, like a fruit cocktail with a little green umbrella and a slice of lime. God, she needed a drink right now. Not soda, or beer, or wine coolers. The stuff that burned her esophagus on the way down, and caused a rush on the way back up. And she contemplated again about how much of herself she'd given to Xanthic, slaved over her desk like a monkey dancing for her master, with calluses on her fingers, migraines twice a week, long hours and longer nights, a marriage on the rocks, an ulcer in the works, and a black book filled with a series of two-date wonders—before her nuptials—that she needed to call upon if her husband decided to make his threat of divorce a permanent resolution. She pictured the papers being served on her birthday, while he bounced around town with a redhead on his left arm, and a grin a mile wide plastered on his face. In the end, she wouldn't have blamed him, but she would have blamed herself.

It wasn't like she hadn't tried, but work always managed to get in the way. Always. She'd even missed her father's funeral due to a minor crisis and a last-minute presentation. Her father died of a heart attack, took an early out three years ago, and she'd missed it—the funeral—because of the big speech the next day. She was in Boston stuffed behind her desk with the cleaning crew running the vacuum, when she needed to be in Pennsylvania. She'd told herself it was worth it, but it wasn't, and if her husband decided to leave her, she'd have nothing left. Nothing.

Her dad had died at his desk. That's what she'd heard later. He couldn't slave hard enough, and now she, Lynette Sommer, of sound mind and even sounder body, resigned herself to the same fate with a destroyed building in her wake. Now here she was sobbing in her car with the windows rolled up and her knees against her chest in the Stuart Street garage around the corner, basement level, surrounded by pillars and not a single pill in sight. If she had a penis, she'd still have her employ-

ment—albeit a vanished existence—and she'd have her
Friday afternoons booked from here to eternity, literally.

Her employer took and took until there was nothing
left. Turning on the ignition and shifting gears and backing up required too much effort, thought, and energy. It
was all about the amount of effort she had given, and
what she had done to please her boss, and look where it
had gotten her: hopeless, jobless, and empty. Her job and
her life weren't worth it—the sleepless nights and constant aggravation—and yet she was more than willing to
give it up anyway, and hand it over gladly, as she offered
her soul to the devil for a promotion and a smile. Sure,
none of what she had been willing to do was good, but
that was the worst of it: her willingness to sacrifice her
life and her relationships for her career. That made her
cough and gag and retch, and it kept the faucet dripping
and her motor running.

She opened the door, snot shooting out of her nose,
tears cascading like waterfalls down her cheeks and de-
positing themselves on her cream blouse—the one that
her boss said he liked the best—and vomited on the
pavement. She didn't know she had anything left to give,
and yet there it was.

တသက

Addison needed a vacation. He hadn't even been on
the scene two hours, and he already knew he needed to
take a leave of absence. He could already see the overtime forms, his boss's smiling face, and the calluses that
would incorporate his feet, hands, and the rest of his
body. He could see it coming—the stink and stench that
permeated the air—and he tried to break free with what
was left of his dignity. He decided he wanted out, before
the circus had even begun, but he couldn't find a way to

break through the insanity—the passenger in his backseat one Richard Lancaster III hadn't helped matters either.

Addison took one shaky breath after another. After the fifteenth gurney appeared, his stomach flipped, his legs shook, and the contents of his stomach turned to acid. He hadn't puked yet, but he certainly pondered the notion. The universe had deposited him in front of the Pru at the exact worst possible time in the history of the fucking universe, and even his nine-millimeter couldn't tip the scales of justice. The level of catastrophe had reached an obscene state, with bodies popping off the ground and from behind glass doors, and the gurneys played on a continuous loop out on a grand stage. And courtesy of the boss at the top this was still his scene.

Even more folks lined the streets than what he remembered moments ago. The survivors, gawkers, and news hounds led the way. He wasn't sure where those bastards had come from, but he would put an end to this right now: It was time to exert his authority. The concrete barrier had developed a few cracks.

"What do you think you're doing?" Addison asked.

"Observing the situation." The reporter wore a pinstripe suit and a full beard with his hair in a state of disarray.

"Do you have a permit?" Addison asked.

Pinstripe stared. "Do you?"

"I don't need a permit."

"Then we don't either," Pinstripe said. "It's called freedom of speech."

"Why don't you free speech yourself somewhere else?"

Pinstripe flipped him the bird. "Are you naturally an asshole, or do you find you have to work at it?"

Addison's hand clenched at his side. "What did you say?"

"I don't believe I need to repeat myself."

A second camera followed the first, and a handful of bodies leaned forward.

"Are you testing my patience?"

"Are you testing my virtue?" Pinstripe asked.

"What?"

Pinstripe waved a microphone at him. "I could scream real loud, claim that you groped or raped me, and you'd have a serious situation on your hands."

Addison glared. "You wouldn't."

Pinstripe took a step forward. "Do you want to test me?"

Addison brushed snowflakes from the top of his head. "Are you actually doing anything useful?"

"Of course." Pinstripe pointed at his compadre with the crumpled coat. "Why? Are you?"

He hated dealing with idiots. "I was."

Pinstripe ran his finger along the front of his coat. "And now you're not?"

"Not at the moment," Addison said. "No."

A crowd stood at attention behind Pinstripe. A barrier divided the ranks, but the crowd leaned forward on every word, with eyes darting back and forth and iPhones at the ready.

Before this evening was out, Addison would probably end up famous on YouTube, Twitter, and all that other shit. He'd have more than one proposition, and a few prank calls to the station if he was unlucky.

Pinstripe tilted his head to the side. "Are you trying to be funny?"

"It's just a natural occurrence." Addison's wife, on the other hand, tended to think otherwise. Her sense of humor had a rather limited range.

"And a wiseass?"

Addison looked over his shoulder for reinforcements:

There were none. "That's all part of the program as well."

"Seriously?"

"As a glass house built near the ocean." He never wanted a glass house, or an ocean view: too many people.

Pinstripe stuck the mike out in front of him. "Maybe you should let it go."

Addison said nothing. The silence between them reached a deafening level, and still the crowd waited with bated breath. A division in the ranks would soon follow.

"You're the investigative lead, aren't you?" Pinstripe asked.

"Are you conducting a survey?"

"In the name of a story. Yes."

Addison's eyes drifted to the faces that surrounded him. "Is there anything you wouldn't do?"

There was an audible pause filled in with an elongated sigh and an exchange of heat. "Probably not. No."

"Then you're just like everyone else."

Pinstripe smirked and held the mike up even higher. "And that's a bad thing?"

Addison stared for several beats, and Pinstripe didn't blink.

And then Addison Thomas executed an about face. He didn't bother with a response, since social media already had more than enough fodder. But he did at least need to act like he knew what he was doing, instead of punching a loud man in an even louder suit on the bridge of his nose. Even though he avoided all contact with the press, he had started a fight, and he had lost. Retirement and The Cape never sounded so good.

Inside the Pru, he viewed the carnage—had nearly tossed his cookies, a couple of sandwiches, and a Mountain Dew—and had walked back outside again, made another pass, had another series of fleeting moments with the stomach bug, and then he'd ordered a group of CSIs to process the scene before his present altercation.

He had no idea how exactly the political puppets would react. The fools didn't seem too interested in his perspective, but as the lead officer, he deserved a little fucking respect, even if he ended up in his present circumstance through happenstance. So what if the biggest case in the history of Beantown had fallen into his lap, and so what if he received all the credit for solving it. He could think of worse outcomes.

ပာပာ

Richard Lancaster III sat in the back of a police cruiser, in front of the Pru, like some common criminal with a four-digit bank account. He'd tried to shift in his seat, bring the handcuffs around to the front—like he'd seen in the movies—but that didn't fucking work, and he'd nearly thrown his hip out of alignment. He'd lost his agility due to his current waist circumference, or he never had it: touching his toes was never a realistic proposition. He'd nearly tossed his back out of whack, and it spasmed like a lizard with herpes. He bent over in his seat, gasped for breath, and cursed red and blue for over a minute, the words flowed faster than the Charles, and his head roared louder than a wind tunnel. He jammed his thigh against the side of the door, and found a new outlet for his fury.

He had no idea of the time with his wrists out of sight, and his phone jammed in his back pocket, but the cruiser had turned cold even with the windows rolled up and the continuous movement. A line of pedestrians passed by, but none had noticed him, or if they did, they pretended not to, even if he did raise his voice on three separate occasions.

He wasn't even dumped in the front, like a proper citizen, and shown some decent fucking respect. The officer dumped him around the corner, away from the press, as women and children walked by with heads together, singing "Kumbaya" and skipping for several blocks. Time moved on, but he did not. And the cop must not have trusted him, because he took the keys and locked the damn doors. Like he was a good enough driver to maneuver the steering wheel with his teeth or knees from the backseat. He'd experienced enough accidents in his life to know how the world really worked. And it certainly worked against Richard Lancaster III. The landslide of life cascaded around him with broken boulders and broken promises uprooting his entire existence and dropping him in the middle of a thunderstorm.

Without the car keys, there was no radio, no lights, and with his luck, it'd probably get dark soon, he'd have to take a piss, and there'd be no way for him to see, let alone get the locked door open, since that was another issue with police cruisers—no way to open the doors in the back except from the front—and so he'd probably end up pissing his pants, with a stain the size of South America slammed against the front of his trousers.

༒

Fucking towel-headed terrorists. He'd heard about them on the news, read about them in the paper, and now Daniel Pinder happened to be one of the first ones on the scene at The Hancock, and therefore he was a witness, a goddamn witness to the American execution and attempted extinction by a bunch of camel jockeys. He'd had about enough of it, and enough of them. Not only did he have to deal with the Middle East—and none too happy about it, thank you, Obama—but he had to deal with the fucking Chinese who were hell-bent on taking over the cosmos. The commie bastards didn't give a shit who they hurt, or who they stepped on, as they stomped, clawed, and broke the laws of human decency on their way to the top, with their cyber-attacks and nuclear weapons and elitist attitudes. Needless to say, he wanted to get even, but he didn't have a plan, or even a way ahead. But he would start by showing those bastards that he wouldn't take this kind of abuse, America wouldn't take it, and that he would fight fire with a hand grenade and a Colt Peacemaker, brush off his American flag, and ring the bells of freedom, using both a towel-head and a commie bastard to bang the metal.

Daniel didn't have to take this shit, and neither did the American people. Sure, he was on the job only six months, and, sure, he was a firefighter, but he was filled with youth and energy, and an alcoholic beverage or two. His bosses, though, wouldn't know. It wasn't exactly a mistake he planned to advertise.

He shoved his helmet against his head, as he raced up one floor and then another with an axe in his right hand. His friends below sprayed the scene with several hoses.

He either had a hero complex, or a death wish.

ᏒᏜᏒ

"Boss, you'd better come take a look at this."

He'd always been called boss, and Addison wasn't quite sure why. He wasn't the one in charge of the fucking precinct, although he'd certainly put in his application years ago, but he was denied. Probably hadn't even been looked at by the political puppets at the top, men who spent more minutes on comb overs than they did out in the field. Instead, the puppets dumped his dreams in file thirteen, along with a handful of Big Mac wrappers, some stale fries, and a handful of soda cups. Addison didn't have to take this shit, but it never managed to ease up.

"What am I looking at?" he asked.

"If I had to guess right now, before it's been at the lab and thoroughly analyzed—"

"Go ahead and guess." Addison leaned over and scratched the bottom of his chin. "It's not like I'm going to hold it against you if you're wrong."

"That's like calling out a number," the officer said. "Even if it's wrong, everyone always focuses on the original number, 'til the end of days that number is cemented in the brains of those who heard it."

"I'm not looking for cement," Addison said, "I'm looking for answers."

"And answers you shall have." The officer paused and turned it with his tweezers. "I'd say it's cloth."

Addison had one hand under his chin and one eye on the prize. "Cloth?"

"Most likely from a shirt or a pair of casual pants," the officer said. "Or it could even be from a purse or a backpack."

Addison bent over a little more at the waist. "What would a backpack be doing on this level?"

The officer shook his head. "I don't know."

His favorite store Lacoste was a shell of its former self and charred barbeque lingered longer in his mind. His knees ached, but he remained in place.

"I'd say we have our first clue. This doesn't sound like a random fire to me."

"No, it doesn't. But, then, you never actually believed that, did you?"

"Probably not." Addison still had no idea what the hell he did believe. Although if he ever did figure it out, he planned to tell his wife in the most expeditious manner and with the least amount of hand gestures.

He stood up, brushed off the soot, and plopped the white mask back in place. He'd always liked this damn building.

"Wouldn't it be something if those al-Qaeda bastards had decided to strike again?"

Chapter 9

His tour bus schlepped along Boylston. Stuck in traffic for the past hour, the culmination of distance traveled was measured in feet and inches. Not miles. Even the fucking exit ramp was a chore and a meandering journey filled with red lights and BMWs. The entire downtown was shut down. Quinn Fitzrelli hoped it wasn't on his account. Sure, he was famous enough, smart enough, and even managed to ride the elusive fame train, like some sex-crazed, money-grubbing whore of a wife. Not that he had one of those, even though the chicks lined up outside of his tour bus like it was the Boston Garden before the NBA finals. Quinn did enjoy it, though, probably more than he should have. That was the price of fame: It was fleeting, but it sucked your cock once or twice before it moved on to the next cowboy with an even bigger gas pump.

He'd dosed off and on, and when he peered out the window, the same view remained, maybe a foot further down the road with a new store for his purview. He had nightmares about being stuck in traffic, not moving an inch, the streets jam packed with a slew of motor vehicles and bicycles, one on top of the other, every inch of roadway covered, the tour bus running out of gas on a country road in the heart of the Appalachian Mountains ten miles from the nearest town. The gig mattered, the screaming fans and topless women—although they didn't normally start out that way—the panties onstage—he had a rather elaborate collection, and he didn't have the heart to throw them away—a few bras, the looks of ecstasy and utter joy that he managed to plant on the faces of the girls with the biggest tits, even if it was only temporary, the ability to forget—alcohol offered him the same indulgence—and the fans, the diehard ones singing his music back to him, quoting him word-for-fucking-word and move-for-move with voices rising toward the rafters. He'd stopped singing many times, and the fans took over the show. And they were happy to do it, thrilled even, and he would sway back and forth with them, the connection deeper than a small-town block party.

He'd once entered the arena with the fans—hoping to cop a feel or four—but he stopped that rather quickly. He'd caused a few of them to trample each other in pursuit of him, women screaming with arms winging, the touching and the grabbing, and the mass of fans shoved in his direction. The security folks liked to tell him his safety was in jeopardy, and that riots, while entertaining, lacked true imagination. What he needed was a little more inspiration and a little less exaggeration.

The onlookers and the hangers-on hadn't appeared yet. Quinn made sure the tour bus didn't have any identifying markings on it, after a fiasco a few years ago. The bus was attacked in Chicago, nearly stampeded by a group of women, beautiful, uncontrollably beautiful with fake tits and tank tops and flip-flops, and even a few men, who might have lacked brainpower and common sense, but certainly made up for it in intensity, and he was lucky to walk out of there without much more than a tipped over tour bus and a few bruises. Over the years, the legend waned, the intensity of the situation discounted, and the story became more of a myth than a reality.

He was here to tell the truth. Not to paint the world in jelly beans, gumdrops, and popsicles. He was here to provide good old-fashioned entertainment, with four strippers—wiggling in black leather pants and red bras—tossed on stage for good measure.

He'd had girlfriends, and he'd lost them. He'd had managers, and he'd fired them. He'd had band members that were no longer a part of the brotherhood, and yet here he was, lead singer of The Sex Maggots, and he would carry on and raise the American flag. A doctor had told him he wouldn't live to see thirty, and he planned to prove the bastard wrong. He'd stage an impromptu concert on the man's gravesite. The record company had balked at the name, threatened to end the band right there before it even exited the front door, but Quinn had stood his ground, and pissed all over the damn waiver. Now he was a goddamn legend with an online presence that rivaled Miley Cyrus. And the record company had him to thank for it. He'd pulled them back from the grave, and into the black, before he'd told the man to shove it and started his own label.

If this was Boston, filled with parked cars and traffic jams, he wasn't sure how he felt about it. He'd stared at the Boston Common and Public Gardens so long he began to wonder if he was in some sort of alternate universe. Restaurants and shops lined one side of the street, and green grass lined the other. But at least he still had his guitar, a pen and paper, and most of his brain—drugs painted the world in multicolored rainbows. Inspiration had struck—not the drugs—and he had no idea when it would strike again. He picked up his acoustic guitar, strummed a few chords, and then a few more, and before he knew it, he sang in his low baritone voice, the words pouring out of him, his mind clearing, his hands moving of their own accord. Once all the words comingled together, he wrote with reckless abandon on the pad with the same silver pen with the click top that he used for all of his lyrics. Call him superstitious, but he was damn proud of it. That pen had inked two number-ones over the course of his career, and Quinn knew he could drum up a few more before it was all over. If he needed a drug-induced fog, he had a manager to lead the charge.

When he took a breath two minutes later, the page on the pad was full, and his brain was empty. He grabbed the nearest glass on the table, and slammed the contents down his gullet. Ten seconds later, the back of his mouth was bitter, but he considered it all part of the experience.

Quinn noticed her legs before he noticed her. The blonde had legs as long as the Nile and tanned skin peeked back at him. She wore tiny lace panties and a thin white T-shirt that allowed him to see the outline of her curves. All of them. Her hair was long and blonde, curly and unkempt, and her face was devoid of makeup. He liked the unkempt look. In fact, he preferred it. A woman just aroused from sleep was the most beautiful sight to behold. He had written two of his hits based on just such an experience, and if the creative muse struck again for a third time, he would welcome it like the prodigal son and slaughter the fatted calf. He loved women, and he despised them: It was the circle of life.

Her pale, pink nipples poked through her shirt.

"What are you doing?" she asked.

She ran a hand through her hair. Her name was Salt or Pepper, or some other condiment. The drugs and the writing helped him lose track, and her voice was thick like molasses.

He wanted to tell her not to touch it, but he had trouble finding his voice, and he had trouble controlling various parts of his anatomy. His libido was a problem, a serious one that led him astray more often than a thousand-dollar-a-day cocaine habit.

"Writing," he said, as if this were his answer to all of his problems, and many times it was.

But there were times when even writing couldn't save his tormented soul. During those times, he preferred the numbing effects of alcohol. It was easy to contemplate a scenario where booze encompassed his daily life. But he wasn't an alcoholic. His old man had been one, and his old man before that, and he had seen the effects of the booze, the toll it had taken on his mother, and heard the stories from his grandmother before she kicked the bucket. But that wasn't him. He would rise above it, conquer it. Not the other way around. Alcohol was an evil bastard that left a tingle on his lips and warmth in his heart.

She lifted her arms up and pulled at her T-shirt. Her hair remained astray. "Do you want to fool around?"

Of course, he wanted to fool around. That wasn't even a valid question. Did he want to watch *Sesame Street*? That was a more valid question, and he could answer it in exactly the opposite way as the question presented before him. A question that lingered on the lips of the women he met more often than he cared to admit, since kissing and telling and locker room stories never provided the validation that he hoped they would. But that hadn't stopped him from trying, and in some cases it hadn't stopped him from caring, even when the mascara ran and the clothes were rumpled and the lips were swollen. He had more condoms stuffed on the tour bus—underneath seat cushions, in the microwave, staring up at him from the floor right next to his bunk bed, in the glove compartment, and stuffed in his wallet—than one would have thought humanly possible.

He even had them stuffed in the refrigerator and the cabinets above the sink. When the tour bus ran, the women popped up like weeds in a cornfield. He'd even woken up in the middle of the night—not to write song lyrics—but because his dick was so hard that it had practically lifted him up off the bed.

He shook his head. "Maybe later."

Her ass twitched like the tail of a dog. "Your loss."

The funny thing was she wasn't even his pickup. She was the drummer's, but all of them, every last one of the hangers-on, always wanted the lead singer, like his cock was sheathed in satin and gold. He didn't even have to be the best looking band member—although he certainly was—and he could have a voice that sounded like the Chipmunks on acid, and even that wouldn't matter, and he could forget half the lyrics, because he was so tripped out on acid, or mushrooms, or ecstasy—although he never had been—that he couldn't even remember the time of year let alone the city. The bottom-line: none of that mattered, as long as he had the stage presence of Bono, exuded the confidence of a Greek god, and fucked like Hercules. Perfect that, and he could pretty much do whatever the fuck he wanted.

 භ

Quinn had one leg on the floor, one on the sofa, and a bottle of Jack in his left hand. A full bottle when he started, now it was less so. With a perfect view of the bus, he leaned his head back and rubbed his cheek with his right hand.

He adjusted his position when the door opened, and one of his bandmates stepped through the threshold. Nicholas Night rubbed the back of his head, face filled with dread, and slammed the door. "What the fuck is going on?"

Quinn lifted his eyes up. "So you're awake now?"

"Of course, I'm fucking awake." Nicholas opened a black curtain, gazed out, and slammed it back. "Why haven't we moved?"

Quinn tipped the bottle to his lips and swallowed. The liquor freed his empty mind. "You've been asleep."

Nicholas stared at his empty wrist. "But the itinerary said we should be at the hotel by now."

Quinn chuckled and then shook his head. He removed his hand from his face and rubbed the bottle. "Since when do you read the itinerary?"

Nicholas charged forward and yanked open the fridge. "I know how to fucking read."

"Never said you didn't."

A head popped out followed by a hand and a jug. He popped the top, and then chugging commenced. After Nicholas wiped his mouth with the back of his left hand, placed the cap on top, and shoved the jug back in the fridge, he turned back to the sofa. "Where's the blonde?"

Nicholas didn't even bother with her name. He had the memory of a centipede, but he was hung like a garden hose, or so Quinn had heard. But it still didn't stop the girls from seeking out the showman of the brotherhood.

Quinn should have mentioned something about not treating women as sex objects, but his heart wasn't in it, and he wasn't sure how accurate it was anyway, since he had a hard enough time keeping his dick behind closed doors and the bottle away from his left hand. There was probably a bit of irony in there somewhere, but he swallowed it long ago.

Quinn brought the bottle to his lips and took another pull. He offered it to the drummer, but Nicholas declined.

"Asleep," Quinn said.

"Did you wear her out?"

Nicholas wasn't upset, not that Quinn could tell anyway. Just curious. Hell, Quinn was curious most of his natural life. It was probably some downside to being creative, something he hadn't known about when he had signed on the dotted line in blood and sweat and misery. But the girls were worth the pain and suffering, most of the time anyway. The few times they weren't he was off to another city to make a few memories.

Nicholas tapped the back of the sofa with his left hand. "Anyone outside?"

Quinn peered out the window. "Nope."

"Good. I don't want to deal with any groupies right now. Besides, we're already fucking behind schedule. I'm surprised you haven't seen Wilford yet, and that he hasn't started raising holy hell."

Wilford was the manager, and he was one irate motherfucker. He'd once cussed out his mother in the middle of a cocktail party. It wouldn't have been so bad, except it was in front of a bunch of retirees, and it was his mother's birthday party. The sorry slut hadn't even known what hit her until after the confetti settled. He'd also once told a club owner to go fuck himself after a particularly harrowing performance and the dumb shit had tried to renege on the last part of the contract. Needless to say, the club hadn't invited The Sex Maggots back. Quinn had considered firing Wilford, but the man got results, even if he was forced to attend the occasional anger management class. His methods weren't always sound, and he made women and children cry with equal abandon. But he was a man with a vision, even if he couldn't see six feet in front of his face.

"Maybe he has," Quinn said, "and we're just not aware of it."

"Not aware of Wilford?" Nicholas shook his head. "Not possible."

Chapter 10

Matthew left the party early. The fucking incompetents still sat by the window, staring into the great abyss that was Copley Square, which was full of flaming fire. Squad cars, fire engines, random pedestrians, and various open-mouthed idiots filled the available space. Death and destruction lay out before him on a giant canvas that covered multiple square blocks. It was his mission, his vision that led them here, and now he needed to execute the next phase of his plan with a rising crescendo and faint echo. Simple really. So far, it hadn't required much effort on his part, but the rest of it would. A brilliant plan, if he did say so himself, but then brilliance, strategy, and ability defined him. He'd once been hung from the rafters by his ankles, and he should have talked and coughed up information, but he hadn't. He had not answered even the most basic of questions.

Matthew was trained in the art of not talking. He'd once gone six days without forming a single sentence, the silence as pure and steady as a waterfall with his eyes forward and his back straight. He lost track of time and space and even his most basic existence in some abandoned warehouse, a warehouse with broken beams and charred windows and rusted machinery, on some abandoned street in some abandoned town. The steel beams ran overhead like a series of complicated mousetraps.

With the walls peeling, the air smelling like mouse drop-
pings, and the pliers hovering inches away from his feet,
before the first toenail was yanked off, he closed his eyes
and thought of all the dead women and children. He
hadn't screamed, he hadn't even turned his head. He
watched with the infinite coldness reserved for a sniper,
perched on some ledge, overlooking some square, taking
aim at some kindergartner, with a missile wrapped
around his small fist and the slightest hint of indecision
in his eyes. It had been a long time since he'd felt that
sense of release. If he was lucky, he would feel it again.
When he opened his eyes, blood slid down his foot onto
his ankle and started in on his calf.

The toenail had grown back.

The recorder punched his pocket every time he took a
step. Matthew threaded through the idiots, nearly invisible, his heart cool, calm, and even, and his hands surpris-
ingly warm, despite the cool air around him. A snowflake
inches away from his hand splashed out upon impact.
The sound of his breathing had leveled off, and he'd
slammed his hood over his head, the ball cap and most of
his face hidden from view. He kept his head down and
pointed in his intended direction. His lips curled into a
sneer, but it was hard to tell, since his face was as cold as
the air around him. A single voice stood out in his head,
reiterating what he had to do. The voice was as steady
and even as a bass drum. He had come this far, relatively
easily in fact, and he wasn't about to lose sight of his destination, not when so much was still at stake.

A voice called out to him, or it was the sound of the
wind? His shoes brushed aside the light dusting of snow.

When all eyes faced the opposite direction, he grabbed
the handle of the nearest squad car. Locked. He cursed
under his breath, turned away, and tried again with the
next vehicle. Same result. Same result with the one after

that. On the fourth try, though, Matthew hit pay dirt, and he dropped the recorder on the backseat, before he slinked away. A strictly in-and-out operation. Not a single cat, dog, or person in sight.

ℰↃℰↃ

John sat behind the wheel. He didn't ask about the recorder, because he already knew the answer. He'd seen Matthew drop it in the marked car, and he'd seen a man in the crowd, slightly off from all the rest with his attention directed in the location of said vehicle with his hat pulled back and a tuft of gray poking out underneath. Not a face that John recognized or that would stick with him. A nondescript face of a nondescript man with a wrinkled forehead. The trench coat was similar to Columbo's and a symbol often depicted in the movies. The coat alone lacked enough warmth to keep the cold at bay. John had stood his ground—the eye contact brief—until the older man turned away first. The entire exchange had taken over a minute.

Getting out of the city was easier than he'd expected at this hour, but then he took the road less traveled, and he abhorred traffic. John didn't like staring at the back bumper of some minivan, with one of those stupid Obama stickers, the ones with the blue lettering and the white background, the ones that made him want to stick his index finger in his mouth and retch through the open window. People weren't particularly smart, and probably never would be, and Obama had destroyed every bit of decency with a wave of his pen. America became more stupid by the day, less intelligent by the year, and a tidal wave of ignorance with each passing decade. It wouldn't be long before China took over, especially since our gold was dropped in their hands with a smile and a wave and a smart salute. The willingness and ease with which it had taken place shocked him worse than having a diaper shoved on his head and being hooked up to the electric chair, the metal bucket blocking out his ability to hear the world around him, and a thousand volts of electricity clicking through his tormented system.

Traffic moved well below the speed limit with 95 jammed like The Stones had decided to play at the Garden—not the old one, but the new one. The one where the Celtics had only managed to win one championship so far and had reached the Finals before ultimately losing to the Lakers. Fucking Lakers. If he was a basketball fan, he might have carried more than a passing opinion. Lately, though, the Red Sox weren't much better. Their collapse that September that shall forever be remembered as the "Fried Chicken and Beer Incident" reached a historic level, and ultimately caused them to miss the playoffs. That shit just didn't happen. Not in Boston, where Fenway Park was a fucking icon, and the curse of the Bambino was lifted on that fateful day in 2004. But the past had come back anyway.

His eyes flicked toward the dash, as one of those dummy lights came on and informed him his tire pressure was low. He slowed down, discovered the one massive pothole on the mile stretch ahead—the Boston roadways notorious for dips and dives and potholes the size of craters—heard a pop, and a scraping noise as his rim connected with the blacktop beneath and scraped sparks high enough for him to see the smoke. He pulled over to the side of the road, uttered a few more choice words, some of which included four letters, and flipped off the ignition. If he had any sort of plan, now would have been a good time to come up with another one. His mission was filled with blocked exits and broken roads.

"What the hell happened?" Mark was in the back with his knees jammed into the seat and his voice reverberated in John's ear. "Was that a flat?"

"It was."

Mark poked the back of the seat with his elbow. "Did you do it on purpose?"

"Of course I did it on purpose." John flicked the steering wheel and let loose a deep breath. "I found the biggest pothole I could find, and I dove right in."

Matthew punched the dashboard. "Why did I bother to let you drive?"

John unbuckled his seatbelt and popped open the door. "You didn't. Besides, I know what I'm doing."

"That's what you said when you drove us here."

Rather than dignify that with a response, John exited the vehicle. While managing to avoid oncoming traffic, he dug the spare and jack out of the trunk, and stomped in the direction of the driver's side. Before setting to work, he rolled up his sleeves, and slapped the jack against the ground. He hummed a little tune as he lifted the car, and loosened the lug nuts, the words lost on him. The melody, however, wasn't. His mind drifted and shifted, skipped and jumped, before it appealed to a higher purpose, a greater need—the man with the plan—and then he managed to quit the whistling, slap the spare in place, drop the Mustang to the ground, tighten the lug nuts, toss the jack and flat in the trunk, and slam the lid.

As he walked to the driver's side, he heard a police car, siren blaring, and he straightened up, jerking his already worked muscles, before the cruiser flew by, heading in the opposite direction, toward the city. A city filled with The Freedom Trail and liberals.

With his eyes forward, Matthew said, "Took you long enough."

John checked his watch: eleven minutes from start to finish.

ↀↀↀↀ

A fence lined the base, most of the perimeter anyway, one with barbed wire at the top. Matthew obtained a map online with a few details of the base, the buildings. The research lab—he was sure—held what he needed to complete the rest of the mission, and he had two nitwits he'd dragged along, in case any trouble ensued, the kind of trouble that took more than a conversation and that could require human shields and sacrifices. The green Mustang was fixed—the flat anyway, he couldn't say the same about the person behind the wheel—the night was clear and filled with stars, the moon full, or nearly so, and problems and nearly as many solutions occupied his mind.

Matthew had talked the two buffoons into wearing all black, despite several protests, strange looks, and multiple complaints, none of which were held for long. The ball caps were black, obtained from a local Goodwill store for only a dollar each, still useable, the pants a bit long and baggy, but he cinched them with a lightly-worn belt. Matthew didn't want the bulkiness of a jacket, and he couldn't find a good alternative—less bulky version— at the Goodwill store. His shoes were built for running. The cool air had chapped his lips, and despite the warm gloves, his hands still managed to go numb in less than thirty seconds.

He'd brought along long strips of cloth for the fence, and he handed his two compatriots a series of strips as the three meandered their way to the barrier, stepping into a ditch as a patrol car passed by.

John stared at the moon. "Are you bloody sure this is going to work?"

Matthew's hands were icicles. He gritted his teeth. "It has to—"

"Why?"

Matthew blew on his gloves and rubbed them. "Do you want to consider the alternative?"

"Not really."

"Are you backing down from the plan?" Matthew asked.

"No."

The wind whistled and flakes smacked his face. "Do you have second thoughts?"

"No."

The questions continued, and so did the answers. Twenty questions would have been easier, and probably more fun. His lips formed a sneer, and his voice reached a low, rich flavor. John's voice droned on and on, and Matthew wanted to strangle the man with his right hand. But he kept his right hand at bay, and he pulled the cap down tighter on his head.

With the guard gone, Matthew wrapped the strips over both of his hands, creating a makeshift knot as best as he could to hold the strips in place. Anticipation filled his heart, and probably adrenaline, too.

He swung his arms, and then he leapt, grabbing hold of the fence about halfway up. He scaled the barbed-wire fence, the cloth digging into the wires at the top, before he dropped like a penguin on the other side, hitting the ground awkwardly as he tucked and rolled, before springing like a Slinky to his feet. He brushed off his pants and smiled a wicked grin. The other two followed blindly, carrying the gym bag, as metal clanked against metal. The two imbeciles hit the ground less awkwardly than he had, maneuvering slightly, without the tuck and roll. The bag struck the dirt with a loud clank, and then a puff of dust billowed up around them.

Mark picked up the bag and slung it over his right shoulder.

"Military?" Matthew asked.

"No civilian," Mark said. "But I watch a lot of bloody TV."

With his body free of the bag, Matthew sprinted hard across the open field—he'd been built to run, even though he hadn't signed on for long runs or even short ones. Mark, carrying the bag, proved the slowest of the three. Mark's breathing was short and jagged, like the scarred edges of a sharp knife. During a brief respite, Matthew slugged him on the shoulder opposite the bag. Mark didn't flinch. The dark building provided temporary cover, and the moon overhead provided more than enough light.

After a few deep breaths, Matthew sprinted once more, while the other two followed.

Weaving through the aged buildings of cement blocks and dirty windows, he slipped once before he righted himself. The night resounded in his ears, the crickets and owls and whatever else had decided to take up residence in the surrounding fields of green. The hill was curved and steep. He pumped his arms at his side and shortened his stride.

ೲೲ

The building was secure, a passcode required for entry. All was quiet around him, except for the wildlife, and before Mark gave it a second thought, he tossed the bag at the glass door. It cracked, but it held, and the bag dropped to his feet, mocking him. It clanked and clattered against the still night air.

"What the bloody hell are you doing?" Matthew asked.

Mark picked up the bag. "Getting in."

"You're going to wake the neighbors."

"Does it look like we have any bloody neighbors?"

"Are you even sure about this place?" John asked. "It looks deserted."

"Maybe not, maybe so. Only one way to find out, though." Mark reared back, and tossed the bag again. The glass cracked again, but it still held, and the bag dropped to the asphalt once more. He could see the weakest pieces, where the glass wasn't as strong as the other areas, and he grabbed a wrench from the bag—although he did briefly consider his shoe which provided no real protection at all—and slammed it through the glass threshold. Glass shattered. Fragments sprayed in every direction. A few fragments barely missed his face, and one struck it before he brushed it aside. A drop of blood along with the piece of glass fell to the ground.

Mark cleared the hole with the wrench, and he stepped through the threshold. Matthew and John followed close behind.

Before them was a set of stairs.

A short time later the three exited the building—it was as old inside as it appeared from the outside, the ceiling leaked in places, the plasterboard overhead was stained with a rainbow of colors, the cement walls old and gray and dim, and the elevator jerked and jumped when it started and stopped, similar to the ground shifting above the fault lines—with all the Semtex—a plastic explosive that could take down a large jetliner— the bag could hold.

Even though the bag held more than it did before, it somehow felt lighter against Mark's shoulder.

Chapter 11

I t seems al-Qaeda has struck again, the full story at eleven."

She'd researched the piece; interviewed multiple sources on the street; poured her heart, mind, and soul into the story; and now she'd witness the fruits of her labor. The teleprompter was her friend, and she would win in the end. The words, her words, would scroll through, and she'd emphasize the right syllables, toss her hair at the right instant, and show the world her bedroom eyes. If so many faces weren't pointed in her direction, she might have masturbated.

Built for sin, Pepper Pen oozed more confidence than her dozen lovers had ever seen. But at least now she could strut her stuff in front of a television audience. She'd never been so turned on in her life.

It was easier than she'd expected, proving her point, and now she'd help engineer a full-blown news media revolution. She'd put in the hours, waited for her chance to hit the big time—Los Angeles, Chicago, or New York City were her targets. She'd seen firsthand what hard work could get you, and she'd clawed her way to the top. She'd even slept with a producer, before she realized that he couldn't do anything for her career. So she'd dumped him, watched him cry on his sofa, his knees clutching his chest, shedding tears the way she'd shed her clothes that first night. She'd even given him head. If she was honest with herself, it wasn't one of her finer moments, and if she had to do it all over again, she probably wouldn't have executed the same scenario. Pepper would have utilized an entirely different setup, maybe even blackmail. She'd heard about its benefits, but she'd never had the courage to give it a go. Instead, she'd tried using wiles and charms, gave a blowjob or three, and look where that had gotten her: "Nowhere" was probably too strong a word, but it was certainly accurate. Her whole body shivered.

She'd been a high school cheerleader, the peppiest of the pep squad, and she'd had a set of lungs that could be heard throughout the stadium. Now she managed to get herself a gig on TV, in front of greater Boston, the top story of the evening, and she'd been at it more than a year—the gig, not the story—giving it her all, and it had resulted in nothing. Well, not nothing, but she'd expected the big three to call, recruiting her with better pay, better stories, and better benefits, and so far, she hadn't had a single fucking phone call. Not one. Of course, the producer—who had been out to get her ever since she'd stopped the relationship—if you call oral sex a relationship—cold, with his pants around his ankles and his briefs forming a tent, she'd decided that she didn't need the headache after all. Had she calculated the math with her head instead of her tongue, she might have focused on the long division. He had threatened as much—a favor parade as dry as a bag of lye—from the comfort of his sofa and with his eyes rolled back in his head. She'd done her own research, despite his best efforts to steer her in another direction—to the crotch of his pants—and she'd been right with her assumptions: He wanted to end her career and bury her at the bottom of the river.

She'd been labeled a screamer by her first boyfriend, who had a dick the size of a septic pump, but she liked to refer to herself as vocal. It didn't hold a negative connotation. Passionate. That was an even better word. She was passionate about her job: Fucking relieved tension.

The interviews had gone well enough. She'd talked to her share of shell-shocked individuals, some of whom were incoherent, and some of whom weren't. Some of whom couldn't have formed a sentence if she'd spotted them all the vowels and a handful of consonants. But it was worth it, every last disjointed sentence. She'd gotten her sound bites, and she'd even decided to give the editing process a go, which was a first for her. Granted, she didn't do all the work, but she'd done a significant part of it. And now she could add that to her resume.

Eat your heart out al-Qaeda. Those Egyptian bastards wouldn't know what hit them.

ᘒᘒᘒ

"So what you're trying to tell me is we had three buildings hit simultaneously?"

"I'm not telling you, sir," Leo said. "It's a fact."

"Don't call me, sir, goddammit. This isn't the military, and I'm not your commanding officer."

Leo decided not to point out the obvious. But when Ward Phillips lost his temper, he lost all sense of rationality. And it was a long way to the top when he had to start at the bottom. He'd worked the shifts no one wanted, even tried his hand at traffic duty, and failed miserably. And now here he was: ready for the big time. Biding his time wasn't as much fun as he thought it'd be. In fact, it was damn near catastrophic at some times, and as boring as having his carpets cleaned at others. But he'd seen it through, and now he stared at a cliff, only he wasn't looking up from the bottom, where the water met the land, he was about halfway up its face, with a climbing rope attached to his back, threading the rope through his pack.

Leo reached in his pocket for a handful of sunflower seeds. His lips watered at the thought, but he didn't have the bag in his pocket.

The office was claustrophobic, jammed with chairs and filing cabinets and bowling trophies. The desk was pristine and immaculate: Ward used a bottle of Windex hourly to give the wood its shine. Handshakes and smiling faces filled the memorabilia wall. The man behind the desk, though, remained devoid of all happy thoughts.

Ward's gaze locked on his own. "What did you find at the scene?"

"Cloth."

"Cloth?"

"Most likely from a pair of pants, shirt, tent, or backpack," Leo said.

Ward threaded his hands behind his head. "Are you saying someone walked into the Boston Public Library with a tent?"

"That's the least likely scenario."

"What do you think?" Ward whipped out the Windex, along with a paper towel, and went to town. "That someone stuffed a bomb down his pants?"

Leo had shut the door, and he stood at attention even now, the smell of cleaning fluids assaulting his nostrils. He rubbed his nose: Crisis solved. "The backpack seems the most likely. But our lab will conduct the analysis."

Ward dropped the bottle below and the paper towel in the trash. "Anything else?"

"Plastic explosives. Or the remnants of them."

"How did C-Four make its way into the Boston Public Library? Did it grow a pair of legs?"

"Again, the initial analysis says it was more powerful than C-Four."

Ward rubbed his chin. "Say what?"

"Semtex."

Ward pointed his index finger at him. "What the hell is Semtex?"

"An explosive popular with terrorists," Leo said. "It's virtually undetectable, relatively stable, and more powerful than C-Four. A half-pound of it could blow up a commercial airliner. And it's reasonably available, as far as explosives go."

Ward rubbed his face with his hands, rearranged a trinket with the edge of his desk, and then moved it back to its original position. "Al-Qaeda?"

Leo flexed his fingers. "I'd rather not jump to conclusions at this point."

"The mayor is going to be up my ass—"

With his hands behind him, Leo scratched his lower back. "Of course."

"And probably the governor as well—"

"I wouldn't expect anything less." Leo hated the governor with every muscle in his body. The arrogant prick was a two-headed snake with a venomous bite.

Ward leaned back in his chair. "Are you stroking my ego?"

"I wouldn't dream of it, sir."

"I told you not to call me sir."

At least he didn't add goddamn.

❧❧❧

He'd never gotten around to cleaning his desk, but at least it was organized. To the casual observer, it looked like piles upon piles of papers, but to Leo Nivea, it was his life story laid out in written form.

A man stood at his desk with a tie wrapped around his neck. He had his hands shoved in his pockets, and from what he could recall, the man's name was Addison. The last name escaped him, even though the lieutenant had mentioned it only moments ago. He'd seen Addison around with the small patch of hair on the top of his head. When Leo slid behind his desk, Addison turned his head to the side.

"Three buildings were hit," Leo said.

Addison glared. "Are you asking me or telling me?"

"Maybe we should start with known connections."

"You don't want to start with al-Qaeda?" Addison asked.

"Are you a detective or a conspiracy theorist?"

"Like you, I'm just looking for answers."

Leo might have found a few on his desk, if Addison hadn't shown up with his chin toward the sky, and the stride of a tiger. The man had confidence written on the inside of his underwear.

Leo picked up a stack of papers. "Well, if you start with al-Qaeda, there's nowhere else to go."

"Maybe it's the only place we need to go."

Leo tossed the pile on the floor and grabbed a fistful of sunflower seeds from his desk drawer. "Are you detecting or speculating?"

"The boss said—"

Addison must have had his own conversation on a separate occasion. Or maybe the walls talked. Leo tossed the seeds in his mouth. "I heard what the boss said. And he's thinking politically not strategically."

"And what are we doing?"

Leo shrugged. He didn't like this any more than Addison, and he wasn't sure he liked the man on the other side of his desk either. "I have no idea."

Leo didn't. Not really. He'd discovered answers, but

then he'd answered entirely different questions, and he'd had more pieces of the puzzle to work with, instead of a puzzle box with half the pieces MIA. He couldn't even say for certain about the cloth, but it was a decent-sized chunk, the size of a sticker, and it felt like the material of a backpack, and if it was a backpack, at least that was a start. Still a long way to go, but at least it pointed him in a general direction. Even though the boss wanted an open and shut case, blaming it all in the name of Allah and al-Qaeda, Occam's Razor never applied when it came to detective work. As for politics, it always seemed to clash with common sense.

The boss being the boss, he wanted to research any and all known connections to al-Qaeda. But then Lieutenant Numbnuts wasn't exactly thinking clearly, and at least Leo had talked him down from just writing it off as al-Qaeda altogether. That had taken exactly twelve minutes. It would have taken longer, but Leo could think on his feet, approach a situation from different angles and separate positions. He didn't trip over himself. In fact, he was articulate. He was on the debate team for three years, and it was one of the greatest experiences of his life. It helped him deal with assholes now. It was predictable—the boss's reaction—and he had taken it in stride. Going over the situation point by point with a calculator and a spreadsheet, Leo discovered more than a few missing exclamation points. He straddled between articulate and belligerent, as needed. The key to belligerence and anger was to use it at the right time and in the right situation. Attacking a situation the way a crocodile might did nobody any good and only created a gaping wound or two.

The debate team helped him through high school, and whether he realized it or not, he might need to call on it again soon. He could see that Addison harbored a certain amount of skepticism, or maybe he had a temporary case of acid reflux. Either way, he wouldn't let the terrorists win.

Maybe the terrorists—he couldn't think of a more appropriate word—were politically motivated. Boston politics corrupted, probably since the dark ages and the founding of this once-proud country, a country now filled with leeches and serpents and assholes. Even if the targets weren't politically motivated, politics at least made sense, provided some brief respite of rationality in an entirely irrational world, where the city of Boston was lit up like a cigar. The hint of smoke lingered in Leo's mind.

∽∾∾

Maybe three random acts happened at exactly the same moment. And coordinating the effort to find out would take some political connections that he didn't possess. He didn't want to be on the phone when the FBI got wind of this one. Addison Thomas couldn't even talk to his ex-wife without resorting to screaming, and he didn't expect the situation to improve. But that was him: all or nothing. He supposed a mental diagnosis might explain what traversed his mind, but he wasn't sure he could handle the results.

Maybe three sets of disgruntled employees exploded simultaneously, working in conjunction or individually, but if that were the case, he didn't see any direct indications of a confluence of events. It would take a while to sort through the bodies and charred remains. Most workers, though, weren't that sophisticated. They didn't shoot random individuals, turn the guns on themselves, and blow the whole building to the Middle Ages. And the Pru was destroyed at the observatory level. So what did that say? That an individual hated Boston to the core: its views, its people, its passion, its politics, and its history.

Well, it was fucked up, he did know that much. He had no idea what the final body count was, but he knew he wouldn't like it.

Authorities confirmed the buildings exploded at exactly the same time. Addison needed to begin researching the employees, occupants, and any and all known connections. Three buildings—Hancock Tower, the Pru, and Boston Public Library—one of which was a popular tourist spot. Yeah, it was loads of fun, and if he needed his toes cleaned, he was sure he could find a pair of pliers.

∽∾∽

What was a recorder doing in his backseat? It wasn't his recorder—the officer had made that determination in the first five seconds—because he didn't own a recorder. It wasn't just that he didn't feel the need to own one: It's that he never felt he had anything important enough to record, and return to it later. He'd done the drunk dial before, and that had ended with disastrous results. He might have had a restraining order placed on him, if he hadn't handled the situation with more tact, since the one he dialed drunk wasn't exactly a person of sound mind. A good lay, sure. Sound mind, no. He had mumbled and rambled and probably tripped over his words at three different points, his voice rising and falling at all the wrong moments and the woman on the other end calling him a dick on four separate occasions, as she lingered on the other end. He didn't remember the conversation, since he was drunk, but he was fairly certain it wasn't one of his finer moments in his otherwise banal existence. The hangover afterwards, though, was something fierce. It had felt like his forehead was going to come out of his skull. The dull ache had turned into a dull roar, and he saw spots for the first half-day, the world a sea of potted plants and ferns and purple roses. A greasy breakfast later, which had taken place around eleven, did help ease the pain and the sidesplitting headache. Agony had certainly been the right way to talk about the situation. That and puking throughout the night, hugging that porcelain bowl like it was his first cousin with his lips hovering near the top and his knees digging into the linoleum floor. He had been just aware enough, or more likely, someone had done it for him, to place a wastebasket next to his bed, so he had rolled over, vomited, cursed, and rolled back. He liked to sleep on his back, but he hadn't that night. He'd slept on his stomach or side, he couldn't remember which, and it had helped the cause tremendously, although his stomach felt like a colony of red ants ran around, and then had taken up residence in his colon.

The recorder, though, wasn't placed by red ants. The officer really couldn't remember if he locked his cruiser or not. He was in a rush, based on the gravity of the situation before him, with blown up Boston landmarks and all, people running around like ants without a hole to go home to, and he had rushed to the scene like someone had just shot him in the ass.

The recorder was plopped between the seats and turned at a slight angle. It appeared relatively new and relatively small. It was silver, and if he was lucky, it was covered in fingerprints. He stared at it, waiting for it to talk to him, but it didn't. He hadn't noticed it when he'd left the scene, and he hadn't noticed it on the way home. It sat in his car all night, and he probably wouldn't have noticed it the next day, except he tossed his gym bag in the back of the cruiser, and there it sat. He breathed in and out, counted from Mississippi to Tennessee, and then punched the play button with a pen he had stuffed in his pocket.

Chapter 12

The studio was tighter than an eighteen-year-old virgin, with the leather on the seat jammed up his ass. Quinn Fitzrelli wore sunglasses, a ball cap, and a "fuck you" grin. He had a flask filled with gin shoved down the front of his leather pants, and he ended up a little harder every time he moved. Or maybe it was the flask. The idiot on the other side of the square table introduced himself with a high-pitched squeal, and the back of Quinn's head rang 'til kingdom come. His seat squeaked along with the man, so of course he shifted every other minute.

"What do you think of all this?" the DJ asked. His name was Steve, or Stan.

"We hope it brings a bigger turnout to the Common," Quinn said. The cramped room was no bigger than the size of his bathroom, filled with knobs and dials and blinking lights. The lights moved and the screens shifted.

Leaning in closer, Steve...or Stan...blinked his eyes. "Don't you care about what happened?"

"Absolutely," Quinn said. *The fuck was he talking about?* "But we have a show to do and a crowd to please." And he had a surge of pressure to relieve.

"Do you believe there's any truth to the rumor that your show will be canceled?"

Quinn rolled his eyes. He hated morons, and he hated

morons with high-pitched voices even more. "Absolutely not. We have a show to do, and we're ready to do it."

"The album?"

"Will be dropped in two months' time," Quinn replied. "If not sooner."

"And The Sex Maggots?"

Quinn flexed a bicep and shifted his cap. "We're stronger than ever."

A single hiccup of silence filled the air and the waves. He filled the void with a screech of his chair and another grin.

"What made you decide to do a free show?"

Quinn pointed at his microphone. The flask dove hard to the left. "The attendance—"

"Who booked the gig?"

"Our manager," Quinn replied. "He books all of our events." He had no idea where the show went next, but he'd figure it out when some cute girl told him. If not, he could always pretend. The tour ended whenever Wilford told him it did.

Two hiccups of silence took up residence in the tight room.

"Were you disappointed by the sales of your last album?"

Quinn swiveled in his chair. "It was a transition for us."

Stan…or Steve…leaned forward. "Is there any truth to the rumor that The Sex Maggots are dead?"

Quinn gave him the finger. "I'm still around, aren't I?"

"Why the Common?"

"This is where it all began," Quinn said. He'd always been a fan of Aerosmith and Steven Tyler, or maybe it was the drugs. It could have been the girls: the drunk ones and the fun ones with edible panties and big smiles. "And Bostonians have always supported us."

"What are your plans after the band?" Steve…or Stan…asked. "A solo album—?"

Quinn flicked the mike. The sound nearly tore his ear in two. "I'll probably be dead."

"What about the rumor that you guys party too hard?"

"We're rock 'n rollers." Quinn lifted his fist in the air. "What do you expect? Should we be hugging your grandkids?" He hated the little fuckers.

"Any final words?"

"Don't forget to attend our show. We're going to party like it's 1969." Sure, it was before his time, but there was still plenty of free love to go around.

※※※

Lynette Sommer didn't even have a dog to go home to. That was all her employer's fault. Her husband, if he were around, instead of out of town, probably would have blamed her. She could picture the red face, the elongated tongue, the way his eyes might have flickered at her, before flickering away, as he pounded down the stairs and hit the T at full speed. Even if she ran her heart out, she could never catch him.

Instead of life on the road, she had an empty condo, and probably a few missing colleagues. And her employer didn't give a damn. If she knew her boss, he'd probably figure out some way to capitalize on the tragedy— assuming he survived—and make it his own. When she really stopped to think about it, the man disgusted her. Even his beady eyes didn't do him any favors.

She'd placed a few empty calls—to the numbers she had plugged into her phone—to a few empty cell phones, and left a few voicemails. The response so far had been one giant goose egg. The result: her worrying increased, instead of dissipating. Horrific thoughts filled the void in her head, and her mind shifted on a continuous loop.

Her condo hadn't been updated in years. All the improvements she expected to make drifted by the wayside in empty promises and lost letters. She could have had a home in the suburbs, a commute into the city, a dog, a cat, and two smiling children. But she had given it all up for an employer that didn't give two shits about her, and a lovely condo minus the lovely improvements. Instead, she bid her time, and what was left of her dollars, on someone else's leftovers. But it was hers, free and clear. On Boylston Street, in the heart of Boston, on a lovely road, in a lovely neighborhood, within walking distance of downtown, and today, she had nowhere to walk. She hadn't even changed out of her pajama pants.

She padded into the kitchen, took a carton of plain yogurt from the fridge, and dumped in a few strawberries. She was out of blackberries. Another trip to the store could have fixed this minor oversight, if she wasn't too tired the night before, and if she hadn't cried all over her coffeemaker. She flipped on the TV, images of yesterday still played loud and proud, a scenario that she would never forget, for more than one reason. Instead, she'd remember yesterday for the rest of her life, and probably come to terms with all of it through the aid of a therapist and a battering ram.

Lynette didn't believe in God. But she did believe in fate, and so she had no idea why she was saved. Although it didn't feel like she was saved, she still felt like she met the brick wall on 93, a barrier invisible to everyone else, but it managed to suck her in, torment her, along with her invisible automobile, and dump her in the Charles on the east side. The car she'd sold years ago, when she discovered it was more of a hindrance than a

help. Now she could rent a Zip car for the day, if she discovered she needed the transportation, but often, that
wasn't the case: Her legs carried her just fine. Cars were
a luxury she didn't need. The insurance, the gas, the
miles, the depreciation. All of it. The look she received
from other drivers when she sat behind the wheel without
using her turn signal, the way it turned some perfectly
normal people completely insane, the way horns honked
and tempers flared, and normal rules of society no longer
applied. That was what she had decided. Her husband,
though, happened to have a different view on the matter.

If she had any female friends, which she did not—
again the work thing—she wouldn't have been surprised
if she were told that her condo resembled a male bachelor
pad. Dark furniture, hard lines and angles, glass, and the
flat screen filled out the scene. She'd bought it two years
ago—the flat screen, one of her biggest purchases, outside of the vehicle she no longer had and the condo that
no longer felt like home—and found she rarely used it, or
even wanted to. Her husband made more use of the idiot
box, when he wasn't traveling, or working late, or hitting
some club downtown in a pinstripe shirt and matching
pants. Although with her recent situation, she might end
up using it a lot more than she ever had before. And that
was okay. She wasn't in a hurry to discover some other
employer with some other plan that required her to give
up the rest of her natural life.

Why had she picked finance? Love of the game. That
was the only reason. And if she stopped to think about it
now, she probably should have picked it for more than
just love. But it satisfied her, welcomed her, and then had
literally taken everything away from her. Except her sav-
ings and a husband that was around even less than she
was. And that would have been okay, if she had a family,
a dog, a cat, or even a hamster to come home to. But that

was impossible. She couldn't even keep a fish alive. The guppy had lasted three months, before she flushed him down the toilet, while her husband gave the eulogy, and she had turned her head away in shame.

ᕙᕗᕙᕗ

Carl Razer had a dog. A mutt. And suddenly the damn dog was all he could think about. That and his girlfriend of two years. She was beautiful. His girlfriend. And she managed to stick with him, despite his smoking, and despite the fact that she had never picked up a cigarette a single day in her life. And she was his. Well, at least he hoped she would be. He had the ring in his pocket, and it currently burned a massive hole, despite the fact that it was in a small blue box, the ring surrounded by purple velvet. It jingled when he walked. When he didn't have it shoved in his pocket, he kept it in a shoebox at the top of his closet out of the line of fire. He had picked it out two months ago, and waited for the perfect time to give it to her. There was no perfect time, he realized, but he had to try. And then there was his dog. Danielle Reynolds—his girlfriend—loved his dog. The mutt. That was what he called him: Mutt. He'd had other, better names in mind, but the name the dog answered to was Mutt, and so Mutt it was. He'd had the dog for four years, and it was hard enough finding an apartment in Boston that would take a dog, that was within walking distance of work, and in an area where he knew he wouldn't get mugged, but he had. The dog had nearly saved his life, warned him of a possible intruder, and barked loud enough so he scared whoever it was off. He had more than earned his keep, and even if he hadn't, Carl loved that damn dog with all his heart. Mutt wasn't much, but he was his. Mutt's fur was shaggy and more than one color and the end of his nose was jammed flat and two of his teeth were more crooked than all the rest.

The dog never seemed to have a sad face, always happy, always ready to play, to love, to do whatever he asked, and bounce in his seat at the sound of the word treat. Mutt snored in his sleep. Not a soft snore, the cute and cuddly kind, filled with bubbles and rainbows, but the kind of snore that made him believe the dog had a sinus infection. Carl had checked him out. Well, the vet had, and the vet blessed him, and handed him back faster than he could say stethoscope. But still Mutt snored. Even still, his girlfriend didn't mind, and if Danielle was willing to make him a happy man and become his wife, he would spend the rest of his days attempting to please her. That is if she would have him. It was never a question of whether or not he would be thrilled to have her, but he had waited anyway, for the fairytale to end, the cigarette butts to accumulate, and for her to find the emergency exit. But it had never happened. Danielle had stuck around. She had even moved in with him, to his grungy apartment, with his dog named Mutt, and slightly used furniture, most of which he snagged from Goodwill. It wasn't like he was a great catch. If he had caught himself, he probably would have paddled away to hit the Charles another day.

And then there was the incident at the library. His one good job—he hoped to make a career out of it—punched him in the gut, and his prospects suddenly looked a tad worse. She was good for him, his girlfriend, and he was lucky to have her, just as he was lucky to be alive. It was by some goddamn miracle that he was still walking around with his shoes tied. Camels. That was what he'd been smoking, although he did have a pack of Marlboros in his pocket as well.

Four different men interviewed him, and he'd told the

same story each time. He had developed patience, either he was born with the gene, or he had developed it over time, until it was harnessed with appreciation and moral support. The men he'd met held both morals and a certain amount of cynicism with slight grins, but mostly it was the coldhearted stare and off-color remark that tripped him up. His voice jumped and dove at all the wrong moments, heart steady in his chest, and his smile was less than genuine.

He'd smoked more than his customary cigarette every two hours. He'd chain smoked the Camels through the course of the interviews, and he considered starting in on the sealed pack of Marlboros. But he'd held off. Restraint had never been his forte. He'd steadied his hands with the cigarettes, his voice calculated and even, the perfect "O" leaving his mouth with each puff, and his hand stopped shaking after the first cigarette. It had turned chilly, after the course of four interviews, the nip in the air bit against his warm skin, skin that had now grown cold. Goosebumps covered his arms, and his teeth clacked in his mouth.

Minor details interested the cops. Each one bit at him, caused him dread, and left him for dead. The string of suspicion never ended. He was looked at as though he was the enemy. He hadn't expected that, but then he'd never even received a speeding ticket, especially since he avoided all forms of vehicular transportation. He didn't trust himself behind the wheel.

He'd called Danielle after the fourth interview, once he'd been told he was off the hook. For now. He was told not to go anywhere, though. Not that he planned to leave the state, or head out west toward the prairie farms and cattle ranches. Buses did that sort of thing, but he didn't want to take a Greyhound to New Hampshire or Maine and certainly not Vermont. He wasn't even interested in a

train. And he certainly wasn't going to fly. Not after what
had happened with the city. He wanted both feet firmly
planted on the ground where he could duck and cover
when the smoke hit the horizon.

With his head slumped, he turned the key in the lock.
The bolts clicked, and then he stepped through to the other side. Danielle met him at the door with her eyes wide.

"You're back late," she said.

He lifted his eyes and kissed her on the cheek. "You
didn't hear?"

"I heard." Danielle lifted his chin higher and inspected
his face. "How?"

"Luck." Carl removed the pack from his pocket. "The
Camels saved me."

She reached out toward him and pulled him in close.
"I'm glad you're safe."

"You're not surprised, though?"

"I felt you," she said.

Her breath was warm against his ear. He'd learned to
trust her instincts.

She touched the side of his face with the back of her
hand. "But it was bad."

He nodded. "I'll probably be moved to a temporary
facility."

಄಄

"I shouldn't have bothered bailing your ass out of
jail," Loretta Lancaster said. She had on dark rimmed
glasses and a no-nonsense expression. Her hair was in
disarray, as were her clothes, and her purse was askew on
her shoulder.

The hallway was long and narrow, and it reminded
Richard Lancaster III of a death sentence with doors ajar
and pictures askew. His lips moved, but no sound came

out. The officer on the other side of the Plexiglas could have melted wax with his hard gaze, and Richard was sure his wallet had more than a few dollars missing.

He threaded his fingers through hers. "Why did you?"

She squeezed his hand hard enough to leave an impression. "Because I was notified while I was eating a piece of Turtle Pecan Cheesecake with the girls, because you stole the tie right out from under my nose in the middle of one of my favorite stores in the whole entire world, and now I'm the one that will have to live with the consequences of your actions. You're a selfish bastard, Richard."

His shoulders slumped. "It's not that bad."

She tossed her purse on the backseat and yanked open the door. "What's going on?"

"I was fired."

She pursed her lips and swallowed. "How long ago?"

Richard stared at the tops of his shoes. "Three months."

She started the car, and slammed it in gear. "You've been keeping this from me for *three months*?"

"I didn't know how to tell you."

She eased up to the bumper of a Benz. "You could have started with the truth."

Richard picked at an invisible spot on his tie. "You've become accustomed to a certain lifestyle."

She stared straight ahead. "Don't turn this back around on me. Don't you *dare*."

Richard's voice inched higher. "I'm the provider."

"Not right now, you're not." Loretta gripped the gearshift hard enough to turn her knuckles white. "We're behind on the bills, aren't we?"

He added music to the equation. She flipped the radio off with a flick of her wrist after removing her hand from the gearshift. "No, we'll make it."

"Are you sure, Richard?" Her voice hit more peaks and valleys than the Appalachian Trail. He inched back in his seat away from the onslaught. "Because the last time you told me that, we were more than two months behind."

"Now it's the same exact situation." It couldn't possibly get any worse. At least he didn't think so, but then thinking about the tie from the Bergdorf's catalog had gotten him in this situation in the first place.

Loretta lowered her voice to a whisper. "Only you're in a bit deeper."

"Probably." He didn't know exactly, but the debts had mounted up with no end in sight, and the man on the other end would come to collect soon enough.

"Don't give me probably, Richard." She honked her horn at nothing and cursed for her money's worth. "You know exactly what you're doing."

"I wish I did, honey."

She'd been outside eating on the patio, that's what she'd said. She was lucky. He could feel it. It was harmless enough, Cheesecake Factory with the girls, a monthly ritual, a chance to catch up on all that was going on in the world, and a chance for him to do a bit of shopping, of quite possibly the illegal variety. Normally, he didn't come with her, normally, he stayed behind, but this time was different. He had decided to come along, to mingle with the common people, and he couldn't help but wonder if he had changed fate in the process, thrown it in an entirely different direction with his selfishness. After all, it had always been about him. In fact, that's how he'd gotten himself fired in the first place.

Chapter 13

W
here were you yesterday?" Reese Xue asked. Matthew held the phone away from his ear. He stood out in front of his place of employment with a grim expression on his face. The overhead camera had a direct feed to her office. He considered offering up his middle finger, but he thought better of it. "I told you—"

"You didn't tell me anything." Her voice sliced like an incisor.

He danced out of the way of two pedestrians with false teeth and canes. "You didn't get my—"

"Of course, I received your message." Her voice took on a monotone quality. The hum of the office thrummed in the background. "According to company policy—"

"Can you not quote company policy for once?" Matthew asked. "I was stressed out. I thought you, more than anyone else, would understand. So I took a day off. One day off to recharge the batteries, to keep myself from going insane, and now here we are having the conversation that I had hoped to avoid." Before he even managed to step one foot in his office. The damn camera was a curse.

A moment of static followed another moment. "It's suspicious." Reese paused and a printer whirred. "Your two buddies called in as well."

Matthew took another step away from the infernal

camera. "Are you saying there's some sort of conspiracy?"

"I have no idea." Brief pause while keys clacked. "But it's suspicious, all the same."

For a small woman, his boss had a large suspicious nature. She also had a rather profound appetite for jellybeans and strange men, often in that order. Matthew took his phone off speaker and placed it closer to his ear. "Did we mention the same reason?"

Her reply was curt. "Of course not."

The two idiots had a certain amount of sense. Not top-notch but maybe not so terrible either. "And besides," he said, "they're not exactly my best friends."

Most days even "colleague" was too strong a word.

The moment of static was less pronounced this time. "So you're denying that you hang out together?"

Matthew offered the faintest hint of a smile. He hoped the camera picked it up. "Absolutely not."

"Because I could pull up cafeteria footage if you don't believe me."

"It's a company break room," he said. There wasn't a single vending machine, and he received a splinter from the middle table. He'd also had his hip jammed more than once by an overzealous coworker who liked to slam her chair into his own.

"It's a sanctuary—"

"It's a square box that's not much bigger than a closet."

"Closets have feelings, too."

"You can't be bloody serious." Matthew paused. "Besides, I've seen your video cameras, and half the time, they don't even work. Why go to all that trouble for something that's broken half the time? Seems like you could spend your resources more efficiently."

Her voice rose to a whole new level and his eardrum whined. "Because half the time it isn't."

She was bloody paranoid, that one. "Do you really not trust us?"

"I have a hard time with trust." Reese tapped more keys. "You weren't anywhere near downtown, were you?"

His voice remained level, even if his heart skipped three beats. He ducked out of sight of the camera and gathered his scattered thoughts. "What are you talking about?"

A door slammed in the background.

"Hancock Tower, the Pru, and the Boston Public Library were all blown to hell and back."

He kicked at a pebble on the sidewalk: He missed. "Are you saying we had something to do with that?"

"I'm not saying anything at the moment," Reese said. "It's just suspicious, is all. You more so than the other two. You're cold and calculating and completely unpredictable."

"Is that why we're having this conversation now?" He tried to kick the same pebble. "Besides, why do you find me suspicious?" Not that he cared, but he had a chance to make amends. "It's not like I'm a political activist, I've never been arrested, and I've certainly never created any chaos in the office." In fact, he blended in about as well as paint on the wall.

"You're a Republican."

He chuckled, despite himself. "Is that all?"

"It's more than enough."

She hung up before he could offer a reply.

ᘓᖇᘓ

John couldn't believe he was forced to go back to

work. After the day he had yesterday, the excitement, the thrill of it all, the way he'd walked right by the security guard, after he'd given him some bullshit story that the idiot had bought hook, line, and sinker. The moron took the bait like the good little fish that he was. John could have told the man anything, sold him any number of stories, and it would have been the most beautiful sound in the world: agreement. Agreement was a beautiful thing, and so was power. The security guard had actually nodded his head, after thinking about it for no more than a brief instant. Acquiescence.

But now he was back in the loan department of Riptide Community Bank, dealing with a boss that hated him, telling him on more than one occasion that she wanted his ass gone, but not finding a reason to excommunicate him. But it hadn't stopped Reese Xue from spouting off, from flying off the handle, her face turning a tomato-red color, her cheeks puffing out like a chipmunk's, and her pen clicking faster than Jesse James's pistol. Control seemed to leave the branch manager at the most inopportune of moments, and now he was back dealing with the tyrant. He'd seen it in her eyes. What he really wanted to do was start with her. It was that belief that could turn a normal situation into an abnormal one. Maybe it was all about the release.

She was in his office a moment ago, all pomp and circumstance, a tidal wave of emotion, and out of it a moment later in her skirt and pumps, her face as hard as granite. Her eyes were slits, and her calves were like two steel rods.

He'd worked for the bank for twelve years, given them the best twelve years of his life, and still Reese wanted to get rid of him with a flick of her hand and an envelope shoved in his lap. She would have canned his ass tomorrow, if she could find a way to make it stick by

Wednesday. Sure, he didn't have many sick days, but then he'd had issues that had needed a bit of attention, medical issues of the prescription variety, and a halfway house with a bare room and rubber walls. The brief moments in between the here and now, captured in the orange bottles with the white labels, those visions that needed a bit of additional attention. His desk was as cluttered as his mind, and his computer monitor had a crack on the right-hand side. It shouldn't have been this difficult. But he was sure there was a pill for it. If not, he could always work out a few kinks with a bottle of booze.

But Reese was a nightmare. She spent more time patrolling the grounds and checking her watch and cajoling the soldiers than she did behind her desk. She was a rabid terror, and she wanted him to fail. She probably even bet on it with her buddies. He'd heard about her gambling problem, and it hadn't surprised him in the least. She always had a grim expression on her face come Monday morning, like every weekend was single-handedly one of the worst weekends of her life, a pleasure cruise that left her treading water without a life preserver. But it didn't stop her from trying, and every Friday afternoon she bounced, hitting the track faster than an alcoholic could find the local watering hole and order the first round. That was the only time peace and quiet permeated the office atmosphere. Short-lived, but at least it was there come Friday afternoon, as regular as a morning shave.

Reese also had an issue controlling her anger. It ebbed and flowed, most of the time ending like a bikini atop a sand dune on the shores of Nantucket. Or exploding like the goddamn hurricane that had devastated New York and New Jersey, and pelted the DC area with enough rain and West Virginia with enough snow to cause heart attacks and a change in weather pattern.

John shook his head. Reese wasn't back yet from patrolling the grounds, not that he expected her. She took her jellybean break right about now, followed by a short-lived disappearing act for approximately sixteen minutes. It wasn't much, but at least he could set his watch to it.

ⓔⓢⓔⓢ

"What the hell do you mean denied?"

Thunder and rain and self-righteous indignation smacked him underneath the chin and pummeled him in the stomach.

Matthew swiveled his chair to the side out of the line of fire. The door to his office was closed, and the sound reverberated in the small room. The man on the other side of the desk leaned forward when he talked.

Matthew glanced down at the application. "It's simple, sir. You don't have the capital to justify the business."

The old man had a face like a terrier and the personality to match. His arms popped out from his sides. "Why don't you speak English?"

"Your liabilities exceed your assets."

"Campbell's Soup has the same problem."

Matthew leaned back and folded his hands. "Maybe so, sir. But I still can't offer you the loan." And he certainly didn't like the man well enough to make an exception.

The old man shot out of his seat before he sat back down. According to the loan application, his name was Eugene. "Are you trying to piss me off?"

"Most of the time, it just comes naturally," Matthew said. "Or that's what a series of previous girlfriends have told me."

Eugene slumped a little lower in his seat. "What am I supposed to do?"

His office smelled like a wet fart. "You're welcome to reapply once you get your debt under control."

Eugene shot out of his seat again. This time he grabbed his cane and slammed it down on the desk. "Are you saying that I can't control my spending?"

"I'm not here to pass judgment."

Eugene's eyes narrowed through his bifocals and his hair glistened. "So denying my loan request is something you like to do?"

"I'd love to make you happy," Matthew said. "I'd like nothing more—"

"Then say yes." Eugene dropped his cane to the ground and shifted in his seat. The chair squeaked, or maybe it was the old man.

The tension in the air rivaled hell on a Tuesday afternoon. Matthew's office reminded him of a boxing ring, or maybe that was the Muhammad Ali photo behind his desk. His carpet was three years overdue for replacement, and his desk was beyond the span of its useful life. The lobby floor, though, gleamed and glistened: A man shined it three times a week. Matthew, however, was forced to vacuum his own office.

"I wish it were that simple, sir."

Eugene reached for his cane again. He had it bumped against the arm of the chair. "Are you trying to be an asshole?"

Matthew's eyes flicked to his monitor. "Absolutely not."

"How many loan requests have you denied today?" Eugene asked.

Matthew looked down at his hands before his eyes popped back up once more. "Actually, yours is the first."

"And you called me down here—"

"Actually, you're the one who wanted to meet face to face." Matthew had granted the request, but he knew from experience that it would end in a fucking disaster. At least he'd never been shot during or immediately after the denial process. But once he was stalked for three days straight before the balance of life was restored.

Eugene pumped his fist in the air. "Are you calling me a liar?"

For a man with a head of silver hair, he didn't lack energy. Maybe he started his day with the little blue pills, and ended it with a smile.

"I would never—"

"Why don't we call this what it really is? Because I'm a minority—"

"You're Caucasian, sir."

The cane struck his desk again. "Now, you really are calling me a liar."

His voice reached the dull tone of an economics professor. Matthew wanted to snatch the cane and shove it up Eugene's ass until only the end remained in sight. "I assure you, sir, I'm not trying to be difficult."

"Maybe you are," Eugene said. The cane hovered once more. "Maybe that's all you ever wanted to be, denying decent white citizens the opportunity to have their dreams realized. Maybe it's all a goddamn conspiracy. Like Cuba or the Russians."

There was a pedestal somewhere, and Eugene was standing on it. "Sir, would you like to talk to my manager?"

Eugene pointed with his cane, and the chair said hello once more. "Absolutely not, you little shit. This is between you and me."

Matthew decided not to point out the obvious: He wasn't that little. "What is?"

"The fucking conspiracy. First, the Mexicans are going to take over America, and then we're going to be forced to change our name to New Mexico."

Matthew's eyes flicked to the ceiling. "It's already a state—"

"Don't get smart with me, you little shit. That's going to be the name of our entire country. We're going to have Mexicans at border patrol, letting the Mexicans cross into our goddamn country, and I'll still be sitting here with a denied loan request, while you loan out your entire portfolio to the goddamn Mexicans, and possibly even the Chinese and North Koreans. You might as well take this great country and shove it in the Atlantic."

"Actually, the Hispanic population makes up very little of our loan portfolio."

"Goddammit!" The cane reared back, and then Eugene tipped over like a candlestick. Before Matthew could come around his desk, the old man was back on his feet minus the cane. "That's not what I'm saying at all."

Matthew looked Eugene right in his beady little eyes. "Then, what are you saying, sir?"

"I'm saying I'm going to come back with a Glock Ten and blow your ass to hell and back. And then I'll sit at the border and pick off every goddamn Mexican I can find."

Chapter 14

I don't like this any more than you do," Addison said.
"You look to me like you're enjoying it."
"It's a breakthrough."

"It's not a breakthrough," Leo said. "This is the lieutenant throwing his weight around, mucking up the goddamn investigation, on some wild goose chase, and the only geese we're going to find are the ones that don't fly."

Addison had a granola bar stuffed in his side pocket and a partner with a mouth stuffed full of sunflower seeds. His partner had an empty Dunkie's cup in his left hand filled with shells. A thermos of coffee in a cup holder and a quart bottle of Gatorade with a wide mouth stood just out of his reach. When Addison needed a bathroom break, the quart bottle came in handy. Certainly handier than wandering off behind a bush, just as the bad guy vacated the premises—a scene used in one of those cop shows he didn't watch. Murphy's Law. It had happened too many times on too many cases—often by some rookie with a small bladder—to think otherwise. He'd also stuffed a couple sandwiches on the seat behind him, and he had a partner who liked to talk while he was spitting shells faster than a wood chipper.

The conversation had a few lulls, but it was otherwise filled with the usual amount of small talk and a decent amount of complaining from his new friend Leo, who wasn't really much of a friend at all. The lieutenant had a massive hard-on for this investigation, and he signed the requisition forms with zest and zeal. Ward probably even salivated once or twice. The day was as free as the possibilities.

An hour or two passed. Addison had trouble keeping track of the time, but he didn't have any trouble with his surroundings. He grabbed the granola bar, peeled back the wrapper, and shoved a large bite between his lips. He chewed and chewed, as he streamlined his thoughts and formulated the remainder of the plan.

Stakeouts were all about the partner. He'd seen that fail. The point man drifting off, his partner snoring, the suspect rolling out in his Ford, or maybe the cop didn't have a partner, another murder happened, a midnight jaunt later, and it was all over, Charlie. Or Susan. And then the poor shit had to live with his mistake for the rest of his life, and the guilt weighed him down like a hammer shoved in his pocket.

Birch trees and a juniper or two lined the street. The houses stood at attention like suspects in a lineup, and a slight curve veered off about 300 feet ahead. The sky was gray, and a thin layer of ice sat atop the hood. He could see the first sign of his breath in the enclosed space, and he tapped the dash. The wind whistled every other minute or so.

Addison stared straight ahead. "But it's a link."

"It's a rather loose one at that."

And it was. One of the employees was a Muslim and a known political activist. He'd spoken out about the government, but it was within an organization that was known for peaceful demonstrations. Sure, it was there, and it had even flashed up on the computer screen, blinking at Addison, when he discovered it, but he didn't feel any better about it. And when he'd mentioned it to the lieutenant, his eyes had grown to the size of paper plates, and he'd wrung his hands in triumph, the smirk getting wider, along with his eyes, and he'd told Addison to follow the thread. Sure, it made no sense, but it wasn't like he'd had any choice either.

The Muslim didn't even have a single parking ticket. He'd never so much as stepped foot inside a jail, other than for the occasional background check. Since Ahmad Jaffer was a state employee, his fingerprints were on file, which made the lieutenant smile even wider, wringing his hands with even more authority, as he leaned back in his chair, nearly falling over, and slamming his head into the concrete wall behind him.

The blasts were lucky, causing as much damage as they did. The city of Boston had never succumbed to acts of terrorism before. One of the groups of terrorists of 9/11 had boarded an aircraft in Boston, the flight to New York a quick jaunt down the coast, with enough fuel in the tank to level a city block. City upon city, an entire conglomeration only a short car ride away, filled the entire Northeast corridor. For the rest of his life, he'd remember where he was at that exact minute the instant the Twin Towers were removed from the New York City skyline. A little piece of America died that day, and no amount of time could resurrect it.

Solving cases was about connections, and loose ones often didn't lead to solid results. But it wasn't his case, as he sat in the cold and snow in a parka staring out into the sun at a house with a crooked shutter and scarred front door. Hell, this was about as far from his rodeo as he could go. And yet it still mattered with every breath he took in the confined space. Because his ass was on the line if it all went to shit. He was the sacrificial lamb on the spit over the fire pit. He'd been around long enough to know how the political game was played, and he hated it with a passion. It wasn't about what was the best solution, or even the right one: What the political game boiled down to was votes and influence.

He'd stared out the window for who knew how long, the monotony of the situation droning on and on like a B-movie in a cash only theatre.

Leo had gone through one mouthful of sunflower seeds, and he had just deposited a second between his jaws, his cheeks and mouth working and spitting and the silence stretching for minutes and minutes on end.

Leo turned his head toward his partner. "How much longer you plan on staring out the goddamn window?"

"As long as it takes." Addison had conducted some analysis, and it wouldn't hurt to conduct a bit more. The silence soothed him: It had the same effect as cleaning his nine.

"For what?"

"For answers," Addison replied.

Leo spat a few shells. "We could just knock on the door."

"We're only supposed to conduct surveillance."

"You always do everything you're told?" Leo spat three shells into the Dunkie's cup, and he blinked like a cat.

"Not always."

"Why not?"

"It's easier that way," Addison said. His entire life revolved around coming in a close second, and for the first time, he actually came in first, and it scared the piss out of him. He took a long look at the Gatorade bottle before he discarded the notion entirely.

"Funny. I'd say it makes things more difficult."

"That's because you don't know what you're doing."

"Well, it's not from a lack of effort," Leo said.

"True," Addison replied. "Just a lack of brains." Spirit filled Leo, but he wasn't sure the man was filled with much else. Enthusiasm, though, he had that in spades, along with a mouth that resembled a Disney cartoon character and a tuft of unruly hair.

"Maybe your brains hit a few speed bumps."

And then Leo closed his mouth again. But it was never a permanent thing. Only temporary. The nightmare was only temporary. The spitting proved repetitious and cumbersome, the cup filling faster than a urine sample.

Addison hadn't adjusted well. That was probably in his file. The lieutenant had slammed it on his desk and used it to chastise him more than once. Addison had no idea what was inside, only that it wasn't good. Most personnel files weren't. He'd had his share of behavioral issues and concentrated outbursts. Not thinking politically or strategically when the end was close at hand. He had a hard time keeping track, of wading his way through the temperature gauges. The man beside him had cranked the heat, due to the drop in temperature outside, and there was no way to change his mind. The heat lingered longer than he would have liked. He was running out of clothes to remove, and what hair he had left was matted down on his head. He was probably closer to sleep than he realized, on the edge of unconsciousness, the sound of Leo's voice ringing loudly in his ears and the constant barrage of spitting shells filling in more than a few blanks. And still Ahmad hadn't moved from his residence.

Maybe this wasn't even the right residence. Sure, it was where Ahmad lived, but that didn't mean the man was there. This would have been easier if Addison had a few more options, and wasn't on the verge of passing out from the heat. Leo, though, had his eyes closed and his mouth open and his lips bubbled every so often.

Addison shut the engine off, contemplated the gray sky above him, utilized the Gatorade bottle for a couple of bathroom breaks, and stared ahead as time marched forward in staccato bursts. Just as he had begun to believe in the entire pointlessness of this particular exercise, an SUV backed out of the pristine driveway on a street with very little activity due to the snow-covered road and suburb mentality. Pursuing the Range Rover wasn't a difficult endeavor, but he needed a plan, with the tricky winter conditions and Boston traffic, should Ahmad decide to utilize 93 into the city. Ideally, he'd have another vehicle backing him up, especially if the man he followed was a trained professional, but this was no ideal situation, and the suspect was no ideal candidate.

Addison turned the ignition, slipped the cruiser in gear, and slipped in behind the SUV as it crept along the street. He pursued his suspect for four minutes, and then Ahmad entered his first roundabout. Addison separated himself from the Rover, and continued his pursuit as the snow crunched and compacted underneath the rubber.

Leo jerked awake. "Why are we moving?"

Addison's voice was clipped and monotone. "The suspect is on the move."

"And you didn't think to wake me sooner?"

Addison sneered. "I didn't want to ruin your beauty rest."

"Who said anything about beauty?" Leo rubbed his nose. "Well, he doesn't drive like a terrorist."

"According to the lieutenant, that's always a first sign indicator."

Leo shook his head. "Well, the lieutenant is an idiot."

"I won't argue with you there."

Addison followed Ahmad for three more minutes. The SUV obeyed all speed limits, and, so far, this was one of the most boring surveillance endeavors ever. Leave it to

the lieutenant to be totally off-base, or out in left field
without a glove.

The Rover flipped on its blinker up ahead, and so did
he.

"What's he doing there?" Leo asked.

It was a strip mall with a Dunkie's on the end.

"Stopping for coffee?"

ოჳ

Ahmad Jaffer had his hands on the table, and his back
to the wall, the one-way mirror sat off just to his right,
the reflective glass doing a damn good job of reflecting.
He placed his hands evenly spaced on the table, and his
eyes stared straight ahead. His left index finger tapped
the table at a steady interval, and his head bobbed slowly
up and down. He hummed a melody as the presence of
solitude was further solidified. The table creaked under
the slightest amount of pressure, and the door was closed
with prejudice and judgment.

He had a cup of coffee in front of him that he hadn't
touched. It smelled like burnt rubber and had the consistency of tar. Before he could grab a coffee at his favorite spot with the orange and pink logo, with the line moving at a steady pace, he was eased to the side, questioned,
and when he had become less than helpful and possibly
agitated, he was shoved outside and into the back of a
cruiser, driven in the direction of downtown, and tossed
in a room that was the size of a hall closet and surrounded with concrete blocks. It was his most memorable
morning thus far, and he had a feeling it was about to get
even more so. His chair was slightly off balance, and his
left shoulder ached more than his right. He had bumped
his head on the way into the cruiser, the experience rather
unsettling and more than a little disturbing.

He had sat by himself for nearly a half-hour when the door opened.

Two men entered, and the last one closed the door. One was older and taller; the other younger and shorter. Neither smiled.

"Do you know why you're here?" the taller one asked.

"An exercise in authority?"

The younger one drummed his hands on the table. "I'm Detective Leo Nivea, and this is my partner Addison Thomas."

"Did you hear about downtown Boston?" Addison asked.

Ahmad counted ceiling tiles. "What about it?"

Leo opened a file and clicked a pen. He asked about recording the conversation. Ahmad shrugged. "Do you find it strange that no one has claimed responsibility for the incidents?"

"Maybe no one wants to claim responsibility."

"Do you have ties to the Muslim community?" Addison asked.

At this particular juncture, Ahmad was rather certain it didn't matter that he was a United States citizen. "What does that have to do with what happened?"

Addison crossed his arms. "We're tracing links to known terrorists—"

"Do you honestly think I'm a terrorist?" Ahmad counted more ceiling tiles. "I'm a United States citizen." He had entered this country fifteen years ago and received his citizenship approximately three years later.

"Political activist."

Ahmad stared at the tape recorder. "There's nothing wrong with that."

"Except when you force your political views on the rest of society."

Ahmad took a sip from the ruined coffee and spat it

back in the cup. His entire body shook. "Who said anything about force?"

"Maybe you should explain your situation a little more
thoroughly."

Ahmad counted more tiles. "Do I need my lawyer?"

"Do you?" Addison asked.

Ahmad rubbed his forehead. "Maybe I want to change
my mind."

"You're more than welcome to seek counsel," Leo
said. His body language, though, implied otherwise.

Ahmad stared at the tape recorder again. "I have nothing to hide."

"Then why the look of worry?" Leo asked.

"Because I have no idea what you're going to ask
next. It would seem to me you have already made up
your mind on what I have, or haven't, done."

Addison balled his hands into fists. "Isn't that the
point?"

"I'm not sure it is."

"How long have you been a political activist?"

"For as long as I can remember." Ahmad was fairly
certain the older one was only a few years away from a
heart attack, if his life hadn't reached that particular result already. His chest expanded and compressed at a
greater rate than normal, and he had excess skin on his
cheeks and jaws that wobbled.

"You were raised that way?" Leo asked.

"It was important to my father."

Leo flipped through the file. "What about your roommate?"

Ahmad's eyes flicked to the ceiling once more. "What
about him?"

"Your college roommate is a known terrorist."

Ahmad clenched his teeth, and stared at the recorder
again. "Suspected."

Addison grinned. "Is there a difference?"

"Vastly so," Ahmad said. "You have a laundry list of accusations, and not many definitive answers. How did you find me—?"

"We have plenty of questions," Leo said.

Ahmad shrugged. "I might not have all the answers."

"I wouldn't expect you to." Leo paused. "But you can see our dilemma."

Ahmad shook his head and stood up. "I think we're done here."

Before the strange, misguided men could utter another word, he was gone.

❧❧❧

Leo picked a seed from between his teeth. "Well, that didn't go the way I expected. You might want to consider how the lieutenant will react."

"Did you actually have anything conclusive other than his shitty attitude at the Dunkin' Donuts?" Addison asked.

Leo ushered Addison out and slammed the door. The narrow hallway was empty, and a quiet calm filled the void. The rest of the doors were shut, and a face stared behind the glass partition with hollow eyes and sunken cheeks. The faint hint of hair gel hovered near Leo's nostrils. He pinched the end of his nose, and counted to three. His mental fortitude lacked a proper direction. "He staged a protest less than a week ago at The Hancock. It was all over the news. Why the hell do you think the lieutenant jumped all over this one?"

"Lots of protests are staged."

"Three people were arrested—"

"But he wasn't," Addison said.

Leo moved to the side as a cart rolled past steered by a

woman with purpose and slim fingers. His back stiffened, and he placed his hand flat against the wall behind him. Insecurity and indecision filled the air. He tapped his pocket with his other hand: He'd left the packet of seeds on his desk along with his bottle of water and possibly a few pertinent details. "A minor technicality," he said.

"Are we through here?" Addison asked.

Tension took over for the quiet, and Leo's collar hugged his neck a little too close. He stretched it out with his index finger. With his other hand, he shoved away from the wall. He stretched out his knee, and stared hard at Addison and his determined expression. A sense of self-righteousness reached out toward Leo, and he batted it away with the blink of his eye.

Ahmad had shown more fortitude than Leo had expected. He sparred with a surly attitude and a determined nature. A flowing current of animosity rose toward the surface, and he needed to pound it down with a mallet. Even though he had never met the man before now, he already hated the bastard.

"We're just getting started."

ౚఇౚ

Leo conducted another search of the database, placed a few calls with a few contacts along with a few media outlets, and jotted a series of notes on his desktop and Android. Other than the protest incident, Ahmad had no direct connection to the three massive structures that were now a pile of rubble.

Thinking about the monstrosity, his pinky finger shook as it hovered above the keyboard. The screen blurred. The music in his head stopped. He blinked, and the world returned to normal. He still couldn't figure out how the Muslim drove around in a Rover, and why he had failed to address the tragedy with the proper amount of respect. Ahmad almost seemed glad by what had transpired.

ฉ∕ออ

"My neighbor is a jackass."

The man had on a cotton, button-down shirt, and his blue eyes were glazed over. He didn't have a bottle of beer in his hand, but one wasn't far away. He said his name was Brad. His blond hair fell into his eyes, and his front lawn was immaculate.

Leo had driven over—Addison insisted on riding along—after his shift when his present search had ended on a whimper.

From what he was told, Addison's had taken a dip as well. The sky had turned dark over Ahmad's street, but it had brightened for just a moment when Brad had bounded down his steps and strolled over.

The pleasantries ended abruptly, and Brad dove right into the deep end.

"Jackass?" Addison asked.

"Yeah, he's always praying—"

Leo's eyes widened. "You have something against prayer?"

"He has one of those rubber mats—"

"A prayer mat," Addison said.

Brad nodded. He pumped his arms at his sides. "And he points it toward Mecca...or some shit."

His partner nodded in return. Leo took a neutral stance.

"He always has this stern look on his face, like he's not getting enough poontang. He smells like contaminated water. And he's praying three times a day, sometimes four."

Leo glanced down at the back of his hand. "Does he speak out loud?"

"That's the creepy part: He doesn't."

"But has he done anything to you?" Addison asked.

Rather than steer the conversation back on track, Leo preferred the side roads where the wind blew and the stories grew. He always learned much more from a head nod than he did from a forceful change in direction. But Addison favored a different script.

"He's always referring to Allah," Brad said.

"As a person?" Addison asked.

Brad nodded, eyes pointed toward the sky. He licked his lips. His tongue was long and pink. "You're damn straight."

"And this bothers you?"

"Well." Brad paused and scratched his chin and then himself. Blond hair flopped into his eyes, but he didn't push it aside. "He threatens our country."

"In what way?" Leo asked.

"He had nothing but bad things to say about George W. Bush, probably the greatest president ever." Brad's voice turned contemplative. "He taught those bastards in Iraq a good lesson, after his daddy backed out with his head between his legs. The son had the balls the father lacked." He pointed an index finger toward the sky.

If there were a flag out front, Brad probably would have saluted it. Leo, however, would have kept his opinion to himself.

"Or maybe it was the other way around," Addison said.

Brad glared with his glazed eyes. "That's not possible."

"Are you certifiable?" Leo asked.

"Possibly. But the burka is just asking for trouble. After all, he points himself toward Mecca and drives a

Range Rover. It's not like he's aligned his priorities with reality."

Leo's mouth dropped open. "What?"

Brad's arms flapped like he was ready to levitate. "You ever met a burka that was screwed on straight?"

Leo took a deep breath. "You do realize burka refers to a piece of Islamic attire."

Brad squinted and tilted his head, right before he strolled away.

Chapter 15

So how did you come up with the name The Sex Maggots?"

"That's a long story," Quinn said.

"We have plenty of air time, and based on your last interview, I'd say we probably need more space to fill."

The room wasn't much bigger than the last one. The buttons, dials, and blinking lights were in different places, and so was the chair. The idiot across from him was named either Burt or Bill, Quinn couldn't remember which. Burt...or Bill...had a loud outfit and a loud voice, and not much else on his skinny frame. His cap was pulled low, and his teeth appeared bleached.

Quinn stared at the blinking lights. "I don't like long windedness."

"Maybe you don't like filling in blanks."

"So we like sex—"

"You're guys—"

"And maggots are the bottom of the food chain. I mean snails probably get more play than maggots. We'd had a little trouble with names in the past, and we certainly weren't going to be named The Johnny Rockets."

Bill...or Burt...leaned back. "Especially since your name's not Johnny."

Quinn pondered this. "Although it could have been, you know—in another life." He still wasn't sure how he felt about the name Quinn, even after all these years. But he did have on his favorite sunglasses and the blinking lights soothed his soul.

"Are you serious?"

"I mean I could come back as a chipmunk, or even a unicorn." Quinn grinned. "Everybody wants to fuck a unicorn."

Burt...or Bill...glared at him. "You can't say the F-word on the air." A pause the size of a hiccup ensued. A blinking light blared red. "And maybe you could sprinkle fairy dust on your private parts."

Quinn shoved a cigarette in his mouth. Bill...or Burt...removed it from between Quinn's teeth and stomped on it.

Quinn flipped him the bird. "Hey, I thought this was my story."

"You're the boss," the idiot said. "And you can't smoke in here."

Quinn sucked in his left cheek and chewed. "So we decided to mash the two together. We thought it would be cool, and we weren't too worried about the questions that would come up, until you decided to take control of the microphone. Besides, it sounds even funnier when you're wasted, or when a busty bimbo has it tattooed on her tits."

Burt...or Bill...smacked his forehead with the palm of his hand. "We do have a bit of air time to fill, and I'm always chasing after a good story. Also, you look like you have a problem living in reality."

Quinn had a thought, and then it left. "Maybe you don't have any stories to chase."

Another pause while the airwaves breathed static. "So that's it?"

"Yeah, pretty much." Quinn shifted in his seat, and the leather squeaked. "Once we got famous, it's not like we

could change the name. The record company had a con-
niption, but that was their problem. Our problem revolved around creating the best album we could. It's all
about the music, you know. Laying the tracks, adding the
vocals, throwing in the harmony, and giving it a cutting
edge, that's where I'm at. A unique sound that no one
else has, and I believe we're there, man."

"But your records don't sound all that different than
anyone else's."

"That's because you're not listening to the lyrics,
man."

Burt...or Bill...suddenly looked constipated. "I try not
to listen to the lyrics."

Quinn pointed at his microphone right before he
flicked it. "Then you're missing out on half the song."

"No, I'm fully integrated to your music, much more
than I would like to be. If I wanted to increase my brain
activity, I'd figure out a way to end this discussion."

"Well, you're a bit older than our typical fan base,
man." The idiot probably had one foot in the grave, and
the second wasn't far behind.

"But I'm still breathing."

Quinn puffed out his cheeks and blew. "Good for
you."

The closet was claustrophobic, and the back of
Quinn's neck was slicked in sweat. He had a massive
hard-on that he needed to expunge in the nearest bathroom, and his last dream involved a midget. In short, he
was fucked.

"You could start your tour anywhere in the US. Why
Boston?"

"Boston is all about the music," Quinn said. "It's
about rock 'n roll, it's about girls and sex and drugs and
getting high and playing while high and creating a sound
that's loud enough to blow off a pair of panties. If you

can do that, you're golden, you know. Life is better with a little beaver."

The DJ slapped his forehead again and groaned, and overeager fans pounded on the other side of the glass. Quinn ignored them.

"I didn't know that was possible."

"Well, we're about to find out, aren't we?"

Bill...or Burt...leaned back again. "And you're not worried about not getting paid?"

"Fuck." Quinn took his voice to another level. The small walls crushed his chest, and his pulse soared. "We're not getting paid?"

"I told you, you can't say 'fuck' on the air."

Quinn blew out a breath and then flipped his hair. "Then maybe I shouldn't be on your show."

"FCC regulations—"

"Man, I don't care about the FCC."

As a commercial break began, Quinn picked his nose. He'd had about enough of this shit. Dealing with retards reminded him of sucking a bowl of Jell-O through a straw, which he'd done once while he was stoned. No hot girls with loose expressions and even looser morals were around, either. The closet with the blinking lights suddenly reminded him of a funeral parlor.

When the break ended, the verbal tap dancing resumed.

"Why free?"

"We want to give back to our fans, man," Quinn said. "It's all about the fans. Without them, we'd be some band in some garage strumming our guitars and getting high and waiting for our big break, you know."

Burt...or Bill...laughed. "Are you sure you aren't doing that now?"

Quinn turned thoughtful. "Only when we're working on new material."

"Any last words?"

Quinn rubbed the stubble on his chin and lifted his sunglasses. "Oh, I almost forgot. If you're one of the first five hundred at the show, you'll be given a cap gun to fight the terrorists. It's an exercise of your Fourth Amendment rights."

The idiot groaned. "You mean Second."

⋐⋑⋐⋑

"You still haven't told me what happened," Richard Lancaster III said.

His wife Loretta, had her feet up, and he rubbed them in order to make amends. Every few seconds or so she let out a low moan, and her eyes rolled back in her head. He was on the floor with his feet tucked against his body, his fingers kneading and threading the bottom of Loretta's foot. The TV was on low, turned to a talk show. The carpet rubbed the back of his leg.

Another low moan. "Oh God, Richard, it was awful. There were women and children screaming. It sounded like a bomb exploded. If we had been eating inside, we wouldn't be having this conversation right now. And the only reason we were eating outside was Yolanda arrived sixteen minutes late, we couldn't have the table we'd specifically requested, and all the other seats inside were filled. It was cold, but I wanted cheesecake, and I'll be damned if I would let Yolanda take that away from me as well. Despite her protests, and there were many, we ended up eating outside. The only ones on the terrace, and only because I managed to protest loud enough for the manager to hear. The wind blew my hair, and my hand froze up like I'd stuffed it next to an icepack. And it was right after we ordered that we heard the explosion. Glass flew everywhere, all over the patio and the concrete walkway, and I thought I was deaf for twelve minutes. The world sounded all garbled and jumbled. I couldn't see at first, and so all I could do was just sit there, with my cold hands and my face freezing. It was gray all around me, and I leaned back in my chair, far enough that I toppled over backwards. Luckily, there wasn't a table or railing behind me, or I'd have been taking one of those fancy ambulances to the hospital—"

He massaged the ball of her foot. "When did the ERTs show up?"

Loretta's eyes flipped open. "The what?"

"The emergency response teams."

She moaned again. "Honestly, Richard, are you going to write a book?"

"I have no idea what I'm going to do," he said. "At the moment, I'm just gathering evidence." He might need it to file an appeal.

"As opposed to gathering ties," Loretta said. "And losing jobs."

"I told you it wasn't my fault." He never could handle stress, and his boss needed anger management therapy. When he asked to be reassigned, he was asked to pack up his crap and get the hell out.

Loretta rolled her eyes. "It's never your fault, Richard."

"Yes," he said, "but this was the first time I've been fired." He also had a sexual harassment suit on his hands, but that was later dropped. The girl was less than stable.

"But you certainly weren't weighing your options the way you should have," Loretta said. "If you'd been a bit smarter, you'd have milked your job for all it's worth, instead of storming off all self-righteous."

Richard cringed and his hand jerked. "I gave that job twenty-one years of my life."

"Obviously that wasn't long enough," Loretta said, "now was it?"

His voice quivered and his hand dropped. He leaned back against the sofa and looked at the TV. "What about what I want out of this relationship?"

Her voice took a chafing tone. "Honestly, Richard, it's always about you, isn't it? I have needs too, you know. Womanly needs that you can't seem to satisfy."

"Well, I'd like to do that a bit more often, and I'm glad you recognize our situation. If you'll follow me—"

"I mean shopping, Richard," she said. "Honestly." Loretta waved her hand dismissively. "There's the internet for that other sort of thing."

His face brightened, and he leaned forward. "So you're encouraging it?"

എന്ന

Lynette grabbed a drink and sat at the bar. The only bar she knew. The lighting was dim, the air was stale, and a layer of grime covered her clothes and hair whenever she stepped toward the light. The bar was called The Slow Swallow, and it was exactly one-half mile from her home. She lived in Boston, and she knew one bar. How pathetic was that? It had been hard, finding the bar the first time. She'd wandered around, nearly getting lost about three different times, but then she'd never been good with directions, and she certainly wasn't about to admit that she needed help from a stranger with a long beard and a crack pipe stuffed in his pants who favored his left leg over his right and ogled her out of the corner of his eye.

She'd wandered aimlessly three streets over and two streets up, not sure why she couldn't just find the entrance to the darn place, with her hair blowing in the wind, and her mind reeling with thoughts of the latest mugging. The cold night air bristled around her. The sound of her beating heart kept time with the music that blared from the luxury SUV on the opposite side of the street with the tinted windows and reflective hood. Each thud of bass reverberated within her and chilled her even more than the night air. She could still hear the drums, some nights, when she really tried, and the night air attacked her right cheek even more than her left. Walking, though, even when she wore high heels on the cobblestone streets, soothed her.

Lynette tapped her hand on the bar in time to a long-forgotten beat. The sound echoed in the small space and a head or two turned in her direction. The oak bar stuck out at an unusual angle in an unusual place on the floor nowhere near the door. But then this bar wasn't about space utilization or clean air or skirts and business suits. It was about good old-fashioned drinking, the impending tsunami, and the largest amount of alcohol that she could consume in the shortest amount of time. The drinks weren't watered down, or frilly. The liquor burned her tongue on the way down, kicking down her esophagus, and wiggling around for good measure. She leaned her head back and smiled, and double-tapped her hand against the oak.

Less than a minute later, another glass slid in her direction. The stale air reminded her of her first apartment, where the radiator gave off an unusual odor, and the landlord touched her arm a bit too frequently, with a bit too much authority, and his leer unsettled her even on her best of days. Here, though, the men left her alone, and she was always one or two seats away from her favorite spot. She preferred the fourth seat over from the left where she had an unobstructed view of the mirror in front of her.

She allowed herself one night out a month. But based on her present situation, and that of her former employer, she had a feeling she needed to increase her visits in the upcoming weeks. She might get plowed, stomped on, run over, and left for dead on the side of the cobblestoned street, one heel less than when she started, but she would have a darn good time doing it, since it was all about the booze and the breeze.

Lynette was fairly certain none of her colleagues were left. Being the only survivor and getting fired placed a significant burden on her shoulders that only liquor could soothe. She'd already shed more than enough tears, and that had gotten her exactly nowhere. Her damn coffeepot and a handful of memories were all she had left of Xanthic. Her phone calls and voicemails remained unanswered, and so she'd given that up altogether. She leaned forward.

The second drink went down even easier than the first.

She could feel a pair of eyes staring at the back of her head, but she wasn't about to turn around. She wasn't about to give anyone the satisfaction. She focused on her drinking, her sorrows, the solid bar in front of her, the women's restroom when she needed it, and the ground below her, should her solid stool rock just a bit too far in one direction or the other. She closed her eyes, sucked down the last of her glass, the rum kicking straight at her ribs, and signaled the bartender for another.

The memory of fire still lingered heavy on her conscience.

Yep, one more sounded good.

Chapter 16

We won't condone the behavior of terrorists. Those responsible for this horrible tragedy will be brought to justice. We will seek the harshest penalties allowed by law, and we won't take no for an answer. The good people of Boston deserve justice. The families of those we have lost deserve justice, and your voices will not be ignored. The Boston PD is working hard on getting us answers, and the FBI has been brought in to tactically take over the case. We have leads to run down, and we have three of our greatest landmarks in ruins." Mayor Joey James pointed behind her. "We have a city yearning for some answers, and as soon as we have those answers, you will hear them from my lips first."

She shuffled another page to the back. Cameras flashed, and microphones waved in her direction. No podium separated her from the crowd below. The sea of faces fixated on her and hung on her every word. Her eyes locked on the eagerness to help her get through the next announcement.

Since the explosions, she had been unable to focus on anything else. Like this wonderful city, her mind was shattered, and she hoped she could salvage what was left. Her bottom lip trembled. "The actions of a few will not destroy the lives of many. We can't let them win. We have to mourn, we have to grieve, and we have to rise

above. This will not be easy—Nine-Eleven wasn't
easy—but we survived. We came together as a people, as
a nation, and we will do the same here. I have already
spoken to the president, and he has declared this a national emergency. He is willing to provide us with all the
resources we need to see this outcome to its final resolution. Our voices have not been ignored.

"We must show these terrorists that they cannot break
our spirit, and that they cannot destroy our minds and
souls. That it's not about us as individuals. It's about
Bostonians coming together and helping one another
through this horrific ordeal, and that ultimately we will
prevail. My office has set up a hotline, and we will hold
counseling sessions free of charge to those affected family members. We already have restoration projects in the
works that will resurrect these great landmarks."

The mayor paused here, and shuffled another page.
Her voice had not wavered. Her message was clear. Pain
and emotion rocketed through her, and with grim eyes
and a heavy heart she soldiered on. She had dealt with
loss before—losing elections came to mind—but this was
a loss that had no manual. "Know this, whoever you are,
we will come for you. The city of Boston will come for
you, and reign down upon you—"

Genuine tears filled her eyes, as the cameras flashed
and video rolled, with reporters shouting questions in her
direction, too many questions for her to even understand
and comprehend, and then the tears stopped, as did the
questions, and she cleared her throat as the clouds parted.
She had her lines in front of her, but she didn't need her
notes to discover genuine emotion. She had foregone the
Teleprompters on either side of her, the podium in front
of her, and even her family. Just the people of Boston and
her united together.

She spoke from the heart, the words flowing out of her

like water from the Great Lakes. She was surrounded by a sea of expectant faces, the smell of smoke and charred remains still close at hand, as death and destruction and sadness hung heavy in the air. It was an impromptu session, and the crowd was bigger than she expected. She couldn't wait. She had to get the words out now, while the words were still close at hand. Moving verses filled with hope and anger, to move the people and the city of Boston forward toward some final resolution. The faces of the men who had caused this horrible tragedy formed in her mind. Sure, they might not have been the right faces, but she wanted to look her mortal enemies in the eyes, and conquer them. She wanted the citizens to come together, to rise as one, to find common ground, and to discover hope once more. Maybe The Sex Maggots concert was the answer. A free show to help the citizens forget, even if it was for just one night, even if it was for only a few hours. Maybe a celebration would restore order to this great place. She wasn't part of the concert planning committee, but maybe it was her best hope. Maybe it was Boston's only hope to survive and rise from the ashes.

"I urge you to come out two nights hence for the concert on the Common," Mayor Joey James said. "It won't be one to miss. Thank you."

"Are you saying you *support* The Sex Maggots?" a female voice asked.

"If that's what it means to celebrate," the mayor said, "and help the citizens of Boston heal, then yes, I'm willing to throw my support behind the free concert. We need to celebrate life, and this city is poised to survive and thrive once more."

"Weren't you against such a festival only a few months ago?" another voice asked.

"I'm against the specific principles inherent in rock concerts, but I support all kinds of music, festivals, and celebrations, and I enjoy a good party just as much as the next gal."

"So are you saying you'll be there?"

For the first time during her speech, she smiled. "I can't endorse a concert and not attend," Mayor James said, "now can I?"

☙❧

The governor had a similar speech prepared. He wanted his voice heard over the entire Commonwealth of Massachusetts. He wanted to take his speech to the airwaves, the radio waves, and when necessary, the tidal waves. He had practiced it—the one his speech-writers had spent several hours crafting, the one sitting on his desk, as he stood off to the side, with a mirror in front of him, as his emotions, intonation, and enunciation transformed—until it was his voice and his words. He had to place the emphasis on the right syllables, he had to concentrate on a deeper voice, since his was naturally high-pitched, which didn't sound right for a politician from the state where JFK had once resided.

He had maneuvered around the past, and he was more than prepared to face the future. He had his political cronies ready to take up the front rows, and cheer him on, no matter what words came out of his mouth, and he had the people behind him, the ones with the cue cards, and the incessant smiles, the ones who would make him, as well as the audience, feel right at home, cheering and stomping and stampeding as necessary. He paced throughout his office, turning circles on the red carpet, and repeating his key points. He had to focus on those points. He couldn't drift too far away from the mainstream, otherwise he would lose his audience, some of whom probably didn't have more than an eighth-grade education. And there were certainly those individuals in Texas and New Mexico that he'd have to worry about, if his speech went national. He'd been on national television before, and he'd done it gladly, along with the right sense of authority, with perfect precision and articulation. But this was different. He needed the citizens of Massachusetts to rise above this horrible tragedy, and he needed to one-up the mayor—that self-indulgent female who looked and acted like a model posing on the runway—since this was about a second term, a second chance to make things right. What he needed was another opportunity to take over the world. And he couldn't do it in the shadow of a former beauty queen with calves as strong as aluminum rods.

"They're ready for you, sir."

He'd employed a military man as his executive assistant. With Hanscom AFB thirty minutes outside of Boston, it was important that he showed support for his airmen, the ones who had given their lives for this great nation, the ones who showed purpose, restraint, service before self, integrity, and courage in the face of personal and professional tragedy, and who would support this nation whether here or abroad, doing it admirably and with the utmost professionalism. But his assistant still spouted "sir" and "ma'am" as if he were in the Marines and the commanding officer was about to lead the charge over Bunker Hill.

It was all about the battle and getting answers and taking no prisoners and doing what was necessary to complete the mission. And he was glad he had an executive assistant who knew what was what. Boston, though, might never be the same again.

৩৩৩

Two years, two months, and two days ago Daniel

Pinder lost his wife. It started out like any other day, and it had ended one step over the tragedy line. One life was lost that day, but it was a life that was extremely important to him. A life that he could never get back no matter how hard he searched for answers. No matter how high or how low his search reached, he couldn't bring her back, nor could he reconstruct the pieces of what happened. No medical team, no EMTs, not even the best medically trained professionals in the world, including all the top hospitals in Boston, could give him the answers he most desperately needed. As for the autopsy, it was inconclusive. Answers had escaped his world. It wasn't for a lack of trying either, with long, sleepless nights, newspaper clippings, and favors called in to the local precinct died on the telephone line. After multiple phone calls and visits, the investigation stalled, and the case died a quiet death with no pomp or circumstance.

He was a firefighter, and the police had lost their sense of urgency.

Unlike her.

The search was fruitless. The endeavor more mind-numbing than he would have ever imagined possible. The memory of her remained strong with him, strong enough to wake him up some nights in a fit of terror and loss, but that memory had faded ever so slightly. Life moved on. He tried to do the same with his face shoved toward the fireplace.

Her car had flipped over, clinging to the guard rail in one last desperate breath. She had died instantly. Her face was covered with blood, one arm pinned at her side, the other arm protruded at an unusual angle, the stereo turned to an R&B station. Her right leg was broken; her left leg wasn't. Blood had dripped on the roof that was now below her, covering the ceiling like a Jackson Pollock painting in large drops, with splatters of red mixing with dark blue, and tiny fragments of bone.

The oddities stuck with him, though. He was unable to extricate them from his mind. His wife never listened to R&B, she was a careful driver, and there were no skid marks, nor a single indication that she had bothered to slow down. But the first arrivals had mucked up the scene, trampling evidence into the asphalt, or losing it altogether in the rain storm that had quickly ensued soon after her car had flipped, and the sky had opened up. The engine was still warm, and gas leaked out of the side of the vehicle, dripping a long line, growing with each passing second.

He wasn't allowed anywhere near the accident—security reasons or some bullshit. He wasn't allowed to leave the fire station without an escort. He had a guard watching over him, to the point that he couldn't even take a piss without the man entering the men's room and holding up the door, and he wasn't allowed to stay by himself. He was put on suicide watch, and he was ordered to take counseling sessions, until he was no longer deemed a risk to himself or the fire department. His wife's case, however, had never been solved. No solid leads. Early on in the investigation, it was deemed an accident, and that was all she wrote.

He didn't have the investigative skills or the wherewithal to see it through all by himself. But that didn't stop him from trying, from searching for answers wherever and whenever he could, as little scraps filled one notebook and then another. It didn't stop him from bending the rules, just a bit, using his knowledge and skills about fires and transferring those skills to police work in the hopes of discovering the truth and seeking justice for his dead wife. But he managed to come up short.

Somehow Daniel Pinder was always two steps behind the power curve, and he was well on his way to a third.

ᘒᘒᘒ

The lieutenant had a bottle of Windex in one hand and a piece of paper in the other. He sat behind his desk as straight as a stone wall. "This is a simple operation," Ward Phillips said. "If you fuck this up, you'll be picking peanuts out of your ass for the rest of your days."

Addison Thomas adjusted his hands behind his back. "An elephant never forgets."

"Is that supposed to be funny?"

"Not necessarily." Addison wasn't offered a seat, so he didn't take one. He had his hands threaded behind his back, and his legs spread apart at shoulder width. He stared at a spot just above the lieutenant's head, and he didn't waver in the slightest even under the intense scrutiny. In fact, he welcomed the challenge.

"If he gives you any trouble, talk to him calmly, hand him the warrant, but don't engage the suspect further."

"What if he calls his attorney?"

"He's certainly welcome to." The lieutenant dumped the bottle of Windex in a drawer behind his desk, and dug out a paper towel. "But that's not going to stop the proceedings."

"You make this sound like a court of law."

Ward lifted his head. "It's more about following through on your actions. You can't leave yourself open to the wrong interpretations." He paused. "It's not about whistling in the dark. This is supposed to be simple. Do you know what you're looking for?"

Addison shrugged, adjusted his legs, and shifted his gaze. "You mean besides answers."

Ward attacked his desk with the paper towel in one hand, and handed over the warrant with the other. "Don't get smart with me. He's a known terrorist with connections to bomb-loving enthusiasts."

"Suspected one."

Ward gritted his teeth. "Don't make this about yourself."

"I'm not." Addison wiggled his left hand, and his shoulder realigned to a more comfortable location.

"Go in with authority," Ward said. "That's why we have a team in place."

"This man has been an outspoken advocate of the president." Addison softened his voice. "Do you really want that on your conscience?"

Ward rubbed harder. "Everyone and everything is corruptible, when it's given the right push."

სოღა

The warrant had come through after a bit of political maneuvering by the lieutenant and mayor's office. It was done at a strategic level that Addison didn't really understand. Sure, Ahmad Jaffer had his share of inconsistencies and issues, and probably more than a few problems, including former friends and irate neighbors and suspect demonstrations, but the Muslim had a family and a steady job and not even so much as a parking ticket. But Addison was a man that followed orders—countless years on the force told him when to keep his mouth shut—and saluted smartly and didn't leave his bare butt dangling in the breeze.

He gripped the warrant tightly in his fist, gathered his partner, Leo, with the sunflower seed fetish, and ambled toward a man filled with an errant set of ideals. Somberness filled the ride over, and the stroll to Ahmad's front door was cast in a web of doubt. But Addison knocked, the door opened, and Leo shoved the paper through the crack. All Addison's doubts and fears were cast aside with one simple push.

Addison conducted the search swiftly and thoroughly, barking out orders to Leo and his men. Ahmad's face registered surprise, shock, anger, and then the slightest hint of calm in less than a minute with each shift a concerted effort on the Muslim's part. Ahmad called his attorney next, and stormed outside while his residence was flipped faster than a queen size mattress and turned inside out.

Addison led one team, the team that discovered C-4 in Ahmad's garage, while Leo and the other team stormed upstairs in a glint of metal and blue. Addison whistled softly as he said a silent prayer to no one in particular.

The Muslim had hidden it out of the way, behind a canoe painted in red and blue that he'd shoved against a back wall. He had the plastic explosive and various lengths of fuses and wires. No detonators. He had enough to blow up a single building on a busy street. But not three.

That concerned Addison, but not as much as it probably should have.

Chapter 17

How did you manage to get expelled this time?" Daniel asked.

"Do you even care, Dad?"

"Of course I care, Kasey. You're my daughter." *And I'll always love you.* Raising a teenager was difficult, raising a teenager without his lovely wife proved even more difficult. Her sandy brown hair, soft curls, and the look of defiance plastered across her face told him to back off. The earbuds jammed in her ears as she scrolled through her phone further emphasized the point.

Her walls were painted black, and she had taken on a new look with her wardrobe, beginning to pay attention to what she wore, and what other people thought about her clothes, specifically boys. Her eyes were trimmed in black eyeliner, and she had the faintest hint of makeup on her face. He asked her to take out her earbuds, and set her phone aside. She groaned, rolled her eyes, stared at him with an icy gaze, and then did as he asked. Life was always a production with her. She reminded him of her mother, and he loved her even more for it.

"But you're never around," his daughter said. Her lower lip bobbed, but her eyes remained hard and neutral. Kasey jammed a pillow underneath her left elbow. "You're always working. You spend so much time focused on yourself—"

"That's not true—"

"Isn't it?" She sat up, pounded the same pillow, and jammed it against the headboard, strangling whatever life was left in it. "Do you even remember my name?"

"Of course I remember your name." But he didn't, not at that particular instant. It would come to him later, though, when his emotions were back under control, and his daughter no longer resembled his dead wife. "Why are you being so dramatic all of a sudden?"

She shook her head and pounded the pillow again. Shifted, readjusted, and then tossed the pillow over the side. "I've always been dramatic, Dad. You just haven't bothered to notice."

He shifted his eyes to the floor, before he focused on her once again. Kasey, his beautiful daughter with the attitude and rebellious streak, always filled with sage advice, and eyes filled with wonderment and awe. "This isn't your first time, is it?" The expulsion weighed heavy on his mind.

"Of course, it's not my first time," she said. "You conveniently forget the other times, because it means you'd have to put forth more of an effort. And you're not willing to do that. Ever since Mom died—"

"I still love you."

The lip quivered again, this time more prominent than the one before. "Of course, you're going to throw *that* card on the table. That's the only card you have left. But you actually have to remember that I'm still here, even though Mom isn't. You can't just show up once in a while, pretend to put in an effort, and then expect everything to be okay. Because it's not okay, Dad. It hasn't been okay for a long time, and the fact that you haven't noticed at all, not one iota, says more about our situation than any actual words, and especially those three little words that you like to use—"

"I understand perfectly." Daniel took a tentative step forward and reached out his hand. "You want attention."

She hopped out of bed, away from him and his hand, made a beeline for the window, and stared out at the world. Silence lingered in the room, as he continued to gaze at the back of her head. Words that should have been spoken were left unsaid. Being a parent scared the shit out of him. Every. Single. Day. Despite his hope that it would get easier, Daniel ended up on a more difficult road instead.

Kasey turned back around. Her voice was uneven. "Dad, you don't have a clue."

"That's what this is about: isn't it? You think I don't remember you, don't appreciate you, and don't want to be anywhere near you. But I do, sweetie, I really, really do. I want to be a part of your life—"

A sigh escaped her lips, and she sucked in her right cheek. She took two steps away from the window. "You're so full of it, Dad. This isn't about you. And maybe if you had taken more than just a few seconds to understand what's going on, you'd realize that."

"It's about Tommy, isn't it?" He'd heard the name mentioned before in the presence of her best friend Shelly, during one sleepover that involved cupcakes and the latest high school gossip. He had eavesdropped out of necessity and for the chance to better understand his daughter. It wasn't that long ago. The name was slathered with the faintest hint of affection and a strong sense of pride. She had smiled then—he heard it—but she hadn't smiled around him, not for more than two months, and the earbuds had remained firmly in place. Losing a wife, and possibly a daughter, with an entire city in turmoil added several points to his cholesterol level, thank you, Obama.

"You're throwing names around like you understand

the meaning behind them. But you're just firing in the dark. You're pulling the trigger, and you're spraying bullets, but that's all you're doing."

Her words said he was wrong, but Kasey's facial expression and lower lip movement said otherwise. He decided not to push the issue more than he had to.

Daniel held up his hands, palms to the sky, his voice soft and even, and barely above a whisper. "Would you prefer that I did?"

⌘⌘⌘

Carl had looked everywhere for Mutt. All of his usual hiding spots, behind the TV—despite the number of wires that he sometimes liked to chew—in the closet that he was able to nudge open with his paw and his nose, on his office sofa and the regular one, in the bathroom where he liked to consume toilet water, because it was cold and wet and easily accessible when the toilet seat was left up—dumb dog—and underneath his desk. No Mutt.

So Carl had taken to the streets. He called out Mutt's name, and he'd walked up and down the block, and around the corner, searching in all of the dog's favorite playing spots, including behind the neighbor's woodshed where he liked to dig with reckless abandon. Unfortunately, there were a lot of gardens, and Mutt always sought those out first. Before he'd even realized it, Carl had walked several blocks and then a couple of miles, calling and screaming, his hands cupped around his mouth, canvassing the neighborhood up and down and all around. No luck.

Losing his dog, and his colleagues, and an entire library filled with books was too much. Sleep, hard enough to come by under normal circumstances, escaped him, and his tortured mind experienced a new level of pain and sorrow. His steps were heavy, his stride short, and his legs moved about as fast as a tub of molasses.

His thoughts turned strained, and so did his voice. His hands whipped rapidly at his sides, in frantic motion, his entire body in constant movement, one giant piston ready to fire, and his voice shook at the thought of a missing dog and a pack of dead colleagues. But Carl marched on as the thick, cold air, smacked against his face, and the sweat pooled against his shirt and underneath his jacket. His legs churned through the soft white powder that barely covered the road and scrunched underneath his rubber soles, and his shirt clung to his chest, as the sound of a car starting up jerked him back to the present.

A voice lingered in the breeze, or maybe it was a dog, and he had a pack of Marlboro Reds jammed in his jacket pocket. The wind tickled, and his nose itched.

His feet started to ache, along with his ankles and knees, and his mind turned to the worst of distractions where screaming and dead bodies ran rampant. Sweat formed around his shirt collar now, the collar strangling his neck, and so he jerked it, creating a passageway. The wind ducked and darted inside, and Carl shivered.

His right foot slipped on a patch of ice, and he stumbled but didn't fall. His left leg held him upright, even as his right leg bent at the knee. His mind stood frozen in time before the tragedy, back to when the teenager in the BC sweatshirt held a black gun at his chest. The threat of violence proved just as bad as the act itself. His heart had the same uneven rhythm, and the kid had the same scorn and indifference exhibited by a common criminal held in the nearest federal penitentiary.

He called out in spite of the wind. But the sound of his voice didn't bring any dogs running toward him, including the elusive mixed breed whose whereabouts continued to remain a mystery as the wind continued to blow.

After Carl's eyes had roamed through the streets, sidewalks, and front yards, he started banging on a few doors and ringing a few bells. He spoke with insistence to anyone that would listen, possibly a futile effort, but it was all he had.

∾∾∾

The foot rubbing had ceased, and packing had taken its place. His wife dumped clothes and cosmetics in a handbag and rollaway suitcase from the master bath and closet with practiced skill while her arms were a continuous blur of motion. Richard Lancaster III had put a hand on her shoulder to stop her, or at least slow her down, but she had slapped it away, and pushed on with her mission. The slap held no maliciousness, but it did cause him to pause and reevaluate his current condition. She had stuck with him through the thin, but now she was determined to take her life in a new direction.

"You're leaving me now?" he asked.

Loretta slammed a few bras in place with a twist of her hand. "You can't seem to take care of yourself."

He held out a hand to touch her, before he pulled it back. "You really don't have any decency, do you?"

"It's not about decency." Loretta grabbed a few more bras and shoved them on top of the others with added authority. "It's about sticking together. That's what we were supposed to do, through thick and thin."

"Well, now things have gotten a little bit thin."

She stopped her packing momentarily and turned to face him with narrow eyes. "They've been thin for a while, Richard. You just haven't been willing to recognize the inevitable. Getting fired for insubordination should have made you stop and think."

The room felt much smaller than it had only moments ago. It never did feel like his room, or house: She had decorated all of it herself. He was a small pea in a large pod. "You and I were a team. When I grew, it was because of you. With you, I was better than I ever could have been on my own."

For a moment, the packing stopped. She nodded, and rubbed her arms. "That's what it was supposed to be."

Richard dropped on the edge of the bed. "What's changed?"

"You." Loretta pointed a finger directly at his chest. "You're not getting any better. In fact, you're getting worse. I had hoped it wouldn't come to this, that you would improve with time. But now here we are, and you've resorted to your old ways. You've put yourself so high there's no room for anyone else."

"I was never a thief."

"You weren't." Loretta had moved on to her underwear, grabbing and shoving it into the bag by the armful. Bending at the knees, she heaved one pile after another into the rollaway. "But you were a liar."

Richard softened his voice. "Honey, that was a long time ago."

"Don't 'honey' me." Her voice rose higher and higher reaching toward the rafters. "Don't turn this around on me." Shrill was a significant understatement. "It's your fault we're in this state. If you had just been better at work, you wouldn't have gotten fired."

Richard held out his hand again, left it lingering in the space between them. But it went untouched and unnoticed. She probably could have strangled a kitten in her present condition. "I gave that company twenty-one years of my life. And I was willing to give it even more." He paused, voice catching, his throat closing. "And then this happened."

She piled blouses on top of bras and underwear and pants. No real method to her madness, clothes poking out everywhere. "Don't blame the destruction of the three buildings for your mistakes. Your firing happened long before this." She nodded her head for emphasis. "You said so yourself."

He lifted his arms palms up. With each blouse and pair of pants Loretta packed, she shut herself off from him a little more. "But I can change." And he would. If it meant she would stick around this time, he would move the Appalachian Mountains. Not go running off into the night again like some lost cat.

"You've said that before."

He lifted his eyes. "I'm *willing* to change."

"I'm not sure you are, Richard." Her voice turned softer. She piled in long-sleeved shirts and sweaters on top of the bras and underwear and pants and blouses, clothes popping out all over the bed, piles jumping and springing and growing with every passing second. "I'm not convinced about the new you. You blame your problems on everyone else but yourself. Now, does that sound like a person willing to change?"

"But it's about more than just me. It's you and I together forever. We've taken vows—"

"Oaths even," Loretta said. "Sure. But it's not about what you want anymore. This is about me." She pointed a finger at her chest and raised her voice to new ground. "And I still have a chance to make things right."

His voice turned soft while hers rose higher. "By leaving me?"

"It'd be a start." She paused, several beats lingering in the small space, while he looked down at the mess of clothes. "This time I'm serious."

A whine entered his voice for the first time. "What am I supposed to do?"

She dragged the suitcase off the bed, slammed the lid down, and ran the zipper around. When it wouldn't close right away, she sat on it, and tried again. This time it worked, and she looked up afterward. "I'm sure you'll figure it out."

He placed both hands against his face. "But you don't have anything…"

She stood up and twisted her hips. "I'll be back for my stuff later."

His eyes widened. "All you need is a suitcase?"

"Two," she clarified. "For now anyway. At least until I get settled."

He stared at her back. "Where are you going to go?"

Loretta yanked the handle on the rollaway and slung the handbag over her shoulder. "Does it really matter, Richard?" She paused, and then used a different tone. "You're too self-absorbed to even realize that I'm leaving. You're too focused on yourself to even understand what is really going on. We've been broken for a while, Richard, and you just haven't bothered to recognize it. You think you can change everything, and everything broken can be fixed. You think you can save the world. You think you're only one small move away from success. But let me tell you, Richard. You're a lot farther away than you'd like to admit, and it's not going to get any better. If you can find another job—"

"If? What's this 'if' business?"

She pulled the rollaway behind her out of the bedroom, the handbag perched on her shoulder. "You're no spring chicken, Richard. I'd rather set my sights on a thoroughbred, not the one that's being led to slaughter."

He rubbed his head. "What?"

"When I almost died, I realized life was too short, and that it was important for me to start living it up. At least while I still have a few good years left in me. Your best years are behind you, not in front."

He looked up at the ceiling. "Where will you go?"

She turned around at the bottom of the stairs, while he maneuvered the steps one at a time. The chasm between them felt like it was measured in miles, instead of feet. His right hand slipped off the banister, and he grimaced. A stair, the faulty one that always managed to give him trouble, creaked beneath his weight.

"Oh, I'm sure I can find a place to rest my head."

The whine reentered his landscape. "Aren't you worried about us?"

"I stopped worrying about us a long time ago, Richard," Loretta said. "At one time you were the best thing to happen to me, and now you're just the aftereffects of a horrible nightmare. Losing your job might have been the best thing for our relationship. Now I get to live my dream, and you can find yours."

"But you bailed me out of jail."

She wheeled her bag out to the garage. He followed her. "I'm not evil, Richard. Just lonely. The long nights you work have certainly taken a toll on me, and it's only going to get worse, since now you'll probably be depressed for half your days, and the other half you'll spend lurking online when you should be peddling your resume. You were always a procrastinator, Richard. It's about time you start living up to your own expectations."

He gripped the doorjamb until his knuckles turned white and ached from the exertion. "You're really going to give up on me?"

She slammed the trunk. "It's not like you're leaving me any choice."

"Why are you still here? You could have left whenever you wanted to."

"Closure, Richard. You need it more than I do. I don't want to leave you flapping in the breeze. From the stories I've heard, you were never good at ending relationships, and I'm not going to do the same thing to you. It's not fair. You deserve to know the truth, even if the truth smells like yesterday's garbage."

The garage door lifted, taking all of his hopes and dreams along with it.

He started to raise his hand, a reflexive gesture, but just as quickly, he dropped it back down to his side.

ᕯᕯᕯ

Carl had a slice of turkey breast in front of him. A rather large slice. Cranberries and mashed potatoes and gravy and green beans and corn were also piled on his plate. He couldn't eat with Mutt missing, but if he didn't shove something down his gullet, it was going to be a long night, and possibly an even longer morning. He stared down. The china plate and silverware clinked together with a sense of urgency, and his mind filled in the blank spaces. His hand shifted in a methodical manner, covering the short space and then doubling back, the circle on his plate widening.

Danielle stared at him, not harshly, but with concern in her eyes. He'd seen that look before, and he knew he would see it again. She had a gentle smile, but even her smile had trouble with this scenario. There was a potted plant in front of him, one he'd bought for her birthday, and somehow it managed to survive, even thrive, in the humid air. His effort, though, went continuously unnoticed, and he forgot to water it more often he remembered. If it had been up to him, it would have died a long time ago. It stared at him, hurt in its eyes, and the lingering sadness it left behind. The same way Mutt would have, if he'd been around. Leaving was an easy thing to do. Staying, though, was much harder.

He placed his elbows onto the wooden table and stared out the broken window. The blinds were pulled back as he peered across the street.

"You're thinking about Mutt, aren't you?"

The table was short, and so were his nerves. "He's probably lost out there. He could have been hit by a car. He won't survive in the cold, and they're calling for more snow."

She poked at a piece of turkey. "He'll turn up."

He dropped his fork. "How do you know that?"

"The same way I knew you would survive," Danielle said. "Instinct. He knows his way home, and when he's ready, he'll come. He's strong, stronger than you give him credit for."

Carl shoved his spoon, as corn and beans collided. "But he's never run away before."

"Maybe he just needs to spread his wings."

He'd had Mutt longer than he'd had Danielle. A confidante. Filled with eager eyes and an overzealous tongue, he was a real charmer. Mutt had the longest tongue Carl had ever seen. He had a mouth that always gravitated toward the nearest bone, and a tail that never ceased to wag. He even ran circles on the living room floor for no apparent reason, a continuous motion of joy.

"He's not a bird."

"But he could be," she said. "It's not always all about you, you know."

The silver spoon clattered against the china. "I know that."

"Do you?" she asked.

He scooted his chair away from the table, separating the distance and easing his mind. "I don't know how you can be so calm."

"You're practically bouncing off the walls," Danielle said. "Someone has to bring you back to reality. If you stare outside any harder, I'm liable to lose you forever."

If he wasn't careful, the table would eat him alive. Or maybe that was just his mind. The tension congregated in his right shoulder. "But you're not worried?"

"It won't make things easier."

He dipped his spoon in his mashed potatoes. He pushed past the point of resistance, and grabbed a bit of gravy on his way back up. He thought about his mess of a life, his mess of a dog, and his former employer. And then the doorbell rang. He looked at Danielle, she looked at him, and neither of them moved. It rang again.

"Maybe you should get it," Danielle said.

Carl heaved a heavy sigh. "Why?"

"It might take a bit of the edge off."

"You have some interesting instincts." But he didn't decline her offer.

"I can give you the long version sometime, if you're so inclined."

Carl dragged his chair back, rose to his feet—on shaky legs—and leaned on the table for support. His elbows locked, and his mind cleared.

"Who knows?" she said. "It might even be Mutt." If she had said it with a bit more feeling, he might have even believed her.

He bowed his head. "Yeah, maybe he learned how to ring the bell."

He yanked open the door—not even bothering to look through the peephole—stared out into the night without really focusing, lost in a sea of black and gray and shadows, before his eyes adjusted to what was right in front of him. "What are you doing here?"

☙❧☙

"Can I buy you a drink?"

Lynette held up her glass automatically, the ice and liquid rattling around in her grasp. It was her second. No…it was her third. And she was fairly certain it wouldn't be her last. A faraway look filled her eyes, and blank spaces filled her mind.

"You're not much of a talker, are you?" a male voice said.

Her head whipped around. The soft, velvet voice matched the man, the eyes smoldering, boring into the back of her head like two individual fires. Her breath caught in her chest, and she swallowed. The liquor bit her on the way down, and her mind bit her on the way back up.

"Are you trouble?" she asked.

"I could be. Why?" His gaze wandered, and then his eyes bored right back into hers. "Are you looking to discover a bit of it?"

She shook her head. "Not particularly. But you never know what tomorrow will bring." At least her coffeepot could help with the hangover, and her mind could remember a few of the sordid details.

"By the way, I'm Tim."

"Lynette."

"So do you come here often?"

Not the best of lines, but she was willing to play along. Maybe it was the end of her third drink talking. "About once a month. It's sort of my contribution to the universe and the local community. And it keeps me out of trouble." The grime, however, ensured regular visits to the local laundromat where the same row of washers always offered the same result: out of order.

He swooped down on the stool next to hers. "Going to a bar keeps you out of trouble?"

"Sometimes it does, sometimes it doesn't. I never really know which way the wind will blow." She held up her index finger. "Right now it appears to be blowing a bit to the east."

His drink was nearly gone, and he'd signaled the bartender for another. No wedding band on the appropriate finger, and no tan line either. Not that she was looking. But his eyes did speak to her in a way that not many men did. She'd noticed his eyes first, as he had hovered above her, but now her view was slightly obscured. His lashes were long, and so was his hair. The strands dipped into his eyes, and he let them linger for longer than she would have thought possible.

Flirting was still a foreign concept to her, but that didn't mean she couldn't try. She drummed her fingers on the bar, stretching them out in between the drumming. She ran her finger around the rim of the glass, as the drink in her hand hovered inches away from her lips, before she set it back down on the bar with a smack. The refill was a good idea before, but now she wasn't so sure. Her hand was steady, her mind less so. Her thoughts scattered like pixie dust at her feet, and her chair squeaked at the slightest hint of movement.

The floor seemed a long way below from where she was prepared to go. The solid stool had developed a crack in the leather.

"Are you always this sure of yourself?" Lynette asked.

He had a wicked grin. "Not always."

"But sometimes?"

"Sometimes," Tim replied.

The bartender replaced her empty glass with another one before she could even argue. Tim scooted his chair just a hair closer to her own, and the whole room spun in the opposite direction. A cloud of guilt weighed heavy on her conscience, and her thoughts shattered on the floor like the dust and the dreams she had left behind. The colleagues she abandoned became a distant memory, and her world remained poised for new possibilities.

Lynette pushed past the instability. "So what do you do for a living?"

"I'm in the insurance business."

She groaned. "That can't be fun."

His head bobbed up and down. "Most of the time it isn't. But you never know when you might meet an interesting party standing on the other side of the door."

"You do a lot of cold calling, don't you?"

"It's not all it's cracked up to be," he said. "The first several dozen hang-ups are always the worst. But it gets easier after that—"

"How so?"

"You learn that hearing no is just a part of the job." Tim swallowed half of his glass, and the ice cubes clinked in response. "It's nothing personal."

She bit her bottom lip. "So you build up a large number of antibodies?"

Chapter 18

The evil man dumped Ahmad in a holding cell overnight. The cops were neither apologetic nor helpful. He had a clean bed—sort of—a metal sink, and a metal toilet without a seat or a lid. It wasn't exactly paradise, but it was probably as close to Mecca as any other cell. He didn't have a roommate, which was a plus. The bars in front of him were made of rusted metal, and the cement floor didn't exactly do his ankles any favors. He'd paced for a while, and he'd taken a break on the bottom bunk. The top one looked even worse than the bottom, the mattress frayed and worn in all the wrong places, so even though he wasn't big on confined spaces, he made an exception. There was a hole in the floor, probably a drain, and there was a sprinkler overhead, the metal rusted like all the rest.

He had dropped to the floor and done a series of push-ups. He'd stopped when one of the guards began to take notice. He recited a few poems—the ones he could remember—and he'd managed a series of prayers, each one played off of the one before it. His mind had drifted this way and that, his eyes stared out into the vast expanse in front of him, and his voice turned hoarse from all the talking. A series of desks, only one of which was currently occupied, lined his vision, and a series of chairs, none of which were of the ergonomic variety, sat behind said desks. His right eye twitched—it happened when he was nervous or scared—and the voice inside of his head, a demon, was ready to explode onto the world, and curse a series of four-letter words. He held the demon back with self-control and mind games.

He climbed on the bed, staring up at the metal webbing above him, poking, and prodding for a sign of weakness. Again, it was more rusted than not, but the webbing held. His lips formed a sneer, and his eyes drooped from the additional stress. The evil man led Ahmad away from the questioning when he had given them nothing. This all stirred from his neighbor, the man with the quick temper and too-loud voice. He was sure of that much. He couldn't remember the man's name, but he remembered his blond hair and sour expression.

His neighbor believed he'd poisoned his dog, despite the dog's incessant yapping and howling, of which Ahmad had complained to the man on multiple occasions. Brad—he did remember—had made a few choice comments, none of which were worth repeating, and then the dog had dropped dead under suspicious circumstances after a long night spent in a flower bed. An autopsy was inconclusive, but the neighbor, Brad, directed his blame over the fence, with his hand—middle finger extended—pointed severely in Ahmad's direction. The man had a large chin and a large attitude, and he didn't know how to smile. His voice was an octave higher than it should have been, and his mouth was a bit wider than his face warranted. His ears were also a bit large and his lobes drooped noticeably from the rest of his face.

Brad wore button-downs, the occasional pair of camouflage pants, and red bandanas that were years past their prime. The man had shaggy blond hair that bounced when he walked. He sniffed a lot, and drank too much, and blamed the rest of the world for his problems, of which there were many. His disposition pointed in about every direction, aside from neighborly, and the drinking and tobacco stained his teeth yellow. He had hair coming out of his ears and an overbite that had never been fixed by an orthodontist. And he leaned forward when he talked or swallowed, with his Adam's apple protruding, and his neck bent at an awkward angle.

Brad had called the cops on him on more than one occasion for various offenses, none of which had involved him visiting a precinct. But the man bid his time, waiting for the right ship to set sail, and the winds to blow in the appropriate direction. Brad had jumped on this whole terrorist scenario, Ahmad was sure of it, and Brad wanted to ride it for all it was worth. Even Brad's smile was false, the one he'd seen on only three occasions that he could recall, despite living next to the man for more than three years—three long and painful years centered around yelling and cop cars and misguided loyalty. The man had gutters that he cleaned in the middle of the summer, blowing the leaves around at five or six in the morning, in cargo shorts and his red bandana, bent over at the waist, and wielding a long hose. He also had a thing for deer. Not a good one. He had some sort of whistle he used, whenever the mood struck him, and he spread his arms wide, and always managed to yell with extra authority, also at random times of the day or night to shoo them off his property. Brad rocked in his chair, when he was in one of his more subdued moments, probably after taking a Valium, or some other prescription his wife managed to shove down his gullet, or crush up in one of his many alcoholic beverages. The marriage was one for the ages, or so he'd heard, with the wedding ceremony conducted on either Nantucket or Martha's Vineyard, in the middle of August, in one of the greatest heat waves of Massachusetts with the humidity hovering near the triple digits. It was probably a sign. She had been beautiful once, before he had aged her two years for every year of marriage.

But the damn dog was dead. And Brad still blamed him for his loss. It didn't matter that Brad let the dog run loose in the neighborhood, and more than once, he'd eaten trash, inedible leaves, worms, or whatever else the dog could dig up. It didn't matter that the dog constantly had dirt on his paws, and that he howled through half the night and into the morning, only going to sleep as the sun was about to break through the horizon and the roosters started calling. And it didn't matter how deeply Ahmad shoved the earplugs into his ears, he still heard every sound out of the dog's mouth, even with his doors and windows shut. The dog yipping and yapping like he'd been shot in the ass with a pellet gun, which if Ahmad had anything to say about it, would have occurred, and probably more than once.

"Wakey, wakey, sunshine," a male voice said.

Ahmad rolled over on the bed, his eyes pointed toward the metal mesh just above his head, the mesh that was a whole lot closer than it was the night before.

He hadn't gotten much sleep, thinking about his ridiculous neighbor Brad and his ridiculous mutt, the howling kept him tossing and turning, and the bed had a mattress that was as hard as a mahogany desktop. The hard, flat pillow wasn't much better, as it jammed against his left ear and the back of his head when he stared at the bed above him. His eyes rolled around his head like grapefruits bouncing down a flight of stairs. His bottom lip trembled, and he looked out, staring through the bars at the monster with the misshaped melon and squinty eyes. No, it was another monster, but similar. Short of hooking up electrodes to his testicles, Ahmad couldn't think of a worse situation to be in, as he was exposed and put on display for the litany of officers that marched through the halls.

If he were a weaker man, he might have already abandoned all hope and cowered in the corner with his head down, before he pointed himself in the direction of Mecca and spoke underneath his breath until the clouds parted and the sky turned blue.

"Your bail has been posted," the officer said.

Ahmad had no idea who would have gone to the trouble to bail him out. Even his wife, his lovely, beautiful wife, would have left him in jail, and even though it was her idea to shoot the dog in the ass, she wasn't the forgiving type. Not when it came to his temper, and the demon that popped forth whenever he least expected it. She would have left him in jail for a few days, before he was able to return home and beg her forgiveness. The sighs, along with the hidden meaning, and the underlying currents, would have set him off on yet another tirade.

Ahmad lifted his eyes and stared at the officer's blue uniform. "Who?"

"Anonymous donor."

"This isn't a blood drive," Ahmad said.

Not that it mattered. He was a free man who was about to put the rust of life behind him and move past the metal barriers that barred his existence.

The officer smirked. "Someone likes you."

Ahmad wasn't likeable. Instead, he experienced regret. Regret for the mistakes he had made, regret for coming to this country, regret for having an idiot roommate who couldn't be bothered to keep his political views to himself, and who Ahmad had considered on more than one occasion duct-taping and shoving in the closet. Fifteen years was thirteen years longer than he ever expected to spend here, but he had a solid home, a solid union, and a steady job that paid for his Range Rover.

Mind-numbing monotony had threatened to rule his world, and passion attempted to fill in a few blanks. A good cause offered up a distinct number of possibilities, and he had a voice here in this godforsaken country that he lacked back home. Boston limited the open spaces, similar to the small, confined space that he was about to be set free of, and where road rage and a lack of turn signals ran rampant. The metal bars clicked open, the bar squeaking and dragging on its track, and the bell of freedom began to ring.

The smell was the worst. Somebody had thrown up in his cell, and there were still remnants of the waste, along with bleach to cover it up—not the best of jobs—and the pungent odor of mold from between the cracks. The bleach made him nearly gag. It wasn't diluted, and that had probably led to his vivid dreams and nightmares of misbegotten neighbors with overenthusiastic tendencies. His grimy teeth were stained from the water. He had a habit of not brushing his teeth twice a day, sometimes not even once. The cold tap water assaulted his teeth and gums, and turned his mouth numb.

Ahmad stepped through the opening with his right foot leading the way. The air around him suddenly clearer, the voice inside his head suddenly muted. He took deep breaths, the gasps piercing his lungs as well as his body, the sounds of silence filling in a few more details. The stench of rot and decay nearly caused his head to jerk back. Coupled with the body spray and loud deodorant the officer painted all over his body, Ahmad was surprised he was able to maintain an upright stance. His lips, however, moved encouragingly, as he mumbled an inaudible prayer.

"What was that?" the officer asked.

"It took you long enough," Ahmad said. "My bail was posted last night, wasn't it?"

The officer's face hardened. The body spray poured off him in waves. "How did you know?"

The metal door clanked shut behind him. Ahmad didn't turn. Instead, he took another step forward and then another.

"Your expression says it all. You didn't want to let me go, but you were forced to, probably somebody higher up. Am I right?"

"What if you're wrong?" the officer asked.

Ahmad stared straight ahead. "I am never wrong."

"That's what you'd like to think, choir boy."

Ahmad marched beside the officer matching him step for step. His body was stiff, and his knees were bent.

The officer's pocket protruded at an unusual angle.

"Is that a phone in your pocket," Ahmad asked, "or are you just happy to see me?"

"You know," the officer said, "it's smart comments like those that caused you to end up here in the first place."

"Wrong," Ahmad said.

This was about his neighbor: the jerk with the too loud dog and too-loud voice. Their first altercation hadn't even been about the dog. It was about the gutters being blown to smithereens at six in the morning on a Saturday in October. The man had on headphones, and he sang as he blew the leaves out of his gutters and into Ahmad's yard, and Ahmad had only seen red, not just about the gutters, or the leaves being sprayed around, or the singing: It had been a combination of all three. He had tried to let it go, but the singing kept getting louder, the spraying kept getting wider, and the blowing increased in intensity, until finally he jerked out of bed on a Saturday, after nearly twenty minutes of miscues, and stomped across his yard, climbed up the ladder—still clad in his pajamas—his face bright red, and screamed for Brad to stop, the ladder shaking and jerking along with him. Ahmad had screamed loud enough that Brad could hear him through the headphones and the blowing and the singing and the incessant barking.

Ahmad had nearly shoved Brad off the ladder. Brad had nearly tumbled to the ground, and probably would have broken a rib, or maybe an arm or leg in the process, and even then Ahmad might have decided it was worth it, just to see the look on Brad's face, when he had exited his reverie and ended up back in reality.

Paying a fine would have been well worth his time.

ᕙᕗ

Ahmad had his second Jose Cuervo in front of him. The gold variety. The first went down easy enough, and he hoped the second one would go down even easier. Music thumped in the background, a song about loneliness and regret, mixed with loud guitars, an even louder singer, and drums that beat like a sledgehammer against a concrete barrier. The music mixed with the alcohol offered him a splitting headache for his trouble, but he wanted to forget his plights.

He slammed the second one back as quickly as the first, and he signaled the bartender for a third. He planned to keep drinking until he lost track of the number of shots, lost faith in reality, and experienced a state of semi-conscious saturation, where the voices he heard in his head no longer talked to him in an expeditious manner, and he no longer heard the leaves blowing and the officers and dogs barking. His left leg bounced up and down, and once in a while his right foot hopped of its own accord. The bar smelled like burnt popcorn, stale pussy, and sweat that had clung to clothes for multiple days. The stool had a large tear in the middle, and it was slightly off-balance. He was slightly off-balance, but he didn't mind this particular turn of events. Ahmad only focused on the drink in front of him, and the one that would come after he finished this one. He had plopped a hundred on the bar—what was left of his walking around money, after he'd downed a plate of Indian food—and told the bartender to keep them coming until he ran out of funds. The hundred would buy him a few more drinks and a few more chances to forget.

He had another hundred in an emergency fund stuffed inside his sock, but he wasn't allowed to touch that money. Not yet. It burned a hole in his sock, but that was where it would remain. All he cared about was that each successive tequila shot tasted better than the one before it, and that the shot glass was relatively clean and the tequila was relatively strong. He recycled the same one. When he was ready for another, he tapped the bar with his fist and waited for the lanky bartender with the crew cut. The bar had fluorescent lights jammed into the ceiling, and the stained wood reflected the light, causing his eyes to blur. His pupils were already dilated.

He wiped his hand across the front of the glass, and his palm came back with a smudge on it. A blemish on his otherwise perfect skin. His lips moved rapidly as he downed the next drink and tapped the bar once more. He had downed three shots in twenty minutes. The tube in the background filled a gap or two between the drinks, his thoughts, and the passing of time. A football game, on the one TV set in the joint, professional, but he wasn't watching the game with any sort of regularity. The other patrons captured more of his attention, and one girl in particular caught his eye, winking at him in such a way that the shot glass nearly slipped from his right hand and deposited itself on the chipped hardwood below.

"Are you looking for a good time, sugar?" the dark-haired woman asked. Her hair flowed down her back, and her eyes were almost black. Her outfit was tight against her body, and two large mounds protruded from her top.

Ahmad hadn't even seen her approach. She moved like a cat. He hadn't even had the opportunity to set the drink back on the bar before she plopped herself down on the stool next to him, her skirt riding high on her right thigh. Her skirt was red and tiny, and her hair was long and dark and supple, like the nipples that were poking through her thin top. She had short nails, the kind that were clipped on a regular basis, and she had wide, full lips, the kind of lips every woman envied, that few women managed without a little extra help. But it was her eyes that were her best feature, the kind of eyes that twinkled in the moonlight, and probably the daylight, too. The tips of her fingers clipped the edge of the bar, before she shifted on the stool, moving a hint closer, close enough that Ahmad could feel the heat coming off of her legs, the curve of her ankles, the three-inch heels that clicked against the wooden bar whenever she adjusted her position, and the gaze that made him feel taller. She had a drink in front of her, but she hadn't touched it. In fact, she hadn't made a move toward it, only toward him, with pupils as wide as a sunset. The dark eyes zeroed in on him like twin laser beams, and he swallowed what was left of his pride.

He adjusted in his seat, nearly falling off the stool, with the drinks iced through his veins like the tap water he had left behind. The crease in the seat snagged on his butt, and he jerked, catching himself on the edge of the bar, the stool going down before he did, and dropping to the floor.

He caught the glass with one hand and the bar with the other. The stool, however, wasn't as lucky.

She lifted her eyes. "Quick reflexes."

Ahmad lifted the stool, and plopped the glass back on the bar. "Almost catlike."

She flicked her lashes in his direction and shook her head. "If you were catlike, you wouldn't have fallen in the first place."

"Even cats strike the ground once in a while."

"Maybe you're less catlike than you think," she said.

The air around him turned heavy, as the drinks rumbled through his veins and his head spun in a counterclockwise direction. Her knee brushed his thigh, and he felt the warmth through his long pants. His bottom lip had somehow turned dry, and he licked it.

"So," she asked, "do you have any money, sugar? I don't work for free."

Chapter 19

The mayor wore a crisp suit, her back straight, not a hair out of place, her heels adding three inches to her already lavish frame. Her smile usually appeared at a moment's notice, but there was no reason for her to smile now. Not even a little. She had her hands behind her head, and a big spread of fruits and vegetables on her desk, and more than a handful of papers.

Her office was more masculine than feminine—to keep up with the men—filled with cedar, cherry, and mahogany. Not to be outdone by her male contemporaries, she included a wall filled with awards, plaques, and plenty of photo ops. She could name-drop relationships with two senators and four representatives, not that it had done her campaign one damn bit of good. If anything, it almost cost her the mayoral office. Had she been a man and slept with women in power, she'd climb the social ladder faster than the next supermodel. She even looked the part.

"Tell me some good news, Bob."

Clipboard in one hand, pen in the other, Bob dropped in one of three seats on the other side of her desk. "There is no good news to report, Mayor."

She dropped her hands from behind her head. "It can't be that bad."

"You've been lagging in the polls ever since that first debate." He glanced down at his clipboard. "The debate where you referred to the other candidate as a cocksuck-er."

Mayor James sighed. "It was a heated exchange."

"Not for him," he said. "Your opposition moved ahead of you by leaps and bounds in the polls. If you hadn't salvaged the comment by circling back on target, our focus for the entire campaign, you'd be lagging in the polls by more than five points."

She stood up and turned toward the window. "I can make up five points."

Bob followed her to his feet. "That was what you won the first election by, Ms. Mayor."

Joey turned around, her gaze pensive. "Don't remind me, Bob. I'd rather savor the moment." It was a huge win, and now it might explode in a cloud of smoke.

She sat back down, and so did he. She crossed her legs, and noticed he followed suit automatically. In sync. She hadn't noticed it before, but now that she had, she couldn't erase it from her mind.

"There's nothing to savor, Ms. Mayor."

Joey grabbed a celery stick from the platter and chewed, her eyes flittering around the room, honing in on the picture of John-John and herself. Neither her best hair nor clothes day, it was still her favorite photo, and she placed it prominently on her wall. "Not right now, there isn't. But soon there will be. You just have to trust me on this."

After she finished the first, she grabbed another stick and followed it up with a stalk of broccoli. Bob, on the other hand, kept his hands away from the platter.

Bob glanced down at his clipboard. "That's all I've done so far."

"Maybe it's not enough, Bob. Maybe you need to be-lieve. Maybe I need to hear you believe." She paused with her right fist poised at attention and her voice at another level. "Maybe the campaign needs to hear it."

"You might be salvaged by this act of terrorism, Ms. Mayor." Her campaign. In the end, that was all that truly mattered. If her campaign faltered, then so did she.

"Say it louder, Bob," Joey said. "Say it louder, so he can hear you." The mayor pointed to the picture on the far wall, the one she had put directly in her line of sight and at just the right angle. John-John winked at her. Not often, but sometimes. Sometimes he even smiled. He hadn't smiled in days, possibly over a week. She, along with everyone else, had to believe. Despite the obstacles against her, she would beat her opponent. She had to. She'd done it before, but this was when a state senator's job—Second Worcester District to be exact—hung in the balance, not the Mayor of Boston. Not the big leagues where she needed to achieve and press the flesh and smile on cue and speak with eloquence and lean forward even when she wanted to lean back.

It had been a friendly debate, or so Joey thought, and then the mudslinging began, and she grabbed the biggest pile and tossed it around like an M-80 on the Fourth of July. As she discovered, this often led to trouble. It had then, and it would now. What felt good at the time always came back to haunt her later. Standing on her moral high ground, she had gotten squashed by the nearest helicopter. Joey had big plans, and she had to play with the big boys. That's what her dad had always taught her: Never back down, never take no for an answer, never let grown men see you cry, and never go down with your bat on your shoulder.

What catapulted her present predicament to another mountain entirely was her affair, brief and consensual, with a US senator—or as she liked to refer to him Number Two. She had believed in the power of the senator, his backing with more than a few good words pointed in her direction, and he had offered her as much, before she went down on him behind his cherry pine desk. He was ready to go with his zipper down and his limp dick fumbling out. No pomp and circumstance. No stained blue dress, no mess, no muss, no fuss. But somehow word had gotten out anyway, probably leaked by the senator himself—the bastard—since he was behind in the latest election poll. She still had the ring of a former beauty queen, and he needed the misogynist male vote. For her trouble and his subsequent deposit—she even swallowed—she had received a black mark on her shoulder, despite the senator divorcing his wife less than three months later. Instead of going for her with her big dreams and even bigger assets, the senator married a well-endowed young aide with dollar signs in her eyes, and the keys to Washington at her feet, for as long as she was willing to get down on her knees. The little temptress smiled lovingly, played the part to perfection, and from what Joey heard, the young aide had started an affair of her own only hours after the ink on the marriage certificate had dried.

The political whims of man-children damn near pissed her off.

Mayor James had wanted a clean campaign, but now she just wanted to win. She wanted to prove to the world that she wasn't just a one-term wonder, and that she could win on the issues, instead of her good looks, and that some pretty boy from Brookline would have to face his own demons.

Her opponent was gay, and she had called him a cocksucker on local TV. Word had spread quickly, probably leaked from his campaign, that she was against the gay community, which wasn't true at all. She loved the gays, supported them with fundraisers and parades. She was as progressive and aggressive as the next gal, and if she had a lesbian sister, she would have fully supported her and possibly even marched in a pride parade with her rainbow flag pointed toward P-Town. It was just her cocksucker opponent that she hated. She still had a score to settle with the fitness freak.

The man ran triathlons for crying out loud. It was all about the competition for him, whereas all she wanted to do was win and finish another term in office, before she sought her sights on bigger and better things. If she were Bill Clinton, the whole blowjob incident would have taken on a whole new meaning, and she could have salvaged the race easily with a documented apology and a sheepish grin. Hell, it might have even resulted in a landslide in her favor.

Instead, she had to rely on the fucking terrorists to help her out with their demented ideals plastered on national television. She could feel herself inching up in the polls. It was all about the crisis and how it was handled and the power behind her next move. That would determine her fate. She was sure of it. If she could manage to pull this off, she had another four years to push her agenda and rise in the political pecking order. If not, she could kiss her opponent's ass on her way out the door.

෨෨෩

The governor had no idea how he was behind in the polls. Three points, and it wasn't looking good. If his wife had managed not to fuck whatever crept across her path and looked at her with more than a hint of longing, then it might not have come to this. If not for that, he'd probably hoist a champagne glass from the top of the polls right now. His first debate had gone well enough. He'd run his opponent across the surfboard, without the slightest hint of wax, while he'd plunged the man's head underwater, and had him spitting bubbles through his nose. And then the incident with his wife had come out. Well, a series of incidents. The whore. She'd had affairs, multiple, over what he assumed was the past two years— he was fuzzy on the details, and he preferred to keep it that way.

He didn't want to know if it was longer. The press dug deep, and the governor placed his hands over his face to cover up the right hooks and jabs. He had enough money to buy up every copy of every newspaper in Boston and several of the surrounding cities and counties, but that wouldn't put a stop to it. In fact, his opponent would probably dedicate a whole series of commercials to free speech and reporter rights. He'd smile like the Cheshire Cat. With the grin unstoppable and possibly even unbear- able, he'd parade around with his head held high and talk about the supposed issues. His opponent was for the working man, and somehow the idiot was three points ahead of him in the polls. The shitbird didn't even know how to spell politics, even if he was spotted the vowels.

The governor couldn't find a single dirty detail on his opponent, and he had his people looking, combing through former employers, colleagues, colleges, and high schools, all the way back to middle school. And he'd managed to come up with zilch so far. His opponent was either a saint, or he knew where to bury the bodies. The man was an Eagle Scout, captain of the debate team, or some shit like that, and he had a set of white teeth that would blind a tiger at a thousand yards. Hell, the man didn't even hunt, or own a rifle, or ever have a gun regis- tered.

As far as his detectives could tell—and he had more than one detective on the case—the man had never owned a gun of any kind. Not even a pistol. In Vermont, he would have been frowned upon for his lack of ability to embrace the great outdoors, but in the Commonwealth of Massachusetts, his opponent was considered a golden boy. If the governor couldn't figure out a way to embrace terrorism, and ride that gravy train all throughout the re-election campaign, and then put an end to it in all forms and measures, his campaign was headed for the toilet. And if his wife couldn't keep her panties on, he had a lot more to worry about than just a failed re-election. Hell, she hadn't even signed a prenup. In other words, he was fucked.

॰৩৩॰৩

His hands strained against the bar, his arms, wrists, and biceps shaking, sometimes even in unison. Music pumped through the speakers. Muscle-bound freaks sur-rounded him, and women in spandex, halter tops, and not much else hit the ellipticals and treadmills like it was an all-you-can-eat buffet.

Matthew lifted the bar twice more—every muscle in his body straining, even the ones in his chest, shoulders, and back—toward the heavens, before he placed it on the rack and stretched his arms. Bouncing up just a little bit slower than when he had sat down, he took a look around and nodded his approval. His shorts were covered in sweat, and his T-shirt clung to his body like yesterday's discarded clothes. His breathing came in ragged bursts, like the steady bullets from a machine gun, his lips posi-tioned in a straight line without any creases or wrinkles. He had come up two short from the last time. Not good.

The idiots beside him had smiles on their faces. The one to his right had lifted the bar three times more than he had, and the one on his left had lifted it twice more. He took a long, hard look at himself in the mirror. His eyes flitted to the not-so-defined muscles on his biceps, the ones he had worked hard at popping out, but still remained hidden beneath the skin. They held back the way he did without even the slightest hint of promise and fulfillment. He hadn't given it everything he had, and it had cost him.

Matthew cursed under his breath, and blocked out the music—some rap song by some rap singer that probably wouldn't be around this time next year—with a hard beat and syncopated lyrics. A white guy. The bloody name escaped him. His hand rested on the free weights before he lifted a middle-sized one with one hand.

John flexed his right arm. "You going weak on us?"

Matthew stopped his humming. "Not by a long shot." He dropped the weight back in place and lifted his chin in the direction of the competition.

John eased the bar onto the metal rack. "Then what happened?"

"My head wasn't in the game," Matthew said. It was true: His mind had drifted elsewhere, and when his heart wasn't in it, his body followed.

"You'd better get back in."

"Or what?"

"You're not going to like the results," Mark said.

Matthew hadn't. He beat himself up more than the other two could have done. This was all about him, and what he lacked. The nightmares had attacked him with the same precision and force that an all-out assault would have. Visions where America was overrun by China and Russia, and he was stuck behind a fence with barbed wire, a close shave, and baggy pants.

He stared hard in the mirror, checking out the merchandise on aisle three, the one directly in the middle with the black leotard and the turquoise shirt and the powerful legs, who attacked the elliptical like some sex-crazed hyena, and whose exposed skin glowed in the fluorescent lights. One who had probably had more than a few misadventures in her day, and whom he could only hope might have a few more in store.

ოოო

The lobby was packed front to back, filled with press and spectators, and even a few friends. Her suit was filled with sharp lines and defined edges, hair perfect, skin clear, and mind shifted into overdrive. Her prepared statement had gone off without a hitch, not even the slightest hiccup, and now it was time for the Q & A portion, where the surprises were sprung on her with shocking regularity. An assistant fielded questions, and she stood ready with the answers.

"How do you feel about the re-election campaign?" a man in blue asked.

Mayor James grinned, showing off her thousand-watt smile. "I like my odds."

"You're still behind in the latest polls."

"That's true," Joey said. "But I have a feeling we're going to make up those figures." Her optimism was contagious, both with the press and members of her staff. If she could believe it, she could achieve it. She didn't strut around in a bikini for the health benefits.

"Why?" another man asked.

"I'm not going to let the terrorists win. This is about winning one for the good people of Boston, the working-class citizens who deserve a break." After her campaign, she'd need one as well. Maybe she could find herself a boy toy who kept his mouth shut and his dick hard.

"So you're fighting back?"

"Absolutely," the mayor said. "I have my best men on it, and I'm in contact with the police chief on a daily basis. This is about more than just a few blown up buildings. This goes to the heart of the American psyche, and we're going to fight back. We have to fight back."

The echo of the words vibrated through her, and her whole body was on fire. The sea of faces stared at her expectantly with hands raised and cameras flashing. The podium lofted her up above the rest, and a small crowd hustled around the back of the throng.

"Are you concerned about how your reaction may look with the Muslim community?"

"Why should I be concerned about the Muslims?" the mayor asked. "This is about righting a wrong, and seeking justice where justice is due. If that means I have to piss a few people off in the process, then so be it." It was time to react and respond with precision.

The questions shifted, and she was prepared for the renewed focus.

"Do you think you can close the gap in the next poll?"

She flashed her pearly whites. "I have a feeling the whole campaign is about to turn around." *Those bastards are going down, even if I have to handcuff them and strut them in front of the courthouse myself.*

"Do you regret your previous actions?"

Her leg shifted behind the podium. A slight twitch. Not enough for anyone out in the audience to notice, but it startled her, and her pause was a second longer than she had planned. "I don't regret anything that's happened. All of it happened for a reason, and without it, I wouldn't be where I am right now."

The murmuring and shifting in the audience increased, and a few heads shifted their focus away from her. Her assistant gave her the signal to end the folly.

Before she could strut away from the podium, another question filled the blank space. "What about your use of the word 'cocksucker'?"

"It came at a particularly heated moment," the mayor said. "I can't change the past. I can only ask for forgiveness. And I hope a moment of insanity doesn't harbor too long in the minds of the voters. But if it does, all I can say is that I'm sorry."

Chapter 20

The briefing room was filled to the brim. Blue uniforms and suits stood one on top of another, stacked together like lettuce and tomato. The temperature in the room shifted away from comfortable. Brutal images of a city torn apart projected on the screen in front, a city beaten from the inside out with a mallet and sledgehammer. And from his particular position, it would only get worse.

The meeting hadn't gone as well as Ward had hoped. Instead of coming together and working toward a common purpose, the dividing lines were set, and the anchor was dropped. Instead of the slotted hour, it had gone closer to two, and now the lieutenant had to meet with Leo and Addison to work out a few of the finer points in the presence of the agents, the ones with matching haircuts and a similar sense of humor who wore complementary ties. In this case, a lack of humor probably suited them best. And if he didn't handle this correctly, he was about to face more than just a proverbial shit storm. He'd have a full-on collision with interdepartmental relations set back about fifteen years.

If he wasn't politically astute and managerially savvy, he'd find himself with his pants pulled down and his ass in the breeze hanging over a barbed wire fence. Not only was it cold outside, it felt even colder inside. With the heat busted, cold air pumped through the vents and he wondered about hypothermia. His lips were numb as were his cheeks.

"I realize we don't have all the answers you'd like," Ward said, "and I realize this situation has spiraled out of control rather quickly—"

"That's an understatement," Leo said.

"But it's nothing we aren't prepared to handle on this end. We have your best interests at heart." Or at least he hoped he did. Ward couldn't say the same for the two men hovering near the door with stoic expressions and horizontal eyebrows.

"Where have I heard that before?" Addison asked.

Ward soldiered on. "The FBI is involved."

"We're taking over the case," Gordon Everly said. He was a small man with a much larger presence and dark eyeglasses. He had lines on his face and a streak of gray in his hair. The watch on his wrist was gold.

Ward shifted position behind his desk. "That's still being negotiated."

Gordon took a step forward, coming out of the shadows and into the limelight. "There's nothing left to negotiate."

"This is about the greater good, the people of Boston," the lieutenant said. "Those who deserve some answers." He paused. "I'm not sure you have their interests at heart." Stuffing his hand in his desk drawer, Ward pulled out the bottle of Windex, along with a paper towel. He held both aloft, and then he proceeded with the rubbing and buffing.

Gordon smirked. "Do we need to have another meeting?"

"I'm through with meetings," the lieutenant said. And he was. Arguing with the little shit would get him a one-way ticket to somewhere like Columbus or Santa Fe where his dreams died on the open plain, and his suits turned to ash. "The meetings have gotten us nowhere."

Gordon's eyes brightened. "Oh, we're somewhere, all right."

The lieutenant sprayed, swiped, and wiped. "What game are you playing now?"

Gordon shrugged. "No game."

The tension in the enclosed space ratcheted up about three notches. No man moved and no mouths were opened. If not for the hiss from the bottle, the room was otherwise silent. After more than a minute, and a nearly clean desk, the lieutenant played his trump card. "The mayor is interested."

Gordon shook his head. "Do you think we give a shit about the mayor?"

"This is about more than just some federal review board. There are lives at stake. Many lives—"

"What the hell are you talking about?" Addison asked.

The lieutenant glared at his subordinate, a man one year away from retirement who was on the verge of being retired a hell of a lot quicker.

On the other hand, that was exactly what Addison wanted. It was simple. The man just didn't give a shit. If Ward were in his position, truth be told, he probably wouldn't give a shit either.

"There was a recorder left behind in one of our officer's cruisers," the lieutenant said. "He didn't come to us right away, but when he did, it was rather troubling. The Boston Common is mentioned, for the night The Sex Maggots offer the Common one free night of debauchery. Or at least that's what the ad claims. And if we don't figure out what's going on before then, this could blow up in all of our faces. If you want to deal with the aftermath—"

"Why didn't you tell us this sooner?" Leo asked. "Why are we learning about this now?"

The lieutenant tossed the paper towel in the trash. "You're learning this at the same time as the rest of our officers. If you want special treatment, then you might want to reevaluate your present position."

"But we're the head of this fucking investigation—"

"How long do we have?" Addison asked.

The lieutenant glanced down at his watch. He really hated this shit. His doctor told him he was about five cheeseburgers away from an ulcer or heart attack or both. "The concert takes place in less than forty-eight hours."

Leo tossed his hands up in the air. "This whole investigation is a clusterfuck."

"You can say that again," Addison replied.

The lieutenant shifted his eyes among the three men, each pair as stone cold as the ones before it. "Do you think this is easy for me?"

"I have no idea what's easy for you."

"You might have left a few answers on the table, but this is ridiculous. What's the mayor worried about?"

"Honestly," the lieutenant said, "she's focused on her re-election campaign. At the moment she's behind in the polls." Politics, though, always proved worse than these jaded conversations. When he needed to summon up some hate on short notice, he could always count on a political whino to help him with his cause. Those poor shits were the lightning rods of society, each one as cunning as the one before. If not for a few missteps and transgressions, he could have made captain by now. But he was stuck in purgatory with no end in sight.

"But she's all about the strong finish."

Agent Everly took another step forward. "We'll need that tape. We'll have our lab techs analyze it."

Ward handed over a copy.

"Is this the original?"

The lieutenant shook his head.

"You're going to give us the original, and you're going to like it."

Addison scratched his chin. "That quote reminds me of *Caddyshack*."

Agent Everly plowed ahead in a clipped, succinct fashion. "Now that you've had your turn, and your investigation has literally led us nowhere, here's the real story. Your terrorist isn't the man that was released yesterday, the man who has ties to the Muslim and Islamic nation. Your terrorist is a part of a known French conglomerate of international interest."

The lieutenant's mouth dropped open. *What the hell?* "You can't be serious." Sure, he hated the French—the pompous asses—as much as the next guy, but those feather-dusters couldn't even defend their own country.

"You've had your turn," Gordon said, "and now we get ours. That's the way this relationship goes. You might not like it—"

"Good, because I don't—" Addison interjected.

"The French?" Leo asked. "You can't be serious."

The robotic voice was back. "We received a tip from a reliable source."

"How reliable?" the lieutenant asked. In his experience, one out of every one hundred reliable tips proved worth his time. The rest were better off shoved underneath his mattress.

"Reliable enough for us to take it seriously." Gordon brushed the front of his shirt. "The French group goes by the initials PN. Otherwise known as Political Nationale. This is the first large-scale incident that they've been a part of, but there have been smaller incidents around the globe with French ties. The connections run deeper than the Niger River."

The fucking French? "Isn't the Niger River in western Africa?" the lieutenant asked.

Gordon offered up a dismissive gesture. "Here's what we know: the French bought the John Hancock Tower, when it was sold a few years ago. Several pieces of real estate within the Prudential Center were purchased by the French over the last several years, and the Boston Public Library banned the works of a French author within the last year. There might be additional connections, but those are the ones we've been able to ascertain thus far."

"Based on that, wouldn't it seem more likely that the French didn't commit this crime?"

Gordon dropped his gaze. "As you're already aware, gentlemen, Semtex was used at the first crime scene, and the blast origin has a French stamp on it. You've also let the first suspect go, and rightfully so. It's in your best interests to turn your focus in another direction. You might be wondering how we know so much."

Leo smirked. "Not really."

"Well, we have intelligence all over the world, and I'm willing to bet you've never considered the French. But make no mistake, the French are our enemies, and there's not much we can do to stop them." Gordon took a breath. "Now, we've identified some assets that are potential targets based on our intelligence, and I'll go over that information with you now."

Gordon handed out three packets, the papers perfectly aligned, each staple in perfect harmony with the top left-hand corner of the page.

The lieutenant decided right then and there he hated the smug little shit.

಼಼಼

Lynette fingered the ring on her right hand. The sun

struck her forehead, and her eyes opened wide. She shielded her eyes with her right hand, and ducked her head toward the ground. Her feet shuffled against the hard pavement, and a feeling of claustrophobia shook her to the core.

The traffic light in front of her blinked from red to green, and she stepped back from the oncoming traffic. She glanced to her left and stared at an unfamiliar face with the faintest hint of familiarity. The whisper of the wind turned her world to ash, and the vast sea of white switched off right in front of her. The uneven pavement turned her left leg a half inch, and her hip bent with the turn of her leg. A dog barked and a horn honked and a small child squealed with glee. The light reflected off the cracks in the landscape, and what remained of her world turned to gray.

A ghost from her past lifted up to meet her, and the wind pushed her just a hair to the right. She tapped a man with the back of her hand, and he apologized before she could offer up one of her own. The faintest hint of a shy smile appeared on her face, and when her chin dipped, so did her left hand. He wrapped his coat tighter around his thin frame and tipped his hat as he stepped away in the opposite direction.

A tourist stopped and asked her to read a map, and she pointed out the end of the Freedom Trail along with the red brick path that offered its own trail of breadcrumbs. The buildings towered above her as she felt small below, and the tunnel of wind whistled through the enclosed space. Lynette's sense of purpose died in the breeze.

Her thoughts drifted and shifted to the man with the feminine hands and the soft ruby red lips. His hips proved nonexistent, and his voice proved deeper than she had first expected, and the hat on his head was pulled low, and when she bumped her forehead against his own, he hadn't offered an apology. He grabbed her around the waist with both hands, and she felt small and insecure beneath his harsh stare and large pupils. She shifted on the balls of her feet, and he slammed the stall door with his left hand, not his right. The lock clicked into place, and she felt a sense of finality in the small space.

Even now the image of confidence remained, and his twisted grin proved even more pronounced in the end. The bang on the door vibrated to her core, and thrilled her to absolutely no end. Lynette smiled now, even though the tryst had occurred the previous night, and despite his inability to pick up the phone, she still filled herself with hope. Had he offered his number, she would have been bold enough to call. The pretty boy look was not lost on him, even though she felt off balance for the rest of the evening and into the break of the morning sun.

He had walked her to her car and stuffed his tongue down her throat as a departing gift, and she had enjoyed every minute of it. The confidence was real, and so was he, and he made her feel alive when she felt dead inside.

The smack of her hand against her hip brought her back to the present, and the bump against her shoulder caused her mouth to open, but the words died against the back of her throat. Her body jerked in a reflexive manner, but she continued on with her forward motion.

She zipped up the last part of her jacket as the breeze took hold. Her car stood right where she had left it. She pressed the key fob, and her car blinked to life right before her eyes.

☙❧☙

She had struck him square on the jaw. The bitch. Carl's ex had a temper that could end all tempers. Her voice was soft, sweet even, but she packed a wallop in her small frame, most of which was toned muscles from those stupid exercise classes that she went to religiously, and a bit of muscle training. But that must have come later—after he divorced her for sleeping around on him—and she had the nerve to say it was his fault. She curried her favors elsewhere from strange men and one-night stands, and Carl was the idiot standing in the middle of a room and wondering what the hell had just happened.

She liked to exert her influence, even once she was out of the picture. She showed up every few months and socked him in the mouth, before she stalked back down the stairs, her arms swinging freely. Vengeance comforted her, and she resonated pure evil. Any decent bone in her body cracked and broke long ago, and her eyes filled with hatred. She had never been a runner, but she certainly had the passion for it. Maybe one too many of the spinning classes had gone to her head and possibly her fist as well. She whipped her head around, and cashed in on his faith and honesty and good nature.

The first punch always hurt worse than the second when her anger was on the verge of cracking her in half. She wasn't a large woman, his ex, but she had enough passion to strain the confines of a rocky relationship. Her voice was soft, but revenge echoed through her core, and bounced like a barbell on a concrete floor. The rage was explicit, and it ended up with him on the flat of his back wondering what the hell had just happened. His head might as well have been stapled to the living room carpet.

Carl hadn't gone to the cops, though. He just didn't have the dedication to put her behind bars. If he really wanted to fix her, he'd have to kill her and bury her body in the park. That's what she'd told him once, in that high-pitched laugh of hers mixing with the crazy and the hate. He had been stuck with her, until he decided to get the hell out of Lexington, and leave her behind with a glass of red wine. It was the best decision of his life, and he was rather surprised he hadn't made it sooner. He liked to refer to it as the beginning of his existence. The point at which his life found its one true course.

Now he had a relationship with a dog named Mutt and a woman named Danielle, and a series of beautiful moments flowed through his mind like a highlight reel on ESPN. Sure, he witnessed the *Twilight* teenager incident, but he could chalk it up to drugs and the lust of young love. Whatever it was, he rather preferred to place the whole incident in the closet, turn out the lights, and shut the door.

⋐⋑⋐⋑

She had left him. The bitch. The next day she'd come back for the rest of her stuff, with movers and a truck. Neither of which he was sure she could have gotten on short notice. It was planned. The whole fucking thing. Probably worked out months in advance the way she mapped out the majority of her life with lists and Excel spreadsheets.

And now Richard Lancaster III had a few mismatched items and the remnants of his wardrobe tossed in the closet where the emptiness alone resonated in waves. She'd even managed to trash the place a bit, taking what wasn't hers, and leaving behind the tattered remains. A penance. That was how his lovely wife thought. Like a demon of the night she had terrorized his life and then walked out the front door with her head held high. But before she reached the street, she turned back around and grabbed whatever wasn't bolted down. If she had a heart once, it turned the color of charcoal and dissolved in a glass of water. She probably used the concoction to water the plants.

His hands shook when he walked through the door and witnessed the carnage. She'd always taken whatever she wanted without a glance back, or even a slight turn of her head, and she had no qualms about it now either. She would do whatever it took to succeed, and he was the fruit fly that she had swatted with a flick of her wrist. He'd seen it coming, but she'd worked faster than he had expected, with more purpose and single-minded determination than she had shown in years, and certainly more passion than she'd ever tossed his way. He didn't even have time to change the locks. Or hire his own set of movers. Or stop to catch his breath. And then it was all over and his entire plan was shoved underneath the shag carpet.

The divorce papers hadn't come yet, but Loretta had probably worked out the most opportune time to deliver the swift kick to the nuts that he knew was coming, going over all the intricate details with an attorney, and right before she handed him a settlement that would make his balls shrivel up to the size of raisins, she would punch him in the gut with her engagement ring.

His hand shook at his side, harder and faster. She had destroyed his guitar, his amp, and all of his old records, the vinyl ones—most of which he special-ordered and most of which were limited-edition runs—and she had discarded the remnants over the floor where the Persian rug had been, if she hadn't carted it out through the front door in broad daylight into the back of a moving truck. He did have all of his clothes, and she hadn't placed her foot through the television like she'd threatened to at one point in their relationship. But that didn't stop the game playing, and the fighting that he knew would ensue even before he walked in the court room and she revealed she had slept with his brother—probably untrue—and had never loved him—probably true. If she were a dog, she would have been a mix of pit bull and terrier. The world was hers, and she would take her piece of the pie, the largest slice with a gigantic mound of whipped cream and chocolate sauce, right before she devoured what was left of his own sundae.

His house was a whisper of its former self. He dropped to the floor, pulled his knees up against his chest, stared at a blank spot on the wall where an oil painting once hung, and contemplated how in the hell his life had come to this.

cงeง

Back in his office, the lieutenant savored the peace and quiet. It reminded him of the calm before the grand-kids stopped by and raised more hell in five minutes than he ever had in five months. His desk glistened, and his eyes danced. The recorder was in his bottom desk drawer on the left-hand side tucked on top of a stack of papers an inch thick.

His computer emitted a ping as he pulled out the re-corder and turned it over in his hand. It was small and black and fit in his palm. No tape, no fingerprints, and a series of buttons on the front. The lieutenant had handed over the tape without a second glance. The agent, howev-er, had forgotten to ask the question, or maybe Gordon had remembered. He didn't even blink when the lie left his lips.

He popped the seal of the bag, grabbed a paper towel from his bottom drawer, extracted the recorder, and grabbed a pen from the metal bin on top of his desk. He pushed play, sat back, and waited. Static followed for three seconds, and then a single voice followed soon af-ter.

"Your continued disgrace of the Middle East will not stand. Imposing democracy and Christianity and free will and women's rights ends here and now. The first three buildings were just a test. But rest assured there will be more. Death and destruction is only the beginning. You will hear from us again soon."

Ward pressed the stop button with the end of his pen. The recording continued on for another two minutes and identified the Common as the next target. He had listened to the recording multiple times and hoped a few irregularities stood out to him, but all he had identified thus far was an American attempting to sound un-American. Possibly from Boston, but he knew one thing for sure: It wasn't the fucking French.

Chapter 21

It was his idea to obtain the Octanitrocubane. Matthew was the one who had suggested it, since he knew the military could take crazy to a whole new level. His dad was prior military, and spent twelve years in the trenches—a cubicle on the third floor—before he'd been let go, in some sort of rightsizing, or downsizing. But any way the military decided to slice it, it was all the same: his dad was shitcanned. Not the kind with the golden parachute, but the kind where you were asked to pack up your desk on a Friday afternoon and vacate the premises by the end of the day. The kind where the looks started well before the ax fell, and his dad rocked himself to sleep at three a.m., hoping that the next truncated maneuver wouldn't be his last. His dad was a financial expert, or that's what he'd told Matthew—and he was inclined to believe it, at the tender age of eight, when the whole world was filled with addition, multiplication, and subtraction. And that's the way this operation had been. The Octanitrocubane was right within his grasp, as the idiot—Mark, but it could have just as easily been John—reached out to grab it.

John was the one with the bright idea to break into a secure facility, and he was the one who decided to repeat the previous offense, attacking the same building, at the same base, in the same research laboratory, while using the exact same entrance and exit strategy. Idiot squared. But as soon as John had tossed the wastebasket through the double glass doors, all hell had broken loose. Matthew had never heard so many damn alarm bells in his life. He was the one on the street, watching for oncoming traffic and military men dressed in green. He'd been nearly blinded by the sea of lights—the bright ones that imprinted a map in his brain—and he'd nearly passed out from the overexposure to his corneas. He couldn't even open his mouth before every bullhorn, siren, and car within a ten-block radius decided to lead the charge. A giant voice assaulted his ears through multiple speakers, as the three little bones in his ear pounded in rapid succession and a splitting headache formed at the center of his forehead.

And the idiot still stuck to the plan. Well, he'd certainly have to give John an A for effort, although he didn't deserve an A for much else. He'd broken through the glass, and he was halfway to home when the first Taser struck him, and sent him to the ground, caving in on himself, and rolling around in the dirt and twitching like a half-dead cockroach. The next one nabbed his buddy, and Mark snail-crawled, poking around on the ground, jutting out his head like a turtle who'd had a few too many drinks on his way toward the finish line. And as the MPs swarmed around, locking down the scene, Matthew managed to set a firestorm heavenward that nearly took out the conference center and the building next to it. The MPs headed off in that direction, and that's when he managed to extricate the two morons, both of whom foamed at the mouth and made a few goo-goo noises and jerked like a pair of geriatric dancers. He executed a double-slap maneuver and yanked John and Mark by the collar toward the awaiting escape vehicle.

As the MPs started firing in every direction but theirs,

Matthew picked up the pace, feet slapping against pavement, his eyes focused two hundred feet ahead, scanning the horizon. The damn Octanitrocubane slipped right through his fingers—Mark had handed it over to him—the alarm bells waking up half of New Hampshire and Vermont.

Matthew's arms pumped at his sides, as he raced through the woods, hopped the fence, and dragged the two babbling idiots with him, one of whom had spit-up on his shirt. A giant gob of mucus followed the gob of goo, and Matthew nearly gagged on the aftermath.

The fence snagged part of his sweatshirt, and he hoisted the two babbling idiots before he heaved himself over the barbed wire. The vehicle was where he'd left it, parked next to the fence, just around the corner, sitting at an odd angle. Matthew popped the hood of his sweatshirt, tossed the two yahoos in the backseat, and eased behind the wheel, peeling out and leaving a quarter-inch of rubber behind, along with a thin cloud of dust and gravel. He jerked the wheel back and forth in the direction of the skid, whipping it around, tires slipping on the wet and snowy road, before executing a perfect three-point-turn, and ultimately heading back the way he had come. He couldn't see the sirens, but he could hear them screaming through the night air, and piercing through what must have been seven counties. The explosion had left more than a few remnants for the MPs to deal with, many of which might be discovered a day or two hence with scopes and night vision goggles. The local cops would remain outside the loop and outside the gate, and the military would go into lockdown mode, which bought Matthew a little time and plenty of space. He didn't have any choice but to drive directly at the lights, the vehicle a cherry-red tomato, the speakers blaring through the cool night air, headlights winking and glistening in his direction and cutting through the black. His hands gripped the wheel like a wet dream, and his mind reeled with various fantasies of head-on collisions and narrow escapes. One of the two in the back hiccupped. Matthew wasn't sure which one, and he wasn't sure he cared.

The sirens petered out. The gate was damn near blockaded with metal barriers shoved into place, the guards staring out into the calm night air with backs straight and guns raised. A half-dozen guards paced back and forth, left to right, as Matthew took the side road a little too quickly, catching just a brief hint of the guard and maybe a stray bullet, before the guard stared a little too hard in his direction with his assault rifle. Before the guard alerted his colleagues, Matthew jammed the pedal to the floor and cursed under his breath, as the men in uniform with rifles slung on their shoulders shoved themselves into armored trucks and cruisers and hit Hartwell Avenue, balls to the wall.

Matthew whipped the wheel around, and then jammed his foot on the accelerator, tires squealing, slipping and then gripping on a half-inch of packed snow, one of the guys in the back moaning, the wheel slick and then firm in his grip, his eyes focused dead ahead, the vehicle bouncing and pounding down the road. The sirens inched closer toward him, as he roared down Hartwell, passing a bike path and stoplights, and dark buildings and street-lamps. He cranked the stereo louder, drowning out the moans and hiccups and sirens, his mind frayed with fits and bits and his stomach took one massive leap, the fragments and words jammed through time, as flashing blue lights painted the sky, and his mouth formed a tight line and he sucked his bottom lip. He took a curve too quickly, whipped the wheel a little too hard, overcompensating, and he bounced off a ditch and a pile of packed snow. His eyes flicked behind him, the cruisers painting the roadway like a single gazelle being chased by a pack of lions. The narrow road was not quite large enough for four lanes, and yet two by two they came with headlights blasting.

Sweat drenched the wheel, his hands slick with perspiration, the bikers and cars and sirens closing in around him, his chest more and more constricted, yet he pushed onward, jerking the wheel left and right around small cars and large ones, some fast and some slow, but all were left in his rearview mirror as his car shimmied and shook with pride. He gunned the engine as he hit the entrance ramp to 95 North, skidding around the hairpin turn, tires squealing, mind reeling, hands fast on the wheel, too fast for the snowy conditions as he careened against the guardrail and scraped the driver's side, metal scraping against metal, screeching in the back and in the front, as his car and heart galloped ahead.

He zipped in and out of traffic, the cars lined up like placemats ready for the next TV meal, red lights and open highway, hopping like a frog through the maze of silver, white, black, and gray—all the colors blending into one. His focus harnessed and his senses intensified as he nipped his bottom lip. Smelling the cinnamon roll he had for breakfast, and remembering the way the taste lingered on his lips, the cup of coffee with a medium body—reminding him of varnish remover—and the way the wooden chair had dug into his lower back, he shivered at a sudden rush of cold wind.

The eruption of gunfire sounded as Matthew held fast to the wheel, the slick surface slipping through his fingers, the heat not pumping hard enough or fast enough to silence his fleeting hands and mind. His eyes flicked to the mirror, as he was rubbed from behind, shoved forward, and right into the backend of a Chevy Tahoe with a blue and white Connecticut license plate. His fingers careened through the hard plastic and his chin bumped the wheel. The men in back yelled, and more gunfire erupted, slamming against the trunk and two bullets struck the rear windshield, shattering the glass as bits and particles exploded inward, bringing with it more cold wind. The words, though, were lost on him, and so were the number of bullets striking the car. More tires squealed, including his, losing purchase in a dicey spot, one painted with black ice and covered with loosely packed snow, as Matthew shoved the car forward through the burning rubber. He yanked the wheel hard to the right, fishtailing, and nearly colliding with a truck with Massachusetts license plates, white with red lettering, with a man in a hat hunched over the wheel.

He took the 95-93 split, veering off to the right, heading south on 93 toward Boston, the engine screaming in protest as he took another turn too fast and clipped another guardrail, the screech cutting through his psyche and those of the men behind. The voices chattered away, those in his mind and those in the back, and he flicked up the heat to knock back the cold air. Immediately, the sea of cars became tighter, the whine of the engine became louder, and his heart beat faster, clipping along with the dial on the speedometer, the car shaking and grinding like an NKOTB backup dancer with a little extra junk in her trunk. He saw a vision of a woman dancing in a black top and thong with her hair thrown back, and her green eyes cutting through the glass, as she shimmied in the median. He blinked once and the image was gone. What replaced it was a pair of taillights winking a little too close, as he slammed the brakes just before impact.

When enough space cleared, Matthew weaved in and out of traffic, around minivans and SUVs like he was meant to do this, faster than a locomotive on an open

stretch of track, ready to finish this race that he had started, as sirens blared behind him.

☙❧

America was a shit country filled with entitlement and
stereotyping and government handouts given to men in
khaki pants with hundred-dollar haircuts. It was a country
filled with wasted opportunity and a sluggish mentality.
It always managed to seek the easy way out and was built
on a sue-first mindset. Ahmad's neighbor Brad was the
epitome of all that was wrong with the American dream.
Brad wouldn't have lasted five hours in Egypt or Syria.
His fragile mind would have disintegrated in the desert
sun, and foaming at the mouth would have quickly followed.

The police worked from a position of misinformation
and attempted rather poorly to catch Ahmad in a lie and
wound what was left of his pride. Like all American efforts—including the misguided invasion of Iraq—the
Americans claimed victory even when defeat stared them
right in the face. The interview room was no different.
Sure, he could have been more forthcoming, and he
should have cut back on the hostility, but he was a man
built on pride and precision, and he wanted to beat the
bastards at their own game. He stared when he should
have feinted, and feinted when he should have stared.

Even though it was difficult to prove, he now feared
he was part of some government watch program and the
dark, nondescript vehicle parked on the opposite side of
the street was a policeman with too much time on his
hands. It was easy to chalk up his fears to too much television, and the nightly news certainly blew his mind with
the series of alleged crimes that made it sound like Baghdad was right in his own backyard.

What kept his mind at ease was he knew his life was about to change for the better, and he was prepared to do battle with the American slugs whom he was fairly certain would come for him once more.

Chapter 22

"Man, I've gotta pee," Carl Razer said.

The line was longer than a Jimmy Buffet concert, but at least he was near the front of it. He wasn't first, because his GPS had lost signal, and he had no idea where the fuck he was. The Big Dig had turned his life into one massive shitstorm, and the bodies still washed up on the shore. But he did have a sea of long legs around him, most of whom were attached to women he could look at for the next several hours or so.

His mind drifted to the rocky shores of Nantucket where the wind billowed the flowing skirts, and the hat jammed on his head had nearly blown away in the ensuing breeze.

The mixture of tights and snow pants and ruffled jackets set his mind at ease and the devil on his shoulder grinned in triumphant jubilee. The voice in his mind gathered in time and space and took him to a better place where the beaches were warm and the air was crisp.

He still wasn't sure how he'd been talked into this rock concert of epic proportions. His damn dog was gone, but both his girlfriend and his best friend had told him he needed to get his sorry self out of the house, and after the wakeup call via a punch in the nose from a crazy ex, he decided he ought to take matters into his own hands.

"Maybe you should have thought about that before you got in line," Arnie Norfolk said.

"The whole point was to get in line early. I feel inspired, and that cold air's hitting my lungs like an assault rifle." Carl's jacket had a hole in the armpit, and the air entered through the slit, and turned his life into rainbows and popsicle sticks. He had started shivering after twenty minutes, and he'd probably lose all feeling in his armpits soon. A snow flurry landed on the back of his hand. He'd left his gloves in the car. But it wasn't the biggest mistake he'd ever made.

"You'd pass out before four. I'd find you on the side of the road, cuddling up against the curb, probably puking your guts out, or dry heaving, dog. You don't stand a chance at no ten miler. Besides, I thought you gave up running."

"I only made you think I did." Carl tapped his forehead. For some reason, it increased his desire to relieve himself and smoke a cigarette, in that order. "Mind games, man. It's all about the mind games."

"What's that supposed to mean?" Arnie asked. "Are you trying to tell yourself that you can't run? Are you looking for some sort of inspiration out there to counteract your lack of fitness ability?"

Carl shivered, or that might have been his bladder. "You don't know how to take a joke." He sniffed the air. It smelled like a wet dog.

"I can take a joke just fine—"

"When is this concert going to start anyway?"

Arnie poked his companion. "Not for another four hours."

Carl narrowed his eyes. "And you made me line up now?"

Arnie waved his hands in every possible direction. "Would you look at the line?"

"Yeah, we have two teenyboppers in front of us, and now more than six-dozen behind us. I feel like I'm at Disney World, and I'm in line to meet Mickey Mouse."

The long legs, though, did put a positive spin on things. But he wasn't about to tell Arnie this. The dude would hump a tree before breakfast and another one after dinner, as long as it didn't slap him. Carl, on the other hand, had higher standards. He needed more than a beating heart and a pair of tits to get his libido train moving full steam ahead, and right now he had all the woman he could possibly handle.

"This is supposed to be their premiere concert," Arnie said, "the start of their upcoming tour." He spread his arms wide and lifted his head toward the sky.

Carl blew out a breath and then watched it float away. He needed that cigarette pronto. "Whatever you say, *dog*. I think you ate a few too many of those 'shrooms you have stashed in your sock drawer. Maybe you ought to lay off them for a little while." Carl slapped a hand underneath his arm to stop the breeze from blowing through. "Maybe forever. When you dream, you need to do it with the lights off and your feet sticking out in front of you. Not while you're standing up and giggling."

Arnie made a face. "I have no idea what you're talking about."

Carl smirked. "You probably wouldn't."

The sleeping bag at the front of the line was a nice touch, and a man leaned against the metal fence with a stogie stuffed between his jaws, as a sour expression painted his face and puffs of smoke emitted from his mouth. Carl sniffed the air and picked up the faintest hint of pure bliss. Beach chairs stood up around him jammed against the wet snow with a thermos or two sprinkling the atmosphere for good measure. Traffic meandered through the crowded streets at a sluggish pace as horn honks and hand gestures filled in more than a few blanks.

"Besides, this is a free gig."

"Man, I don't care," Carl said. "It's four hours before the show, my lips are already numb, and I'll probably lose all feeling in my fingers soon. Plus, I gotta pee like some thoroughbred who took an extra water break and went around the track one too many times after the fifth race."

Arnie waved a hand in front of his face. "Then go pee."

"I can't exactly leave you by yourself. You'll proba-bly do something stupid like take a few more 'shrooms and call it an 'eventful experience.' And then I'll find you hanging on the sidewalk spewing. With you, it's all about the evasive maneuvers and the forced grins."

And then when the Disney World teenyboppers admin-istered CPR, Arnie would attempt to remove his pants and hump a stump. The fool had more visions than a blind man who rubbed the crystal ball a little too hard.

ᘒᘖᘒ

Addison Thomas couldn't believe folks were already lined up for the show. The line wrapped down Boylston Street like a snake, past both T-stops, and around the corner. A line filled with kids, kids, and more kids. Like all the colleges and universities in Boston were let loose at the same hour on the same day, and for the exact same purpose. It would only get worse. He hoped he didn't need his Taser.

The first signs of intolerance filled the air, and he had already seen one man with his hands waving in nonspe-cific patterns who leaned a little too hard to the left. His mind was alert, and so was the dog at his feet.

The dog, a German shepherd, sniffed in a specific pattern, with a specific purpose. The dog was on a leash, and he had nose receptors that were five thousand times more powerful than a human's. If the dog hadn't scarfed an entire stick of butter—wrapper included—he'd even call the animal smart. But it had, and now he wasn't so sure the dog would make it through the evening without offering the butter back.

The dog had his face in the grass and snow and his butt in the air, and he meandered through the green and white with relative ease. His pattern was not specific, as he zigged and zagged and tugged at the leash with plenty of authority. The dog weighed more than eighty pounds—before the stick of butter—as a sense of determination filled the air.

As he continued to focus on the sniffing, he hadn't looked up or even barked once. A squirrel could have danced on the ground with a hula-hoop strapped around his waist, and the dog would have looked right past him and continued on with the task at hand. The lines had blurred a while ago, at least for Addison, and he had hoped that it wouldn't come to this.

The entire area was closed off to crew and cops and dogs. He had a long night ahead, he was sure of that much, although he tried not to think about much else, including the dog and the stick of butter, and the sea of upright figures holding leashes in their right hands. The air was brisk and the snow flurries danced through the cool breeze like kites on a string.

So far none of the dogs had found anything. Not that he expected them to, but it didn't hurt to try, right? It was all about the effort. Something like ninety percent of life was about showing up.

If it was, he needed a refund.

CRCRD

Nearly four hours later, the lights went down, and the stage lit up. The front row was as beautiful and majestic as Carl had imagined it to be. He could no longer feel his fingers and toes, but he was told it was all part of the experience. It wasn't his first concert, but it was his first concert on the Common. He'd had a Dunkie's earlier from a food truck on the outer edge of the Common, but it didn't offer up more than a brief caffeine boost. The cream and sugar did manage to make him feel better, if only temporarily.

He had struck up a conversation with two girls who were high and floating on cotton candy clouds during his third smoke break.

He pressed his face near the stage, and the girl behind him had bumped his butt more than once. He had glared at her over his left shoulder, and she stuck out her tongue. Her boyfriend had on a skull cap and a black leather jacket with a red emblem emblazoned on the front. The guy to his right smelled like he hadn't showered in over a week, and Arnie—on his left—had already elbowed him twice in the ribs.

"Can you believe this shit?" Carl asked. "Where're the prim and proper showgirls—"

Arnie rubbed his forehead. "I didn't know showgirls could be prim and proper."

A guitar roared onstage, and Carl lost all hearing in his left ear. "You have no idea—"

The riff ripped through the night for twenty seconds and drowned out the sound of his voice. The sweet smell of weed cozied up to his nostrils, and lingered there throughout the riff.

Arnie opened his mouth, and shook his head. He leaned in closer. "You're right, I probably don't. But I don't think you do either."

Carl leaned into Arnie and raised his voice. "Have you seen the dogs?"

Arnie grinned. "You mean the one that sniffed your crotch earlier trying to get a taste. You might want to think about not stuffing meat inside your jeans."

"You have a warped imagination." *Or maybe it was sense of humor.* When it came to Arnie, Carl could never tell which was which. The man didn't know when to say when.

"What about a sense of humor?" Arnie asked.

"Yeah, that's warped, too," Carl said. "You have any idea what the dogs are doing?"

A drum solo ensued, and the crowd roared. Then, the guitar found another gear, and Carl figured he might burst an eardrum before the night was over. Maybe he could claim disability, and go on tour with the band. One weekend filled with debauchery ought to do the trick. Nah, he'd better make it two. He heard The Sex Maggots had a collection of panties that could fill a walk-in closet. The fantasy was replaced by reality, and he couldn't imagine a life that didn't have Danielle right in the center of it. Her grin still managed to make him come unhinged, and he hoped the feeling never left his body.

Carl stuffed his hands in his pockets and swayed, even though it wasn't that type of song. He'd already gotten bumped twice, neither of which was by an attractive blonde or redhead. He felt close to all the crazy idiots around him, and distant at the same time, even with his nose pressed next to the stage. When the singer took a running leap, the crowd went nuts, and Carl saw bodies go down left and right like checkers.

He grinned because he couldn't think of anything better to do. He hoped the girl behind him in the too-tight top decided to flash her breasts before the night was over. He had his camera ready for just such an occurrence. He'd always appreciated a good pair of tits.

"Besides the dog sniffing my crotch," Carl asked, "have you seen anything else going on?"

Arnie shoved a dude with a facial tattoo. "What am I? A reporter?"

Carl nodded and leaned in closer. "You are, in fact, a reporter."

"That was a dream from a long time ago, dog," Arnie said, "I used to have a huge crush on Katie Couric."

Carl sniggered, and made some sort of honking noise. Maybe he had a sinus infection. "But that all changed when you hit college?"

"Exactly—" Arnie slapped him on the shoulder and cuffed his ear. "—I grew out of that phase, dog. Now I'm chasing after Heidi Klum."

The song ended, and Carl shook his head. A roar through the crowd followed the last note, and his head nearly exploded. "Good luck with that."

Arnie grinned like one of the teenyboppers. "She and Seal split up."

"Good for them."

Arnie pointed at his chest. "No, good for me, dog. You have to believe, otherwise you're never going to achieve."

"Like crotch sniffing?" Carl removed a cigarette from his pack, stuffed it between his lips, and lit it with the flick of his index finger from the lighter in his right hand.

Arnie might have sniffed a crotch or two in his day when he was high on 'shrooms, and couldn't remember his own address or phone number. And he'd wandered around lost on the quad during another particularly troubling instance. But he always managed to find his way back. Carl figured the drugs were a semi-enlightening experience, and he wanted to be around when the haze turned gray. Other than a nicotine fix and the occasional drink, he stayed away from the serious shit.

"What kind of friend are you?"

Carl leaned in closer and slapped Arnie on the ear. "The kind that calls you out when you're being fucking retarded."

"Maybe you should work on not being so honest."

"Nah," Carl said, "that's not going to happen."

The energy from the stage reverberated through Carl in waves, as the singer hit a particularly high note and then followed it up with vocal vibrato. The guitar charged through a series of licks, and then it all ended with a cymbal clash.

Arnie giggled. "As for the dog, though, he might come back so you and your crotch should be ready." His head turned sideways. "I thought you had to pee."

"That was four hours ago. Just how many of those 'shrooms did you take before we arrived? Did you eat the whole baggy?"

Words were spoken to the crowd, and then the band onstage bowed. A man tossed a pair of sticks into the crowd, along with two or three guitar picks, and the horde roared in response. Carl was bumped from behind one more time. He turned around and gave the girl the finger when her boyfriend had his head turned in the other direction.

"Show time was supposed to be an hour ago," Arnie said.

If it hadn't been for Arnie, Carl could have mourned in peace and rediscovered hearing on his left side. The drum beat out of time in his head, and he'd gotten jabbed in his kidney during one of the five or six melees. Sure, it was supposed to be fun, but he didn't need this shit. He had more important business to attend to, like Danielle with her long legs, tight butt, and massive cannons he'd been searching for all of his life. Her three-inch heels would have added to his already massive erection, and her winking smile was forever etched in his brain. He didn't need drugs to develop his own fantasies and wink at reality.

"That was the opening act," Carl said. "You aren't missing anything."

"But I like opening acts. I like getting fired up before the main event."

"Don't you mean 'eating up'? You might want to consider a new plan of attack."

At least Carl would remember the experience. The girl behind him had slapped his ass in the ensuing mayhem, but he kept his hands to himself.

ⱷⱻⱷ

Leo had a great view at an entire lawn filled with tight butts. "Why am I the one dressed like a woman?"

"You don't like your skirt and pumps?"

"I like my regular attire." Leo still didn't know how he'd gotten talked into dressing like a woman, but he knew he'd remember the experience for the rest of his life. He had shaved his face, but he had drawn the line at lipstick.

"Dude, your regular attire involves wife-beater T-shirts," Addison said.

Leo stood small at the back of the venue, undercover so to speak. But he knew Addison would enjoy the concert a lot more than he would. He'd turned down multiple propositions, had a drunk guy check out his butt, and a third individual had tried to cop a feel, this one a woman with a penchant for stumbling. She did have an interesting body filled with a little extra meat on top and around her middle. Her thighs were muscled, and her lips were purple.

"So?" Leo asked.

Addison had on a suit so stiff and bothered it should have been abandoned in the 1960s. Supposedly, it was vintage. Instead, it smelled like mothballs, and it was covered in a fine layer of dust. The handkerchief in the front pocket was a bit over the top.

"The lieutenant associates wife-beater T-shirts with a man who cleans his shotgun on his front porch."

Leo adjusted the bottom of his skirt. "I don't have a shotgun or a front porch." Currently renting, he didn't think he'd be able to afford a flat in this life or the next. But he could admire from afar. He had hoped to catch another glimpse of the woman with a few extra pounds on her, but she had mysteriously disappeared. It was possible she had gone in search of a refill, or more promising opportunities.

Addison clapped Leo on the back. "That still doesn't excuse the wife-beaters."

"Women dig the wife-beaters," Leo said. "Didn't you get the memo?"

The opening act…the name escaped him…was loud, and there was a mosh pit in the first several rows, but otherwise it might as well have been The Grateful Dead, except with louder guitars and a whammy bar. The drum solo was a nice touch, and so was the guitar one. The dudes resembled sticks with heads, and a resounding energy resonated off the stage in waves, making him half-dizzy from the experience.

Intermission was filled with just as many moving parts and bodies, and Leo searched for what was out of place. With his back against the nearest tree, the bark stabbed his soft flesh, and his mind whispered in two different directions. Longing and regret and the faint hint of car exhaust filled the night air.

"You look good in the skirt and pumps. But you should lose the cigar."

Leo stomped a heel on the grass, and came up with a patch of dirt. "That's the only way you're able to spot me, am I right?"

"Have you ever seen a woman in a skirt, pumps, and stockings smoking a cigar?"

Leo flashed a set of white teeth and a shit-eating grin. "I'm not ready to admit the error of my ways."

"I'm sure you're not," Addison said, "but that still doesn't make it legal."

Leo took a puff and then another. He edged his back away from the bark and the tree. "How are we supposed to spot anyone, anyway? It's not like we can cover the entire Common."

The men were placed at strategic positions around the Common. Since it was easier with a partner, the men were paired up. Only one man was dressed like a woman, and it was a bet Leo hated losing more than wearing a Jets jersey.

He'd lost track of the number of men dumped on the Common, but the number hovered over thirty. The stiff suits and occasional blue caps stood out like prostitutes in Connecticut.

"Would you rather try," Addison said, "or should we just give up now?"

"I vote for giving up now," Leo said. "That way I can get out of this damn skirt."

"Oh, I don't think you'll have to worry about someone getting you out of your skirt later." Addison smacked his lips. "You'll leave a definitive mark on society, that's for sure. Probably scar several individuals for life."

Leo squinted at the lights and the prospective mosh pit. "Did you even hear the band?"

"Is that even the point?" Addison asked. "I thought the point was to get drunk, or stoned, or both."

Leo stood over an hour now, and his knees were killing him. He didn't know if it was the standing or the high heels. His underwear had jammed against his butt crack, and he probably deposited a tissue or two on the snowy landscape somewhere. And if he didn't know better, he'd say his makeup was running. Damn bets. If he lost another one, he planned to just pay the fine and move on with his life. Even if it pushed close to three hundred dollars, he'd starve himself for a week just to make ends meet.

"Why is this show still going on anyway?"

"Haven't you ever heard the phrase 'The show must go on'?" Addison asked.

"Yeah, but I didn't think it would actually work."

The last concert he'd attended was Genesis. The Phil Collins drum solo duo was the highlight of the entire show, and he'd use it to judge all future drum solos. From what he'd seen so far, there would never be another one like it. The guitar solo was adequate, but it wasn't much to look at either. The cigar, however, helped settle his nerves and made the snowflakes dance.

Addison looked at his ridiculous partner. "Are you going to keep your shirt on this time?"

Leo smirked and took another puff. "You like it when I take my shirt off."

"You might want to keep in mind that you're wearing a skirt—not that that's ever stopped you before—but it is something to consider."

The mosh pit filled, as Sharpie banners were thrust in the air with great fanfare. A rumbling filled the mob, as the lights blinked five or six times. An AC/DC song cut through the air, and the mob roared in response.

"This concert is tied into the mayor's reelection campaign," Addison said. "It's all about getting another four years of office. Dirty politics doesn't come cheap."

"Who said anything about dirty politics?" Personally, Leo hated politics, and he wasn't a big fan of the mayor either. She was too pretty to be trusted. Former beauty queens that made his eyes weep only added to his constant state of confusion, and her ability to steal nearly ten years off her true age made him realize her dance with the devil must occur on a near daily basis. If the devil ever won, he had no idea what would happen next.

"When has the political game ever played fair? Besides, you know how close the mayoral race is. She believes her entire campaign rides on this show. It's the first one on the Boston Common, and she hopes it won't be the last one either." Addison scratched his chin. "Could you imagine the uproar if she had cancelled the show? It's only been advertised for the past month."

Another cheer reverberated through the crowd, as the lights dimmed. Leo wondered if it had to do with bare breasts. He'd never met a pair he didn't like. Being a woman, if even only temporarily, afforded him certain opportunities that he could never get away with without the dress and pumps. His stare was no longer lascivious. It was filled with contempt and bordered on jealousy of the highest order. He had even practiced his look in front of a mirror just in case.

Leo nudged his partner. "You're happy that I'm wearing a skirt, aren't you?"

❧❧❧

The mayor leaned forward in her seat to better enjoy the experience. "How are my numbers looking?"

Her front row seat was even better than she had

hoped, even if she had a temporary setback in her hearing. The opening act was loud and enthusiastic and filled with testosterone and sweat. The jeans were skintight, and the lead singer strutted around like a jaguar in a cage. Were it not for the political ramifications, she might have considered a possible nighttime feeding. But as it was, she decided to pass for political reasons. Her libido grimaced in response.

The mass of men that surrounded her gave off a particularly potent odor, and she sniffed the air with a sense of longing. Her heightened arousal caused her to shift in her seat and a slight flush in her cheeks. While the opening act had long since departed, her libido had not taken a similar dive. Instead, the air felt charged, and so did she. All she wanted to do was pound her cocksucker opponent into the ground, and then have a little fun of her own with a young stud who was free and clear of all emotional entanglements and who had more than a few bedroom talents that she could exploit.

"Do you really want to discuss this now?"

Joey James grinned. "Maybe not. But they're looking good, aren't they?" Like the men that had been on stage. The air practically levitated around her.

Bob nodded.

She was already having a near-deaf experience, along with an increased amount of feedback from the speakers. She'd managed to secure the seat herself, with the help of a rather fortuitous manager who fixated on former beauty queens. And it had been worth it. This show would put her campaign over the edge and parachute her all the way to the ground. The competition had been fierce, and the bloodbath was far from over, but it was all about her name being announced as the winner on election night—nothing else mattered. Joey James could practically feel it, the win pulsating through her body, commanding the stage the way she had in a pink bikini some years ago. Or maybe that was the feedback from the speakers again. It was hard to tell where the feedback ended, and she began.

Winning, though, was more important than a temporary hearing loss.

As the lights dimmed, her spirit soared, and she squeezed Bob on his left shoulder, her long nails digging toward the bone. Bob, though, didn't even flinch, and she managed her first small smile in response.

Chapter 23

Quinn could feel the energy of the crowd pulsating through his veins. That's what he played for, that's what he could never seem to get enough of, and his spirit soared as the crowd roared. His hand shook with anticipation…or drugs. But that didn't mean he was finished. It only meant his senses were heightened, his awareness sublime, as adrenaline surged toward his extremities.

The stage and his voice were perfect; the venue, crowd, and band were in perfect harmony; his energy peaked after his recent sexual conquest. He'd passed out for several hours, had multiple cups of green tea to go along with the drugs and the sex. The opening act had stirred the crowd into a pit of frenzy, sex, and rock anthems. The blonde in the second row had bowling balls stuffed in her bra as she bounced up and down, and he had dual redheads lined up for after the gig waiting in a state of flushed anticipation and near-naked existence. If life got any better, he'd need a respirator.

His band was amped and ready to play, or locked and loaded—the term he preferred—a mixture of adrenaline and heroin floating around in his veins and bubbling beneath his skin. He'd been ready, ever since Wilford, the band's manager, secured the gig with a handshake, a fifteen-page contract, and a half-dozen phone calls. He'd perfected his moves: the dips and jerks and flips, the speaker jumps, and the microphone stand twists. You see, it was all about giving the audience something they had never seen before, even if it meant additional hours in the recording studio or the local gym. That's why Madonna was still around. She had a perfectionist complex, and if he was perfectly honest with himself, he did too. The best ones always did. He worked on the high notes and lows, and he gurgled carbonated water four times a day.

As Quinn stepped on stage, it was the loudest sound he'd ever heard, an uproar, like the sound of a jet engine at Logan. The surge of adrenaline went up another level on the Richter scale, and he threw his head back and lifted his hands toward the heavens as his T-shirt rose above his waistband. This was what he lived for. The crowd. The fans. The pheromones and the sexual energy. None of the other bullshit: not the greedy conglomerates, the record deals, the critics, the haters who said he was a washed-up loser, a has-been, or a never-was. He silenced the critics when he hit that first high note, and for an hour and a half every night, he kept those self-righteous bastards at bay, and his heart hovered in the right place.

He had visions. Sometimes even aspirations of what his life might be like with a woman on each arm and one on her knees. He couldn't picture a life where he wasn't on some stage performing, entertaining, and making a name for himself where the crowd adored him and a busty lass tossed the occasional undergarment in the direction of his head.

He hit the first note right, nearly perfect. It was important, that first note. It set the tone for the rest of the concert and his confidence. It was a lack of confidence that held him back at times, the constant need to please and receive pleasure, to seek the adoration of an admiring crowd, a group of female fans who thrust their pushed-out breasts in his direction and yanked up their shirts in an admiring wave of bare breasts and pale nipples. But he was better now. That's what his therapist had said. Making progress. He had lived the ultimate dream, and come back from the subsequent crash with an admiring flash of black eyelash and red lipstick. It was all about the high. The thrill. The constant rush of affection and longing looks offered up with glassy eyes and glowing skin.

Quinn commanded the stage. He owned it. For an hour and a half, it was his. Performing scared him the same way a stripper with an AK-47 would have, both exciting and terrifying at the same time with the slightest hint of unpredictability. But no matter how hard he tried, he couldn't seem to get enough. The high rushed forth, as the next note crossed the threshold.

It was all about the desperation. Even in his own music, if he managed desperate just right, it worked. Always. If he left something on the table, anything, the song blew up in his face like a water balloon. He heard a whisper in the crowd, a murmur, and he gripped the microphone stand with both hands. The lights flipped on, and the crowd flipped into a frenzy with bodies pummeling one another and shouts echoing toward the lofted stage. He glided across the stage with the stand in one hand and his other arm raised.

The next notes came even easier than the first, and before he knew it, Quinn danced across the stage, the crowd cheering, his legs vibrating, the music pulsating, the guitar riffing, the drums and rhythm and bass guitar all playing in unison. It was utter perfection, and then the song ended. He greeted the mass of bodies, and the mass shouted back with a roar of gratitude.

Nicholas smacked his sticks, and the next song began just as loud and proud as the one before it. Quinn moved with elegance and ease and circumnavigated the stage with his mouth open and the words flowing out one right after another. He leapt forward, and the crowd followed suit. It was all about the survival, the constant healing, the creative process, the highs and lows, the ebb and flow, the self-doubt, and the energy that the crowd returned for his life's work. Each note was just as powerful as the one before it, and soon he had forgotten about the bowling ball blonde and the dual redheads.

Even his own mother told him he'd be dead by now. She'd shown him charts and pie graphs that choreographed his imminent demise. Rock gods who peaked faster than a bottle rocket and crashed back to earth exploding upon impact and leaving a small crater in their wake were his major source of happiness and inspiration. Graphic videos of explicit sex and horny teens helped fulfill his dreams. She predicted suicide and his immortalization on a plain white tombstone. Pessimism ruled her domain. That was the only way she survived, with self-guided righteousness flowing through her arms and legs. If she didn't destroy him, she'd destroy herself with mixed drinks and burnt cigarettes. Maybe if she had one more son, it'd have been different. But he was the only one, and a damn miracle he'd come in the first place.

eɔeɔ

The cigar left Leo's mouth and struck the ground. "What the hell is that?"

Addison shook his head. He'd finished one Dunkie's, and he'd managed to score a refill between sets. If it would have done any good, he would have flashed his badge and displayed the faintest hint of sympathy. "Are you high again?"

"There was never a first time."

Other than being high on life, Addison kept his feet

firmly planted on the ground. But he leaned forward for good measure. "What are you looking at?"

Leo pointed. "That backpack. It wasn't there on our last round."

"Maybe you were dreaming again," Addison said. "You gotta work on that whole sleep, not-sleep ratio." And so did he. The more the terrorists won, the more he was inclined to break the rules. Bureaucracy wasn't built on rule breaking, nor was it managed by creative thinking.

"It's only just begun."

Addison scratched his chin. "What the hell is that supposed to mean?"

Threading through the packed crowd hadn't been easy, even with a man dressed as a woman, and a cigar dangling from his lips.

He'd flashed his badge—the one he wore around his neck for just such an occasion—but the stoners and miscreants had only giggled before the body slamming, tangents, and food chewing resumed. Shouting followed in equal measure, and Addison's forehead slammed to the beat emitted from the stage. This was more exercise than he had gotten in the past two weeks, and he hated that his heart rate had spiked. And if he was being truly honest with himself, it wasn't easy to walk with a coffee cup in his hand either. The caffeine, however, made his blood flow more freely.

Leo picked up his cigar and wiped it off before shoving it back in his mouth. "I saw it on a bumper sticker once."

"The backpack?" Addison prompted.

"Yeah, right," Leo said, "like I said, it wasn't there before."

The backpack was your standard, off-the-shelf variety, black with two straps in the back. It leaned against a tree, and not a single soul surrounded it. Other than being inconspicuous, it offered no other redeeming qualities.

Addison nudged his head in the direction of the individual moving expeditiously through the crushed horde. His hair was blond, and his clothes were dark, and his posture was stiff. "And what about the man running away?"

"There is that, too," Leo said.

"He doesn't even look high."

"No, he doesn't," Leo agreed.

"It's all about the acid trip, you know," Addison said. "You've probably been taking a bit too much acid yourself."

"I don't bother with that shit."

"You bother with a lot of shit." It was how Leo Nivea ended up in a skirt in the first place. With the cigar currently protruding from his lips, he bunched his hands at his sides.

Addison took another look at the backpack, before he focused his attention on the tall blond man skirting away. His brain cleared, as did the smoke, and he took off running after the nondescript man who currently weaved his way through a sea of unfamiliar faces.

Addison pumped his arms at his sides, puffed out his chest, and yelled, grunted, and bumped his way through the stoned throng. The blond man increased his casual pace with his skinny frame and not a single look in his direction.

e/ɔe/ɔ

Leo spotted a similar backpack. When he stepped closer, it was the exact same one. All the details right down to the zipper and abandonment issues. He shook his head. What the hell was going on? This time he didn't see anyone walking away, and it was damn near impossible to chase after the individual last time in his pumps and polyester skirt. A man with blond hair, tall, gangly, some might even say sinewy had a specific gait, like a specific plan, and a specific purpose behind the specific strategy. And he wasn't high. Not that Leo could tell.

He'd lost the cigar and the pumps in the first pursuit and several tissues from his bra. Sweat cascaded down his face, and he had a large bruise on his right side. A clutch of women had pointed in his direction like he was a fawn being laid on the altar. The sound of erratic guitar playing filled the cold air, and his legs wobbled with each step he took. He hunched over, and the black bag continued to point in his direction. He opened his mouth, but no sound came out, and shame replaced triumph. The pack glanced up at him before it gave him the finger.

His left toe had swelled up, and his wig had gotten twisted around on his head. His elbow was jammed against his side, as he took one tentative step forward and then another. The cold night air assaulted his lungs, and he'd ripped a hole in one of his stockings. The gaggle of women had turned in his direction.

The drum beat out of time, as his heart slammed against his chest. Claustrophobia wrapped him up in a warm embrace, and a large hand groped his behind. He turned around and slapped the swollen face, and the man grinned exposing a missing tooth. His missing shoes caused him great aggravation and possibly two blisters.

Leo actually enjoyed chasing ne'er-do-wells, but not in pumps and skirts, with his feet swollen. He wasn't sure where the skirt had come from—not that he had bothered to ask—and he didn't really want to know either. What he wanted to do, though, was put this entire mess behind him, and move on with his life, with the miscreants behind bars for the next fifty years of their lives.

With his attention focused once more in the pack's direction, he edged close enough until he could reach it with his outstretched hand. It was propped against the bark of the tree, and when he reached out his hand, the bag shifted away from him. He reached out his arm once again, and unzipped the pack. What he discovered inside was a series of wires and plastic explosives and a possible death sentence. He stepped away and clicked on his radio.

❧❧❧

Quinn had visions, aspirations even. He'd been stuck in a rut, changing, drifting from one moment to the next, bouncing on a wave of transformation and a sea of silver. He stuffed his hand in his pocket and rolled around the loose change, before he pulled his hand back out again. He reached out to touch, toward the audience filled with moving parts and lingering bodies and wide-open mouths. Quinn had his pants tighter than a model's ass in the middle of a runway, and his loafers caressed his toes and made his feet smile.

An ocean of moving bodies bounced from one moment to the next with restless energy and drifting thoughts. And then the moment was gone, and he was back in the present, with the speakers blaring, the base pumping, his voice reaching a viral scream, the audience moving and swaying with hands in the air, the faces of the females in the front row, most of whom wanted to be with him with tight T-shirts and toned abs. The expressions of lust inspired him, and he danced with greater precision and purpose as each lyric left his mouth in perfect pitch.

He granted a few favors, and if Quinn was honest with himself, he knew he'd grant a few more before the tour was over, before the last bottle of booze was gone, and before he pissed the remaining drugs from his system. As for the dudes, they wanted his life, to be him for a day, or week, or month, as the females—some of whom had boyfriends or significant others—lined up outside his tour bus, several blocks deep with lace undergarments and short skirts. Blonde ones and dark-haired ones and everything in between lined the streets.

The mic comforted Quinn, as he gave the gig everything he had, leaving nothing back, letting his projection become their projection, letting his mind drift and sway, the same way his hips jutted and the audience shimmied and beautiful breasts spewed forth.

It was intoxicating. No matter how many gigs he did, no matter how large the crowd, it was all about how he felt, how the audience fondled his ego when he took the stage, when he reached out with his arms, embracing every last bit of it, hoping that it might last for just a moment longer.

But it never did, and the inevitable crash led to a night of surrender and compromise and meaningless sex before the next gig and the next high took its place.

No matter where he was, though, this was exactly where he was supposed to be, where he was supposed to hope and dream and embrace whatever came his way. The music, the lyrics, the fans, the musicians, the aging of the band, of himself, the way the music industry changed and the audience transformed, and yet he still embraced it. All of it. It was the only way he could survive.

It made sense.

Nothing else did.

And then the purity of perfection morphed into shit.

ഇരുന്നു

Three explosions rocked the Common. The blast reverberated above the music, the flashes of light intense, as flames shot in the air, along with earth and dirt and red and black. The smoke was intense, and his nostrils flared. Quinn covered his mouth and coughed more than once before he dropped to his knees. His head dropped, and when he picked it up, he saw the crowd running and colliding and dipping and diving and shoving with mouths open. The constant thrum of a fan filled the background. Panic and despair created chaos. A state of confusion surrounded him.

His lips moved; his feet and knees wouldn't. Despite all the movement around him, the body parts that were flung in the air, the bleeding that painted the sea of green and black, the torn bodies and torn souls, he lifted himself up and stepped forward. The lead in his feet caused his whole body to drag.

The smell was worse than anything he'd ever smelled in his life. It smelled like burned skin and broken dreams and burning leaves. The intensity of it, the need, the desire, the way it reached out to him and overpowered everything else around him nearly caused him to drop to his knees once more. The smell intensified to rotten eggs and decay, and it nearly suffocated him.

His heart hammered against his chest. It was chaos, as bodies and souls collided and masses were trampled and the never-ending stampede paraded onward. He couldn't hear out of either ear, and the disorientation caused him to stumble and sway on the bent stage. Snapshots in time packed his existence, a moment that throttled and shook his core took over, and he toppled forward in a blind pursuit of the right side. In the midst of the melee, he tripped and went down on his right knee and jammed it against the hardwood. He opened his mouth, but no sound came out, and no one seemed to notice. He turned his head this way and that looking for the other members of The Sex Maggots, a stage hand, or Wilford, but none of them were around. He was all alone in the smoke-filled tomb, and he wondered if this was truly the end.

All Quinn could do was think about the concert, the mass of people, the confined space, the open air, the heart of Boston, the ebb and flow, the cap guns that had been passed out but hadn't been fired, the constant thrum of fans lined up hours before the show, the dogs sniffing every piece of open space with ears perked and noses to the ground. And the men, suspicious ones that he hadn't been able to approach, filled in the gaps of the throng and skirted like cockroaches at the first sign of trouble. The men in uniform couldn't get to them fast enough. But worst of all he couldn't shake the image of the backpacks planted in the crowd that had exploded during a particularly loud crescendo.

Nor did he have any idea what the hell had just happened.

Chapter 24

Carl hated crowds, and he hated disorganized crowds even more. He had a bruise on his right side to go with a throbbing headache and sense of disorientation. He also was slightly dehydrated from the alcohol he had consumed, and he was fairly certain the smoke hadn't helped matters. The line was longer than his entrance into the concert with a bottleneck at both ends and a series of minions stuffed around blue uniforms and a gust of wind looming on the horizon. Enough cops surrounded the insanity for him to take notice even in his slightly disoriented and inebriated state. The smoke seeped through his open pores, and through the holes in the armpits of his jacket. For the record, he didn't like snow either, as flakes dotted his nose and the top of his jacket. He had tasted a couple of the little assholes by accident, and he gagged and shuddered and spit on the ground near his feet.

Smoke covered his hair and caused a brief sneezing fit, and his eyes had watered more than once. The only saving grace was the ass—currently stuffed into white snow pants—on the woman three groups in front. Her long blonde hair flowed down her back and stopped at the exact point where her ass jutted out. He tried to think of something to outwit his libido, but all he could think of was rabbits and weed, and then rabbits smoking weed, and the end result was that he was harder than at any point in the preceding thirty-six minutes.

If the line moved any slower, he'd age ten years before he reached the end of it. But the blonde with the beautiful ass would live on in infamy.

"What the hell's going on?" Carl asked.

"I think we're in lockdown mode."

Carl's friend consumed a few too many 'shrooms, but he was apparently still coherent on the Common in downtown Boston. "Lockdown mode?"

"You see all those policemen by the exits—"

Carl narrowed his eyes and scratched the side of his face. "So what?"

"It means nobody's leaving."

"The hell we're not," Carl said. "I'll show you how it's done." Patience was for the common folk, not the ones with library cards and steady jobs and a pack of cigarettes stuffed in his back pocket.

Carl marched up to the man in the blue suit—a series of grunts and murmurs and irritated gestures and vulgar comments followed— the suit with the creases still showing, and the shifty gaze and soft face. The cop's cheeks puffed out, and his glasses were tight on his face.

A twitch of cold entered through the open end of Carl's jacket, and he fought to keep his composure. "I need to leave. Now."

"You aren't going anywhere," the cop replied.

Carl took a step forward and hunched up his shoulders. "Why the hell not?"

In most situations, stepping toward a cop was a bad idea. In Carl's world, forward motion was the most confident one, and he had his eye on Boylston Street. He still hadn't forgotten the teenager with the hooded sweatshirt and the small black gun that was an extension of his arm.

"Because you're a witness."

Carl felt a tap on his shoulder, but he ignored it. "To what?"

"Are you mentally retarded?" the cop asked. "To what took place here tonight. If you need me to spell it out for you further—"

Carl's tone was clipped, even, and his shoulders inched up even higher. "I don't have any idea what you're talking about."

"You have it written all over your face," the cop said. "You have a surge of adrenaline, but when that passes, you're not going to like the end result."

"Yeah, and I'm slowly coming back down to earth," Arnie said. "You might want to try it sometime."

Carl had no idea his friend had followed him, and that Arnie currently hovered near his right shoulder. More murmurs and grunts circulated through the crowd, and a female voice called him an obnoxious dick. Carl hoped it wasn't the one with the perfect ass, otherwise he might have to stuff a little something extra in her mouth.

"You know," Carl said, "if I scream loud enough, there won't be a thing you can do to stop me." He felt the pairs of eyes intensify, but he ignored them. He also chose to ignore the throbbing pain in his temple, the one behind his right eyelid that spread to his left. He fisted his hands at his sides, and his arms began to shake with adrenaline and aggression.

The cop looked over his shoulder before he leaned in closer. "Who says I want to stop you?"

Carl leaned back on his heels and dropped his shoulders. The tension left his body in one smooth motion. "What are you after then?"

"I'm after the truth," the cop said. "And I want to do whatever I can to find it."

"What if it's not even us?" Carl asked. "What if we're not even the ones who were involved?"

The cop shrugged his shoulders. “I didn’t say that you were, but it’s nice of you to offer an opinion.” The cop adjusted his glasses. “No, what I’m really focused on is what happened here this evening.”

“You’re crazy, man. You know that don’t you?” Carl took a step back. “Yeah, you do, and you don’t even care. Maybe you don’t care at all. Maybe you’re just pretending to care.” His right hip suddenly developed a mind of its own, and he started worrying that the left one might follow suit. The cool breeze shimmied through his jacket. All the anger and fear he felt earlier from his encounter with the sex-crazed teenager bubbled to the surface.

“You really are high, aren’t you?” The cop had a gun on his hip that jutted out at an odd angle and a canister on his other one. The look made him seem even larger than he already was, and the soft cheeks rumbled when he spoke.

“I haven’t taken any ’shrooms,” Carl said, “if that’s what you’re worried about.”

“Clearly all you’re really doing is wasting my time,” the cop said. “I’m not into that sort of thing, thank you very much.”

He turned around and disappeared back into the crowd. Carl, on the other hand, opened his mouth, but no sound came out.

Quinn had seen more than enough blood and pummeled bodies. He still hadn’t heard any screams, other than the ones in his head, but maybe that would come later, and maybe his vision wouldn’t seem as blurry as it did right now. Shock. That’s what some shrink would have said before he asked for a check the size of Rhode Island. He couldn’t shake the images out of his brain, though. The ones that came in fits and starts across the broken TV screen, as his head pounded and his skull throbbed. He stumbled back to the bus with his eyes amiss and his heart slamming and his fingers twitching. He needed to take the edge off before it was too late.

The heroin had left his system. It was replaced with doubt and fear and gray hallucinations. A woman in white had her arms wrapped around his neck, and her tongue slithered out of her grapefruit mouth. He had his head thrown back on the makeshift sofa, and he had a pillow jammed just below his waist. He had passed out with his mouth wide, and he jerked awake when he felt long feminine fingers rubbing below his waist. He shoved the hand away and opened his eyes. The image was split in two, and the look of compassion and desperation was lost on him. She slinked away with her head hung low, as the nightmare continued once more, and darkness turned in his direction.

Quinn had counted on leaving the crowd and his compadres behind, next to the amp and speakers when he first stepped onstage to the roar of the crowd, where the gap in the festivities was fleeting, like his existence on this earth. He had sung the right notes, and his band had struck the right chords, and the audience voiced the words back to him. It was beautiful and wonderful and sensational. It was a great crowd. The largest one he had ever seen and played before. Better than his most vivid dream, the one where he received a blowjob by three different women with three pairs of luscious ruby red lips. It had almost happened once. He was so close, but yet he was still miles and miles away from reality. No, that wasn't right. A stupid song stuck in his head and flipped his brain cells. The lyrics and melody tripped over one another in some mixed-up harmony where the words and phrases were filled with clipped and forgotten praises.

His head pounded, and his spirit dropped faster than a broken elevator. Fear was his only salvation.

The woman in white was back, and this time her hands were even bigger than before. The bus lurched forward, and he smacked his head on the arm of the sofa. He cursed once with his mouth open wide, and the wheels beneath rumbled on. Red was painted on top of the white, and a series of screams erupted from the woman's mouth. Her shoulders were locked and so were her arms, and her mouth formed a thin, tight line.

The high was real. What he felt afterwards was emptiness and relief. That was the best part, the only part that really seemed to matter. He had thrown everything into that concert, and now he had nothing left, not even a bottle to touch to his lips. It felt as though his life had just ended, and the gap was as wide as the Charles with the shore far away and growing more distant with each passing second. He wouldn't even know where to find himself again, or if he had ever really existed. It was hard, and he had done his best to fill in the gaps. Large stretches of time smacked him in the face. Memories should have helped him, if he hadn't managed to lose a few of them along the way, and he was fairly certain he would lose a few more.

The trampling haunted him more than all the rest. He couldn't discard the madness and sadness. Maybe that's why he needed more drugs.

憄憄

Addison hated interviews. What he hated more than anything in the world was talking to idiots, and unfortunately, he had to deal with a lot of morons, most of whom couldn't form coherent sentences, talked in circles, or were higher than a prostitute in six-inch heels. The two idiots he conversed with now were no exception to his stereotypical tendencies, and if he could have discovered a way to speed up the conversation, he would have gladly pushed the fast-forward button and then followed it up with the delete key.

"Why don't you tell me what really happened?" Addison asked.

"We s—saw a dude," the shorter of the two said.

His name was Carl. The other one was named Arnie. Arnie had a far-off look in his eyes, and Carl's expression wasn't much better.

Arnie nodded and pursed his lips.

"What kind of dude?" Addison asked.

"A tall one?" It was a normal response disguised as a question.

Thank you, Bing Crosby. "Are you asking me or telling me?" Addison rubbed his receding hairline and licked his chapped lips.

"W—what?" Carl now had a faraway look in his eyes, and his pupils were dilated. He also shook every two minutes and coughed after every third sentence.

"What happened after that?" Addison prompted. He needed a shot, preferably from a gun not a glass, and then a drink, or vice-versa. His conversational skills needed a breather.

"The dude left," Arnie said.

He was the taller of the two and skinnier. He reminded Addison of a tree branch. Arnie, though, shook less frequently than his partner.

"But he left something behind," Arnie added.

"A b—backpack?" Carl asked.

"Look, you came to me," Addison said. "You told me you saw what happened. Just how high are you?"

"Are those angry trees?" Arnie asked.

"Disappointed, maybe."

"You really shouldn't h—hold back your true feelings," Carl said. "It's like holding back a sneeze, man. Sometimes it's good to let those things out."

Thank you, Bing Cosby. "Is that what you're doing?"

Carl smacked his lips together. "What are you talking about, man?"

Addison shifted on the balls of his feet. "Are you letting your sneeze out?"

Arnie looked up. "Who are you again, dog?"

Addison pointed at the middle of his chest. "I'm the one with the badge."

"Is the show over?" Carl coughed and clutched his stomach.

Addison rubbed his receding hairline one more time. "Okay, I think we're done here."

"But I'm just getting started, dog," Arnie said. "He was a blond dude."

"And he was tall." Carl bent over at the waist and coughed some more.

The two idiots shared a conspiratorial smile. Addison wondered if he had a second pair of handcuffs on his person, or maybe shoved in his glove compartment. He was fairly certain that wasn't the case.

"Exactly, man, it's like we're connecting."

"We're not really connecting at all," Addison said.

If these two weren't stoned, he'd hand over his badge right now. On the one hand, he could arrest them and stuff them in the back of his car. On the other, he didn't really want to deal with the pile of paperwork. And he had a never-ending line in front of him that wound its way through the Common and reminded him of a rattlesnake.

"I have answers for you, dog." Arnie burped and then farted. "You're looking for answers, right?"

Addison turned his head away and counted to eight before his gaze swiveled back around. "Why are you here anyway?"

"Because I wanted to hear live music," Arnie said. "The Sex Maggots are the bomb."

"That's what went off, man," Carl said.

The conversation between the two morons continued onward.

"The backpack?"

Carl nodded. "Yeah, it was one of those b—black ones with the straps. And the dude wore a suit, which seemed a bit off to me. I mean, it's a concert, am I right? Concerts are all about the music, not about what you're wearing. Instead of taking the time to dress up, he should have taken the time to dress *down*."

Addison pinched the end of his nose. "Maybe he wanted to show off."

Carl rolled his eyes. "Dude, that's ridiculous."

Addison stuck his hand up in the air with his thumb pointed behind him. "I think we're done here."

�⋯

"This line can't move any faster? What the fuck is taking so long? Are you fingerprinting every mother-fucker in this line, or what?"

His long hair whipped around his head, and the unruly fan exerted light pressure with his right hand. The line had a mind of its own, and he was caught in the middle. The cop at the front was a man in woman's clothes, and he had a sharp nose. His feet were bare, and his skirt was too short. He also had a patch of mud on his right knee, and he had a twig sticking out of the top of his head. The police force had taken a turn for the worse.

"It's called statements," the officer said.

"I've got your statement right here." The unruly fan bent over at the waist and dropped his pants. The cold hit his butt like acid reflux. He closed his eyes and embraced the sting, the wind between his legs, the stares, and the dropped jaws. When it was over, he laughed. Not one of those little laughs, but a big one, one that would have marked him as crazy. But the unruly fan didn't care. Not about that, or the line, or the stupid concert that had ended way too soon, with the cold and the snow and the frosted flakes painting his face. He didn't care about the explosions that had gone off, or the car backfiring, or his heart pounding, because less than two hours ago, he observed a woman with her lips firmly pressed to the breasts of her friend, and the image continued to dance through his brain like a never-ending conga line.

But then it had all ended in a series of screams followed by a stampede, and he was no longer able to witness the lesbian twins. He had cursed the bright red devil himself.

I mean, really, the set hadn't even lasted two hours. What the fuck! It's a good thing he hadn't paid for it himself. As it was, he had to wait in line the whole night twice.

The unruly fan yanked his pants back up, and the crowd cheered. It was the first time anyone had ever cheered for him, and a feeling of warmth and self-importance replaced the cool sensation. If he hadn't been focused on the crowd—the group of people, the endless piranha wave in front of him, the line moving at a snail's pace, the snake that had formed in the grass, a long snake, never-ending, a fucking retarded snake that he was ready to hit over the head with a giant mallet—he might have taken a bow, or maybe dropped his drawers again, or stuck his hands in the air in celebration.

He'd always wanted an encore.

e/∂e/∂

Matthew sipped his vanilla latte and smiled. A little smile, but justified nevertheless. Maybe that's all it ever was, but he'd make it good enough. He had to. It had blown up, the Common, the way it was supposed to in a blazing inferno and a screaming stampede. A beautiful thing, damn near amazing, he thought, as he took another sip of his latte, this one tasting even better than the last, lingering longer, the vanilla tickling the back of his throat. His vacant eyes searched the dark horizon, and he squeezed his lips. The sound of bloody hyenas filled his ears, and the muffled minions continued their wave through the park. The crowd had thinned out, but it had grown more restless with each passing second.

The backpacks had exploded right on schedule, not a minute too soon, or a minute too late. It was beautiful the way the cattle slammed into each other, the herd bucking and weaving through the open plain, their mouths open in shock and awe, the lemmings running into each other and grinding each other to the green and white, cascading to the mass of multicolored carpet spread out before them. Matthew savored the way the cops had closed off the scene, how smoke had drifted toward the heavens, the riots, the lattes one right after another like clockwork, and the series of messed up druggies pounding through the haze.

A few had stepped away from the crowd, and tried to charge through the barrier. A couple were tased, and they twitched on the ground for a good minute before the authorities hauled them into the back of the nearest cruiser as Matthew's lips moved wider.

He snorted. The fucking lemmings. The cretins crept through the darkness, as his coffee cup continued to provide a hint of solace. The glass steamed from the contrast of hot and cold, and his vision was distorted, but he kept the highlight reel moving forward, as the chair to his right grew colder.

Body parts were tossed aside, individuals had caught on fire, and still the pandemonium ensued like a broken switch. No one seemed to have control, not the cops, not the stoners and moaners with unlocked jaws and distant expressions, and not the mayor and her security detail.

Even the people in Starbucks had made a run for it, cascading out the door, moving like cattle down the streets of Boston, the entire Common in chaos. It bloody amazed him the way it had all come together. He could smell the smoke and the despair and the hurt and the fear from where he sat by the window, the latte nearly sealing his caffeinated fate, nearly bringing him over the edge once more, as his mind shifted back and forth through time. All of it was wonderful, even better than he had expected, and he knew the passion would only increase with time.

෴

The recorder banged against his pocket, jingling around like loose change, or a set of car keys. John had enough espressos in his system to do some serious damage, and he leaned forward in his stride, his gait moving east, his strides long and sure and filled with pride as his feet smacked the cobblestone.

Pride had gotten him to this point, and he wasn't about to let it down. He was close to the edge, to the brink of insanity, but he had found his way back, discovered the truth—whatever that was worth—and he was ready for wherever it might lead him next.

John had his innocence, a sense of purpose, and the firm belief that he had the right vision leading the way, even if Matthew had his head stuffed up his own ass.

Self-importance was the only thing that would save him. He had a firm belief and a firm hand shoved at the center of his back. Sure, it was a metaphor with a vacant expression, but it pushed all the same. He turned his head low, and his hood up, and his shoes punched the pavement.

The end justified the means. That's what he kept telling himself. Over and over the message played in his head like a broken record. He had big dreams with even bigger aspirations, and he always tripped over his own two feet. It was one listless moment to the next, to him being here, walking toward the cruiser, recorder in hand, with his hood slammed over his head, his hat bouncing, his vision obscured by the nearest light pole, the traffic signal blinking, and downtown as quiet as an empty tomb.

He slipped through the silent crowd, unnoticed, untouched, his head down, his eyes forward, the recorder patting his leg and brushing up against his thigh, his mouth formed in a tight, determined line, as the uneven street massaged his feet. Looking over his shoulder and peering behind, he noticed no eyes in his direction. Covered in his deception, John was safe. He jerked the first door he came to with the white cars lined up in a row. Locked. He tried another one. Same result. In fact, he tried the whole line of cars on one side, none of which opened for him. He cursed once and then again before he jammed a pebble with his foot.

The night caressed the side of his face, and he searched the black for a hint of weakness. The darkness pushed back. He was about to give up, to discard the whole charade, and dance away when he struck pay dirt. He dropped the recorder on the backseat, and then he slinked away, slipping unnoticed through the crowd once more.

Chapter 25

He had a ham sandwich stuffed between his thighs, and his eyes plastered to the front windshield. He turned the car off, and he considered bringing out his sunglasses. Leo shook his head, his long hair falling into his eyes, before he shoved it out of the way with one quick movement of his hand. His lips formed a sneer, right before his eyes flicked off his ham sandwich and to the nebulous region between the seats. He had a Gatorade bottle next to him, half-full of lemon-lime sticky goodness. He had a partner beside him, a man who hadn't said much, and who was probably the least talkative man he had ever met in his life.

Leo didn't mind, though.

The catastrophe at the Common had forced the department into reactionary mode. The mayor had phoned and chewed out the captain, who had then called the lieutenant into her office and shut the door. Leo heard the verbal tongue lashing a floor below right before the entire squad was shoved in a conference room and another round of screaming ensued. Leo's head felt like it was ready to explode, his chair shook, and his mind was blank. Ward had raged and ranted for the better part of five minutes before he stopped to take his first coordinated breath and sip from the mug on the table next to the podium.

The lieutenant had stood with his lower back resting against the table, and the room was filled with a cluster of silence and confusion and collective gasps. Leo's mind had wandered for a minute until Ward wound up for his second round. Panic from the top down had officially set in, and the lieutenant was ready to latch onto whatever came his way. A rush analysis resulted, and the strip from the discarded pack had turned out to be from the Sudan. More than one witness had commented about a Middle Eastern man skirting through the crowd with dark hair poking out of a cap. More than likely this was more fabrication than reality, as eyewitnesses were notoriously unreliable. Even more witnesses, however, had offered up a collection of blonds into the fold, and the voice on the tape was clearly American, but this didn't persuade the lieutenant away from his Middle Eastern rabbit hole.

Ward's stubborn mentality often reacted badly when he was cornered and faced the possibility of political annihilation. He cowered in the corner and lashed out with his claws and dragged down whatever poor soul happened to be around. The Middle East happened to be the easiest target, and he happened to hold the proverbial flare gun. Ward was a better paper-pusher and political candidate than a policeman, and he could sell a Middle Eastern man to the higher honchos more easily than he could a mysterious blond man who preferred tape recorders and microcassettes. It was all about what Ward could sell, not what made the most sense.

In short, the lieutenant was an idiot, but he was a smart one with political aspirations and a keen eye for government work. This meant he was guaranteed a captain slot, as soon as one became readily available. Until then, Leo had to cave in to Ward's every whim. His mind had continued to race, and the blanks were soon filled with a series of dots and dashes. He had gathered the quiet one—otherwise known as Addison—from his metal desk the next day, and the two were placed on permanent surveillance duty with an unlimited number of overtime hours approved. It was sheer madness, but then the government was often known for bureaucratic idiots.

He was sworn to protect the innocent, but he wasn't so sure about the idiots.

Leo hadn't seen any movement within the confines of the residence. He hadn't heard a single cricket, although he had noticed a few fireflies, the kind he used to catch in glass jars when he was younger. His hand shifted to the gearshift, caressing what he thought was the expanse between his seat and the next, the voice in his head ringing louder than a radio station at full volume, his shirt pressed, creased, and already beginning to wrinkle against his chest and back. His voice formed a loud crescendo in his head. He thumbed through the CDs he had stashed in the dashboard compartment, and when his partner woke, Leo leaned his head back and took his turn.

If it was all the same, he would have preferred a different game. Sure, Leo had managed to keep his head above water, but Addison Thomas had more than a few screws loose and a shady attitude. The man foamed at the mouth, snored, and stared down the barrel of an insubordination charge if he wasn't so damn close to retirement.

❧❧❧

The mission was simple: watch the house until the bastard made a move. The lieutenant had placed his entire surveillance budget in one location with the strict instruction of taking down Ahmad. The warrant didn't grant home access, but his prior explosives and an eyewitness or two did justify departmental services on a Cheerio budget.

Addison opened his eyes, and discovered he had somehow managed to end up in a horizontal position with a glob of spit on the right side of his mouth and a massive headache that had tunneled inside his forehead.

The lieutenant was an idiot, but he was a determined idiot. He had probably sniffed a bit too much Windex and swallowed when he should have spit. But the authorization to abduct Ahmad at the first sign of trouble did provide him with a certain amount of hope given this godforsaken world. He had come prepared with a few supplies in the trunk, and he wanted nothing more than to make the Middle Eastern fuck scream at the top of his lungs. Getting him to confess might prove challenging, but Addison had more than enough patience to succeed at his task. Roughing up a prisoner provided him with an added sense of security in this troubled world. He'd taken a knife to the stomach from a pimp in Dorchester, and he wasn't about to have that crap happen again. If he couldn't convince Leo to wrap his hands around the dark necked man, he'd complete the task himself.

The front door opened on the quiet street with Ahmad shuffling on the porch in a bathrobe with a prominent protrusion on his left hip. The fuck turned in the direction of the nondescript car and released his middle finger toward the sky. Instead of sitting idly by, Addison shoved his door open, galloped toward the steps, faster than he had moved in over two months, grabbed Ahmad before he could gather his morning paper, and dragged him by the collar down said steps and out into the street. The fuck didn't go lightly. He screamed and cursed and handed out elbows like they were nickels on Newbury Street. He called Addison a bastard and a sonofabitch and a fuck and a cunt and a Catholic priest—that one hurt worse than all the rest—and he squirmed like a rainbow trout at the end of a long line.

Ahmad in his blue bathrobe with a pistol around his hip that poked him in his right side—carrying a concealed weapon without a permit in a state that didn't take such crimes lightly—attempted a roundhouse kick and a sucker punch, neither of which landed, and instead, the small man with the even smaller brain was knocked flat on his ass and dragged like he was hogtied in the middle of a rodeo. Ahmad lost consciousness for a moment—the fluttering of the eyes was a dead giveaway—before he regained it, and started cursing and rumbling all over again. One neighbor appeared and then another, and Addison did his best to reassure the elderly couple in matching khaki outfits that there was nothing to see and that all was right with the world. This had the desired effect of offering up a bit more attention to the situation, before a younger couple came along and helped the older couple back inside, and then all was quiet on the street with the three sycamore trees.

During the brief bout of unconsciousness, Leo had popped his head out of the vehicle, and walked behind Ahmad on the other side just beyond arm's length. The protection was unnecessary, and Addison told him so, but the young shit wouldn't listen.

Addison had briefly considered the notion of hanging Ahmad from one of the sycamores. But that plan managed to lose its luminescence when the elderly couple first appeared. With witnesses, it made bad much more difficult, and frankly, he wasn't sure he was ready for the extra paperwork. The forms were long and complicated, his patience much less so.

☙❧

The warehouse was empty, and procured for just such an occasion. The call was made to the lieutenant, and

Addison was given the throttle and a full tank of gas. The Middle Eastern man with the sour expression was left to consider the sinful nature of his erroneous ways, while the call was made and the wooden chair was dragged from one side of the floor to the other. Otherwise the room was empty and a rusty odor permeated the dark expanse. When the call ended, Addison marched to the empty vehicle, popped the trunk, and removed a series of white towels, a dirty sock, zip ties, a canvas bag, a length of rope, two empty jugs that he planned to fill with water, and a Zippo lighter that he'd purchased at the mall.

The lieutenant was unaware of the lighter.

He returned to the warehouse at the same pace and with the same sense of determination.

Addison grabbed Ahmad around the neck, and jerked his head down. The bag went over Ahmad's head easily. Addison's hand reached for the man's throat, cutting off his supply of oxygen and causing a slight protrusion of his beady eyes. Addison's voice was a steady monotone, the inflection not really moving or swaying too far from reality, as his lips formed a tight line after each uttered phrase.

Ahmad reached out, grabbing at nothing and missing everything, as his hand dropped and his voice shook. Addison had a look, a stare he'd perfected, as Leo stood by his side, congregating around the puddle on the floor, the puddle that the man with the bag over his head had made. Addison gripped his side, the ache much stronger than before, as a feeling of redemption pulsed toward his core. His mission was focused, intense, the sea surrounding him a pool of red, mixing with orange and gold, and he blinked away the harsh light from the broken fixtures. He zipped his jacket up tight, close enough that it jammed against his throat and rubbed beneath his chin.

Addison yanked hard on the bag, dragging the man along beside him toward the chair in the center of the room. Ahmad's cheeks moved, but no words came out. His hands—beautiful, manicured, the nails clipped to perfection—flailed about with each thrust and drag of the canvas bag. Addison's muscles bulged, as he stuffed Ahmad in the seat with the back of his knees bumping against the solid wood, securing him with plastic ties and a length of rope. Ahmad struggled and mumbled, despite the dirty sock jammed in his mouth, jerking about and flopping around like a rabbit. His black eyes were dead, and the whites licked out toward the light.

ᘓᕲᘓᕲ

Ahmad's presence filled the room, and the stench from three hours of being tied to a chair left a foul odor that highlighted the other stenches that had come before it. The chair had flipped on its side at some point in the three hours, and Addison righted it with a flick of his arm and a shove of his shoulder. His face remained neutral, and so did the face of the man staring back at him. The stare off continued for more than a minute.

The tape was ripped, and the sock was yanked out.

"What do you want from me?" Ahmad asked.

Addison spoke with distinct clarity. "We want you to talk."

The man said nothing. The stare remained the same.

Addison dangled the dirty sock in front of Ahmad. "We plan to help you along."

Ahmad's eyes lit up at this, like flames that had slowly burned to life. His eyes bounced around the room, nearly everywhere except at the man in sunglasses standing right in front of him. Addison slapped the side of Ahmad's head.

"Maybe you should make a move," Addison said. "The right one."

Ahmad shook his head. It flopped all around, and his eyes became liquid pools where only hard ones existed before. "You have no idea what you're doing."

"That's the problem, my friend. We know exactly what we're doing."

With Ahmad's hands tied behind his back, the sock was stuffed inside his mouth, and Addison emptied a gallon jug over the towel, Ahmad spitting and gagging, his nose running, his legs kicking out beneath him, his eyes as big as a Gatorade bottle. Ahmad kept kicking and jerking while the entire jug was emptied. When the deed was done, Addison stepped back and admired his handiwork.

Once the gagging ceased—Ahmad at one with his fate—the towel and sock were yanked free.

"Are you ready to talk?"

Ahmad's eyes were less clear. "You're a bastard."

"Maybe I am," Addison said. "But I'm also a persistent one."

He slammed the towel and sock home, the ritual repeated once more. Ahmad bucked, his legs jerked like the upended legs of a turtle. When Addison removed the items this time, retching followed the spitting, gagging, and hiccupping. Water cascaded down Ahmad's front, pooling at his waist, the water tainted and mixing his own urine.

"What have you got to say for yourself now?"

Ahmad's eyes had even less fight this time. "You're still a bastard."

Addison slowly shook his head and waited. He glanced down at his watch, as faint light reflected off the harsh face. The second hand turned and his insides burned. He wasn't overly pleased with what he was doing, even though his orders were clear and distinct and left no room for interpretation. The man currently at his disposal was just a tool, a vessel, even if his innocence was garbled and jaded.

Life and spirit had drifted from Ahmad's eyes, and his features were distorted by the vacant light. His skin was pockmarked, and veins popped out of his thin arms. His unruly hair tossed about his face, and his lips were chapped from the cool air and the sun's tentacles. A shield of quiet covered the room, and still the feeling inside him burned.

When the man finally did talk, it wasn't what Addison had expected him to say.

ℰↄℰↄ

Four hours later the man tossed Ahmad in a holding cell, his phone call and his morning newspaper forgotten. There was a tattered sleeping bag on the floor. No bed. No pillow. The toilet looked like a medieval torture device with claws and fangs. His right eye flinched against the harsh light streaming through the window, the bulbs brighter than the light he had previously been exposed to. And for the first time in nearly a year, Ahmad Jaffer started to cry. Tears silently cascaded down his cheeks, the saline touching the corner of his lip.

His head rang louder than the cell phone he had left behind at his empty residence on the quiet street. His legs had cramped during his time in the chair, and he had lost his mind for the second time. Whatever he had hoped to accomplish, he had let slip away, and in its place a feeling of emptiness stood at attention. What he still didn't know was why, or what would become of his twisted fate, but he did hate the bastard in the dark sunglasses with every ounce of his weight, and he would have preferred to smash the prick with a brick.

The man provided Ahmad a pen and a piece of paper to go with his empty bag and the evil toilet. If he were given the opportunity, he would have signed his life away without a moment's hesitation.

Chapter 26

The bastard never called her. Well, he'd never gotten her number. She'd been too drunk at the time, staring at her tequila shot with more than a hint of longing, having already forgotten how many shots she had taken, only remembering the liquid as it slid down her throat and mixed with the anger. The sound of his voice reverberated long after the moment between them had passed. He jerked her shirt to one side when he kissed her in the bathroom—the men's room of all places—but it had been exciting and wrong on so many levels. Lynette Sommer had reared back and tossed him against the stall door, right before she slipped her hand down his pants and curled her fingers around the hard muscle striving for her attention. When he tried to touch her, though, she didn't let it go any further and shoved him away with both hands. She had licked her lips after she'd shoved him away and batted her eyelashes in a manner of casual indifference with the slightest hint of desire.

The power had given her a sense of freedom, and she smiled at it even now. She had never executed a bold plan before, and then followed it through until her fantasy shattered. The strange man with the soft skin and the enlightened eyes that focused so intently on her face made her feel more powerful than she ever had before.

The excitement enlivened her spirit, and then the moment passed like a discarded piece of fruit. The image crackled, and emptiness took its place. The empty, raw feeling in the pit of her stomach remained.

He had vanished and played it nonchalant, not even looking in her direction when she exited the men's room. It wasn't like she'd executed men's room incidents on a routine basis with a long line of strangers. This was her first time. What had she seen in him anyway? He did have a certain swagger, hands folded in his lap, and he'd turned to Lynette in such a manner, with a slight upturn of his mouth, a look of confidence and chagrin, and when he grabbed her hand an electric current shot through her like it was Christmas Eve on the Boston Common. She shook her head, the image flitting from her mind like the wings of a butterfly.

She should have seen this coming. He was a little too perfect, his hair a little too straight, his arms a little too pressed at his side, his lips a little too full. And then there was that smile: It was passionless, and filled with contempt. She could see it now, clearly. She had been wrapped up in the feel of him against her body, the way his body was nestled against hers, the look in his eyes, and she wasn't worried about the fact that he was too pretty or too confident. He had zeroed in on her, she could see that now, and singled her out from all the others. It was an act. An act to slip his hand beneath her panties, but she had grabbed his wrist before it had slipped below the cotton fabric. She shook her head, angry with him, but even more angry with herself.

She wasn't like this.

He had approached her and cultivated her with smooth words and smooth ideas, his delicate hands tapping the bar, inching toward hers, and she had played the game with the sultry expression she had practiced in front of a mirror for just such an occasion. Done the dance, hoping that it could turn into some sort of romance, something more than just a fleeting glance or a trip behind a stall door, and the press of one body against another.

A momentary thing.

A fleeting one.

One blink and it was gone.

ℰↄℰↄ

"You're going back to school," Daniel Pinder said.

Kasey shook her head. "I'm not going back to school, Dad."

"You can argue with me all you want, but my word is the law."

Kasey stood with her hands on her hips and her chin thrust out. "You sound like Judge Dredd."

Daniel nodded. "Maybe I am Dredd."

"Well, if you are, then you need to work on your impersonation," she said.

"Why are you arguing with me?"

"Because, Dad, the kids are going to make fun of me. It's not exactly the ideal situation."

He'd known it was about a boy. It was always about a boy with his daughter, and she'd gotten a little too intimate with him in the gymnasium. Confined to her room, she had barely even complained, even as he took every electronic device he could think of away from her. He had found her there, in her room staring up at the ceiling with tears rolling down both cheeks and her face partially muffled by a white pillow. The sobbing was silent, but the tears were not.

He said he loved her. That's what Kasey had told him, and Daniel wanted to strangle the little shit. He had gotten to some base, maybe it was second—baseball had never been Daniel's sport—but all he knew was that he wanted to reach out and hold his daughter, comfort her in some manner that might lead to her happiness, instead of this feeling of dread. If he could make all of this go away somehow, he would snap his fingers and rid his daughter of her sadness.

Somewhere along the way, though, he'd lost control. She'd stopped being a little girl, and she'd grown into a woman. And he knew she wanted to rebel and flip her finger at the man. He understood that. He'd rebelled, too, when he was her age, and it was all about how his parents didn't understand him. Daniel wasn't exactly the world's greatest father. He was never around, he didn't understand what she needed, and then there was that whole selfish factor that his wife and daughter liked to play off of, that he put his career ahead of his life and family. But he was trying dammit. He tried harder than he needed to, every damn day, and still he came up short. Every. Single. Day.

Maybe if he had started the whole father process sooner, instead of coming off the bench in the eighth inning with his team already down by five runs and two outs on the scoreboard. He could make up the runs, but he couldn't make up the time.

Richard Lancaster III hopped on the T with the common folk and misbegotten teens with the fluorescent backpacks and fluorescent hair. He discovered a spot in the corner, and stared out through the clouded glass at nothing in particular. A monotone voice resounded overhead, and the train lumbered out of the station. Metal ground against metal, as the train clicked and clacked along the open track.

The strange voices garbled and jumbled together, and he rubbed his forehead with the palm of his right hand. He pulled his cell out of his pocket, unlocked it, opened a random app, and closed it once he realized he had no signal. He mumbled an incoherent phrase under his breath, and the woman on his right slinked away to an empty chair. Before she left, she offered a strange look of fear, and he offered her a blank face in return.

A small son of a gun bumped Richard's shoulder with an errant elbow. He glared at the kid, but the kid wouldn't look at him in reply. When the train stopped for what must have been the seventh or the eighth time—he lost count—he stood up on rickety knees, his expression pained, and he lumbered through the open doors and out of the station.

Upon reaching the outside, sunlight struck his face, and he experienced the first hint of freedom. It was a welcome addition to his otherwise tainted universe.

❧❧❧

Carl coughed, sputtered, and spit on the ground. He shook his head, but his world had turned a hazy gray, and his lungs hovered on the verge of extinction. He couldn't find Arnie, and the sidewalk felt uneven beneath his feet. He shuffled his feet at a slow, awkward pace. He swayed one direction and then another, and even his back hurt. His pupils were dilated, and his skin appeared to have changed colors. He rubbed his nose, and then he coughed once more into his open palm.

The world spun, and his dizziness grew. He grasped the air before he grabbed a tree and held on tight. Bark and air slipped through his fingers.

"What the hell is the matter with you?"

"Huh?" Carl replied.

"You aren't right in the head, dog."

"My lungs are on fire."

"You didn't do any drugs," Arnie said. "You smoke some funky cigarettes?"

Carl tripped over his own left foot, and executed a perfect face plant on the sidewalk. Arnie tapped him on the back, but Carl had no air in his lungs to respond, and his world faded from gray to black.

ℯↄℯↄ

Quinn stared at the needle in front of him, at the flame dancing beneath the spoon, and at his hands that made the flame dance. The light shifted. His eyes lit up, swaying, his hands were solid, focused on the task in front of his face, holding the spoon and the light in place. His lips pursed, concentrating on what was the most beautiful mission he had ever accomplished. The perfect mixture blended into the spoon, before it found its way to the needle, and into his arm. His eyes lacked their regular hue, and a crust had formed on his lips. He had dark, purple circles underneath his eyes, and sallow skin wasted away beneath his thin frame. His eyes were spotted, and despite the nakedness around him, all Quinn could focus on was the dancing flame, the spoon, and the liquid melting, bubbling.

The flame rose and so did his spirit.

The hand with the spoon shook slightly. He licked his lips, and his hand shook just a bit more. His eyes flicked from the spoon to the woman sitting next to him on the sofa. She'd expressed an interest in what he was about to do, her eyes dancing across the hollow of his face. She had on a thin white cotton shirt and nothing below her waist. Waiflike. So small that she could have danced on the spoon with the liquid bubbling and his mind racing and his thoughts scattered and frayed. Her eyes had the same freakish tint as his own, and he could feel her energy surrounding him and pushing him forward.

She leaned into him. "Do it, baby."

Quinn grinned and licked his lips once more. "Do you want some?"

Her head bobbed. "You know I do, baby."

"What are you willing to do for it?"

Her eyes were hooded before him, her shirt riding up and giving him a taste of her depths below. She licked her lips and scooted toward him, the shirt riding higher, her eyes locked on the spoon, and on him. Her voice was dark, distant. "Anything you want."

And then she did. She dropped to her knees before the hand and the spoon, and put her mouth on his dick, giving him the best blowjob he'd had in the past three hours, as he sucked in one deep breath and then another, and his heart beat faster and faster. The long needle winked at him, waiting for him, hoping he would show it the same courtesy that she showed him now with her lips and her tongue and her warm mouth, the way her mouth moved up and down his shaft, the warmth and suction, her little tongue darting in and out licking the head with just the right amount of pressure.

His eyes glazed over, his focus waned for just a minute, and Quinn spilled some of the liquid onto the carpet.

"Goddammit!"

Despite the liquid in the needle and the look of horror on her face, as she peered up at him with wide eyes, her long, dark lashes flicking at him, her long blonde hair dancing across her face, his eyes flamed, and then his mouth, and then the rest of his face. But her mouth, though, remained focused intently on the task at hand, the bobbing and motion and warmth and suction, and then it was all too much for him.

Rage boiled up from down below. He dropped his gaze to her succulent mouth, the liquid pooling on the carpet, his mind drifting in an entirely different direction, and punched her in the face. Her head jerked back, her jaw opened in surprise and shock, but still her teeth managed to scrape across his shaft.

She hadn't completed her task, the tease. And then there was the issue with her teeth, so he slugged her again. She toppled over the coffee table, her head struck the hard surface as she flipped end-over-end on her way down. He could see that her eyes were wide in shock and fear. She was afraid of him.

Chapter 27

Leo held a Taser in one hand, and his sanity in the other. He wasn't sure which one would win. It was easier to shift his weight to the left and his sense of pride to the right, as he stared at the man who wasn't all that much different from him. When Ahmad had opened wide, he'd jammed an athletic sock between his jaws, and slapped duct tape over his lips. If he hadn't been staring a promotion in the face, he would have walked away ages ago. But now he wasn't so sure, and the man beside him wasn't telling any tales.

"Maybe we shouldn't do this," Leo said.

"What's the issue?" Addison's tone was clipped, and his eyes were wild.

Leo and Addison stood on one side of the bars, and Ahmad sat on the other, Ahmad's back was jammed against the metal, his hands tied, the tape woven between the gaps, and his cheeks were puffed out at the edges.

"There are no issues."

"Then why the hesitation?" Addison asked.

The lieutenant had spoken to Leo, the pep talk and implications and insightful innuendoes, the promotion well within his grasp. "There is none."

"Then what's the problem?"

"Is this really necessary?" Leo asked.

He didn't remember ever torturing a prisoner, even

one who carried concealed weapons and spat at him
when he wasn't duct taped and submissive. Addison
stood alone for the start of the torture, but Leo couldn't
make the same argument now.

The walls shrank, and the distinct sensation of claustrophobia took over. He gulped in one breath and a second one followed soon after.

"Do you want the promotion or not?"

"Of course I want the promotion," Leo said.

By Leo's estimation, he'd earned sergeant detective
more than a year ago. But he still hadn't proven it to the
higher ups. As for Addison, he was merely a means to an
end, a man who had one year left before he walked away,
and Leo wanted to offer Addison his elbow.

"Then you need to color outside the lines."

Leo's spine stiffened. "That's not what they told us in
training."

"Maybe you shouldn't focus on the training," Addison
said. "Maybe you should focus more on what's happen-
ing right now. It's not about you, it's about reality. You
need to beat the system, before the system beats you."

Leo glanced down at the back of his hand. "Is that
your new catchphrase?"

"You can call it whatever you want," Addison said,
"but it works, and that's all you need to know."

"I don't like the idea of planting evidence."

Ahmad jerked against the rails, his hands and head
bouncing. His grunts increased in size and length, as his
head shifted.

"Then don't do it." Addison lifted his shoulders before
he dropped them back toward the ground. "You know
he's guilty, right?"

Leo replaced the Taser. "It's not about guilt or innocence. It's about following the rules. Guidelines keep the
system in check." He believed in the system.

Addison stabbed a finger into Leo's chest. "It's not about you, it's about winning. And that's really all you need to know."

Leo glared at his supposed partner. "Frankly, I need to know a bit more."

Even from the back, Ahmad looked like he'd been tossed in a pit before a tractor rolled over him. He was bruised and battered, and Leo had never signed on the dotted line for police brutality. But fear had shown its ugly little head, and he felt more dead than alive. The sound of Addison's voice cut through the hallway, and reminded him of a demon perched on his left shoulder.

"Frankly, I've known a bit less, and it has worked just fine. If you believe in the innocence of these individuals, then maybe you shouldn't be here."

Leo shook his head. "That's a bit dramatic, even for you, don't you think?"

"It really boils down to the reality of the situation, and the unreality you are currently facing. If you think you're going to win by following the rules, you won't, but if you're willing to bend the rules once in a while, you'll reach the promotion that's been staring you in the face. It's more about preparation, not aggravation." Addison scooted back as a female detective passed through. "You see the difference, don't you?"

Leo shrugged. "Maybe I do, maybe I don't." He pointed a finger in Addison's direction. "But I'm certainly not going to tell you about it."

❧❧❧

Ahmad had been left in the cell all night long, sleeping on the cold, hard floor, the rotted sleeping bag beneath him, rolling around, the concrete cold on his side, his thoughts straying, as images of his torture reappeared,

the warm sunlight poking through the bars and the darkness. He flipped over, ramming his ear on the concrete,
and he cursed under his breath. His heart hammered in
his chest. He was hot, then cold, then hot again. The sunlight streamed brighter, as his head jerked away from the
light, and then he slept again for what seemed like
minutes. And when he woke, a shadow lingered over
him.

"Are you ready to talk yet?" the older detective asked.

"Why?" Ahmad asked. He had missed a meal or two,
and was therefore lightheaded. The menu featured pork,
and he had handed it right back with a shake of his head.
Whether it was done on purpose, or not, made no difference, the end result was still the same: hunger.

"I just thought you might have something to say."

"I have a lot of things to say," Ahmad said. At least he
didn't have the duct tape jammed around his mouth or
hands. The man ripped it off before this discussion, but
he didn't quite remember when. The hours blended together, but he still remembered each scream.

"I always want to listen. I'm here to help, right?"

Ahmad's eyes flittered away and scurried up the wall.
"Like an auditor?"

"Only better."

"Yeah," Ahmad said, "you carry a gun and a badge
and you have white towels and buckets filled with cold
water." The retching was the worst of it, though. He
would never forget the way the contents of his stomach
emptied, and the smell of hate that lingered long afterward. He could overcome the pain, but not the shame.

"I'm sorry about that."

Ahmad gripped the bars with both hands, his forearms
and wrists flexed and his mind tripped over each thought
in his head. "No, you're not."

The older detective shrugged. "You had to know we suspected you."

Ahmad gripped the bars so hard his knuckles turned white, and the pain in his head transferred to his hands. "Is that all this is to you? Some wild goose chase?"

"I prefer the tamed goose chase."

"You're not funny."

The older detective flinched for an instant. "Neither are you."

Ahmad backed away until his back was pressed against the cold concrete, and the pain had transferred once more. A pause as long as the Nile ensued. The distance between the bastard and him felt like a chasm. Ahmad stepped away from the concrete, and paced about the small space. His hands waved about his head, and his lips moved, but no sound came out. And then the bastard broke his trance with his large mouth.

The older detective glared. "You really didn't learn anything from last night, did you?"

Ahmad paced some more. "Is that what this is about?"

"Maybe if you stopped to listen, you'd realize this wasn't about you at all."

Chapter 28

Addison had one hand on his hip, and the other on the doorframe.

The lieutenant had neither his Windex nor a paper towel visible, but it also didn't mean he had entirely discarded the notion either.

Addison had learned that from personal experience. "Our man isn't talking," he said.

What he needed was a vacation. He might have developed a stress-induced ulcer brought on by terrorists with large explosives and split personalities. He hated what had become of his life, and more importantly, what hadn't.

The lieutenant's office was cleaner than a church on Monday, and the scent of daisies filled the air. "Maybe you haven't tried hard enough," Ward said.

"I've broken every rule I can think of—"

The lieutenant pointed his index finger at the heavens. "There are fewer regulations since The Patriot Act—"

And Godzilla used to be an itty-bitty lizard. "That's not the point."

The lieutenant's eyes flicked to his monitor. "Then what is?"

"It's not getting us anywhere," Addison said. "We might want to try a different approach."

"Might?" The lieutenant folded his hands on top of his

desk and perched his face above his hands. "Or is that what you want? This is all about you, isn't it?"

"It's about much more than that," Addison said. "This is about discovering the truth before it's too late. You heard the tape. You have to realize what we're up against." And if he had perfected another second place finish, he could have continued the game behind the scenes, instead of being first in line.

The lieutenant spread his hands. "We're up against much more than that. It's about saving lives."

And probably another phone call from the mayor. Addison shifted in his seat. "I realize what's at stake here."

"Then why are you pushing the issue?"

"It's the only way to get results." Uncooperative suspects weren't exactly his specialty, but Addison did have a large fist. "This is about results, isn't it? As you said, it's about more than just saving lives."

The lieutenant squinted. "Maybe you need to sleep on it for a while."

"I've been sleeping on it," Addison said, "and it's certainly not getting me anywhere. The odds are stacked against us. We've had multiple explosions—and who the hell knows how many more are planned—and we've got nothing to show for it, other than a terrorist with red eyes, a broken spirit, and no moral code. He's not interested in saving himself or others. And I'm not sure how we can beat that—and him. I've tried everything I can think of, and I still feel like I'm missing a thread. There has to be another way. You have to see that." Addison pushed on the chair, at least the chair didn't push back.

"Are you trying to cause problems?"

"I'm trying to find solutions," Addison said. "Surely, you realize that. That's why you and I are having this conversation right now. Otherwise, I can think of a few other ways to handle things. That's what this is all about, right? Handling the situation."

Addison hated rules and exaggerations, and men from countries he could never hope to understand.

"Are you trying to piss me off?" the lieutenant asked. "Because if you are, you're certainly doing a damn fine job of it."

The lieutenant was one self-important shitheel.

Addison scratched his lower back. "You know it's not always about you, right?"

"Maybe it is. Maybe everything in life is about me. Maybe that's the difference between you and me. Sometimes it's important to focus on those differences, otherwise I have no idea where—"

"Probably six degrees from where we are right now." *And a long way from anywhere useful.* But it wasn't like Addison had an image to uphold nor did he plan to kiss any ass on his way out the door. Instead, he planned to smack it with his elbow.

Ward dropped his hands and lifted his eyes. "Our guy isn't talking?"

"Maybe there are other ways to get him to say what we need him to say," Addison said. "Although he did sign a piece of paper, there has to be a better way to force the truth out of him, right?"

The bottle of Windex made its inevitable appearance and the spraying began. Ward scrubbed the top of his desk like his life depended on it. "Do you even know what you're doing?"

Addison had wondered that himself on more than sixty occasions.

⊱⊰

Most days Addison hated his job, some days more

than others. But he was in it for the paycheck and the pension, even if the salary stank. But he did have his sunny disposition to turn his life upside-down, now that his wife was no longer around. She'd probably leave him a roll of toilet paper.

He glared through the bars and the Muslim glared back.

"What do you want?" Muhammad asked. No, it was Ahmad.

"The truth."

Ahmad shook with rage. "Have you brought more white towels with you, or are you going to use a baseball bat? Maybe you have a pair of pliers in your purse. Or another piece of paper stuffed in your back pocket."

Addison gripped the bars with both hands. "This isn't about towels—"

"Then what's this about—"

"Answers."

Ahmad paced in the small space. "You saw how well that worked for you the last time, didn't you?"

Addison narrowed his eyes. "Maybe we can approach it from another angle."

"You still think I'm your guy, don't you?" Ahmad asked.

What Addison wanted was a simple solution to a much bigger problem. "Do you want to be?"

Ahmad stopped pacing and leaned away. "Not particularly."

"Then maybe you can give us something." Even if it was the wrong answer, Addison needed a sense of purpose, a change in direction.

Ahmad had his thighs pushed against his chest, and his head propped on the top of his knees. "What are you after?"

"The truth." Addison had known criminals to offer it up before, but it wasn't usually on his watch. He needed a lighter touch, or at least that's what his therapist had told him once. He'd stopped seeing her.

Ahmad had a curious expression on his face. "And you're not here to beat it out of me?"

"I prefer calm discussions." But Addison did have a Taser on his belt, and he knew how to use it. The Taser even had a charge.

Ahmad wiggled his toes. His shoes were off, and so were his meds. "I didn't realize you had a calm bone in your body."

Addison took a step back. "I try to keep an open mind."

Ahmad peered down at the ground. "What about the floor?"

Addison rubbed the top of his head. "What about it?"

"I don't like it."

"I'm sure you don't," Addison said. "But it can't always be about you, can it?"

"You know," Ahmad said, "I could say the same about you."

With his next move, Addison closed the distance between the bars and Ahmad. "Are you trying to make me angry?"

Ahmad opened his eyes and blinked. "I'm just trying to get a handle on you. You do know what the definition of civility is, don't you?"

"I know a lot of definitions to a lot of words," Addison said, "but that doesn't mean I'm open to a discussion." He kept his knees in check, even though he wanted to open the gate and offer up a prayer to Ahmad's groin.

Ahmad closed his eyes again and put the back of his wrists on his knees. "Who says I'm looking for answers?"

Silence wrapped its arms around Addison's neck and squeezed. He closed his eyes and blocked out the pain. "It's written all over your face."

"Maybe you have done a lot of hiding over the years," Ahmad said. "Maybe you haven't done a good job of being honest with yourself."

"Who said anything about being honest?"

"That's what life's all about," Ahmad said, "isn't it? Honesty is good for everyone. I might have even seen that on a bumper sticker once."

"You might have seen a lot of things," Addison said, "but that doesn't make them true."

Ahmad opened his mouth and emitted a low, steady pulse. "It's complicated."

"Of course, it is. Life is always complicated. If it were easy, everyone would have it all figured out, and we could just go through the motions. You know, like bowling."

Ahmad's eyes flipped open again. "You seem to think you have all the answers. I'm not sure how well that's worked out for you."

❧❧❧

"There's another recorder," Addison said.

The lieutenant had passed along the news during a period of emotional turmoil, and time had only added more kerosene to the fire. The slap on the back was out of control, the smug expression even more so, while his face had the hint of cherubic glee.

Leo wasn't particularly happy about the first one. The second one didn't offer up any warm thoughts either. The cop who dropped it off had an inferiority complex and a smile that was always too large for his face.

Leo's hand shook as he fingered the package, his eyes flicked over the recorder, analyzed it in the same manner that he analyzed any other piece of evidence. It was the same size, shape, and color as the original. His hand shook, and he dropped it. The man next to him, a friend, caught it before it struck the cold, hard tile. The look in Leo's eyes was one of pure hatred, the kind he normally reserved for rapists, child killers, and pedophiles. He jammed his hands in his pockets, hoping for a mint or a stick of gum. He had neither. He bit down on his lower lip.

Addison slapped him on the shoulder. "Are you all right, man? You look a little pale."

Leo bit his bottom lip. "My stomach feels like it flipped over twice."

Addison removed the hand from Leo's shoulder. "Maybe you should sit down."

Leo breathed in and out deeply. If he could have offered the mayor his resignation, he would have at least briefly considered the notion. Smiles were always a little hard to come by. Problems, however, proved much easier. He forced a smile. "I'll be all right."

"You should play it in the squad room," Addison said. "Everyone should hear it. It might be the only thing that brings us back to reality."

⊱⊰

The voice was the same: same accent, same inflection, same emphasis, and same mispronunciation. It was on purpose. It wasn't the voice of the man Leo had in custody, the one with the broken spirit and folded knees. What happened when the end didn't justify the means? It stung. Leo had hoped to find answers, hoped that the man was somehow involved, but now that was a moot point, the kind that stuck out in his mind and slapped the hands of time. Leo hadn't slept since he heard the voice recorder that first time. The nights of tossing and turning poked holes in his skin. He didn't want to believe in the severity of the situation. He didn't want to concern himself with the consequences. Hatred played with another's emotions, and it only added to the possible consequences. Maybe he should have said no to Addison when he had the chance.

The pain was intense, severe, and complicated. It attacked him at his very core and surrounded his middle. It attacked both arms, before he shoved them in his pocket. He had two bottles of generic pills in his desk, and he decided he needed to take one of each. His current problems—the ones that revolved around sleeping, a loss of appetite, a loss of movement in his arms, and the sharp pain that felt like he jerked one or both his arms out of socket—congregated outside of his mind. The socket part threw him. He'd never broken any bones or even dislocated an elbow.

He played the tape again, this time with only himself and one other person in the room, and he stared hard at the recorder, as the numbers counted down before the tape finally clicked off. It was a mockery, the investigation. Fueled by political power and precision, it revolved around hanging a man from a tree. Whether Ahmad was the right man for the job, or not, was totally irrelevant. Instead, it was all about the symbol the man created, and what it would mean for the entire city of Boston to slam shut the latest book on terrorism. If nothing else, it would send a message to the rest of the world that nobody messes with New England and walks away unscathed. As the blood pooled on Copley Square, Leo would keep his head pointed toward the ground.

The last piece of information was the date on the tape: It had been recorded while Ahmad, suspected terrorist, was under the thumb of Boston PD. That was what caused the nerves in his head to pinch, his insides to become his outsides, and his arm to hurt like a sonofabitch.

He really did hate this shit.

❡❡❡

The nights were worse than the days. Screams interrupted his sleep, and pain resounded long past morning as one day blended into another. The gaps in the metal bars provided Ahmad with the slightest hint of hope before the fleeting image vanished right before his eyes. The two men who held him in custody were idiots of the highest order, but one idiot was definitely more dangerous than the other. He lost his sense of compassion a long time ago, and his hatred grew with each passing moment.

His beloved heritage was a sham to the Americans, as even his citizenship was called into question. One line of questioning bled into another, until his brain was about to explode. His spirit dwindled, and the three walls shrank around him. He'd never conducted a terrorist act, even in his mind, and the thought of chaos offered up a level of sadness to his already thin frame. Sure, he'd conducted his fair share of protests, and he'd ended up with a crazy roommate, but that was the university's mistake, not his. He had never felt more alone in his life than he did right now.

What destroyed his soul was the sense of revenge that he couldn't seem to get past, as it ate away at his intestine one chunk at a time. He had gripped the bars until his knuckles turned white, and his hands had cramped from the exertion. He had done a few pushups on the floor to break up the monotony, and conducted a few sit-ups after he had worn out his arms. He had paced the small space and pretended he was on the outside of the metal and concrete cocoon.

Officers had paraded past his cell, one asshole after another. Some wore a uniform, some did not. One man in particular had slathered on the musk, while another smelled like a chimney. The crumpled appearance of one blue uniform caused him to shake his head in disgust. This particular vision would live on inside of him long after he and the officer had parted ways.

It made him think of the man he had met at the airport nearly fifteen years ago who stood on one side of the partition while he stood on the other, and scrutinized his passport with nothing short of a magnifying glass. The look in his eyes was hostile at best, and it only added to his underlying anger.

If he could find a way to thrive in this unreceptive environment, he'd have his ticket to freedom.

Chapter 29

Sleep drifted away from him these past few days. Had Leo tied both hands behind his back, leaned his head on the pillow, and listened to the sound of the ocean, the little sheep would have found him—not that he could hear the ocean from his apartment, or even the sound of waves. But he could hear the pigeons in the morning, and rats most evenings, along with the sound of his neighbor's bedframe hammering away at his bedroom wall in twenty-minute staccato bursts.

Leo hated rats and pigeons and rickety bedframes and sounds of pleasure.

The headaches came later and with more force than a tornado in a trailer park. Each one lasted a little longer than the one before it until Leo could no longer separate the pain from reality. It was the unreality of his existence and this universe of mass explosions and piles of dead bodies that troubled him more than the pigeons and the rickety bedframes. The recorder had spoken to him in mixed metaphors and hidden agendas, and the voice tried to disguise a Midwestern accent. The pain was acute, severe, and too intense for words. If he wasn't on duty, he could have used a drink, or possibly two.

The SAC, whose current residence was an onsite conference room surrounded by a mountain of paperwork and a laptop, summoned him via the interoffice intercom.

Weaving his way through the piles of desks and paper-work, Leo targeted the back conference room with the glass windows and pull down blinds.

Filled with an L-shaped table, countless chairs, one phone, and inspirational sayings, the conference room radiated authority and submission. The screen on the wall was blank, but Gordon's face was not.

"Do you know why you're here, Detective?"

"No, I don't believe so, sir," Leo said.

Gordon pointed at a chair perpendicular to his own near the head of the table with a wide back and armrests.

Leo sat. When he leaned back, the chair leaned with him. "What can I do for you?"

Gordon looked up from his notes. "I'm here because we have a situation."

"You have situations all the time—"

"This is about more than a pissing contest, Detective." Gordon's tone was sharp. "I just want you to know that upfront."

"Because you think I might have reservations about your true motivation?" Leo had minced words before, and he'd never been keen on the FBI. It was a long story, the majority of which covered misplaced jurisdictions and piss-poor political favors.

Gordon pushed his glasses up higher on his nose with his middle finger. "Do you want to do this the easy way or the hard way?"

"Isn't that a line from a movie?" If it was, Leo couldn't remember which one.

Gordon nodded. "It might very well be."

Leo shifted his position, and the chair wiggled with him. "And what do you think?"

"I think we're about right where we need to be," Gordon said. "You and I."

"You need my help?"

Gordon adjusted his glasses one more time with his middle finger, the ring on his right hand catching the glint of the light. "I might."

The tension in the room could have strangled a kitten. Leo placed his elbows on the table and interlocked his arms. The chair squeaked when he leaned back, but his thoughts remained firmly in place. He offered Gordon a devious expression before he discarded it in favor of a more controlled one. His collar was even tighter than the room.

An endless ocean of questions floated through his mind in rather horrific fashion.

Gordon's expression turned icy. "If you're not willing to give it to me—"

Leo's head popped up. "What?"

"See, now we're getting somewhere." Gordon looked down at his stack of paperwork. "We had a situation at Hanscom Air Force Base."

Leo's eyes widened. "That's a bit out of our jurisdiction."

"I believe it is," Gordon said. "But if you're willing to make an exception—"

Leo yanked on his right cuff. "Why?"

The question seemed simple enough, but life was often anything but. His opponent proved that particular point in his three-piece suit and the thin gold chain dangling from his neck.

"Because we had an incident."

"I believe you already said that."

Gordon squinted. "You might want to calm down. You're making me nervous."

Leo tried to slow down the myriad thoughts plowing through his mind, but his effort failed, along with his jackrabbit heart rate. His neck throbbed, his pulse accelerated, and his skin felt cold and clammy. His shirt shrank, and so did the room. The silence continued. Maybe he should have had that drink when he had the chance.

Leo shifted his position again. "Okay, what is it?"

"We had a break-in, on base, the individuals in question attempted to obtain Octanitrocubane through illegal means. There was a pursuit, and the SF lost them."

Leo's brain was as clogged as a drain pipe. "Who?"

"Security forces."

"I didn't think the military gave up—"

"They're not trained in the art of high-speed pursuits. It wasn't that they gave up. They lost their lead. They backtracked, attempted other maneuvers—"

"And ultimately failed," Leo interjected. "Is that it?" His shirt collar loosened of its own accord along with his sense of claustrophobia.

The SAC nodded. "Pretty much."

Leo decided not to ask where the information had come from, why a sergeant or lieutenant or major hadn't come to brief the situation himself, and why the FBI knew before the local PD. These were valid questions, certainly, but none of which would have helped the situation, and all of which would have only led to additional questions.

"And now you're hoping we can provide you with a few more details."

"Or maybe we could trade information," the SAC said.

Leo coughed. "Why?"

"You're looking for terrorists, right? And those terrorists have struck again. And you've probably hit more than your share of dead ends. I'm guessing it might have something to do with your angle, am I right?"

"What are you talking about?" Leo asked.

"We thought the terrorists were French," Gordon said,

"based on a few loose connections, and based on a tip that we received from an outside source, a source that has given you absolutely no additional information, am I right?"

Leo slumped down in his chair. "And you've decided to change the music now?"

"I'm trained to read people as well as you are. I can connect a few dots, and I'm always willing to entertain new opinions." Gordon spread his arms wide, and his glasses adjusted of their own accord. "One might even say I'm flexible."

Leo's eyes narrowed. "If what you're saying is true, then you're an asset."

Gordon poked at his glasses one more time. "If you want to call it that—"

"What do you suggest?"

"Maybe the men we are looking for aren't French. And if they happen to be the same ones who tried to obtain Octanitrocubane, I'd say we're dealing with some slippery individuals. If we do entertain this new thread, and that's still a big if, I'd rather not have to deal with a bout of political backlash, and have my sphincter handed to me on a silver platter. I don't care how good our theory looks on the outside. What I do care about—"

"It doesn't look all that great on the outside either."

"The men that broke onto Hanscom exhibited none of the habits of the French, and all the habits of men of Irish descent to include the hint of an accent. Plus, I caught a hint of blond hair, and not the kind that is dyed either. These men were also well over six feet tall, all three of them. There's a good chance they are related."

"How did you discover all this?"

The SAC waved a hand in the air. "That's not important. What is important, though, is that we keep the political backlash to a minimum. I'd rather not deal with the paperwork."

ভ৹ৼ৹

"Well, at least you discovered this recorder sooner," the lieutenant said. "Still couldn't be bothered to lock your door, though. You know one of these days you might discover more than just a recorder on the back seat."

The officer's spine stiffened. "What's that supposed to mean?"

"It's supposed to mean that you're already more trouble than you're worth, and you're heading even closer into the wrong neighborhood." The lieutenant shuffled a stack of papers on his otherwise immaculate desk. "Once that happens, there's no way to get you back out again. If that was even a possibility before…"

"Because of the recorder?"

The lieutenant jabbed a finger at the errant officer. "This isn't the first time you messed up. If I were a betting man, I'd say it won't be the last time either."

"The other recorder?"

"Why don't you forget about the recorders for a moment? You nearly killed a seven-year-old in a high-speed chase." The lieutenant held up his hand. "I don't care that she ran out in front of your car and I don't care that she chased a soccer ball into the middle of the street and I don't care that the car you pursued nearly ran her over as well. All I care about is you." His voice picked up speed. "That's all I can control. That's my entire universe, and right now things aren't looking too good for you. You're also having problems at home, aren't you?"

The officer picked at the front of his shirt. "How did you know?"

"Because when your home life sucks, your work life doesn't get much better. Trust me, I know a thing or two about that. That might even be why you've forgotten to lock your cruiser door twice, and that may be why you never lock it again, but at some point you need to take control, reclaim your home life, and do a better job at work. If you can't manage to work all that out—"

The officer jerked like he'd been slapped in the face. "Is that all?"

"For now it is, yeah," the lieutenant said. "And leave the recorder with me. I'll take good care of it. You've already listened to it, haven't you?"

The officer nodded right before he ducked out the door.

Ward stared at the recorder for a full minute, not really sure who was winning the battle. If he could figure out a way to control the situation, he could figure out a way to regain control of his life. If the terrorists won, and the mayor lost her reelection, he might find himself on the nearest street corner with his thumb up in the air, waiting on a taxicab and a better life and a pension that wouldn't come for several years.

He couldn't believe the terrorists were out there, that all he'd been able to do thus far was eliminate a few possibilities, and that he hadn't been able to reach any specific conclusions, expose the terrorists for what they had done, and put this whole mess behind him, reelection campaign or not. If he wasn't careful, the tornado might upend him, and drop him on his skull. He wasn't sure he could wade through the political quagmire without getting his pants muddy.

He flipped on the recorder, and listened intently. When he was done, he leaned back in his chair, rubbed his temples, closed his fist, shook it, and banged it on his desk. Then he repeated the process all over again. He scooted his chair to the right, and silenced the voices in his head.

Digging out the bottle of Windex and a paper towel, he took a few calculated swipes across his desk before he tossed the wet towel in the receptacle.

Why hadn't he seen it before?

What was the matter with him?

He needed to come up with a new profile, and he needed to come up with it right now. If that didn't solve his current predicament, he needed to hand in his resignation and apply for a greeter position at the nearest Wal-Mart.

Chapter 30

"What are we looking at, Gordon?"

Bodies packed the briefing room front to back, images scrolled on the board in front of him, and he had a front row seat to the madness. Ward hated the sense of loss he felt, and that the recorder had managed to determine his fate after a single play. Listening to it twice hadn't brought him the peace he had hoped it would, instead dread and right angles and window cleaner filled his life. Despite his willingness to plunge right in, he couldn't manage to get his desk clean enough. The error of omission was the only sin he had committed in recent memory. But he did believe in second chances, and he believed the fate of Boston rested on his shoulders.

The FBI had called the meeting, leading the charge with guns blazing and lines drawn in the sand with sticks and swords, even though the image of three landmarks burning to the ground was still implanted in his brain, and the multiple fires lighting up the Common only further decimated the situation. He hated being wrong.

The lieutenant still possessed the tape recorder, along with the other two. All three were dusted for fingerprints, and all three had come back lacking. He had already shifted his position in the chair twice, with the result less than satisfactory each time, but like the case, he somehow still held out hope for success. His optimistic tendencies kept his world painted in oranges and reds, as the sunlight streamed through the nearest window.

"We are looking at three highly-trained individuals," the agent said. "Individuals who infiltrated a military base, individuals who had Octanitrocubane on their minds, one of the most powerful conventional explosives known to man, before disappearing down Hartwell Avenue and hopping on 95. Even though they weren't successful, they did manage to escape leaving a trail of military cavalry in their wake. They are of Irish descent, based on facial features, hair, and body type. Other than causing chaos, we haven't identified any other political motivations. These men infiltrated Hancock Tower, the Pru, and the Boston Public Library, along with the Boston Common, on the night of one of the most highly anticipated concerts of the year, a concert endorsed by the mayor, and where you provided security. Despite being warned about the explosions, you still weren't able to stop them. So gentlemen and women, we are not dealing with amateurs out for a date night. You might want to keep that in mind the next time we engage."

"Maybe they just got lucky," Addison said.

"Luck is the least of our problems right now," the lieutenant said. "If we don't stop them before their next target, the mayor is going to hand us one giant shitburger, and the governor might hand us another. This goes higher than solving a crime. Now it's political." And politics was often where he drew a line in the sand. He hated the political weasels that had taken control of his favorite city, who lined their pockets with stacks of hundred-dollar bills.

"What else do we know?" Leo asked.

"These individuals appear to be choosing their targets carefully," Gordon said, "and they're picking the biggest targets for the maximum amount of damage. It's about them trying to prove that they're better than us."

The lieutenant grimaced and shifted his focus. "Well, so far, they are."

"True, but that's going to change," the agent said. "They're also choosing highly visible targets that are relatively close to one another. We are dealing with three spree killers, gentlemen, but this isn't your grandma's spree killer. This isn't Waco or Oklahoma City—"

"It better not be," the lieutenant said. He hated Texas, and as far as he was concerned, Oklahoma wasn't much better.

"These individuals don't have grudges with any particular person or group or business, and there are no obvious connections among the bombings. They're obviously close by afterward, as you'd expect them to be, and they are relishing in their success. That's what this is about for them. That's why we are receiving the tapes, and that's why they are going to strike again. They are not satisfied, gentlemen. These men want nothing more than to give us the middle finger, and watch us trip over ourselves in anger and false consternation."

Hating the FBI was harder when Ward knew they were right. But given the right motivation, he could stick up his middle finger just as easily.

⁰ℑ⁰

"If you listen to the recorder slowly," the lieutenant said, "you hear more than one voice." He motioned to the guest chair on his right.

The lieutenant commandeered Leo after the briefing, while his head still swam with explosions and a semi-arrogant FBI agent. The lieutenant's office was previously sprayed and the hint of Windex still lingered in the air.

Based on the amount of it, an already stressful situation ratcheted up about two or three notches.

Leo covered his nose for several seconds. "In the background?"

"I'm not sure it was intentional."

Leo raised an eyebrow. "Whose voice?"

"The governor's."

Leo raised the other eyebrow. "What the hell are you talking about?"

The lieutenant clapped both hands together. "I'm trying to tell you—"

Leo sat up straighter. "What are you trying to tell me?"

The lieutenant tossed both hands in the air. "This was taped at one of the governor's rallies."

The Windex remained hidden away, waiting on another day.

"What does that mean?"

The lieutenant placed both hands on his desk and leaned forward. "It means we have an even bigger problem than we initially realized."

"Are you saying the governor is involved?" Leo nearly fell out of his chair. "That the governor staged explosions to gain political support for his re-election campaign?"

"That's one possibility," the lieutenant said.

There was an elongated pause, and Leo shifted in his chair twice. No matter which way he turned, the back dug into his spine, and emitted a squeak with every shift.

Leo thought for a minute. "What do you think?"

"What if this was about ultimately attacking the statehouse?"

Leo must have had some wax buildup that had gone undetected by his last Q-tips. He tapped near his right ear. "Excuse me?"

"Maybe all of this has been leading up to the ultimate execution. If this group attacks the statehouse and wins, the entire city of Boston could be in jeopardy. We'd have a political calamity, and the entire state might find a reason to evacuate. I could imagine the President getting involved, and a mass exodus from this great city."

If Leo hadn't needed a vacation before, he certainly needed one now. When this was over, he considered an elongated one in a place where he could sit back, relax, and enjoy himself. He heard Cuba was beautiful this time of year. He might even invest in a good cigar. "And they haven't made any demands?" Leo asked.

The lieutenant shook his head. "None that we're aware of."

Leo peered down at the desk. "And there were no demands on the recorder?"

"Absolutely not."

The lieutenant mentioned that he had listened to it twice. He did not offer to listen to it a third time.

"And you find this difficult to swallow?" the lieutenant asked.

Leo nodded. "Extremely."

"Do you have more than a hunch about this?"

"I wish I did," Leo said. If he had, it would have made his life easier.

∾∾∾

His arm itched. Like fire ants were in full-on assault mode, or like he had a bomb inside his chest that was about to explode. His right eye twitched. Quinn had taken enough meds to kickstart an elephant, and still his eye trembled and shook. Not when he danced onstage, singing for his drugs, with the crowd of supporters larger than any Central Park concert he'd ever seen, but now, when he was in the bedroom, with a needle next to him, a lighter, the drugs, and a woman on his arm. Well, not just one woman, because it was important to have more than one, each with breasts that stood at attention like good little soldiers. He eyed the spoon in front of him, the needle to his right, and the plastic bag to his left. His eyes danced at the concoction, and a melody formed in his head.

He had the bedroom door closed and the music loud enough. Their latest album—the one that was about to hit the shelves in another week, the one that was prepped months ago in the studio, for this specific purpose—filled him with excitement. The Sex Maggots' existence rode on this album, this sayonara in the sun, this beautiful, complicated disaster that had come together in an extreme moment of clarity, purpose, and one humungous overdose.

The girl on his arm wiggled gently, and his hand shook with the anticipation of what was to come. His mind reeled, forwards and backwards, slipping in and out of control, just as he had slipped in and out of consciousness. It had been a wild ride. He had the distinct feeling he was just getting started, and that wasn't just the drugs talking. He had waited, anticipated that this moment would come, and now that it was here he wasn't sure what to do with it. It was a beautiful thing: the concert—not the explosion and the blood—the fans, the excitement, and now the after-party. The beautiful women who clung to him, who managed to hang on to his every word, who looked to him as a godlike figure with a voice that could touch angels. He had a picture in his mind, a fleeting image, that kept his dreams just out of his grasp. He reached out toward it, as the doppelganger evaporated, and he turned his head away before a flicker out of the corner of his eye drew him back.

Her breasts swelled, and her panties slipped down to her ankles. A patch of bare landscape drew his focus, and his mouth opened. He had trouble deciphering the pictures, and he had even more trouble when he floated above dry land. It all became a fantasy. Every last little bit of it. She smiled at him, not one of those half-smiles but one of those full-blown deals where her lips parted and her white teeth flashed even whiter, and her tongue flicked out of her mouth like a beautiful seductress. Her skin was milky white, and so were her thighs. The moles existed but not prominently so, and her hair had fallen into her eyes, covering them, as she reached out her arm toward him with her fingers trembling. But maybe that wasn't real either.

The spoon was real, and so was the fire, and so was the voice inside his head that told him to let go. The siren slipped her hands beneath his waistband, as Quinn sought out the rest of the fantasy, and his tongue flicked out of his mouth.

His heart skipped along, probably missing a few beats in eager anticipation, and his mind swelled like an overripe pumpkin, and his arm bounced up and down, unable to stop, or even slow down. Bubbles formed in his mouth and on top of the spoon.

His bandmate sat on the other side of the room with his back to the door, watching and waiting for his turn, as the music increased in intensity in the background. The smell of burnt metal, burnt popcorn, a blown fuse, and some sort of chemical compound mixed in with all the rest, as he held the needle steady in his hand and pulled back the plunger. He breathed in and out. Once. Twice. As steady as a surgeon performing his first operation of the day with a little extra kick for good measure.

He smiled, one of those Cheshire Cat grins, as the sound of eager anticipation and triumph filled the air.

The needle went in smooth and easy beneath his skin, the liquid shooting through his veins, as his eyes rolled back in his head and he slumped toward the floor. The girl next to him laughed, or what sounded like a laugh, but maybe it wasn't a laugh at all. Maybe it was a gasp, as his eyes rolled back further, round and round inside his head, and then Quinn heard nothing at all.

こうこう

The voice of eager anticipation filled the sofa seat next to her. The receptionist with the headset wrapped round her head had as much cheerfulness as a dying flower. The room was half-packed with souls in suits and ties. The magazines were all a month behind. Lynette hoped her cloudy crystal ball had experienced a drop of clarity. The TV played coverage of the latest bombing on the Common, and the footage was scattered with the carnage and confusion that had plagued the horrendous situation.

Lynette turned her head away and focused on the magazine before her head spun even more out of orbit. She still had flashbacks to the Hancock, and the pavement hugging that had ensued and the river of tears that followed. She had tried calling more than once, but only voicemails followed, and she had given up and attempted to move on. But that had ended in a bathroom stall disaster that she preferred to forget with a man who wasn't who he said he was. The man was a bastard, and liquor was a fleeting friend that never called her back.

The interview was scheduled for an hour, but her previous experience led her to believe sixty minutes was too much time when talking about herself. Talking fast was a common habit when she was nervous. But her head danced with the possibility of a date with Fidelity, and she was ready to put her acquired skills into play. She hoped the firm respected her particular talents—optimism had served her well before—and if it was good enough for Peter Lynch, it was good enough for her.

When the receptionist called her name, Lynette dropped her magazine and looked up into the eyes of a man with a small red stain in the middle of his tie.

෴

The empty house reminded Richard of a tomb, and the sea of dead bodies that played across the news only added to his despair. The rooms were only half-covered, and another third of his possessions were broken in the ensuing melee of his wife's poorly timed exit. She had called him once, but the conversation was strained, and it sounded as though there were a thousand voices in the background. Richard Lancaster III bowed to no man—or woman—and the ensuing disaster that had now become his existence only made him hate the TV dinners and boxed lunches even more. Eating out proved less enticing when the other side of the table was empty, and the wait staff viewed him as a half-crazed loon who needed a few friends and took pity on his very existence. The anticipation of dating made him want to regurgitate his Lean Cuisine and microwaveable pizza.

The photo he preferred most of all was pillaged, and smashing a hole in the wall with a hammer only made him stare at the emptiness left behind. The ants marched up and down his intestines, and stealing a sick day only made his stomach turn even more. The sofa was bluer than he was, and his voice was constricted in the back of his throat. The screaming last night didn't help matters, and the parade of thoughts helped matters even less. His face itched, and his shoulders slumped, and a sense of defeat began to take hold.

As long as he still breathed, he'd find his revenge.

❧❧

Carl woke up with a tube wrapped around his head, and his arm attached to another tube, which was attached to a monitor. He blinked, and his head exploded in a cascade of pins and needles. He was horizontal on a bed, and the room lacked any personality. It wasn't familiar, but then little explosions continued to go off in his brain, and he had no idea what was real and what wasn't. He saw white and a flash of light. The monitor emitted beeps, and a tray of untouched food stood at the foot of his bed when he lifted his spinning head.

He breathed in and out a few times, and the roaring in his brain became a dull ache. The spots on the ceiling reminded him of ink blots, and the splashes of black merged into one. The machine started to hum, and he followed suit with a low baritone of his own.

A woman's voice pierced the fog. He lifted his head and squinted at the light...and nothing. He inched his head forward ever so slightly, and the woman's voice turned more insistent with hints of compassion and sympathy.

"Are you okay?" she asked.

Carl reached out to rub his head, and the tube moved with him. "Where am I?"

She offered the faintest of smiles. "You're okay. I was worried. The doctors..."

Her cheeks glistened, and he lifted his hand. "Who are you?"

She hiccupped. "You inhaled so much smoke."

He did smoke, didn't he? He couldn't remember where he'd put his cigarettes. "My smokes?"

"You really want that now?"

He wasn't sure, but he thought he did.

⌑⌑⌑

"We will find these terrorists," the mayor said. "You have my word. This is about peace and happiness and the American way. This is about freedom, a sense of belonging, it's about harmony and giving the city of Boston what its people so rightfully deserve. The people of Boston deserve the opportunity to wander the streets, to come out of the darkness and the shadows, to run in the Boston marathon if they so desire, without constantly looking over their shoulders, being spared an infinite number of problems that have arisen, without seeking out answers where there might not be any answers to find. This is about your sense of truth and hope. You shouldn't have to lay down your lives, and if the Boston police force can't find out what the hell is going on—"

Addison blinked. "Did the mayor just say hell? On the air?"

"The entire force will be replaced."

"Please tell me that wasn't just spoken on the air," Addison said.

"The shit is going to hit the fan now," Leo said.

"Maybe it already has."

Addison's desk was crowded, and Leo crowded him even more, standing just off of his right shoulder, as the video feed progressed on his monitor. The mayor continued her jaunt from the top step of City Hall, with a sea of reporters just below and cameras flashing every other second. Her pantsuit was pressed, and so was her hair.

"I don't know about you," the mayor said, "but I do not want to live in fear for the rest of my life, based around an enemy that I'm unable to identify. This does not help me sleep well at night. In fact, it hasn't helped me sleep at all. I've wrestled around with this problem for the past few nights like many of you have, of that I'm sure. And we're going to discover the answers together."

Chapter 31

Mark rushed the front door, and the other two took the back. Silence covered the street, not a single car, cat, or dog to be heard. The wind whistled, but it was still quiet enough, as the sound of soft anticipation filled the empty moments. He whistled, the call anticipated by the other two, and then he was through the front door, barreling his way inside, not even bothering to be subtle about it. He lifted his head, and his eyes shot forward.

The clerk behind the counter had a shotgun pulled up and hovered above the laminate, but Mark was faster. He had his gun ready with his finger on the trigger, and he fired off a shot, striking the clerk in the shoulder, spinning the fat man around. He fired another shot below the first, and the man's mouth opened wide, before he went down hard against the counter, his face planted against the laminate. The fat man let out a scream, followed by a series of curses and obscenities that decreased in volume, and then a sigh, and then nothing at all. Mark took out the monitor in the far-right corner with his next shot, the screen a spider web of broken glass. The feed stopped midstride, and the camera went black. And then he leaned on the counter for support, a rush of adrenaline shaking his entire body, his right-side quivering more than his left.

His side ached. He hadn't run that far, just an all-out assault toward the front door, his hands and arms pumping. He'd run farther before, most of the time he ran four miles a day. But the short distance had thrown him off, yet his side still screamed, rocketing outward, the scream becoming louder and louder, the world swirling faster and faster, and he had no idea what the hell had just happened. It had all gone according to plan, including the fat man behind the counter with the shotgun who was a step or two behind. He savored the moment of triumph.

What had led Mark to this particular place at this particular point in time was a series of events too long to mention, and now the entire right half of his body was on fire, and he didn't have any way to douse the flames. He clutched his side, and his legs gave way. Confusion entered the scattered pieces of his mind. He reached out his other hand to steady himself, but his fingers slipped through the empty air.

"He's been hit," Matthew said. Or it could have just as easily been John. Two faces blurred into one. And somehow Mark managed to forget where he was, what he was doing, and why he had run straight at a fat man with a two-barreled shotgun behind the counter.

⌾⌾⌾

"What the bloody hell are we supposed to do now?" John asked.

Matthew looked down at Mark who currently bled out on the stone, the shot having struck him on the right side of his stomach. "We have to continue the mission."

John glanced down at Mark who groaned and then burbled and then groaned again. "What the bloody hell does that mean?" John asked.

"I think you know exactly what it means."

John grimaced. "We can't just kill him."

"He knew the risk going in," Matthew said. Mark started to open his mouth, and Matthew slapped his hand over it. "It was a distinct possibility. And now that possibility has come to reality. If you can't handle—"

John's voice rose. "He'll survive. All we have to do is take him to the hospital."

Matthew shook his head and glanced at a bag of potato chips. "That's not an option. You know that, I know that, he knows that."

Mark opened his mouth again: It didn't last long. Blood seeped out of his mouth as well as his side.

John looked Matthew dead in the eye. "Well, I'm not going to do it."

"Did I say you had to?"

Matthew really hated the weak, merciful individuals who lacked spine and apathy, and even a basic way of life. He should have seen this weakness coming. Maybe it was there all along, and he had failed to recognize it. Well…no matter, he had the chance for success staring at the middle of his forehead.

"Well, I'm not going to watch either."

"No one said you had to," Matthew said.

His partner, the pussy, ran outside. John couldn't get out toward the gas pumps fast enough. It didn't matter that he'd nearly passed out at the sight of blood. The clerk that was a second faster than anticipated, his partner who was just a second too slow, the man bleeding out on the stone, underneath the harsh yellow lighting that gave his skin a sallow glow.

Matthew held Mark's head, the man's lips moving, the blood pouring out all around him, his T-shirt seeping and leaking blood, and dripping onto him as well. There was no way to avoid the blood. Mark's whisper was too soft to hear. He had led a less than honorable existence, and had failed in his duty. A certifiable moron who didn't deserve to live. He was shot by a fat man with saggy jowls behind a counter and that was all there was to it. Nothing more, nothing less. Matthew placed his hands in his jacket, pulled out his small caliber pistol, pointed it at Mark's forehead, and pulled the trigger. He picked up the spent cartridge, crossed himself, and left the body behind, the bleeding continuing for only a few seconds longer before the heart stopped altogether.

⁂

John's eyes narrowed outside the front door. "What the hell are we supposed to do now?"

"Finish the plan," Matthew said. He had two idiots on his watch. At least now he was down to one.

John raised an eyebrow. "How?"

Matthew tapped the backpack on his shoulder. "I have the Semtex."

"Are you sure?"

"Of course, I'm sure. Do you want to check for yourself?"

John shook his head. "Why are you making this so bloody difficult?"

"I'm not making it difficult at all," Matthew said. "I believe you're trying to add layers of difficulty that aren't there. And now you're challenging my authority."

And Matthew hated it. Every minion that walked the earth deserved to be squashed and taken down a notch.

John shook his head. "I wouldn't dream of it."

The wind blew and a bout of silence ensued. He clicked the fob, and the doors unlocked. Matthew slipped inside, while John tapped the hood of the car. Once the idiot slammed the door, Matthew peeled out just as a car pulled in.

"But you've bloody thought about it."

"I just don't see why he had to die."

Matthew's voice turned to ice. "We are not going to have this conversation again." The meek deserved to die: It was as simple as that. Not only did the strong have the right to rule, it was their privilege.

"But we never had this conversation the first time."

"Exactly," Matthew said. "And it's going to bloody stay that way."

John stared straight ahead. "So I guess that's it then?"

"Exactly," Matthew said. "The plan is to finish the job, and when we're done, you and I can both claim victory."

"I may never sleep again."

"That's certainly your prerogative."

John tapped the dash. "Why do you always have to make things so difficult?"

Matthew tuned out the distractions, and focused on the road ahead with its bends and curves and roundabouts, as torn pavement, smoking vehicles, broken billboards, and empty gas stations rushed by. Each vehicle had its place, and his was over on the far-left hand side. Traffic zoomed forward. He had his eyes on the prize, the junket ahead with its gold roof and stone staircase. He had just killed a man, and had an idiot passenger to his right. He had passion and whatever remained of his integrity.

Matthew felt the presence of evil, and he welcomed its embrace with open arms. The clouded windshield distorted his view, and his companion lacked all pretense of common sense. The world distorted his message, and his vision blurred toward fantasy. The self-important Americans didn't deserve to live, as they flexed their muscles time and time again.

Every path was paved with failure. The men and women fattened their bank accounts and their waistbands at the expense of the less fortunate.

All of it, including the minions, lived to question his authority.

John adjusted his seat belt. "Do you think this is going to be easy, boss?"

"Easy peasy, shotgun sneezy."

"Shotguns sneeze?"

Matthew tapped the steering wheel. "Are you trying to be funny?"

"Most of the time I don't have to try."

"Why?" Matthew asked.

"Because it's normally right there for the taking." John gripped Matthew's shoulder with his left hand. "Just like this situation."

Matthew's eyes flicked to his right. "You know, if you take your hand off my shoulder, I won't be forced to break it."

"Sorry, boss, just a habit."

Matthew wasn't sure it was. "And not a very good one either," he said. "I've managed to kill people for less." He didn't point out that he just had.

John tapped the dash once more. "You could always try."

ഐഐ

Addison had his gun in his holster, his radio thrummed at his side, his brain slammed against the vast expanse of his forehead, and he had more than his share of problems and fewer answers. He had started seeing spots, the doctor called them stress spots, and his hearing was more than a little off. Again, the stress. He was over-eating—stress related. And he hadn't slept—stress. It wasn't much better that his hearing had gone to piss, and he had a wife that had already threatened to leave him for being more in love with his job than her—her words. Flowers hadn't smoldered the flames, and neither had the multiple counseling sessions with a woman that hated him.

It was more difficult, challenging even, but he was ready to face the trials and tribulations presented, to go down with his radio, gun, and flashlight. In that order.

The cars, many of the unmarked variety, parked around the Common, and many of his colleagues had taken up residence at the Starbucks in one corner while the Statehouse stood some distance away.

The triumvirate, or the gathering of the three, was about to take place at the Massachusetts Statehouse. It was one of the few high-priority targets left in Boston, and the only target that made any sense once the governor was ruled out as a possible suspect. It was all suspect, a gamble, but it was the only gamble that made any sense. And it was worth the risk, and both the lieutenant and captain approved.

The cruisers were pulled around corners and alleyways, and the men and women held coffee cups and newspapers and scrolled through cell phones with their free hands. The pacing took place on crowded sidewalks filled with tourists and joggers and men in suits and women in skirts and blouses. Snowflakes littered the sidewalks and roads, and the surface below was slick from ice and slush.

Apprehension filled the ride over. He had a partner that had perfected the silent treatment, who had probably spent a number of nights working on the formula, with his eyes pointed toward the prize and his fingers perched inches away from the dashboard.

Addison had nearly run down a blond in a silver Jetta, with a sliver of an attitude and a propensity for changing lanes. Horns honked at one point, and he had come damn close to using his siren with just a flip of the switch. But he held back. The hostile state of overzealous and aggressive drivers existed between this life and the next, and he needed to find his proper place in the melee.

The wind whistled around him, and his spirit was crushed like a battering ram. If he was right, that still meant he'd face one hell of a gunfight. And if he was wrong, he might have to push his retirement paperwork, gun, and badge across the lieutenant's desk even sooner.

What he lacked in passion Addison made up for with his hard-hitting personality, thank you, Bing Crosby.

His hip felt like it was about ready to cave in at his side. He dragged his left foot a little more than his right, the slightly off-balance stagger—that's what the guys at the precinct had called it—was his signature. He preferred swagger, like Clint Eastwood and John Wayne.

The lieutenant authorized all personnel for the maneuver. He referred to it as "all systems go." One endless sea of cruisers and heads poking out of windows and bodies surrounding the perimeter and lining the front doors of Starbucks, with paper cups, ready to move in at a moment's notice in waves of blue and black.

Addison had the button, and he wasn't about to push it too soon, the way some of his buddies had done, firing at little girls or little boys who weren't carrying more than cap guns. When adrenaline rushed through your body, when it was dark out, and when you were already on edge because your eight-hour shift had suddenly turned into eleven, and when you'd heard about your buddy being shot only two weeks ago, it was easy to make a mistake, slip, and then the whole universe changed.

The butterfly effect. He had seen guys turn to the bottle, others turn to psychiatrists and pills, and still others turned to sucking on the barrel of their own nine-millimeter.

☙❧

Matthew felt the presence of a hundred eyes looking in his direction, even as his feet pushed forward against the pavement. The walk through the Common soothed him, and the light music helped his brain go numb. The light snow scattered about, and the trees looked like sticks with hands raised toward the gray sky. His feet were already numb, and so were the back recesses of his mind. The air whistled around him, and whispered up from the ground.

More cops hovered on the edge of the Common than usual, and the Common was less crowded than was typical for this time of day. He smelled a rat, and it wasn't the idiot walking next to him.

"What the hell's going on?" Matthew asked.

"What are you talking about?"

Matthew continued to stare straight ahead. "What's with all the fuzz?"

John rubbed the end of his nose. "I have no idea."

"They're waiting on us, you fucking moron," Matthew said. "You might want to keep up. You didn't spout off at some local bar last night because you had a few too many drinks and you were in the company of some blonde-haired, blue-eyed masterpiece, did you?"

"I'm smarter than I was last time, boss."

"Are you?" Matthew asked. "Because now I'm not so sure." He had laid out the ground rules, and it had still blown up in his face. The bastard had let him down, like all good bastards did, and now he was left with the consequences.

The cops didn't move, but their eyes did, as one wave of cops begot another. None stood directly on the chipped, rocky stairs, but he counted a number of interested parties lingering near the dome. Matthew stood at the edge of the Common, and uttered more than a few choice words.

"What are we supposed to do?" John asked.

"What do you think?" Matthew replied. "We can't go anywhere near the Statehouse now, thanks to you and your big mouth. I hope she was bloody worth it."

John rubbed his nose again. "I'm not really sure I remember."

Matthew expelled a pent-up breath. "Great, that's even better."

"But it was fun, though," John said. "I do remember that much. And maybe she wasn't the second coming of Jenny McCarthy, but she was a hell of a lot of fun."

"You made sure you got your fun."

John nodded. "Exactly. See, now you're getting the picture—"

"No, I'm not sure I ever did get that particular picture." Matthew glanced around. "We need a distraction."

"I'm not even sure they're looking in this direction."

"Maybe not," Matthew said. "Maybe you're exactly right." Of course, it was a lie. His entire life filled with one lie after another, as the shit piled higher and higher.

"So what's the distraction?"

Matthew didn't even hesitate. "I'm going to shoot you."

John shook his head.

"You should have thought of that before you went after the blonde." Matthew had always hated blondes: the attitude, the hair, the sense of entitlement. Blondes didn't have more fun. Blondes sucked the fun out of everyone else around them.

John's eyes widened. "You mean, you wouldn't have shot me?"

Matthew's hand lingered near the outside of his jacket, and his eyes remained focused on the man standing just to his side. "Hindsight is always twenty-twenty."

John lifted the top of his jacket to expose his weapon. "Not if I draw first."

Matthew whipped out his piece a fraction of a second sooner. He pulled the trigger, without even a brief hesitation. The sound was deafening at close range, the small pistol bucking like a bronco, his mouth closed in a tight smile, as a whisper of bliss covered his otherwise immaculate face. All eyes looked in his direction, recognizing the sound of a gunshot, and Matthew did the only thing he could think to do. He took off.

He slammed the pistol into his waistband and kicked his legs out, shoving forward, head up, eyes straight ahead, his knees cracking and his heart beating, and the wind kicking up around him, slamming against his face, as his feet slammed against the pavement, an endless stream of slamming feet and distorted voices and before that slamming doors and screaming, and probably finger pointing, and it was all he could do to keep shoving forward, the gun still lingering close to his thigh, his hand still shaking slightly. His left hand went numb. It could have been the wind, adrenaline, the cold, or the pursuers that he could hear breathing now, edging closer and closer, as Matthew hustled up the stone street, a sea of brownstones smiling back at him, the walkups with front doors facing the road. The hill was longer than he expected, steeper than he remembered, and he hoofed up the incline with the wind pounding his eyebrows, his legs and arms pumping, the endless stream of breathing behind him, the ground slick beneath his feet. The steps behind were an endless melody, and the voices turned from surprise to disgust to rage to a series of belated commands. Matthew didn't bother looking around, he just kept his arms and feet moving, until he heard shouting and a voice told him to stop, to surrender, and then a warning shot fired into the air as he kept up the running.

People on the sidewalk—some with kids and some without, some walking toy poodles and basset hounds and dogs that looked like rats with fur, *fucking Chihuahuas*—stood with mouths agape. He'd started out taking leaps and bounds and now he slowed down, his feet stuck in the slush and sliding across the ice.

Beacon Hill had more of a slant than he remembered, as he continued his ascent and uttered a cadence of choice words as the frenzied pursuit continued.

He pumped his arms and kicked out his legs, and now his body moved, but his position didn't. Now he ran in fucking place before his head slammed to the pavement, and the handcuffs slammed on his wrists while his hands were jerked behind his back, before he was shoved upward, and his shoulder felt like it had popped out of its fucking socket, and he screamed and cursed at his pursuers and the stupid pedestrians with the rat dogs and beady eyes and looks of surprise. Brute force ensued, and pain followed. A cheer roared through the crowd and smirks were offered by the men in uniform and doors were open and shut as the watchful crowd grew.

Madness without the pomp and circumstance and fireworks. And then somebody spoke in a calm voice about his rights, like his rights mattered when he didn't have either one of his brothers left, and he would spend the rest of his days rotting in a jail in a county in western Mass, or wherever the fuck he went where the bars were metal and the food was terrible. To bleed out in his bed courtesy of a roommate that was bigger and stronger than he was.

The end.
The bloody minions had won.

About the Author

Robert Downs aspired to be a writer before he realized how difficult the writing process was. Fortunately, he'd already fallen in love with the craft, otherwise his tales might never have seen print. Originally from West Virginia, he has lived in Virginia, Massachusetts, New Mexico, California, and now resides in Colorado. When he's not writing, Downs can be found reading, watching movies, traveling, or smiling. To find out more about his latest projects, or to reach out to him on the Internet, visit the author's website: www.RobertDowns.net.